Ring of the Or'tux

Ring of the Or'tux

A Qyaendri Adventure

Brian S. Pratt

Ring of the Or'tux
Copyright 2008 by Brian S. Pratt

For information concerning books written by Brian S. Pratt, or
where to obtain them in either paperback or eBook formats, visit the
author's official website at:

www.briansprattbooks.com

ISBN-10: 0-9843127-5-7
EAN-13: 978-0-9843127-5-7

Books by Brian S. Pratt:

The Morcyth Saga

The Unsuspecting Mage
Fires of Prophecy
Warrior Priest of Dmon-Li
Trail of the Gods
The Star of Morcyth
Shades of the Past
The Mists of Sorrow*
*****(Conclusion of The Morcyth Saga)**

Travail of The Dark Mage
Sequel to The Morcyth Saga

Light in the Barren Lands
***Book 2** Forthcoming 2010*

The Broken Key

#1- Shepherd's Quest
#2-Hunter of the Hoard
#3-Quest's End

Qyaendri Adventures

Ring of the Or'tux

Dungeon Crawler Adventures

Underground
Portals

Non-fiction Works

Help! I don't Want to Live Here Anymore

This one's for Mr. DeYoung.
A teacher who made learning fun.

I'd also like to thank Alvin Lochan who came up with the general idea for my cover and did the preliminary artwork upon which the final design was based. You can see his original artwork on my website:

www.briansprattbooks.com

Chapter 1

On a plane of existence unattainable by living mortals sat the High Temple of Casdralla. Within its sacred halls resided the greatest of the Qyaendri who served the goddess. These beings, immortal and powerful, had the ability of traversing between the planes upon which the gods resided and the ones their mortal worshipers inhabited. Having such beings in their service was the only way in which the gods could affect what transpired on the numerous inhabited worlds of the universe.

In a never ceasing stream, the prayers of Casdralla's worshipers were brought to the High Temple. Lesser Qyaendri were always among her people, ever watchful and listening to their needs. When a prayer was given up to the goddess they brought it to the High Temple, and there the decision was made whether or not to grant the follower's prayer.

Prayers ranged widely from the mundane to the grandiose. Those which flowed from great need, or were in line with the philosophy of the goddess, were the ones most likely to be granted. Those of a selfish nature such as wishing ill on another in order to prosper, or for money to buy items of little import, were summarily rejected. Whether large or small, each was brought to the High Temple for consideration.

Many Qyaendri were always in and about the High Temple for there were many worlds upon which Casdralla's influence had spread. Some worlds numbered followers in the millions, while others held but a handful. No matter the size, each was accorded the same amount of diligence by the attending Qyaendri.

This day was no different than any other, though days as mortals thought of them had little meaning in the High Temple. Qyaendri came and went with prayers both large and small. Those which had been deemed worthy, were assigned lesser Qyaendri that would return to the world from which the prayer originated and do their best to fulfill the worshiper's need.

Needless to say, some prayers needed to be answered by more experienced Qyaendri. Those were the prayers which had a much more encompassing affect, or were directly linked to the worship of her followers; ones such as the choice for the next High Priest, or dealings with neighboring kingdoms, those sorts of things.

Once in a very great while, communication to the High Temple comes not from the worlds of her followers, but from the goddess herself. Only three of Casdralla's Qyaendri ever had direct dealings with Her. Those three had served her the longest and proven their faithfulness and judgment over the millennium. Rarely were they seen within the High Temple. For the most part, they appeared only when they were there to gather high ranking Qyaendri and a cadre of Celestial Warriors for a mission to a world wherein Casdralla held little or no influence. Such missions were how she continued spreading her influence throughout the universe.

Of the three, Xi was senior and had served Casdralla longer than the memory of any other Qyaendri could recollect. Not for a thousand years had he graced the High Temple with his presence. And so, when he appeared within the Rotunda of the High Temple before the goddess' statue, it was greeted with great surprise and anticipation. For surely, his presence foretold an event of possible world shattering import. Word of his presence spread like wildfire through the ranks of the Qyaendri.

Those Qyaendri on their way back to worlds to answer prayers, or simply to watch over the faithful, stopped when they were made aware of his appearance. Prayers were left waiting as each and every Qyaendri converged on the High Temple in the hopes of being one of those chosen to aid Xi in whatever his endeavor may be. While it was true, those of minor standing in the hierarchy of Casdralla's Qyaendri had little chance of being chosen, one never knew. And so, each came and waited as Xi stood there quietly gazing out over the assembled Qyaendri.

Finally, his eyes settled on one of the Qyaendri. "Daeson," his deep, base voice intoned.

A murmur ran through the assembled Qyaendri as the one upon whom Xi's gaze was fixed made his way forward.

Daeson's heart, if Qyaendri were to have such, pounded in his chest with pride and exhilaration for having been picked. As he made his way forward he could feel the eyes of everyone upon him, some joyful for him, others envious.

He wasn't a high ranking member of Casdralla's Qyaendri, but had proven himself throughout the years and was now what in human terms would be considered a sergeant of sorts. Daeson held a modicum of authority and oversaw a cadre of the lesser Qyaendri.

Coming to stand before Xi, he knelt down on one knee, bowed his head and asked, "What does our Lady require of me?"

An expectant hush fell over the gathered Qyaendri as they waited for Xi's reply.

"Have Larus returned to the High Temple," Xi commanded.

Daeson couldn't believe at first what he had heard. Xi wanted him to bring Larus back? His first inclination was to ask why, but he dared not do so. If that was what their Lady wanted, then that is what he would do. Raising his head, he looked at the ancient Qyaendri. "It shall be done," he replied, giving Xi another bow. When he brought his head back up, Xi was gone.

On a world far removed from the High Temple, a boy worked in a field cutting tall grass with a scythe half again too large for him. The youngest of five sons, he was thought to be a little bit addlepated.

He was often withdrawn and rarely had dealings with others his own age. This gave his mother and father grave concerns for his future. Now eight years old, he should be taking a more active role in life, but instead, seemed to be withdrawing more and more. He tended to work alone and was lost when forced to work with others. That was why he was here, alone in the corner of the field, cutting grass to feed their livestock. Next to him stood a wagon partially filled with grass already cut. Once it was completely filled, Allen could return home.

"I don't care what you think," he said to his friend.

"Yes you do," replied Stymie. Though no one else could see him, Stymie was Allen's best friend. They had been fast friends for two years now, and Stymie was the only one with whom Allen would talk outside his family.

"School is stupid!" Allen said as the scythe cut a small swath of grass.

From where Stymie sat on a nearby stump, he sighed as he watched his friend pick up the cut grass and lay it within the wagon. "School is not stupid," he argued. "You get to meet people and make friends."

After tossing the grass into the wagon, Allen turned to his friend. "I don't like people," he replied. "No one understands me."

This has been a common conversation between them for some time. In the fall, Allen would be starting school as do all youths in his community when they reached their eighth year.

"They will," replied Stymie. "You simply need to give them the chance to get to know you."

Returning to cut more grass, Allen gripped the scythe and paused before cutting a swath. Without looking at his friend, he whispered, "I'm scared."

Stymie hopped off the fence and came toward him. "I know you are," he replied. "But I'll be there with you." When Allen turned to look at him, Stymie could see the fear in his eyes. Even a small tear had begun to make its way down his cheek. The dread he felt at being forced into social contact with others had grown steadily as the first day of school began.

"I don't know what I would do without you Sty," he said.

Then as Stymie always did when Allen grew melancholy, which he had begun to do less and less since Stymie's first appearance, he hopped onto his hands and began gyrating around. When a smile broke across Allen's face, he flipped back onto his feet and launched himself toward the boy. Giggling and laughing, the two rolled about in the tall grass as they wrestled.

When they finally broke apart, the melancholy which had taken hold of Allen was gone. Stymie knew Allen was in for a hard time once he began school. Over the past two years, he has seen Allen emerge from his shell bit by bit. By the time school began, it was Stymie's hope he would be ready.

"You always know just what to do," Allen told him. Stalks of straw intermixed with his shoulder length brown hair made him look quite comical.

"That's what I'm…" began Stymie when his attention was caught by the sight of someone standing across the field looking in their direction. A sharp intake of breath followed as he saw a faint glow shimmering about the figure.

Larus' time wasn't nearly over yet. When he had come in answer to the prayers of the boy's mother two years ago, he had been charged with helping Allen emerge from within himself and be able to have a more active role with those around him. In Larus' mind, the resolution of Allen's mother's prayer hadn't yet come about. To remove him from Allen before his mission was completed could undermine everything he had worked to achieve with the boy.

Staring across the field to where Daeson waited, he inwardly sighed. Creating a simulacrum of himself to remain with Allen, he hurried toward Daeson.

He came and knelt on one knee before the superior Qyaendri and bowed his head. "What does our Lady require of me?" he asked. Such was the ritual question a subordinate Qyaendri always asked a superior.

"You must return to the High Temple at once," Daeson replied.

"But," argued Larus as he came back to his feet, "my work here is not finished."

"I realize that." He paused a moment as he glanced back to where Larus' simulacrum sat near Allen. "Xi has requested you to return."

"Xi?" he asked, shocked beyond measure that a lowly Qyaendri like himself would even be known by one such as Xi. "What…what does he want of me?"

"He would hardly explain himself to me," explained Daeson. "All I know is that you are to return to the High Temple immediately."

It was with no small amount of trepidation that he heard those words. Once before he had been summoned back to the High Temple and it hadn't been for congratulations on a job well done. Rather, it had been due to the disruption he had caused on a mission where they had striven to bring Casdralla's enlightenment to one of the many worlds filling the universe. He could see that Daeson remembered as well. Daeson had been one of the leaders of their group and had lost much standing within the Qyaendri hierarchy because of him.

"But, what of Allen?" he asked.

"Allen will be assigned another Qyaendri," Daeson told him. Directing Larus' gaze back to the boy, he showed him where another Qyaendri had already taken his place. In every aspect, the new Qyaendri looked just like the 'Stymie' Larus had portrayed. It didn't appear Allen even noticed the difference.

Larus looked on with mixed feelings, not the least was sadness at being parted from Allen. Many of the Qyaendri disliked being the ones who fulfilled the lesser prayers and would have jumped at the chance to put behind them such an ignoble job as being the playmate of a small boy. Larus on the other hand enjoyed these types of jobs. True, he had originally been part of

Casdralla's Celestial Warriors, and had shown great promise before the incident which had preceded his earlier summons back to the High Temple. But where he was happiest was out in the field helping to make the lives of his Lady's followers better. He held great empathy for them.

Turning back to Daeson, Larus sighed and nodded. "I'm ready," he said.

"Before we return," said Daeson, "let me just tell you that I don't know why Xi would request you. There are many others who are wiser..." he paused and stared at Larus as if daring him to argue, "and more dedicated."

Larus knew that Daeson didn't like him, and he felt guilty for having been responsible for all the troubles Daeson had gone through because of him. Frankly, he too was rather astounded that Xi had asked for him.

"Whatever he may have in mind for you to do," continued Daeson, "give it your utmost attention and stay focused on the job at hand. I don't want you to mess it up like you did before."

"I won't," replied Larus. "I've learned my lesson. I'll stay focused on whatever my task is to be."

Daeson continued glaring at Larus for a moment before nodding. "See that you do." Then with that, he and Larus left Allen's world and returned to the High Temple.

Upon their return, they found the High Temple even more crowded than it had been when Daeson departed. Word must have spread throughout the ranks of Qyaendri that Xi had appeared and something momentous was in the offing.

None spoke to the pair as they made their way toward the rotunda where Xi had so recently appeared. The Rotunda was the general meeting area within the High Temple. Seven statues of the goddess were evenly spaced in a circular formation around the outer fringe. An eighth statue, dwarfing the others, stood majestically in the center. It was toward the central statue that Daeson and Larus proceeded. As they drew close, Xi appeared.

Larus and Daeson dropped to one knee and respectfully bowed to Xi in silence. They remained that way until Xi spoke.

"Larus," resonated Xi's deep voice.

Larus raised his head and gazed at the most ancient of all Casdralla's Qyaendri.

"Our Lady's people are faced with great difficulties in the times ahead," he said. "Her presence on their world may come to an end."

"No!" several of the Qyaendri among those watching exclaimed.

"What does our Lady want of me?" Larus asked.

"To save her people," he replied.

"How?" asked Larus. *The fate of her people on an entire world was going to rest in his hands?* Where most would feel only the greatest sense of pride in being selected for such a job, he instead felt grossly inadequate with just a touch of fear.

Reaching out his hand to Larus, Xi replied, "Take my hand."

Larus reached out and laid his hand upon Xi's palm. As soon as contact was made, they disappeared.

When they were again corporeal, Larus discovered that he was in a very strange place. The air was the same as what he had experienced on most of the other worlds to which he had traveled in Casdralla's service. It was an arid place with sand and round shaped weeds which tumbled as the wind blew. Larus gazed to the horizon and found a range of mountains rising to the sky. Between where they stood and the mountains were more sand and dirt, a few small trees, and the odd bird.

What made it so strange was the uniform, black road that lay on the ground before them, and the building situated on the other side. The black road was unlike any he had seen before, with a strange yellow stripe running down the middle and a single white line adorning either edge.

The building across the road was rather squat, looked dirty, and in disrepair. A tall pole in front had a large squarish sign that bore the inscription: *Good Food---Gas.*

"Where are we?" Larus asked. Other than the strange road and the building, there were no indications that people inhabited this place. "Is this where our Lady's people live?"

"No," Xi replied. "On this world, there are none who worship our Lady."

Larus glanced at the other in surprise. "Why am I here then?" he asked.

"There is one here who can help our people," explained Xi. Glancing to Larus, Xi continued. "You have a single year of this world to locate the one and prepare him for what he must do."

"Him?" asked Larus. "So am I to understand that I am to find a man?"

Xi didn't reply. "We have made arrangements for one person to be selected and removed from this world," he further explained. He glanced to Larus and said, "Only one."

Larus nodded gravely. He understood that whoever was selected would be the only chance they had. "Part of our agreement is that you in no way attempt to bring our Lady's influence to this world. You will not interfere with its people. Confine your actions with locating, and training the one who must save our Lady's people."

"I understand," he replied. Then he felt energy flowing from Xi to him and what needed to be done, as well as the information to impart to the one chosen, was made known to him.

"You have one year," Xi said then vanished.

As he stood there in the aftermath of what he had learned, he thought of the great responsibility entrusted to him by the mighty Xi. The fear he had earlier felt at being summoned by Xi faded away only to be replaced with pride and a sense of purpose. *Yes*, he said to himself. *I can do this!*

Glancing around at his surroundings, the first question that came to mind was, *'What manner of people lived here?'* He bent down to touch the black road running along the ground in front of him and was surprised to find it hard, yet slightly malleable.

"Interesting," he said to himself.

Then his attention turned toward the squat building. Stepping toward it, he walked across the black road to investigate. Often times, an examination of the native architecture would reveal insights into the inhabitants of a world.

Out front were two small obelisk looking structures about five feet high. They had tubes of a firm substance that was attached to them at one end. Passing the obelisks, he made his way to the building.

It had several windows whose glass had long since been broken, all but one were boarded up. The front door was a latticework of metal which he found to be unusual. Looking inside, he saw barren stands and tables. Small animals the size of his hand with a long tail, rats he thought they were, could be seen making their way across the floor. Whatever this place's original function had been, it was deserted now. Realizing he wasn't going to learn anything further there, he returned to the road.

Glancing down either direction failed to gave him any indication as to which way he needed to go in order to reach the nearest town. Determining that the path to the right traveled slightly downhill, he decided to try that way. Stepping upon the black road, he set out in search for the one who would save Casdralla's people.

Larus had been walking for a little over two hours, all the while contemplating the information Xi gave him to impart to the chosen one. First and foremost was the language of the world in question. Whoever the chosen one turned out to be, it was a given that his native tongue would not be that of the world to which he would be taken. Also, there was a general knowledge of the world which would prove invaluable, as well as basic skills he may need along the way.

Then a sound began to develop behind him, bringing him out of his reverie. It was growing louder by the second. Glancing back the way he had come, he saw what looked to be a fast moving carriage hurtling toward him. *What propelled it?* he thought. There were no horses drawing it and the carriage rode low to the ground. It was black and shiny. Along the side were what looked to be red flames, but were in actuality simply an adornment.

As he turned toward the fast moving carriage, he could see two people riding inside. "Well, this was easy," he said to himself as he waved to them in greeting. It was nice of Xi to have placed him where he was sure to encounter the chosen one so readily.

He stood upon the road waving but the carriage failed to slow down. Almost as if those within didn't see him, it approached and then with a gust of wind, roared past. Larus was startled when just as the carriage was passing by, it let out with a very loud, very unnerving sound that lasted but a second.

As the carriage sped down the road away from him, he ceased waving. Standing perplexed for a moment, he tried to figure out what happened. Then from behind him, another roaring sound began to be heard. Looking back, he saw another carriage heading quickly toward him.

This carriage was unlike the other one. Where the first one had been black and shiny, this one was kind of a brownish color. Only one person was within it, and behind the area where the person sat, was a long open area that resembled a box without a lid.

Larus stood there as the carriage roared toward him. Always the friendly sort, he again waved. To his astonishment, the carriage let out with an unpleasant squealing sound as it began to slow. At its current rate of deceleration, he realized the carriage was going to stop next to where he stood.

As the carriage let out a final ear piercing squeal as it came to a stop, Larus looked through the carriage window and saw an older man inside. The glass of the window suddenly began moving down and smoke belched forth. "Are you lost?" the old man asked.

Larus wasn't sure how to respond so remained silent. *Could this be the chosen one?*

"Do you need a ride?" the old man asked.

"Yes," replied Larus. "I would find that most welcomed."

The old man waited while Larus simply stood there for a moment then said, "Well, don't just stand there." Motioning to the other side of the carriage, he added, "Get in."

"Oh, right," replied Larus. He quickly moved around to the other side and opened the door. The opening apparatus was unlike any other he had ever seen, but readily deduced its function. Climbing inside, he sat next to the old man then closed the door. As soon as the door shut, the carriage roared back to life and they began moving down the black road.

"What's your name?" the old man asked.

"Larus," he replied.

The old man grinned. "You can call me Pete," he said. Reaching up to the panel before him, he pressed a button and music filled the inside of the carriage. It was loud and its sudden appearance startled Larus.

As the old man pulled forth a small thin circular tube, Larus reached up out of curiosity for the button which seemed to have produced the music. Pressing it, the music abruptly stopped.

The old man applied a flame to the tube and smoke began to issue from it. He glanced to Larus and asked, "What, you don't like county?"

Country? Thinking fast, Larus replied, "I like your country very much."

"Then why did you turn it off?" the old man asked.

"Off?" asked a confused Larus.

"Yes," replied Pete. Reaching up, he pressed the button and the music reappeared. Pressing it again, the music vanished.

"Oh!" said Larus as he realized what the man was talking about. "You mean the music."

"Yes," said Pete, giving Larus a sidelong look.

Larus gave him a grin and pressed the button which caused the music to once more fill the carriage. The novelty of creating music by pressing a button intrigued him.

"Are you okay?" Pete asked.

"I am fine, thank you," Larus assured him.

Pete held forth his hand which held a small package with more of the round tubes and offered him one. "Want a smoke?" he asked.

Larus shook his head. "I must decline," he answered. He had encountered various means in which people inhaled smoke given off by burning vegetation, but never once had he enjoyed it.

Pete shrugged and said, "Suit yourself."

They rode down the road in silence for a bit, Larus completely enthralled by the novelty of riding in a horseless carriage. Turning back from watching the landscape zipping by, he caught Pete casting glances toward him. "Is there something I can help you with?" he asked.

Shaking his head, Pete said, "No." Then a moment later, "You're not sweating."

"That is true," replied Larus.

"But, it's a hundred and fifteen outside," the old man stated. "And you were walking beneath the sun."

"I don't perspire," he explained.

"Some kind of medical condition?" Pete asked.

"I suppose you could call it that," he replied.

While Pete had been checking him out, Larus had been weighing the chances of Pete being the chosen one. It didn't take him long to rule him out as a candidate. Using the senses all Qyaendri possess, he could tell the man had extensive problems with his lungs. In fact, Larus would be surprised if he lived through the week. He wanted to help the man for it was within his power to do so, but Xi's warning about not interfering with the people of this world prevented him.

Larus sat back and again looked out the window at the world passing by. Arid, barren, lifeless, he felt the chances of finding anyone suitable in such a land extremely remote. He knew his Lady's people were counting on him to find the one to save them. But where could that person be?

As they continued down the black road, they began encountering other carriages coming from the other direction. Not one of them looked the same. He was fascinated by the apparent need for variety these people exhibited. For the most part, places he had been sent to help Casdralla's faithful tended to be all the same; the people, sights, and sounds. But here, things were different.

"How far are you going?" Pete finally asked.

"I'm not entirely sure," he replied.

"A free spirit huh?" the old man guessed.

Larus shook his head. "No, that I am not."

The response wasn't what Pete was expecting. Shrugging it off, he said, "Well, I'm only going another couple miles. My son and I have a booth at the fair where we sell produce."

"Fair?" asked Larus.

"That's right," he replied.

"Will there be many people there?" he asked.

"A *fair* amount," he said, then laughed at the play on words.

"Excellent," Larus commented. "That would be an ideal place in which to start." He began thinking about how he was going to go about winnowing the people he was to meet down to the few who may fulfill the criteria for the chosen one. Before he had it figured out, his attention was drawn to a town appearing out of the horizon further down the road. As they drew closer, a sight appeared some ways from the town off the right side of the road that he had never seen before.

There was a large wheel going round and round yet not going anywhere. As they drew closer still, he saw people riding upon seats attached to the inner surface of the wheel. Then other sights, equally strange and wonderful caught his eye. "What is that?" he asked.

"That's the fair," explained the old man. "What, ain't you never seen one before?"

Larus shook his head. "Not like that," he replied.

"Shoot, that's a small one," he said with a chuckle. "Out here in the middle of nowhere, you can't wrangle the big amusement companies to come. But this one suits our needs and provided a place for the young'ens to have fun."

Not really paying much attention to what Pete was saying, Larus was taking in the wonders coming at him through the window; the lights and the people. And the *energy!* He could feel it radiating out from the fair. Only extreme emotions could generate such an outpouring of energy from mortals. Fear and love would do it, but he didn't feel any of that coming from there. Something else was causing it.

As Pete pulled from the road they had been traveling upon onto another smaller one, they covered the last of the distance to the fair.

Larus' eyes were trying to take in everything the fair had to offer. He then caught a whiff of an odor coming from outside the carriage. It took him a moment of searching before he found the correct mechanism and rolled his window down to better experience it. Baked bread, only sweeter with a hint of something else. As the window came down, so too did the noise enter. Larus was beside himself with the sights, sounds, and smells of the fair.

Pete followed the smaller road to one of the entryways where he came to a stop. A lady stood near the gate and approached Pete's window. "More produce Pete?" she asked.

"Yeah," he replied. "My boy called and said they were running low."

The lady looked over to Larus. "Who's your friend?"

"Found him wandering along the side of the road. His name's Larus," Pete explained.

"Walking out in this heat?" she asked.

Pete nodded. "Yep." Revving the engine, he said, "Talk to you later."

"You take care," she replied warmly.

Making their way slowly through the fairgrounds, Larus was overwhelmed by the sights and sounds. Never in all his experiences had he encountered anything like this on a mortal world. When Pete brought the carriage to a stop, Larus opened the door and left the cab. In the back of his mind he heard Pete calling his name but he was too enthralled by the energy bombarding him from every side to pay any attention.

The gleeful cries of children, the amazing odors emanating from dozens of sources, all added to the sensory overload he was experiencing. It was unlike anything he had ever experienced on a mortal world. Moving deeper into the fair, all he could think of was Pete's comment that this was small. He couldn't help but wonder what a large one would be like.

Chapter 2

A lone traveler was riding along the road that wended its way eastward through rolling hills. This part of Casdra was sparsely populated with only the occasional farmsteads dotting the land. Further east rose the mountains through which the road would ultimately go. A cool breeze blew down from the peaks, easing the heat of the summer day.

Father Thomas was on his way back to the village of Billin where he was proud to be the spiritual leader. Every three years, Casdralla's priests were required to spend time at the High Temple for a period of fasting and purification. Then once completed, they would return to their home temples, recharged in spirit and ready to continue the work of the Lady.

Riding his mule across the hills of the lower region of Casdra, the land in which their holy Lady held sway, he passed the time by recalling many of the theological discussions in which he partook. Such learned exchanges of ideas were a rare thing in his home temple and that was part of the reason he so enjoyed his time at the High Temple. The priests with whom he served on a day to day basis in Billin were not necessarily the brightest of those called to the Lady's service. Billin being a small town with a small temple, it didn't draw many of what many would consider deep thinkers. The only one with whom he could discuss the more abstract theoretical ideals was Brother Frey. But he tended to be rather peripatetic and spent most of his time traveling between temples, being a more hands on priest than most.

All in all, Father Thomas was quite satisfied with his life. The birds were singing and the light breeze aided in keeping the summer heat tolerable.

Sometime tomorrow he would be back in Billin. Nestled in a high valley along the shore of the prettiest lake one could ever hope to see, Billin inhabited the most tranquil, and beautiful area Father Thomas had ever encountered. That was why when he had heard of the passing of the Father in charge of the Billin temple, he quickly volunteered for the position. He loved being in the mountains and away from the hustle and bustle of the city. Dabbing away the sweat beading his forehead, he would also be glad to be away from the heat of the lowlands.

It was still early in the day when the road began to rise on its way toward the upper elevations. Casdra on a whole was a land of rugged terrain and deep forests. Almost completely encircled by tall mountain ranges, the greater part of Casdralla's domain was accessible only through a single mountain pass.

Father Thomas had made his way through that pass four days ago and then spent the better part of a day visiting a friend who was a priest at the temple in the walled city of Xith.

Xith was by far Casdra's largest city. Situated as it was on the southern border, the soldiers garrisoned behind its fortifications had protected the pass leading into the heart of Casdra for centuries. With its massive wall protecting it, they could sally forth and attack any army which dared try to invade into the heart of Casdra. The last such assault was three centuries ago and the invading army had been decimated so severely, they had eventually given up and returned home in disgrace after losing more than half its men.

Their country was strong, its people prosperous, the world was as it should be.

As he continued along, the road gradually grew steeper as it made its way to the summit. At times it would switchback on itself and grow quite steep. Every time he passed through this section of the road, he would offer a prayer up to the Lady for those traders hearty enough to dare this route of steep incline and narrow switchbacks. For without them, his village would experience grave hardship.

Hours went by as he worked his way to the summit. A hunter's cabin stood not far from the road just over the summit on the eastern side. In the winter, hunters from Billin would come and use it as a base. During other seasons of the year, it was a way-stop for travelers, a place where they could escape the cold of the mountains and take their ease during the night.

Father Thomas always made it a point to stop there whenever he traveled to the High Temple or visited his friend in Xith. Rarely did he encounter another person sharing the cabin during those times. It afforded him a final period in which to commune with the Lady before returning to his duties. And as he crested the summit and the cabin came into view not far down the road, he saw that this time was to be no exception. It was shut tight against the elements and had the look of being deserted.

Behind the cabin was a small stable where he housed his mule. He offered a prayer of thanksgiving to Casdralla when he discovered oats for his mule. They must have been left by the last traveler.

But such was the custom in Casdra. It being for the most part a mountainous and rugged country, way-stops such as this one were not uncommon. Whenever a traveler stayed at one, custom dictated for them to leave what they could for the next traveler. Because who knew when someone's need would be great? The Lady favored those who helped others.

Aside from the oats, Father Thomas discovered plenty of chopped wood stacked inside near the fireplace, another benevolent act by the previous occupant. He stacked several of the smaller logs within the fireplace and soon had a warm fire burning, its warmth quickly banishing the cool of the upper elevations from the cabin.

Once the fire was able to continue burning on its own, he took his pot and went outside to where a small creek made its way past the cabin. There he filled it a quarter of the way with water.

The sun by this time had fallen behind the western peaks and the day was once more giving way to night. Father Thomas took his time on returning to the cabin. The peace of the moment filled him and it was in times like these that he felt closest to the Lady.

When at last he returned inside the cabin, he went about making a stew from the last of his supplies. As he waited for it to become ready, he gazed from the window, enjoying the tranquil view of the trees and mountains.

Tomorrow he would be home.

In the morning before he left, he offered a blessing for the next traveler. Since priests normally weren't expected to chop wood, this was their way of contributing to the way-stops. Anyone who encountered a way-stop that was ill prepared for them knew that a priest had recently spent the night and that they would be blessed. True, there were some who took advantage of the custom and took without giving, but they faced a reckoning for their actions when they departed this world.

Once the blessing had been said and he was again atop his mule, Father Thomas resumed his progress toward Billin. His spirits were high as he worked his way down from the summit, fully enjoying another of the remarkably beautiful days that were so common to this region at this time of year.

He rode for several hours before encountering another traveler. The man was on foot further down the road and making his way toward him. Walking with head down and steps coming in broken rhythm, there was something about the man that made Father Thomas uneasy. Nudging his mule to a quicker pace, he hurried forward. He had covered most of the distance and was about to shout a salutation when the man took a misstep and fell to the road.

Father Thomas immediately slipped from the back of his mule and rushed forward, his concern growing into something more. Even before he reached the man's side, he could see that his clothes were torn and stained red with blood.

His first thought was that the man may have run afoul of bandits. Though not very common along this stretch of road, it did happen. "My son!" he cried as he reached the man's side.

Raising his head, the man looked up. "Father," he said.

Father Thomas gasped in recognition when he recognized the face staring up at him. "Jesop?" he asked in worry. Dropping to his knees, he reached out for his long time friend. "What happened?" he asked. "Who did this to you?" Dried blood matted Jesop's clothes in several places. There was a wound on his head, a bump that appeared to have been caused by contact with a blunt object.

Jesop grabbed the front of Father Thomas' robe. "They're gone! Everyone is gone!"

Fear from deep within the priest began welling to the surface as Jesop spoke. "Gone?" he asked. "Who?"

"I tried..." he began then stopped as the light in his eyes began to fade.

"Jesop!" yelled Father Thomas. Bowing his head, he closed his eyes and prayed. "Lady, who watches over her people as does a loving mother, let not this good man leave us!" When he opened his eyes, he saw Jesop looking back. "Tell me what happened," he said softly.

"They came in the night," Jesop explained. "With clubs and swords they came and took everyone they could find." He started to fade again but strength returned to him and was able to continue. "I tried to save them!" he shouted. "But there were too many." Tears appeared in his eyes as he said quietly, "They took my Valia, ripped her out of my arms as I tried to shield her. She was but a girl!"

"Who did this?" Father Thomas asked.

Jesop didn't reply. His turned his head toward him and sobbed.

Father Thomas held him as he cried. Inwardly, he feared for his people, for Jesop had been one of those who lived within Billin. He was amazed that given his injuries, Jesop had made it so far. Giving silent prayers to the Lady for the safety of his people and for her to protect them, he held the man until his cries stopped. When he loosened the embrace, he found that Jesop had died.

He said another prayer for Casdralla to ease Jesop's passage to the next world, then set about burying him. Father Thomas desperately needed to return to Billin and find out what had happened, but first he would give Jesop the proper burial he deserved.

It took him almost half an hour before Jesop was properly in the ground. Standing by the grave, he offered another prayer then returned to his mule and continued the last stretch home as fast as possible.

An hour later he saw the smoke. Two more hours found him upon the crest of the ridge overlooking Billin and saw what remained of his once peaceful, beautiful village. Not one building remained intact. Whoever had done this had set fire to everything. He sought where his temple had once stood and found only a charred remnant.

A glimmer of hope sprung within him when he saw people moving amongst the smoldering remains of their homes. Nudging his mule into motion, he hurried down to the town.

Daeson was aiding in processing prayers of the faithful as most Qyaendri do from time to time when another of the Qyaendri appeared before him. "Daeson!" the Qyaendri exclaimed. "Xi has returned!"

"Xi?" he asked.

Nodding, the Qyaendri said, "He wants you to come."

Without saying anything further, Daeson vanished and immediately appeared within the High Temple where he made his way to the Rotunda. The temple was crowded to the point of bursting with curious Qyaendri. As he came forward, their ranks parted to allow him a path to the center by the statue of their goddess where Xi waited.

Xi said not a word as Daeson approached. As he came before the most ancient one, Daeson dropped to one knee and bowed "What does my Lady want of me?" he asked.

There was a moment of quiet expectation as everyone within the Rotunda held still to hear Xi's reply. "It is time," his deep voice announced.

Daeson raised his head and saw Xi holding his hand out toward him.

"Take my hand," he said.

Coming to his feet, Daeson reached out and took hold of Xi's hand. In that instant, they were gone.

In a world very much different to that in which Father Thomas hurried to help his people, Larus laughed. He had done much laughing during the past year spent on this world. The people inhabiting this particular world were basically much the same as those he had encountered on every other world to which he had been sent during his time in Casdralla's service. It was what they had done with the world that so amazed him.

He had learned much of this world and its people since his first arrival: radio, television, candy bars, the list was endless. These people had a way of living which transfixed him as none other. From the simple country fair, he had made his way to a more populated area where he planned to search for the one to save his Lady's people.

But soon after arriving, he discovered a place that made the fair seem boring in comparison. It was something the locals called an 'Amusement Park'. In it were things the locals called 'roller-coasters' and other 'thrill rides' which soon had him procrastinating in his mission to find the chosen one. After all, he did have a whole year didn't he?

One of the attributes of the Qyaendri was that when they were around mortals, they were prone to pick up the habits and attitudes of those mortals. Most Qyaendri were able to use this ability to better deal with the mortals they were trying to help. Knowing how mortals thought and felt gave them an edge when attempting to answer their prayers.

However, some like Larus, tended to be more influenced in their own actions by the habits and attitudes of the mortals around them. His susceptibility to being thus affected had played no small part in why he had been sent to help the boy Allen. The little boy lived in a sparsely populated rural community and Larus would have minimal contact with humans. Now though, with thousands of people surrounding him and being constantly bombarded by their thoughts, emotions, and the basic drives of all humans, he was ill equipped to deal with it.

And that is why, a year later, Larus had done very little in the way of finding the chosen one. In fact, for the last three months, he hadn't even thought about his mission at all. Going from one experience to another, he became an addict of this world. Not from drugs or anything like that, but rather from a deluge of experiences so overwhelming, that they were all he could think about.

A year to the day of his arrival on this world, Larus was seated in an old, rundown movie theater watching a Three Stooges' marathon. Aside from himself, there were only fourteen others in the theater. On his lap was a monster bucket of popcorn from which a steady stream of the crunchy goodness found its way into his mouth. Resting on the seat next to him was a half eaten box of bonbons, a pop that was all but gone, and the nachos he planned to eat a little bit later.

There was something about the men on the screen that was hard to resist. Their antics brought forth laughter from him the likes of which he had never experienced. Currently, he was watching them trying to get a block of ice up a tall flight of steps. Every time the block of ice reached the top, it had melted to a fraction of its original size. And every time, he would laugh. Then, they positioned themselves to relay the block of ice to the top. Each moving quickly, they were finally able to get the block of ice to the top intact. When Curly held it up to show the other two they had succeeded, it slipped out of the tongs and shattered on the ground.

Larus broke into laughing so hard, he could barely breathe. When he was finally able to control the laughter and returned his gaze to the screen, he found the picture to be frozen.

"Hey!" he hollered up to the projection room. Glancing to the square through which the picture emerged, he tried to see what, if anything, was going on in there.

About to get out of his seat and head out to the lobby to tell someone, he noticed everyone in the theater wasn't moving either. That was when he saw someone standing nearby in the aisle looking straight at him. A soft nimbus of light radiated from the man. It took only a moment for him to recognize Daeson.

At seeing the Qyaendri, the enormity of what he had done, or rather not done, struck him like a load of bricks. The presence of another Qyaendri did much to negate the accumulated affects of the mortals on this world. He realized the time was up and that he had done nothing in finding the chosen one.

"I've come to bring the one to save our Lady's people," Daeson told him.

Fear coursed through Larus. He had failed! There was no chosen one!

"Where is he?" asked Daeson.

Panic filled him. He could be banished from his Lady's presence for this! And what of Xi? What would that mighty one do to him for having failed? Visions of consequences too terrible to mention ran through his mind.

"Well?" asked Daeson. "Don't tell me you failed again." His expression darkened.

"No," lied Larus. It just came out. He had never lied before, ever. Yet there he was, lying! Before he could stop himself, he blurted out, "The chosen one is ready."

Surprise appeared on Daeson's face. "Truly?" When Larus nodded, he asked, "Then where is he? Time is short for our Lady's people."

His mind froze. What could he say? What could he do? Then, out of the corner of his eye, he saw a man frozen in the doorway leading from the theater. The man was returning from the lobby with a bucket of popcorn in one hand and a drink in the other. Pointing toward him, Larus said, "That's him."

Daeson turned to look at the man and said, "Good." Moving toward him, Daeson reached out and touched the man on the arm.

As Daeson and the man disappeared, Larus moaned, "What have I done?"

Father Thomas was numb. Only a few of his people had survived the attack. Those who had been lucky enough to find refuge in the surrounding forest told tales of men appearing in the dead of night. Wielding clubs, they felled everyone they encountered.

Here and there as he passed through the pitiful remnants of his once beautiful village, laid men who had fought to save family and friends. Their bodies hacked and stabbed, some beyond recognition. Whoever had done this had shown no mercy.

They had come for his people, taken them toward a fate Father Thomas wouldn't allow himself to contemplate. A steady stream of prayers issued forth from the priest as he moved from body to body. Not only were they of the men who fought in defense of their village, but also of the old and infirm.

"Why?" a woman cried out to him. "Why would they do this to us?"

He looked her way and saw a woman cradling the head of a man in her lap. As he gazed into her tear streaked face, he recognized her as Clarissa. She and the man whose head she cradled had exchanged vows but a month ago. Theirs had been a life of promise. Now she was a widow.

Shaking his head, he said, "I do not know."

"It was them damn Ullentites," stated a crusty old codger. Ogger was one of the oldest living residents in Billin and had been the boil on many backsides during his protracted years. "Always knew they were no good."

Ullen was the nation to the south. Ruled by a king, they and Casdra had enjoyed many years of peace and prosperity. During his recent time in the High Temple, Father Thomas had heard unsettling rumors surrounding a recent shift in the power structure of Ullen. He had paid little heed, now much to his regret.

"Carey!" "Mort!" A woman cried out in anguish as she moved through the charred remains of Billin in search of her children.

Father Thomas continued to sink lower into sadness, his world crumbling around him. All he could think of was that he had not been here when his people had needed him the most. Self deprecating guilt and mind numbing emotional pain sought to take his will from him. Then, almost as if a hand reached inside him and brought him back to his reason, he knew what he had to do.

Moving with renewed determination, he made his way toward what was left of his beautiful temple. Offering prayers and words of encouragement to all he passed along the way. The temple door was gone, as were the walls and ceiling. Fire had taken everything but the stone fireplace and the adjoining wall.

Passing resolutely into the still smoking remains, he made his way toward where the wooden altar had once stood. The silver chalice, the golden statue of the goddess, none of the precious, sacred objects had been spared by the invaders. They had stolen them all. His heart broke at the desecration to his temple, but he persevered until he reached the area just before where the altar had sat.

Charred sections of the crossbeams and ceiling were lying crisscrossed upon the floor. Taking hold of the uppermost beam, he began clearing them to the side. For hidden beneath the floor was the most sacred of all the artifacts which his temple had held.

"Father Thomas?" a man asked.

Pausing in his work, he turned to see Ogger standing at the edge of the ruined temple. The old man was looking at him.

"Could you use some help?" he asked.

Father Thomas was taken aback by the offer. In the fifteen years he had served in Billin, this was the first time Ogger had ever offered to help anyone. "Yes," he replied. "I could and thank you my son."

Ogger made his way to the Father's side, and with his help, the floor was soon cleared of debris.

It didn't look as if the secret compartment had been discovered. The fire which had destroyed his temple had scorched the wood of the floor and warped it slightly but appeared still intact. Kneeling down, Father Thomas pressed in the two places necessary to open it. When it popped open, it only opened half an inch. Then Ogger was there with a knife and wedged its blade into the side of the secret compartment's lid. When he pried the lid open, Father Thomas saw the purple velvet pouch and breathed a sigh of relief.

"What is that?" asked Ogger.

"This, my son," Father Thomas replied as he took the pouch and stood up, "is a piece of the very first temple ever built on this world to Casdralla." Opening the pouch, he pulled forth a piece of wood three inches long and one wide. To Ogger it looked like nothing more than part of a wooden plank that had been chipped away from a larger piece.

Father Thomas let the pouch fall away as he held the sacred artifact. "I am going to beseech our Lady to help our people," he explained.

Ogger nodded. "Is there anything I can help you with?" he asked.

"No," replied Father Thomas. Holding the artifact reverently in his hands, he fell to his knees and prayed. "Great Mother Casdralla, your people need your help this day…" As he prayed, he could feel the holiness of the piece of wood he held seem to magnify and envelope him like a warm, comforting blanket.

Pouring his heart and soul into the prayer, he beseeched her to watch over his people, that they may be safe and quickly returned to their loved ones. "…let them know you walk with them great Lady. Help them, I beseech you." With the utterance of the last word, he grew silent as tears streamed down his face. Finally giving into the emotions which have plagued him since first learning of the attack, he clutched the piece of wood and sobbed.

His sobbing continued for only a short time before a warm sense of calm settled over him, a feeling of safety akin to that of a fearful child being comforted by a loving parent. "Father!" he heard Ogger suddenly cry out. There was something strange in his voice, something he had never heard in it before. Opening his eyes, he was startled to see two men enveloped by a radiant glow standing before him.

"A Qyaendri!" he exclaimed. For the man on the right could be none other. Though they looked as any man one would expect to encounter on the street, a Qyaendri had a certain aura about them that any priest could immediately recognize.

Father Thomas was awed beyond words. Never in his time as a priest had he come face to face with one. While it was true he had been taught that they were the intermediaries between Casdralla and the mortal world, he had always harbored doubts as to their existence. At the High Temple where he had just recently come from, there were many murals and statues depicting Qyaendri. He had always hoped they were real. And, now standing before him, was one. Fear intermingled with awe at being in its presence.

The man standing next to the Qyaendri was an odd sort. His dress was unlike anything Father Thomas had ever seen before. In one hand the man held a bucket containing an unknown substance, while in the other was gripped what looked to be a container.

Remaining on his knees, Father Thomas bowed his head. "Mighty one," he said with as much reverence and respect he could muster. From the corner of his eye, he saw Ogger and several others down on one knee.

"There is a task which this man must complete," said the Qyaendri. "You, Father Thomas, must aid him in whatever way you are able."

"But what of my people?" began Father Thomas when suddenly, the Qyaendri disappeared. The glow encompassing the man faded with the Qyaendri's disappearance.

The man stood there with eyes wide for a moment as he looked first to Father Thomas then to the burned out husk of the temple. Then a small noise escaped him as his eyes rolled up into his head and fainted dead away.

Chapter 3

As the man hit the soot covered floor of the temple, Father Thomas rushed forward. Upon reaching his side, he saw that the man still breathed. He had merely fainted and remained uninjured. Turning to where Ogger knelt he said "Help me carry him somewhere more comfortable."

"Kyn's place out in the woods was untouched," offered one of the bystanders.

"Good, we shall take him there." With Ogger's help, Father Thomas lifted the unconscious man and carried him from the temple's remains.

Revitalized with hope, Father Thomas had thrown off the cloak of despair which had settled upon him. Obviously, the appearance of this man was the answer to his prayer. This man of unknown origin would somehow be instrumental in the return of his people.

"What was that?" Ogger asked once they emerged from the temple.

"I believe it was a Qyaendri," replied Father Thomas. "A servant of our Lady."

A hushed murmur passed through those accompanying them. Throughout their lives they had heard tales of the wondrous creatures, but never in all their days had they expected one to materialize in their midst.

"Have everyone gather at Kyn's," he told them. "When the stranger awakens, we'll discover how we shall bring about the return of our people." Moving quickly, he and Ogger brought the man to Kyn's home and laid him on the bed. Kyn had been one of the men who fell during the initial moments of the attack.

A water filled bowl and towel were brought to clean the soot from the stranger and his clothes. And such strange clothes they were too. The shirt was made of a material softer than wool. Brown in color, it bore a bear's face with indecipherable symbols stitched in an arc over its head.

His pants were dark blue and made of a sturdy material. Perhaps the greatest oddity about the man's apparel was his shoes. Never before had any seen their like. They only came to the man's ankles and were tied with a long cord looped through circular, reinforced holes. Altogether it made for a very odd and strange appearance.

While one of the village women cleaned the man, another came in carrying the items the man had been holding when he appeared. "Father," the woman said as she came forward with them.

"Give them here my child," he said. Reaching out for them, he took the bucket and container from the woman. A strange aroma was being emitted by the contents of the bucket which he found to be not entirely unpleasant. Inside were a multitude of small yellowish-white objects. Setting the bucket on the bedside table, he turned his attention to the container. The outside was blue and white with strange, unfamiliar diagrams inscribed upon its surface. Moving the container, he could feel liquid sloshing about within. Setting the liquid filled container next to the bucket, he turned to those assembled in the room.

"These must be the man's food and drink," he said. "Perhaps given to him by the Lady." That elicited a murmur from the onlookers.

"It might be wise to let him rest," Ogger said.

Father Thomas nodded. "I shall remain here with him," he told them. "The rest of you continue in your search for any others who may have survived." As the villagers started to leave, he said, "Ogger."

The old man stopped and turned back toward him.

"Thank you for your help," he said.

Ogger nodded then continued out from the room.

Once the door was closed and he and the man were alone in the room, Father Thomas watched the rise and fall of the man's chest. In his mind, he contemplated the events culminating with the man's appearance. Praying for strength to do what must be done, he pulled a chair next to the bed, sat down, and waited.

Man, what a dream that was, Hunter thought. Rolling over, he tried to settle into a more comfortable position but failed. For some reason, his bed wasn't very comfortable.

His room was dark and he glanced around for the clock but failed to find it. He then looked over to where the red standby light on his monitor should be glowing in the dark and couldn't find it either. "Great," he moaned to himself. "Power's out."

It was still dark so there had to be another hour or two before he would be forced to get up for work, not that he wanted to. In the back of his mind he knew that with the power out, his alarm wouldn't sound and he would probably oversleep. *So?* he thought. Perfect excuse to sleep in.

Rolling over yet again, he tried to find a comfortable position. That's when he became aware of what sounded like breathing coming from within the room. Instantly he snapped fully awake and held still while trying to ascertain whether or not his imagination was playing tricks on him. After a few moments, he heard it again. Then he heard other noises coming from outside which gave him the impression of several others.

The first thing that came to mind was looters taking advantage of the blackout. *He was being robbed!* Not if he had any say in it. Whoever was in the room didn't appear to be moving. In fact, the breathing noise seemed to be coming from the same place. Whoever it was, was remaining in the same spot. *Why?* Hunter couldn't figure that out, but he wasn't going to waste time thinking while his few meager possessions walked out the door.

Between his mattress and box spring nestled a 9mm handgun. His father had given it to him shortly after he left for college. He was pretty good with it, having spent time out on the firing range every once in a while with his friend Mitch.

Moving his hand slowly, he slipped it over the edge of the bed and inched his way toward the space in which his gun was hidden. To his chagrin, his hand encountered the bed frame before the crease between his mattress and box spring. Raising his hand back up, he sought the crease but for some reason, couldn't locate it.

Cursing silently, he figured he was going to have to do this the old fashioned way. Hoping the intruders didn't have guns of their own, he slowly sat up on the edge of the bed. As he came to his feet, he continued to concentrate on the sound of the other's breathing. It remained unchanged. *Curious.*

From outside he heard muffled voices speaking to one another but wasn't able to make them out. *One thing at a time*, he thought. He had to take out the one in the room first. It still didn't sound as if the one in the room was moving about. Unwilling to take the time to ponder such an anomaly as an immobile intruder, he readied himself to pounce.

Turning toward the sound of breathing coming from the one in the room he sprang into action. He no sooner took a step than his bare foot forcefully struck a hard object. Aside from the massive amount of pain such a blow elicited from his toes, the unexpectedness of the encounter knocked him off balance. Crashing into a nearby table, he smashed it to pieces on his way to the floor. As the still intact section of the table fell upon him, he resisted the urge to cry out in pain due to the throbbing of his recently stubbed toes.

The sound of the crash startled Father Thomas awake. The candle which had been burning on the table had gone out and the room was pitch black. "Ogger!" he cried as he scrambled to his feet.

His first thought was that someone had made an attack on the stranger. But when Ogger and several others burst into the room with a lit torch, they quickly realized what had happened. The stranger had left the bed and took a misstep in the dark.

Father Thomas pulled the table off the stranger only to have the stranger strike him in the stomach. Doubling over from the blow, he stumbled backward.

The stranger grabbed a section of the broken table and wielded in like a club as he limped backward to place his back against the wall. Moving the club back and forth, the stranger looked as if he expected Father Thomas and the others to attack him.

Out of the corner of his eye, he saw Ogger move forward toward the stranger. "Stay back!" he ordered the old man.

Ogger stopped and glanced his way. Upon seeing the priest motioning him to back off, he fell back several feet.

Father Thomas turned his attention to the stranger. He felt no anger for being struck, for he too would be unnerved to suddenly find himself inexplicably in foreign surroundings. Raising his hands with palms facing the stranger in a disarming gesture, he said, "We are not going to hurt you."

The stranger looked to him, his eyes slightly wild. Then the stranger looked to Ogger and the others before continuing to pan around the room. As his gaze moved, his expression turned from determination, to puzzlement, and then finally to one bordering on fear.

"Are you okay?" Father Thomas asked in a gentle, reassuring voice. Again, the stranger's gaze turned to him but made no other reply.

"I think he's not all there," observed Ogger.

"Quiet!" exclaimed Father Thomas quietly, all the while keeping his gaze fixed on the stranger.

"What is your name?" he asked. When again the stranger made no reply, Father Thomas moved one of his hands to his chest. Pointing to himself, he said, "Father Thomas." Again, no response.

Glancing over his shoulder, he realized most of the survivors of the earlier attack were crowding the area just within the room behind him. Turning to Ogger, he said, "It might be best if I dealt with him alone."

Ogger nodded. "You may be right father." Turning to the others he said, "Alright, you heard him. Everyone out." Moving forward he began ushering them toward, then through, the door.

"Do you want me to stay?" Ogger asked.

Father Thomas shook his head. "No," he replied. "But leave the torch."

"As you wish." As he came to the door and gently persuaded the last of the villagers to leave, he wedged the end of the torch into a crack in the wall, then walked out.

Once the door closed and he was alone with the stranger, Father Thomas could see the stranger begin to relax.

What is going on? Hunter tried to make sense of what he was seeing. He was not in his room. Rather, it looked like he was in some sort of cabin. The walls were made of logs and the furniture crude. *How did he get here?*

He held onto the piece of wood he was brandishing as a weapon while his mind worked to come to grips with the situation. There were at least ten people here other than himself. The one before him seemed to be the leader. From the way he was dressed in a robe and had short hair, he looked like one of those cultist leaders. Could that be what happened? Are they going to brainwash him and make him sell flowers at the airport? Hunter figured they were going to have to kill him before he would ever allow that to become a reality.

The leader spoke to him in some foreign language, but he couldn't make any sense of it. It sure wasn't Spanish or any of the others he had encountered over the years. He did relax some when everyone but the robed leader left the room. Hunter figured he could take the leader if he had to, but then what?

Not far from where he stood was a window. He began edging his way toward it to see if could figure out where he was. The leader stood still and quiet as he crossed over and looked out. He couldn't see much more than that they were surrounded by trees. Those who had been in the room earlier were congregating together nearby, a few cast glances his way.

Many looked to be in mourning. Men as well as women were crying, some spoke in anger, all in all the mood outside was not good. A second glance revealed that more than one bore fresh bandages that were stained with blood. Turning his gaze back to the leader, his confusion only grew.

As soon as his eyes met the other man's, the leader again pointed to himself and very slowly said, "Fa-ther Tho-mas."

"Father Thomas?" queried Hunter. His question elicited a smile and a nod.

The leader again pointed to himself and said, "Father Thomas." Then the leader pointed toward Hunter and looked at him questioningly.

"Hunter," he explained. "My name is Hunter."

"Hun...ter?" the leader asked.

Hunter nodded. "Yes," he replied. "Hunter."

The leader smiled and said, "Hunter."

"Okay," Hunter said, "now you know my name." The leader nodded when he paused. "What am I doing here?" The leader looked blank at the question. Then, he pointed over to a table near the bedside. When Hunter glanced over, he saw his drink and popcorn from the theater.

That sparked a memory. He had just arrived for the last half of the Three Stooges' marathon, bought his popcorn and drink, then had gone to sit down. After that his memory grew fuzzy. He faintly remembered walking through the door and into the theater. Then nothing until he woke up here in the dark. It didn't make any sense. If they kidnapped him, why bother to bring his popcorn and drink?

The leader spoke again and again gestured toward the popcorn and drink.

Hunter shook his head. "I don't want any, thanks," he said. "What I do want is to get out of here." The leader looked blankly at him for a second then nodded as he spoke several words.

"Do you understand what I am saying?" Hunter asked. The leader again paused a moment before nodding. Hunter remained quiet as the leader spoke, then nodded. "I don't know how I got here, but I want to leave." As it didn't appear that his life was in peril at the moment, he lowered the piece of wood.

As the leader spoke, Hunter nodded every once in a while in an attempt to placate him. He didn't know what was going on, but he hoped that by keeping this guy happy it might afford him a chance to escape. Thoughts went through his mind about cultists and how one documentary had detailed how a man managed to escape their clutches by pretending to go along until an opportunity presented itself for escape. So nodding and giving a small smile, he listened to words he did not understand.

"Hunter," Father Thomas said, "my people are in great peril. The Lady has brought you in answer to my prayers." Pausing, he waited until he saw Hunter nod before continuing. "We must hurry if we are to rescue my people." Again, Hunter nodded during a pause.

"Are you a wizard of great power?" Father Thomas asked. Relief washed over him as Hunter nodded. "Praise the Lady," he said.

Pointing again over to the man's food, he said, "We brought this for you should you require sustenance. Or can you eat our food?" A nod. "You can? Excellent." He gave Hunter a smile which was returned. *This is going better than I had imagined*, thought Father Thomas.

"We should hurry," he said, "before those who took our people have a chance to get too far away. They already have half a day's head start on us." When Hunter nodded, he turned his head toward the door and hollered, "Ogger!"

The door immediately opened and Ogger entered. Fear sprang anew in Hunter's eyes which Father Thomas was quick to alleviate. "It's okay," he said in a mollifying tone. "He's a friend."

"Everything alright Father?" asked Ogger. He glanced from the priest to the man against the wall.

"Yes," he said. "I think I've explained the situation. He's willing to help." Turning back to Hunter he asked, "Aren't you?"

The appearance of the second man worried Hunter at first. But when the leader, who's name he believed to be Father Thomas, turned back to him and spoke reassuringly, he relaxed and nodded again. The old guy seemed harmless, at least for the moment. Hunter felt the need to placate his captors until he could make a break for it. Until that time he would go along with anything as long as he didn't get hurt or was forced to do something immoral. At that time he would turn from a willing, passive captive to one bent on immediate escape by any means necessary.

After several exchanges of words, the old man passed back through the doorway. At that time, Father Thomas turned back toward him and began motioning for him to follow. Backing through the door, it was obvious he wanted Hunter to follow him from the room. Having little other recourse, Hunter moved away from the wall and cautiously followed him through the doorway, the piece of wood still firmly clutched in his right hand.

There he found another room which looked to be the cabin's living room with a small, crude kitchen off to the side. The lack of refrigerator and other modern amenities led him to believe this cult must not believe in modernization. There wasn't even so much as a television, radio, or lights. He looked to the walls but failed to locate any switches or power outlets.

When he reached the doorway leading to the outside, he paused. Almost twenty people were present outside, standing still and watching him. "Okay," he asked, "now what?"

Father Thomas spoke to him in his indecipherable language, again motioning for Hunter to follow. Geared to flee at a moment's notice, he stepped from the cabin. After three steps, he saw a woman approach him and came to a stop.

The first thing he noticed about her were her red eyes and the tracks tears had made in the areas of soot covering her face. She came toward him with what looked to be an old fashioned satchel. Stopping an arm's length away, she held it out for him.

Hunter glanced over to Father Thomas and saw him nod for him to take it. Reaching out, he took the satchel from the woman. She began speaking to him as tears welled anew. Then, panic seized him when she rushed forward. But it quickly dissipated when she wrapped her arms around him and began sobbing almost uncontrollably. Two of the other women quickly came and pulled her away. Something was greatly troubling these people, though for the life of him he couldn't figure it out.

Three other women came forward. One gave a satchel to Father Thomas, another to the old man, and the third to a younger man. When he saw the three of them sling their satchels across their backs, he did the same.

"Are we going somewhere?" he asked.

The crowd of people grew silent as every eye turned back toward him. Father Thomas came forward and laid a hand on his shoulder. He spoke for a few seconds and afterward waited with an expectant look. Not knowing what else to do, Hunter nodded. Immediately, the crowd collectively sighed in relief, many directing smiles his way.

From out of the trees came a man with a bow slung across his shoulders. The people grew silent once more as the man came and spoke with Father Thomas. Pointing back the way he had come he spoke quickly and urgently.

The effect of his words was immediately apparent to those assembled. The momentary happiness they had exhibited deteriorated quickly back into sadness, some even breaking down into sobs once more. When the man finished speaking, Father Thomas laid a hand on his shoulder and nodded. After speaking a few more words which sounded encouragingly to the crowd, he turned back to Hunter.

By this time, Hunter was thoroughly confused. What he was sure had been a cult didn't really act like one. On the contrary, they seemed to be in a great deal of distress. Either way, when Father Thomas spoke to him again and indicated they should follow the man with the bow, he didn't know what else to do but acquiesce. Until he figured out what was going on, he better play along. But the first chance that presented itself, he would make a break for it. Somewhere out there had to be a phone where he could call for help.

Father Thomas fell in behind Lurri, with Hunter close by. Ogger and Kyle, the younger man who was to accompany them, brought up the rear.

"They've made camp in the foothills," explained Lurri. A local woodsman, he had returned from a hunting trip not too long after the marauders had finished their business in Billin and headed south. He had immediately followed in the hopes of affecting their peoples' rescue, but the force had proven too strong. Once the enemy had made camp, he hurried back to inform the others and perhaps organize a more able rescue party. Imagine his surprise when he was told of the stranger and the way in which he had arrived.

Moving quickly, they soon returned to the charred remnants of their village. The sight of which caused the stranger to stop in his tracks. One building still burned while the others were either still smoldering or had been reduced to a pile of ash.

Father Thomas came and put a hand on the stranger's shoulder. "This was our village," he explained. "Most of our people have been captured by those who did this." The stranger glanced at him with an odd look in his eye. Then he silently nodded.

"Come," Lurri said. "We haven't much time. If we don't hurry dawn will come before we can reach them."

"And if that happens," added Kyle, "our chances of doing anything effective will be gone."

"You are correct my son," Father Thomas agreed. Turning to the stranger he said, "We must hurry." With a gentle tug on his arm to get him going, Father Thomas had the stranger moving once again.

As they left what had been his home for many years, Father Thomas offered another silent prayer beseeching help up to the Lady.

"Looks like Larus came through this time," said Ftheril, one the Qyaendri Daeson had authority over.

Standing unseen by the mortals making their way from the ruined village, Daeson nodded. "Perhaps." He and Ftheril watched as the mortals left the vicinity of Billin and began making their way down the river toward those who held their Lady's people. "Watch them," he told the Qyaendri. "Let me know if anything should develop."

Ftheril nodded as one of the lesser Qyaendri left to take the priest's latest prayer to the High Temple where it would be considered. No sooner had the one left than another appeared. Priests always had at least one Qyaendri in attendance at all times. In certain times of crisis or turmoil, there could be more. "As you wish," Ftheril replied.

Daeson cast one final glance to the mortals before they disappeared into the trees. Then he left this world, for there were many Qyaendri attending numerous errands that required his attention.

Chapter 4

Hunter was now even more confused. The last hour of travel along the banks of the river gave him ample opportunity to ponder the situation. He had already come to the conclusion that the people whom he saw shortly before he and the other three left for who knew where, must have belonged to the torched village. The sadness, the smell of char which clung around them, all indicated the two must be related.

But what happened? Assuredly, the number of people who once lived there must have numbered more than what he had already encountered. His initial theory that they might be a cult was beginning to fade in the logic of the situation. He seriously doubted they were cultists. What they really were still eluded him, but one thing was certain, they had recently gone through a traumatic experience. Of that he was sure.

However, that still didn't explain his presence or how he even arrived. Wherever he was, it was very far from civilization. The town looked like something out of an old history book. No sign of power poles, sewers, or any of the other trappings which one would associate with modern times. The thought that they may be kin to the Amish came to mind. Perhaps some sect of theirs with even more of a traditional and isolationist mentality.

Whatever the reason, no matter how nice they seemed, the fact remained that he had been brought there against his will, and they were in no small part involved. He had been kidnapped, no way around it. He must get away before becoming mired in whatever troubles they were having.

The moon and stars lit the way as they made their way quickly along the banks of the river. If it wasn't for the man with the bow, he would have already made a break for it. But the thought of a feathered shaft impaling him through the back kept him docile. At least for the moment.

The four men he was walking with talked quietly amongst themselves. A couple times they made attempts to include him in their conversation, but after several fruitless endeavors, ceased trying. He was too engrossed with his own thoughts to try and figure out what they were saying anyway.

After another couple hours of walking on the uneven banks of the river, Hunter's feet were complaining. The shoes he wore, while comfortable in his day to day activities, left much to be desired when traversing across rock and root strewn ground in the dark. Both ankles hurt and he thought a blister may be forming on one of his big toes.

When they came to where the river passed through a small clearing, the man with the bow suddenly stopped and raised his hand. Hunter and the others came to a stop as well. "What?" he asked.

"Shhh!" the man with the bow said to him. Then the bowman turned his attention to Father Thomas, and after a brief exchange, hurried forward alone.

Hunter glanced to Father Thomas who in turn spoke to him. When he paused with an expectant look, Hunter shrugged and nodded.

Father Thomas nodded in return then turned his attention back to the trees through which the man with the bow had disappeared. The old man as well as the young also held their attention fixed on where the man had disappeared.

Hunter eyed to the trees, and when the bowman did not immediately reappear, came to the conclusion that this may be his only chance. So edging ever so slowly toward the trees he began putting distance between himself and the others. Just when he was about to turn and flee, the old man glanced in his direction. Hunter froze.

"Here now," Father Thomas heard Ogger say. Turning his gaze from the trees, he saw that the stranger was now some distance away from them. He was about to ask what he was doing when the stranger gestured toward his groin and indicated his desire to relieve himself. Father Thomas nodded which prompted the stranger to turn and head toward the nearest tree.

"We need to stay together," Ogger said quietly to Father Thomas. "It isn't safe for him to go off on his own. Lurri said those who have our people are not too far away."

Father Thomas moved his gaze from the stranger to Ogger. "He's only answering the call of nature," he replied. "And besides, Lurri said it was a mile or more to their camp. I seriously doubt if they would have anyone out this far."

"You never know," said Kyle.

After first glancing toward where Lurri had disappeared into the trees, Father Thomas returned his gaze to where the stranger was taking care of nature's business. When he failed to see him, he gestured for the younger man Kyle to make sure he was okay.

Kyle hurried over and quickly disappeared into the trees only to emerge a moment later. "He's gone!" he exclaimed.

"Damn!" cursed Ogger. "I knew it!"

"Lady protect him," Father Thomas quickly prayed. Then to the other two he said, "We must find him."

They were just about to begin the search when Lurri appeared from out of the trees at a run. In his hand he held his bow and an arrow. "They're coming!" he said. Pausing, he turned, put arrow to string, then fired into the dark back the way he had come. A cry was heard indicating the arrow had found its mark.

Turning back, he quickly scanned the area then asked, "Where's the stranger?"

Pointing off in the direction which the stranger was last seen, Father Thomas started to explain when Lurri grabbed him by the shoulder and propelled him in that direction. "Pardon Father," he said. "But there isn't time for talk." As if to accentuate the point, the sound of men crashing through the forest began to be heard.

"Go!" Ogger urged as Lurri took the lead. Making sure Father Thomas was moving quickly before him, the old man followed with Kyle right behind. No sooner had they entered the forest and the river disappeared behind them, than shouts from the river's edge broke the stillness of the night. To their fear, more shouts answered from deeper in the forest ahead.

Lurri had another arrow in hand but thus far didn't have a target at which to shoot.

"We must find the stranger," urged Father Thomas. "Our people have no hope without him."

With a glance over his shoulder, Lurri nodded. It was unlikely the stranger would head toward the sounds of the enemy. So altering course away from them, he led their group deeper into the forest.

After giving them the slip, Hunter quickly found a thicket in which to hide and hunkered down. Looking out from between two bushes, he saw that the one with the bow had rejoined the other three and they were searching for him. It was after they had raced past his hiding place that he heard the sounds of others in the woods. Not knowing if they were friend or foe, he remained where he was.

As he laid low in the thicket, the forest back toward the river began to brighten. Through the trees, he saw dozens of men moving about, some bearing burning torches. If he had harbored any hopes that it might have been the police, they were dashed when he saw the men holding the torches.

They were of average height and dressed like someone you would find at a medieval renaissance faire. Dressed in brown leather armor with a steel helmet, each wore a sword at their hip while a couple carried bows.

He obtained a really good look at them when a group of nine broke off from those by the river and entered the woods to follow after Father Thomas and the other three. They passed very close to his hiding spot but failed to realize he was there. As they passed, he overheard them speaking in an unfamiliar language. It might possibly be the same as that spoken by those he had been traveling with, but he couldn't be sure. Remaining where he was, Hunter watched and listened.

After the men moved off, he glanced back toward the river and saw light from at least two torches moving about. There had to be over fifty men out there, each dressed in armor and bearing swords.

Try as he might, he couldn't make sense of it all. Again and again he tried to recall the events back at the theater and what happened prior to his awakening in the cabin. In the back of his mind he briefly entertained the idea that he was no longer on Earth, but dismissed it as having watched too much television.

Could I have had an accident? A seizure maybe? Perhaps I'm lying unconscious in some hospital bed having a narcotic induced hallucination. If so, why can't I be having one of lovely ladies on a sunny beach?

As much as he liked the idea that this may all be a dream, he couldn't bring himself to believe it. Everything was much too clear and detailed. Reaching down, he used his hand to scoop up some pine needles and dirt from the ground. *Yes*, he thought to himself as the smell of pine and earth came to him, *much too real.*

He waited in the thicket until the men congregating by the river began to move off downriver. Once they were gone and the forest was once more dark, he emerged. Somehow, he had to get out of here. But which way?

Upriver led to the burned out village where he had awakened. Moving downriver would run the risk of encountering the armed men who had just left. The thought of entering the forest and moving laterally scarred him too. He was no woodsman and it was a certainty that he would quickly become lost in such a dark and close place.

After several minutes of indecision, he made up his mind to follow, at a distance, the group of men who had just moved off downriver. It was taking a chance, true, but there was always a possibility they could lead him to civilization. As he moved toward the river to follow the group of men, he carefully made his way through the underbrush, working to keep as silent as possible.

Every sense was alert for the presence of others. Upon reaching the riverbank, he looked downriver and saw the glow from the torches held by the men. Trying his best to shadow the men without giving away his presence, he continued downriver after them.

He hadn't gone very far when the sound of men crashing through the underbrush came to him from deeper within the forest. Pressing himself against the bole of a nearby tree, he held still as three men emerged from the trees some distance downriver from him. They were on their way toward the river. In the darkness, he couldn't see them very well, but could tell they were moving fast.

Then from deeper in the forest, light appeared as more men began approaching. One of the men paused and glanced back. Whispering to the other two, he pointed to the water. In a matter of seconds, the three men were at the water's edge and quickly began making their way across to the other side.

Hunter remained immobile as the other group of men drew closer. In the light of their torches, he saw that they were part of the armed larger group. A dozen boiled out from the forest and one was quick to discover the three in the water. Shouts sprang up as all but two of the men entered the river to follow. The two remaining on the shore, each bore a bow and quickly put arrow to string. As soon as their arrows were in place, they drew a bead on the three men in the water and fired.

He stood there in shocked silence as the bowmen pulled another arrow from quivers across their backs and readied another shot. These men were not part of some medieval club or faire! Hunter watched in fearful shock as the two bowmen loosed their second volley. A cry from the river said one of their deadly missiles had scored a hit.

Straining his eyes, he sought the three men in the moonlight. When he saw forms beginning to climb from the river on the far side, there were now only two. In a flash they raced from the riverbank and entered the forest on the far side.

The two bowmen had loosed another round of missiles before the two men had managed to disappear into the trees. Now with bows held high over their heads, they began entering the water to follow their fellows in pursuit.

Hunter remained frozen against the bole of the tree until the men had crossed and the light from their torches had disappeared into the forest on the far side. *They killed the man!* True he had no definite proof the man was dead, but there could be no other explanation. *Is that what will happen should they find me?* The forest suddenly was an even more fearful place than what it had been. Visions of arrows flying from the dark only to impale him from behind had him looking over his shoulder constantly.

"I have to get out of here!" he said to himself. All thoughts of following the men downriver vanished. Turning about he began heading back upstream. Those people back at the village may have had a hand in his kidnapping, but at least they hadn't tried to kill him. At the moment, they were the lesser of two evils.

As he walked, his mind began putting pieces of this crazy puzzle together. First, there was a village that had been burned to the ground. The people of the village were extremely distraught. Now there were men, soldiers by the looks of them, who were killing people. It didn't take a genius to deduce that the soldiers may have been the ones to have destroyed the village. After all, they were moving away from there and had a decided lethal attitude.

Could his presence within the village have something to do with it? The robed one who called himself Father Thomas had taken him south along the river. Along the very course these men were taking. Why? It was obvious these men with armor were better equipped than anyone he had seen in the village. Were they going to hand him over to placate them? Did they expect him to defeat their enemies? He would have chuckled at the thought if he wasn't already caught up in a situation that could very well mean his life.

Moving alongside the river, he ran as fast as he could. It wasn't easy as the terrain was hilly, wild, and the forest grew right up to the river. Fear propelled him. His ankles that once had merely ached were now protesting quite painfully. His arms, face, every exposed piece of skin began to sting as he forced his way through the underbrush.

Imagined enemies were behind every bush. All thoughts of trying to move silently steadily gave way to the overriding fear that was taking away his reason. *He had to get away!* Every step was one more step away from the deadly arrows. Every step was another step away from meeting the same fate as the man who failed to emerge from the river. So intent was he on getting away, so overwhelming was his fear, that he failed to hear the sound of men converging on his position.

When the voice shouted, he glanced back over his shoulder and saw four men racing through the darkened woods after him. Panic seized him and he ran for his life. Dodging around trees and through bushes that left red lines of pain along his skin, he fled.

Behind him, the man called out again, most likely ordering him to stop. But so consuming was the fear he felt that all the man's cries did was fuel the panic which held him. Glancing back over his shoulder again, he saw the four men hot on his trail. Then as he turned back to continue his flight, a partially exposed root snagged his foot causing him to fall head first into the trunk of a rather large and sturdy tree. With a crack, the lights went out.

In between the trunks of fallen trees, two men hid. Around them they could hear the sound of movement throughout the forest. Voices called to each other indicating that the hunt was still on.

Where the stranger was Father Thomas hadn't a clue. Alone with Ogger, he sent his prayers silently up to Casdralla. One for Lurri who had fallen before they made it to the river, impaled by two arrows. Another for Kyle who had entered the river with them but hadn't emerged. His hopes of seeing him again were slim. Lastly, he prayed that the stranger would escape the enemy and be able to affect the release of his people.

"I think they may be moving off," Ogger whispered, intruding upon the priest's silent prayers.

Father Thomas brought his prayers to a quick close and then listened. It took but a moment for him to agree that it sounded as if those searching for them were beginning to move away.

"What should we do Father?" the old man asked.

"I…I do not know," he replied. Then, "We must still search for the stranger and hope he has not yet been captured."

Ogger peered over the fallen trunks and could see the light from the searcher's torches moving away through the trees. "Do you even know where we are?" he asked.

Father Thomas shook his head. "No," he answered. "I am so turned around I couldn't even tell you which way the river lay."

Pointing off to their right, Ogger said, "The river's that way."

As Ogger stood, Father Thomas came to his feet as well. "The stranger has to still be on the other side," he stated. Glancing to the old man, he added, "We are going to have to make our way back across."

"I thought you might think that," replied Ogger. Off to their left the light from the searchers' torches was now all but obscured by the trees and bushes of the forest. "At least they're moving away from the river."

Emerging from their hiding place they began working their way back toward the river. Straining every step of the way for the sound of another's approach, they safely reached the bank of the river. Above, the moonlight filtering through the forest canopy gave the flowing water and the area adjacent to it an ominous feel. Their imaginations turned shadows into attackers which did little to assuage their fear.

They found the river to be narrower than the place where they had crossed earlier. Much too deep for them to safely make it across in the dark. Ogger pointed upriver and said, "I think we crossed further that way."

"Very well," agreed Father Thomas. "Let us hurry."

Moving out, Ogger took the lead. Clutched in his hand was a thick section of limb that he came across while hiding. Though not very affective against bows or swords, it at least bolstered his courage and allayed somewhat the fear he was feeling.

They kept to the riverbank while working their way upstream to find a suitable place to ford. In the forest all around them on both sides of the river, lights were seen moving through the forest as the enemy continued their hunt. Father Thomas sent another prayer to his goddess that they would be able to avoid the searchers and find the stranger. If his people were to have any chance at all, he had to find that stranger.

Across the river to their right, one of the lights of the searchers began to grow brighter. Another minute of observing the light revealed that they were paralleling their course while at the same time edging closer to the river. Ogger brought them to a halt.

"Should we return downriver?" he asked.

Father Thomas gazed to the approaching light. It had now come close enough that individual soldiers could be seen moving through the trees. There looked to be about six.

When he didn't receive an answer, Ogger said, "They may be looking to cross as well."

Closing his eyes, Father Thomas prayed for guidance.

One of the Qyaendri watching over Father Thomas took possession of the prayer and in the blink of an eye brought it to the High Temple. Moving through the throng of Qyaendri upon similar business he made his way to the Chamber of Decision. This was where each prayer was brought and considered by Qyaendri whose experiences allowed them to make decisions according to their goddess' wishes.

Immediately Father Thomas' prayer was taken and considered. The Qyaendri who had brought it waited only a second before the decision was given. Knowing what he had to do, the Qyaendri returned to Father Thomas. All of this was done in the span of three heartbeats.

As so many times before, he felt a calming come over him, a sensation he took to mean his prayer had been answered. The calmness seemed to flow toward him from downriver. Opening his eyes he turned to Ogger and said, "Downriver."

"Are you certain?" Ogger asked.

Nodding, the priest replied. "Absolutely. But we must hurry." Accompanying the sense to head downriver had been the feeling that time was running out. With Ogger once more in the lead, they hurried south.

Twice more feelings of calmness came over him, and each time he felt the need to alter course. Finally, they reached an area of the river which was wider than most. Ogger glanced to Father Thomas questioningly on whether to cross or not. When he received an affirmative response, began crossing to the other side.

Torchlight was seen sporadically off in the forest on either side of the river. They hurried across and then Father Thomas directed them to continue south.

"But that's the way the main force of the enemy lies," argued Ogger.

"Nevertheless," countered Father Thomas, "that is the way we must go."

Ogger saw the absolute certainty in his eyes and nodded. Grumbling to himself, he turned and began heading south, still clutching the foot and a half stout section of limb.

They traversed the forested bank of the river for a quarter mile before lights finally appeared out of the darkness ahead. Ogger brought them to a stop and turned back to Father Thomas. "I don't think it would be wise for us to go any further," he warned.

"Our Lady has guided our steps this far," he replied. Remaining motionless, he waited for the calmness to settle over him and show him the way to go. But this time, the calmness didn't come.

Offering a prayer of guidance, he again waited. And again, direction from above failed to materialize. Opening his eyes, he turned a worried expression toward the old man. "I..." he began then saw forms appear out of the darkness to the south.

"Run!" Ogger yelled and propelled the priest back the way they had come.

Father Thomas stumbled at first then managed to get his balance and fled. Behind them came shouts from their enemy indicating they had been found. Ogger let out a cry of pain as he hit the ground. Father Thomas glanced back for only a second to see the old man crashing to the ground. The shaft of an arrow was imbedded in his thigh.

"Go!" Ogger yelled as he regained his feet. Raising the stout limb, he turned to face the oncoming soldiers. "Damned Ullentites!" he shouted. "Raze my village will you!" Glancing over his shoulder he saw Father Thomas standing there. "Get out of here Father!" Then flashing him a grin, he turned back to face the soldiers.

"May our Lady protect you my son," Father Thomas prayed as he turned and raced away. He didn't make it very far before he heard Ogger shouting obscenities at the Ullentites. His tirade lasted only a short spell before being silenced.

Father Thomas paused only a fraction of a second before hearing soldiers approaching from where the direction Ogger had made his stand. Fear for himself now overrode every feeling he had. Raising the hem of his robe, he redoubled his speed. For a brief moment he entertained the fantasy that he might actually be able to pull away and escape, but motion in the forest ahead of him quickly dispelled that illusion.

"Stop right there!" a soldier commanded.

Two men held bows while another ten moved to encircle him.

Father Thomas came to a stop and frantically looked for a way out. As he offered a prayer beseeching Casdralla's aid, he was struck in the back of the head and rendered unconscious.

Chapter 5

Father Thomas regained consciousness just as they were entering the soldiers' camp. Two men carried him, one man had him by the shoulders while the other gripped his ankles.

"Put him with the others," he heard one of the soldiers say.

This close, he could easily tell the men carrying him were from Ullen, the kingdom bordering Casdra to the south. It was as Ogger had told him upon his return from the High Temple. At the thought of Ogger, he looked around for the old man but failed to find him. Fearing the worst, Father Thomas prayed.

The soldier carrying him by the ankles noticed that he had come around and informed a man in a sharp looking uniform who quickly came to his side. By the cut of his uniform and air of command, he had to be a high ranking officer of the Ullen Army.

Before the officer spoke, Father Thomas heard people crying and sobbing. Glancing in the direction to which he was being carried, he saw where his people had been gathered together. A ring of soldiers stood guard around them, every one in two held a bow.

"Are you one of those priests of Casdralla?" the officer asked.

Father Thomas turned pain filled eyes toward the officer. "Why have you done this?" he asked, ignoring the officer's question. "We are a peaceful people."

Placing a hand on the man leading the pair carrying him, the officer brought them to a stop. "He can walk from here," he told the two soldiers.

As the man at his feet lowered them to the ground, the officer said, "I don't like it when my questions go unanswered."

With the back of his head feeling as if it was going to crack open, Father Thomas stood and turned toward the officer. "Yes," he replied. "I am Father Thomas, one of the holy ordained Priests of Casdralla."

Nodding, the officer replied, "I thought so."

"What is your intention in regard to my people?" he asked.

"Don't worry priest," the officer said, "we have no intention of harming them. In fact, your welfare is our greatest concern." The way he said 'priest' spoke volumes about the contempt he held for him.

His people began taking notice of his arrival, many crying out to him. As he and his captors reached the circle of soldiers standing guard around the captives, the officer pushed him through to his people while at the same time saying, "Unhealthy and broken people make poor slaves."

Stumbling through the ring of guards, he joined the people he had intended to save. They sat on the ground with hands tied behind their backs. Young and old alike were similarly bound, all that was except for a few women clutching babes. Faces of despair and sadness gazed at him. The sight almost broke his heart right there. People he had known for years, some having dedicated to the goddess at their births, looked to him for some glimmer of hope.

All he could say was, "Casdralla is with us. We are not alone in this." But words that had once held such comfort sounded hollow even as he spoke them. How could the Lady allow such peril to visit her people?

Then hands suddenly gripped him and his arms were pulled behind him. A coarse length of rope was tied tightly about his wrists. Struggle as he might, there was no preventing his hands from being bound.

Once they were secured, Father Thomas was shoved forward roughly to the ground amidst cruel laughter. Those of his people near him looked on in shock at the way he was being mistreated. Having for so long been a man of authority to them, to have him treated so ignobly brought home their situation more than anything else. None dared move to help him as he worked to bring himself upright.

Lady, Father Thomas beseeched his goddess, *come to the aid of your people!*

His prayer left him but was not taken by a Qyaendri. For Casdralla's Qyaendri were being barred from entering the enemy's camp. A ring of Qyaendri serving the god Theroch whom the Ullentites worshiped stood in their way.

It was one of the rules by which Qyaendri abide that held them at bay. Since the worshipers of Theroch held the greater numbers within the camp, Casdralla's Qyaendri were technically forbidden from entering. To do so would be tantamount to starting a war between the two gods and none would dare do so without direct instructions from a higher authority.

Under normal circumstances this rule was flagrantly disregarded by all Qyaendri and incursions by rival Qyaendri were often overlooked as they all did it. When their god's worshippers needed them, they were there no matter where they may be. The only time this rule was enforced was when a rival god's Qyaendri make it a point to enforce it, such as now.

Theroch's Qyaendri keeping them out were not the run of the mill Qyaendri either, but rather those dedicated to the enforcement of their god's will, especially against other Qyaendri. Practiced in the art of celestial war, these Qyaendri were capable of destroying other Qyaendri, especially those of a lesser stature.

One of Casdralla's Qyaendri had been sent to the High Temple informing the higher ups of this new development. To the dismay of those Casdralla

Qyaendris waiting impotently outside the camp, they were instructed to make no attempt to breach the ring of Theroch's Qyaendri. In effect to stay out. Many prayers coming from the captives were fading away since there were no Qyaendri able to take charge of them. A prayer left to itself only lasts a short time before fading away into nothingness.

"Father."

Father Thomas had been sitting with eyes closed and head hanging down for some time. Mind all but numb by the recent events, he had been wallowing in a pit of self-deprecation.

He had been so sure the stranger was going to rescue his people. Now, the stranger was who knew where, he himself had been captured, and those who had set out with him and the stranger from Billin were unaccounted for. He knew for certain that Lurri was dead and was fairly sure Ogger and Kyle had met the same fate. The fact that Ogger hadn't been placed with the rest of the captives seemed to indicate he hadn't survived his encounter with the enemy soldiers.

"Father."

Raising his head, he opened his eyes and looked upon his people. Fear and uncertainty marred many visage, but there was a spark of hope and concern mixed in there as well. Now that he was with them, things didn't seem as bad as they had been.

From one to the next, his gaze passed over them, noting who was there and who was not. Having them depending on him for emotional support if nothing else, he mustered a reassuring grin. "Casdralla will save us," he told them. "Our Lady will not abandon her people to such a fate."

Such was the tone of belief he put into his words, that many faces once laced with fear, grew calmer. A kernel of hope entered many a heart as he smiled, a smile he himself did not entirely feel.

The enemy camp was still active as men came and went. It wasn't long before he saw a group of soldiers emerge from the woods carrying a limp body. Father Thomas' eyes widened and his heart practically stopped in mid beat when he realized the stranger had been made captive as well. He was certain it was the stranger they carried by the clothes the man wore.

Unconscious, the stranger was being taken toward a cluster of five tents. He couldn't hear what was being said, but from the way they were acting, Father Thomas realized the enemy considered the stranger of special importance. Considering the strange attire he wore, he could well understand why they did.

As the stranger disappeared inside one of the tents, Father Thomas offered up another prayer to his goddess.

Ftheril stood amongst the Qyaendri ringing the camp. He had watched the party as they left Billin, and the subsequent chase through the forest. Ftheril knew the importance of the stranger Larus had selected to save Casdralla's people on this world, and he was surprised at the relative ease in which Larus' Chosen One had been captured.

Now to discover that the stranger had been removed to a place he could not follow, and that was guarded by the Celestial Warriors of Theroch, gave him grave concerns. Rarely do opposing Qyaendri stand in the way of other Qyaendri who were gathering prayers. For those Qyaendri who block others' prayers, tended to have their followers' prayers blocked in retaliation. Such situations often degenerated into all out war between the two sides before becoming resolved.

He grew worried when no Celestial Warriors of Casdralla came and joined those in attendance among her Qyaendri outside the camp. That, coupled with the fact the stranger was in the hands of those who had attacked their people, prompted Ftheril to seek out Daeson. Something did not feel right.

Needless to say, when he found Daeson and informed him of all that had happened, Daeson was less than happy. Anger smoldered within him, and for one of the Celestial Warriors, that was a fearsome sight. Ftheril was glad the Qyaendri's anger was not directed at him.

"What should we do?" asked Ftheril.

Eyes filled with fire and damnation turned upon him and he quailed at the sight. "Return and keep watch," Daeson replied.

"As you wish," Ftheril said, just before vanishing.

Larus!

Daeson knew he would mess it up. Why Xi entrusted such an important assignment to one such as Larus was beyond the Qyaendri's vast experiences to comprehend. Larus had been removed from the cadre of Celestial Warriors defending the faith of Casdralla because he was ill suited to such a task. Always becoming distracted at the wrong time, or putting off what needed doing until the last minute. One such as him had no business even being among the Qyaendri of Casdralla.

Such was Daeson's anger that when he left the world upon which Ftheril found him, an outpouring surge of energy exploded in a mammoth fireball. Later when the locals came to investigate what had occurred, they found a crater ten feet deep.

Things had gone from bad to worse for Larus since Daeson had appeared for the Chosen One. Wracked with guilt over having failed his goddess, not to mention lying, he had withdrawn in on himself. *He had lied!* That was an abomination among the Qyaendri and those caught lying were typically banished from their deity's service.

Visions of being cast out and other possible repercussions caused him to seek to hide on this world. In the back of his mind he knew it would do no good for if they wished to find him, they would. Irregardless, he sought to disappear, to become lost in the multitudes inhabiting this world.

Finding a city with an enormous population, he hid in an attempt to conceal his shame, his soul torturing failure to his goddess. He could still remember when he first entered Casdralla's service. For a human it would seem an eternity, but for him it was like it happened yesterday.

What pride he had felt. To be able to serve one of the Great Ones was the single most cherished accomplishment any Qyaendri could ever hope for. Taken from the plane upon which all Qyaendri have their origin, he was brought to the High Temple and there, joined the ranks of those serving Casdralla.

Shame and pain wracked him as again the knowledge of throwing it all away came back. *My Lady!* he cried silently. Why, oh why, had he lied! Fear was intermixed part and parcel with the shame. Xi had picked him. Out of all the Qyaendri serving Casdralla, he had been selected. Not only had he failed her, but he had failed Xi! Visions of that mighty one's wrath wracked him continuously.

"Larus!" the cry came, shocking him back to the here and now.

He could feel more than see the presence of another Qyaendri. The Qyaendri was searching for him and drew ever closer. Fear surged through him. Fear at what was going to happen. And so he fled.

Before he had a chance to flee, the full power of a Celestial Warrior fell upon him, rendering him immobile and powerless. Never before had he felt such fear as when he saw that it was Daeson who had hold of him.

"Don't kill me!" he screamed.

"No," Daeson said, coming forward. Energy fairly crackled about him as he approached Larus, so intense was the anger he felt. "You are to be returned to the High Temple," he explained. "And there your fate shall be decided."

"My fate?" he asked, though he knew the answer already.

"Yes Larus, your fate," he replied. "The one you selected to save our Lady's people has been captured and is most likely dead." Glaring with all the anger and fearsomeness a Celestial Warrior possesses, Daeson's gaze bore into Larus. "Your ineptitude has doomed our Lady's people."

"I didn't mean to!" he exclaimed.

"We were only allowed one from this planet," he accused, "and you wasted it!"

"I'm sorry," cried Larus. "I...I..."

"Save it," Daeson said. "It's time we returned." Then both Qyaendri left the world of the Chosen One and returned to the High Temple.

Larus materialized in the center of the Rotunda before the large statue of the goddess. Her visage appeared crestfallen as he turned his gaze upward. Then motion from out of the corner of his eye drew his gaze toward the fourteen Celestial Warriors encompassing the Rotunda in a circle. Beyond them were row upon row of Qyaendri each looking upon Larus with scorn.

"Larus," Daeson said in an authoritative voice, "you stand accused of dereliction in the performance of the sacred duty given you." Pausing for a moment, he allowed the assembled Qyaendri to murmur among themselves a moment before continuing. "You are furthermore accused of speaking falsehoods in an attempt to conceal the fact that your duty remained unfulfilled."

Staring into the eyes of Daeson, he could see there would be no mercy for him. Coming from the assembled Qyaendri, he felt their contempt for him as a palpable force. Beings, who once counted him a brother, now looked upon him as the lowest of the low.

"What do you have to say for yourself?" asked Daeson.

Larus raised his head and turned woeful eyes upon the senior Qyaendri. What could he say? Every word Daeson uttered was the truth. In a voice that was barely audible to the surrounding Qyaendri, he replied, "I wanted nothing more than to serve the Lady. There is nothing to say other than…I am sorry."

"You have been a poor servant of the goddess since you first entered her service," condemned Daeson. His tone left no doubt as to his feelings for Larus. "Your actions, or rather your inactions, have doomed her people. The fact that you committed falsehoods shows you to be a false servant of the Lady, She who values honor and truth above all."

Every word spoken was as a dagger piercing his innermost being.

"Now," Daeson said, "you must pay the price for what you have done."

Larus looked upon him with growing fear in his eyes. He knew that he could possibly be destroyed where he stood. With eyes locked to those of Daeson, he felt the power within the temple growing. Fear gnawed at him and threatened to take his will. Then inexplicably, peace settled over him as he came to realize there would be no avoiding what was to come. This was his fate, and if it be what the Lady willed, then so be it. He deserved nothing less for what he has done.

The ring of Celestial Warriors, each an entity of enormous power, seemed to enlarge as Daeson called upon them to aid him in administering Larus' punishment.

Standing with back straight and now wearing a look of acceptance, Larus faced destruction as he felt power passing from the ring of Warriors to Daeson. Then he was struck with the full force of their power. Pain the likes of which he had never before felt ripped through him. No longer able to remain erect, he collapsed to the floor. As he lay there writhing in torment, he heard Daeson say, "May you suffer as those whom you have doomed will suffer!"

The agony spiked, increasing tenfold as he felt something within him being torn asunder. Then there was nothing.

When the sun dawned the following morning, Father Thomas and the others were awakened as soldier moved among them untying their hands, but not before shackles were attached to their legs. Then they were given a most unsatisfying meal of gruel before getting underway. He had hoped the stranger would be put in with him and the others at some point, but such was not to be. Instead, he was tied across a horse's back. Worry gnawed at him, for once the stranger was secured across the horse's back, he remained unmoving.

"On your feet!" one of the soldiers commanded.

Crack!

The snapping of whips elicited cries from those who hadn't come to their feet quickly enough. Father Thomas received two blows before scrambling to his feet. One young man complained that with their feet in shackles and hands numb from having been left tied all night, that it was difficult to rise.

Crack! Crack!

Blows rained down upon him as the young man struggled to his feet. "When we say get to your feet," a soldier yelled to the young man, "get to your feet!" *Crack!* The young man was repeatedly thrashed until he made it to his feet. Blood flowed freely from the numerous welts visible through his shredded shirt. None dared complain after that.

Once the captives were ready, there was a crack of a whip and the captives were in motion. Talking amongst the captives was discouraged with blows from the whip, and it was a silent, sullen group that headed south to an unknown fate.

They continued to follow the river south the rest of the day. Around noon the soldiers brought them to a stop and another meal of thin gruel was given to the captives before they once again resumed their march.

It was shortly after the noon break when the stranger regained consciousness. At first he was quite vocal, speaking profusely in his foreign language. But after repeated blows from the soldier's whips, he quieted down.

At least he still lives, Father Thomas thought quietly to himself. *While there is life, there is hope.* Putting one step in front of the others, he prayed to his goddess for guidance and to deliver them from their bondage. He also prayed for the stranger. That the stranger would have the strength to free his people.

Glancing again to the stranger, he saw that the stranger's shirt was stained red and had been almost shredded by the whip's blows. *This is a mighty wizard? How could one who has the favor of the goddess as this one assuredly must, allow himself to be so treated?*

Father Thomas thought back to when the stranger first appeared and the events immediately following. He **had** arrived in the company of a Qyaendri, there was no denying that. His dress and speech marked him as one from somewhere else. But thus far, he hadn't exhibited anything one would expect from someone delivered by the Goddess. There must be a reason for the man to arrive just after the attack on Billin, and Father Thomas refused to believe otherwise. He would have faith in Casdralla. And so he walked and waited.

By the end of the day, they arrived at the town of Rie. It was the southernmost village of Casdra on the eastern border before entering the kingdom of Ullen. The captives were dismayed to discover that it too had fallen and its people taken. The smell of char was still in the air from the devastating fires that had burned it to the ground. Many began wailing and crying until the whips started to fall. Such an emotional display would not be tolerated.

The captives were marched through the town to the road heading west. Many of them once had friends and relatives living there. Even Father Thomas had been to Rie on numerous occasions, visiting with the priests of Casdralla. He looked to where the temple had once stood and saw what he thought may have been its blackened, stone chimney standing as a lonely sentinel.

None of the residents were to be seen. Father Thomas prayed a silent prayer to Casdralla for their safety and well being. Though from the looks of things, such was unlikely.

Once past the outskirts of Rie, the soldiers had them move off the road and settle in for the night. Again, a single bowl of gruel was all they were given for food. Vile as the stuff was, when Father Thomas was given it he ate it readily, such was his hunger.

It was a more somber mood among the captives than the previous night. The reality of their captivity was finally sinking in. A few whispered conversations sprung up periodically, but as soon as a whip carrying soldier came their way, it stopped.

Most of Father Thomas' time was split between trying to offer what comfort to his people he could, and of keeping an eye on the tent wherein the stranger had once again been placed. A guard was posted outside, and every once in a while, one of the ranking soldiers would enter.

Early in the evening, screams could be heard coming from the tent. Each one would cut through Father Thomas like a knife. He didn't know exactly what they were doing to him, but he had a good idea. Most likely trying to interrogate him and being frustrated by their inability to understand the man. At least the screams let Father Thomas know he still lived.

By the time darkness had completely settled in, the screams came to a halt. If it wasn't for the guard still posted outside the tent holding the stranger, Father Thomas would have been concerned. As it was, he figured they wouldn't guard a tent holding a dead man.

Somehow in the hours that followed, he managed to fall asleep. Wracked with dreams of disquieting intensity, Father Thomas hardly seemed rested when the sky began to brighten and the soldiers made ready to leave. Another bowl of gruel and they were on their way heading down the road to the west.

It didn't dawn on him at first, but then he overheard a whispered conversation between two others in which one commented that the road they were on would take them to the heavily fortified city of Xith. Xith of course being the city that guarded the sole pass leading into the mountainous region that comprised most of Casdra.

Hope began to resurface as they grew to believe their captors were taking the wrong road and that help would soon be forthcoming. But such hope was dashed in the late afternoon. For emerging out of the horizon far to the west, was an Ullen army over ten thousand strong on their way north. Their captors turned them from the road and moved to intercept the larger force.

"They mean to lay siege to Xith," one man whispered in trepidation. Not for a hundred years had anyone dared to assault the walled city. So thick and fortified were its walls, that it didn't seem as if this army had a chance. But then they saw the siege equipment trundling along behind the marching soldiers: dozens of catapults, ballistae, even a few larger catapults with massive arms capable of launching an incredibly damaging attack. Even so, many of the Casdrans felt not even that would breach Xith's walls.

"Blessed Lady," Father Thomas prayed, "save your people." He knew that if Xith were to fall, the whole of Casdra would be laid waste by the Ullentites. For Xith controlled the pass and the enemy would not be able to launch an attack into the interior of Casdra while Xith still stood. But as more of the siege equipment came into view, his surety of Xith's defenses waned. Could this be why the stranger had been brought? Was he to be the instrument in which Casdralla would save her people? Father Thomas glanced over to where the stranger was walking behind one of the wagons.

His hands were bound and a tether tied around his neck was secured to the back of the wagon by a length of rope. He was guarded by four soldiers who kept on all sides of him. This was the one to save her people? The more Father Thomas thought about it, the less likely it seemed. All he could do was trust that She knew what She was doing.

Chapter 6

Consciousness slowly returned. With it came an awareness of cold and discomfort. Opening his eyes, Larus discovered he lay alongside a dirt road in the middle of nowhere. Clad only in enough cloth to cover his loins, the morning air continuously leeched the warmth from his body.

Larus sat up and took in his surroundings. He was on a grass covered plain that stretched to the south and west until finally disappearing into the horizon. To the north and east were hills which eventually became a tall range of mountains. The road running beside him came from the east and disappeared into the predawn gloom of the west.

"Where did you send me?" Larus asked as he came to his feet. Shivering, he tried to ascertain upon which world he now stood based upon what his immediate surroundings could tell. Then it hit him. *He was cold!* He had never been cold in all his years. A hollowness within him made itself known as his stomach grumbled. At first Larus couldn't fathom what was happening, then he remembered dealings with humans during past times on other worlds. They often mentioned their stomachs grumbling when they were hungry.

Hunger? Is that what I'm feeling? Fear grew within him as he tried to use the power which was the legacy of all Qyaendri to squelch the grumbling in his stomach and banish the cold, only to fail.

"No," he said in growing horror as the reality of his situation sank in. He was no longer Qyaendri! Hands began shaking at the enormity of his loss. Soon it became unbearable. Knees buckling, he dropped to the ground sobbing.

"My Lady!" he cried out in anguish as racking sobs issued forth in ever greater intensity. Not only had Daeson removed him from Casdralla's service, but he had stripped him of everything that made one Qyaendri.

"I'm sorry!" he cried. Wrapping his arms closely about himself, he curled into a ball and repeated over and over, "I'm sorry."

"Would you consider that a prayer?" one of Daeson's Qyaendri asked him.

"No," Daeson replied. "He did not direct it toward our Lady."

He and the other Qyaendri watched Larus as he lay sobbing piteously next to the road. Daeson had thought seeing Larus like this would have brought him satisfaction in that justice had prevailed. But now, seeing the pitiful sight before him, he held compassion for the one time Qyaendri. For compassion was one of the virtues Casdralla held dear.

"He's one of them now," Daeson told the other.

Nodding, the other Qyaendri replied, "I understand."

As Larus' apologies degenerated back into woeful sobbing, Daeson departed leaving the other who was set to watch Larus. After all, he was still one of Casdralla's people, only now part of the mortal world. And whenever one of her people were in anguish or going through hard times, a Qyaendri would be present.

The other Qyaendri looked upon Larus with both compassion and uneasiness. For there before him was what could happen to any Qyaendri who failed the one they served.

Two hours after the sun had risen, Larus remained lying in the dirt trying to come to grips with what had happened to him. At one point to verify that he was in fact now one of the mortal world, he grabbed a rock and scraped it across his forearm. The pain that action caused, along with the welling of blood, convinced him more than anything else that he was mortal. For nothing of the mortal world could harm a Qyaendri.

Sadness eventually turned to anger. Anger at Daeson, anger at Casdralla, and finally anger at himself. He knew in his heart that Daeson was not at fault, he had simply done his duty. Daeson could never have reduced him to being mortal on his own, and definitely not within the High Temple without the blessings of Casdralla. She never would have allowed one of her followers to be treated thus, unless he deserved it. His mortality was proof of Her displeasure.

The risen sun quickly banished the cold, but did nothing to alleviate the grumbling of his stomach. He knew from previous dealings with humans that without food, his body would grow weaker until finally failing altogether.

Dying. The ending of his existence. He had never really contemplated such a thing before. When he had been a Qyaendri, such a thought had been irrelevant. Qyaendri were immortal barring unforeseen circumstances. But now that he was mortal, such a fate was in store for him.

During his time as a servant of Casdralla he had aided many who had shed the coils of mortal existence on their way to the Hall of Judgment. Every deity had a place where the faithful were judged, though each had a different name for it. There the mortal's soul would be judged according to how it lived. Those having lived according to Casdralla's doctrine would pass on to the rewards she bestows on her faithful. Those found wanting in their devotion went…elsewhere.

A kernel of hope began to grow as he considered the possibility that maybe he wasn't forevermore separated from his goddess. True, he had been banished and reduced to being a mortal. But, if he couldn't serve her as a Qyaendri, perhaps he could still do so as a mortal. Then, when he died, he would join the ranks of her faithful. *All was not lost!*

However, there was one major flaw in his plan. Before one could be counted a follower of Casdralla, he must first be blessed by one of her priests. At which time, he professes his devotion to her and from that moment on, to be hers. After that it would be a piece of cake. Who better than one of her former Qyaendris knew how best to live in order to be judged favorably after death?

With hope rekindled, Larus leapt to his feet. "Now," he said to the world at large, "where can I find a priest?" The thought occurred to him that this may be a world in which Casdralla had no followers. If that was the case, his mission would be harder but not insurmountable. He would first need to start a temple and gather followers. Then once sufficient followers had dedicated their lives to following Casdralla's doctrine, he would have them consecrate him as High Priest and he would be in.

Having a plan and course of action definitely made him feel better about the prospects for his future. He just needed to discover if Casdralla had a presence on this world or if he would be forced to initiate one. Priests would be where the people were.

Scanning the horizon, he couldn't see any evidence of people other than the road. But seeing as how roads linked human populations, he had but to follow it. Now the question was, which way? East or west? For the most part, Casdralla's people tended to gravitate toward the hills and mountains, so Larus turned toward the east and began making his way to the hills in the distance. Once he located a town or village, he would begin working to bring his plan to fruition.

For the next hour he walked, all the while working out the details of attracting followers should such a need become necessary. So into developing a plan of action was he that he failed to notice the large group of men appear out of the horizon to the south. When he finally took notice of them, it was with great relief. Now, he could find out what's what. Altering his course, he left the road and hurried forward to greet them.

Before he made it very far, six riders broke off from the main group and rode to meet him. They wore similar uniforms and each had a sword hanging at his hip.

"Greetings," Larus hailed them as they drew close. Coming to a stop, Larus gave the six riders a courteous wave and offered them a smile. His smile gradually faded when the riders failed to return it.

"Are you from Xith?" one of the riders asked. The other five quickly moved to encircle Larus.

"Xith?" questioned Larus. "Is that a town near here?" His friendly demeanor turned into worry when he realized the men had now completely surrounded him. And none of them were smiling.

The rider speaking to him nodded. "It's a large, heavily fortified city a couple days north of here," he explained.

"No, I'm not from there," he replied. "Actually, I'm not entirely sure where I am."

A rattle of metal drew Larus' attention toward the rider to his right. He saw the man holding a pair of manacles attached by rope. "What…what are you going to do with that?" he asked.

"These are for you," the rider said. "Special made jewelry all the way from Ullen." Guffaws and chuckles came from the other riders.

"But you don't understand," Larus said, backing away from the rider holding the manacles, "I have no quarrel with you gentlemen. I'm looking for a priest of Casdralla." When the man with the manacles nudged his horse forward, Larus nervously said, "I don't want to hurt you."

"Hurt us?" laughed the one with the manacles. "I don't think we have much to worry about from one such as you." Sliding off his horse, the rider began moving toward Larus with the manacles held out toward him.

Larus backed up further as he kept focused on the approaching man. The other riders moved in closer, tightening the circle. Each rider now had a cudgel in hand. His newly acquired mortality and loss of Qyaendri abilities made him fearful of engaging these men despite his earlier boast. If he wound up getting himself killed before finding a priest of Casdralla, all would be lost.

With the available space growing smaller by the second, Larus had little time left to react. Dodging to the left in a mad dash for freedom, he raced toward a gap between two of the riders. The nearest rider struck at him with his cudgel. Moving to avoid the blow, he failed to avoid the falling cudgel of the other rider and was struck in the side of the head.

Dazed, he continued in his attempt to flee, making it through the ring of riders before a second blow landed between his shoulders and knocked him to the ground. Then they were on him. Struggle though he might his strength was no match for theirs. Hands gripped him and held him immobile while the manacles were attached to his ankles. His arms were pulled roughly behind his back eliciting a cry of pain and then were bound with rope. The end of yet another rope was tied around his neck before Larus was hauled back to his feet.

"See," one rider quipped, "we didn't get hurt." The other riders laughed. Taking the other end of the rope attached around Larus' neck, the rider mounted. As soon as the riders were mounted again, the one holding the rope began leading Larus over to the large body of men who were still moving north.

Larus, forced to follow or be dragged by his neck, hurried to keep up despite the manacles restricting his legs' mobility. He wouldn't have minded dying right then and there, but couldn't afford to allow himself to expire before finding a priest of Casdralla.

Moving at a quick pace, Larus kept up with the rider all the while wondering how he would find a priest of Casdralla now. Captured, alone, and from the looks of it being taken toward an army on the move, boded ill for him.

He was led toward the army where the rider leading him departed from the other five and took him toward the rear of the marching men. There he found others bound in a similar manner as himself being led in long lines. He figured there had to be several hundred captives like him in all, both men and women. To his surprise, some of the women were carrying babes.

"Got another one for you," the rider said to a soldier walking at the fore of the lines of captives.

The man looked Larus up and down and nodded. Taking the rope from the rider, he said, "They've been coming in all day. Surprised there hasn't been any response from Xith. They have to know by now that we're coming."

Shrugging, the rider said, "Perhaps they are afraid to come out from behind their walls."

"Perhaps," the soldier said. Turning his steed, the rider headed back to rejoin his fellows.

"Follow me," the soldier said as he turned to lead Larus toward the end of the line of captives.

"But," argued Larus, "I'm not a part of all this. You have no right to do this!"

Crack!

Pain erupted across his back as he was struck by a whip. "Insolent dog!" Glancing behind him Larus saw another soldier readying his whip for another blow.

"That's enough!" the soldier leading him shouted to the other. "I think he's learned his lesson." Turning to Larus he asked, "Have you?"

Pain was a new experience for him and he definitely didn't want to experience any more. Nodding, Larus kept quiet as they continued toward the end of the captives. The faces of the other captives by which they passed were sad, dejected, and fearful. "Stay quiet and do what you're told," the soldier told him, "and you won't be lashed. Cause problems and we'll flay the skin from your bones. Understand?"

Larus nodded miserably.

Once they reached the end of the captives, the rope tied around his neck was secured to the captive in line before him. Then without a word, the soldier turned and made his way back to his place at the head of the captives.

The man in line before him was middle aged and had several lines of angry red welts scoring his back. "What's going on?" Larus asked the man quietly. A slight shake of the man's head was all the reply he received.

Walking with manacles wasn't easy but after several minutes he began mimicking the shuffling gait which the other captives used. Once he had that down it was much less of a strain to keep up.

The captives were strung in a dozen lines behind the main body of soldiers. Behind the captives rolled siege equipment and a supply train with its own compliment of soldiers. At least he didn't have to walk behind them. It was bad enough breathing the dust kicked up by the soldiers marching at the head of the army.

With nothing else to do but to keep following the man before him, Larus found his gaze roving over the other captives. Through the dusty haze, he saw the men and women tied to the lines. They were a sullen, downcast lot. Understandably so given their circumstances.

When his gaze moved to one individual further up the line to his left, his roving gaze stopped. The man was wearing robes and looked to be a priest. It was hard to tell as the back held no insignia and was torn in several places presumably the result of being struck by a whip.

If the man were a priest, perhaps he could find out from him where a priest of Casdralla could be found. Not that the information would do him much good right now. But if there was one thing he had learned in the course of his existence, it was patience. There would come a time when escape from this situation would be possible. Until then, he would learn what he could and be ready when the opportunity presented itself.

Larus looked for other robed individuals among the captives but discovered there was only the one. He had to somehow get close enough so he could speak with him.

They marched all that day with but one stop when he was given a bowl of gruel. His arms were freed so he could eat but the manacles remained. While he ate, the rope about his neck was removed and he was properly secured to the line of captives.

Near sundown, the army was brought to a halt and the captives were gathered together in a close group while another round of gruel was fed to them. Though still attached to his place at the end of the line of captives, he managed to get a little closer to the robed man. Unfortunately, he still remained too far away to be able to communicate with him without alerting their captors.

Since his capture and placement in the captive line, three more individuals had been brought and placed in line behind him. One, a young man of early years, continued voicing his protestations and had to be repeatedly whipped before he would stop. Another man who had been a captive since before Larus joined them tried to get the young man to be quiet, and received two strikes across the back for his efforts.

Taking another bite of gruel, he glanced back to where the young man now sat quietly. There was a look of determination on his face that Larus knew meant trouble. When the young man noticed him looking his way, his eyes narrowed. He met Larus' gaze until Larus looked away.

Larus knew the young man would try something at some point. Most likely getting himself and others lashed or killed. His spirit wasn't the type that would easily take to captivity. Larus cast another brief glance back and hoped the young man wouldn't do anything until his own situation was improved.

Larus ate the gruel that did little to assuage the hunger cramping his stomach. He turned his attention to where his manacles were attached to the length of rope joining all the captives in his line. On the outside of the manacle binding his right ankle was a metal loop. The rope held a matching loop to which his was attached. If he wanted to remove himself from the line of captives he would have to sever the rope. Only problem was, he had nothing with which to accomplish the feat.

His attention was then drawn to where soldiers were beginning to move down the line, collecting the bowls. Using his fingers, he quickly scraped the last of the gruel from the bowl before it was taken from him. It wasn't good, but he needed to keep up his energy. When the soldier came to him, he silently held up the bowl and it was taken from him.

After the soldiers completed collecting the bowls, the captives began lying down to rest. The camp around them was being set up for the night. At this point, Larus noticed the robed man frequently gazing over toward an area where several tents had been erected. He couldn't figure out what was there that held the man's interest. But over and over the man would turn his gaze in that direction and stare for minutes at a time.

Larus looked too, but other than tents and soldiers passing between them, there wasn't anything out of the ordinary. Again he turned his attention back to the robed man. He had to get over there to talk with him. But how? Attached as he was to the captive line there wasn't any way. So close, only to be restrained by a ring of metal that back when he was a Qyaendri would have been no barrier at all.

Frustration quickly turned to anger, anger which smoldered all the hotter for being impotent to do anything about it. Reaching out, he vented his anger on the only thing available, the one thing which was keeping him from reaching the robed man, the ring attaching him to the line. He looped both forefingers through it and started jerking on it hard.

Immediately, the men secured to the line on either side of him moved as far away from him as they could. One man saw a guard notice what Larus was doing and tried to get him to stop but Larus wouldn't listen.

Nothing could breach the red haze of anger that had him in its grip. Nothing that was until a line of pain flared to life across his back. "Stop that!" the soldier cried out. Again the soldier's whip scored across his back. It wasn't until the whip laid a third line of pain across his back that he let go of the loop.

When Larus glanced back over his shoulder at the soldier, the soldier said, "Don't ever do that again. It won't do you any good, the iron's too strong."

The soldier stared at Larus until the anger subsided and Larus nodded understanding. Then the soldier moved off down the line, head roving to and fro as he kept watch on the captives.

Back throbbing and most likely welling blood, Larus laid down on his side. The anger had degenerated into a feeling of loss and despair, the adrenalin rush produced by the anger had worn off leaving him feeling empty and hollow. Those nearby glanced toward him with concern but made no move to come to his aid or comfort him. They didn't want to risk feeling the soldier's whip. Closing his eyes, Larus laid there and tried to ignore the pain.

Sometime later, after night had fallen, Larus awoke to the sound of men shouting. Sitting up, he discovered a good portion of the soldiers nearby were donning armor and moving quickly to the northern end of the camp.

"Something's going on," a voice said quietly.

"Yeah," added another.

"Maybe our soldiers are finally fighting back," whispered the first.

"I doubt if we have enough men to repulse an army this size," stated the second.

Larus didn't know one way or the other, and frankly he didn't care at the moment. His attention was turned toward the robed man who was again staring toward the tents. All he cared about was somehow finding a way in which to speak with him. His inability to reach him produced feelings of frustration.

Turning his attention once again to the rings securing him to the captive line, he considered venting again. But the thought of another taste of the whip prevented him from carrying out his desire. Striving to find the patience which he once had in abundance, Larus looked over to the tent area where the robed man kept casting glances.

His eyes eventually settled on a tent before which stood a single guard. He finally concluded there must be something within the tent that was important to the man. A friend perhaps? An enemy?

As he focused on those questions in an attempt to put his frustration behind him, Larus found his gaze once more settling on the rings binding his feet to the captive line. After several moments of contemplating the significance of the guarded tent, while simultaneously having his gaze directed toward the rings, it occurred to him that something was odd.

Then it hit him. The ring he had earlier vented his frustration upon for which he had received three lashes was more elongated than the other. He was sure it had been circular when he was first attached to the captive line.

Curious, he looked to make sure no soldiers were near, then bent over to take a better look. The elongated ring appeared to have been bent out of shape. Not only that, but the metal on each of the inner surfaces where it was elongated showed an indentation. Fascinated, he reached out and took hold of the ring in both hands. When he gripped the elongated sides just as he had earlier, his forefingers settled into the indentations. It was a perfect match!

How could this be? No human had the strength to physically manipulate iron, at least not in such a small piece as was the ring. Back when he was captured, he had struggled against the rope yet had been unable to break free. But yet, what he saw before him was incontrovertible. The ring had originally been close to a perfect circle, now it was not. Somehow he had stretched the ring when he had vented his anger earlier. But how?

Could this be because of what he used to be? A Qyaendri would have no problem in mashing iron like putty. However, when he awoke on this world, he was mortal. There was no denying that fact. When the men had captured him, he had been helpless to prevent it. There was no way he could have affected metal then, but he could now? He had to know for sure. Maybe Casdralla was looking out for him. Thinking on what he had done that led to his being in this situation, he thought that unlikely.

Glancing around again for the soldiers, he made sure none were near then tried exerting his strength upon the metal of the ring. Taking a firm grip with both hands, he mimicked the way he had pulled upon it before. After a minute of straining upon the metal he took a good look at the ring and was pleased to note that it was even more misshaped. Despite himself, he couldn't prevent a grin from appearing on his face. Perhaps things weren't as bad as he thought.

After another quick check to make sure his efforts continued to be unobserved, he worked on the ring again. This time he didn't stop until the ring broke.

The men on either side of him in the line of captives had their attention fixed on the goings on in the soldier's camp. During his struggles with the ring, they had cast glances his way but didn't seem too concerned with what he was doing. After all, if he wanted a couple more lashes with the whip, that was his business.

Now that there was a gap in the ring, Larus worked to widen it enough to be able to slip the ring connected to his manacles out of it. Once that was accomplished, he turned his attention to the manacles binding his ankles.

He had less leverage to work with in breaking these apart. While working to free his ankles, Larus came to the conclusion that come morning, there was going to be one less captive for the soldiers to worry about.

Chapter 7

In the wee hours of the morning, the camp was quiet but for the snores of men. A few were about, guards, sentries, those who had to keep an eye on the captives. Of those who had departed to the north earlier in the evening there had been no word. One other was awake as well. Though if by chance one of the guards were to look his way, they wouldn't see anything out of the ordinary.

Larus was lying still, his gaze fixed unwaveringly upon the nearest guard. At the moment, the guard was glancing his way, making sure the captives were quiet. Then when the guard's gaze turned to another quarter, Larus resumed inching his way along the ground toward the robed man.

It was painstakingly slow, but he couldn't afford to take the chance of anyone discovering what he was about until he had talked with the robed one. The man had to be a priest, and could very well be his only hope of discovering whether or not Casdralla had followers upon this world.

Almost halfway there, he had to make sure not to disturb the captives he passed. For should any awake and discover what he was doing, and that he was free of his manacles, their reaction would assuredly draw the unwanted attention of the guard.

Sliding a few feet along the ground, pausing only when the guard looked his way, he would then resume his progress once the guard's gaze left him. Little by little, he worked his way ever closer until finally, was close enough that he could reach out and touch the robed man. Twice more he scooted before coming close enough to be able to converse with him in hushed whispers. Reaching out, he gently touched the man's shoulder.

The man snapped awake and started to sit up before Larus grabbed him by the robe to keep him from rising. "Stay down!" he whispered. The robed man tensed as he looked upon Larus, then slowly relaxed and complied.

"Who are you?" the man asked.

"Someone in need of your help," replied Larus. That reply seemed to satisfy the man.

"How may I help you my son?" he asked.

My son? That cinched it, the man was definitely a priest. "Do you know where I could find a priest of the goddess Casdralla?" he asked.

The man's eyes widened in surprise. In the situation they found themselves, this was probably the last question he expected to hear.

"Yes," he replied. "I do know where one could be found."

Larus was beside himself in excitement. Casdralla already held a presence on this world. He wouldn't have to go through the long and arduous task of creating the religion from scratch. "Where?" he asked.

The man reached up and touched his chest. "Right here," he explained. "I am Father Thomas, priest of Casdralla."

"Oh Father!" he exclaimed a bit too excitedly. Off to his right he saw the nearest guard turn and look in their direction. Both he and the priest held still while the guard searched for the source of the disturbance. His gaze roved across them and the other captives nearby several times before the guard turned away. When Larus again brought his attention back to Father Thomas, he saw the priest looking at him oddly. "What?" he asked.

"Were you sent by our Lady?" Father Thomas asked.

"What are you talking about?" Larus asked. He was confused by Father Thomas' question. "Why would you ask that?" Then out of the corner of his eye he saw his hand. Or rather, how his hand was surrounded by a soft, nimbus-like glow. The glow was that of the Qyaendri. Surprised to say the least, Larus immediately suppressed the glow and it disappeared. Such a nimbus-like glow surrounded each and every Qyaendri. Whenever they were around mortals they tended to suppress it so as not to give themselves away. Mortals often acted unpredictably when in the presence of what they didn't understand.

Turning back to Father Thomas, he said, "No. I was not sent by 'our Lady'. In fact, I came to you in order to receive your blessing and be able to serve the Lady with all my heart and soul forevermore." He could see Father Thomas' gaze roving over him, searching for the nimbus which was no longer evident. He hoped the priest would believe he had imagined the glow.

Finally reaching some sort of conclusion, his gaze came to rest as he again looked into Larus' eyes. "This is hardly the place for such things," Father Thomas told him. "The blessing of which you speak is long, requiring many gestures. I doubt if our captors will allow us sufficient time in order to complete the ritual."

"Can't you just wave your hand or something and have it done?" Larus asked. His excitement at finding a priest of Casdralla diminished greatly when he saw the priest shake his head no.

It was one of the peculiarities in dealing with mortals that on every world, the rituals performed by Casdralla's priests differed. On some worlds, what Larus had requested was a very simple matter. All you needed was for him to state his desire, the priest would acknowledge it, and that was that. But on others, as this one seemed to be, more elaborate rituals had been developed.

Larus knew he couldn't make the priest take shortcuts. For if the priest didn't believe the ritual valid, it would have no affect, and Larus would be no better off than he was now.

"I am afraid you shall have to wait until our circumstances change," Father Thomas said sadly. Then his eyes grew wide as he for the first time noticed Larus was not bound by manacles. "My son," he began, "how...?"

Larus stopped him by putting a finger to his lips and giving a quick shake of his head. "That's not important right now," he whispered. His mind was churning as it worked to quickly contemplate this new development. If the ritual required more time than what they would have among the captives, then they would have to do it somewhere else. Someplace that would afford them sufficient time to complete the ritual. And for that to happen, the priest would have to accompany him when he left the camp. Reaching out, Larus took hold of the man's manacles.

"What are you doing?" Father Thomas asked. He was very much confused by what was happening. He had earlier observed the man being brought in and attached to the captive line. Now he was free?

"I'm getting you out of here Father," the man replied.

Father Thomas grabbed hold of the man's hands then removed them from the manacles attached to his ankles. As the man turned to look up at the priest, Father Thomas said, "I cannot leave my people in their time of suffering."

The man's face grew determined as their eyes locked. After a moment's silence, the man said, "You could do more for them by coming with me and raising the alarm."

"But...," he began to argue as he turned his gaze over the sleeping forms of his people. The people who looked to him for comfort and hope. How could he simply abandon them in their time of need?

Then as he turned back to deny the man's request for him to join him, Father Thomas caught site of the tent in which the stranger, whom the Qyaendri had delivered in answer to his prayer, was held.

"Look Father," the man was saying, "I know it's hard for you to leave these people, but you must!"

Father Thomas offered up a prayer for wisdom in making the right choice, though he already knew what he must do. Casdralla had sent the stranger to save his people, and as long as Hunter remained a captive of the Ullentites, such would be unlikely. If he must abandon his people to save them, then so be it. He must stand firm in his faith.

Releasing the man's hands, he said with no little emotion in his voice, "Very well. I will go with you." He saw the man's eyes light up at his words. "But first we must rescue someone."

"Who?" the man asked.

Father Thomas pointed toward the tent. "A man is held within," he explained. "We must bring him with us."

"Are you crazy?" the man asked. A little too loudly as it turned out. The guard turned and looked their way again. He and Father Thomas held still on the ground until the guard once more turned his gaze elsewhere.

"No," he replied. "Only the rescue of the man within that tent would convince me to leave my people."

Larus could see the determination in the man's eyes. He wouldn't leave unless whoever was in the tent came with them. For just a moment he thought of absconding with the priest despite his objections anyway, but then thought of his ultimate goal. If he took the priest against his will, how likely would the priest be to perform the ritual making Larus one of Casdralla's followers? There was nothing for it. If he wanted the priest to come along willingly, they were going to have to rescue the man within the tent.

"Very well," replied Larus. Taking hold of the man's manacles, he began working to free him.

"What is your name my son?" Father Thomas asked.

"Larus," he replied.

"Thank you Larus," the priest said.

Larus merely nodded as he worked on the metal encircling the man's ankles. To his surprise, his ability to rip apart the metal had increased. In a matter of minutes, he had both of Father Thomas' legs free. It would seem he was throwing off the shackles of mortality and regaining the abilities of a Qyaendri.

"Come on," he told Father Thomas, "let's go." Then he saw the wonder in the priest's eyes at his ability to break apart the manacles binding him.

"Father?" a voice said behind Larus. Glancing back, he saw a young woman staring at him and the priest.

"Lynndra," Father Thomas said quietly, turning his attention from Larus to the woman.

"What's going on?" Turning her gaze to Larus she asked, "Who are you?"

"I have to leave," Father Thomas explained. "He is taking me to get help."

"What?" she exclaimed with no attempt at being silent. "You're leaving?"

"Shhh!" Larus urged. Glancing over to the guard, he saw him looking straight at them.

"You can't leave!" she cried as she sat up.

Others around them were beginning to stir, having been awoken by the woman's cry.

"Be quiet!" commanded Larus as he motioned the woman to lie back down. The guard was now making his way toward them. The look on his face said there would be hell to pay.

"Calm down Lynndra," Father Thomas said reassuringly. "I do this for the sake of our people."

"No," she cried softly.

"What is going on here!" demanded the guard as he drew closer. In his hand he held his whip, ready to thrash anyone at the slightest provocation.

By this time over a score of the captives were awakened and sitting up. As soon as the guard spoke, many of them immediately laid back down. To Larus chagrin, Lynndra was not one of them.

Father Thomas cast a worried glance toward Larus. The look he received in return was hard to make out.

Larus came to his feet and turned to face the oncoming guard. "Be ready," he said quietly to Father Thomas. Out of the corner of his eye, he saw the priest nod. Turning his attention fully onto the guard, he caught sight out of the corner of his eyes other guards hurrying toward them.

"Get back on the ground!" ordered the guard. Raising the whip, he struck out at Larus.

Trying to grasp the fast moving whip, he held still. The whip connected and was snatched back out of his reach before he could grab it. He was only moderately surprised when the area upon where the whip struck produced only a small amount of pain that was quickly gone. More proof that he was moving further from the coils of mortality which bound him.

"Down!" the guard yelled.

"No," he replied.

Again, the whip lashed out toward him. This time however, the whip seemed to slow ever so slightly as it came forward. Reaching out, Larus caught the end. Before anyone realized what was happening, he had yanked on the whip and pulled the guard off balance.

Springing into action, Larus leapt forward and caught the guard. Wrapping one arm around the man's head, he twisted and broke his neck. Then pulling the man's sword from its scabbard, he let the body fall.

"Let's go," he said to Father Thomas.

Father Thomas came to his feet quickly and looked at the people he was abandoning. "May the Lady protect you all," he said as feelings of guilt practically consumed him. It took every ounce of will he could muster to move from those placed under his protection.

Hands reached out and gripped his robe, faces looked up imploringly for him to take them too. Faith in the Lady was the only thing enabling him to continue. "I'm sorry," he said, as he pulled his robe from the grips of people he had lived with for years. Tears fell from his eyes as he saw one mother holding up her babe toward him. He almost gave in and took it, but then the sound of swords striking together brought him back to what was of paramount importance. The rescue of the stranger sent by the Lady to save her people.

Larus was engaged with two guards, a third lay dead on the ground. Hands of those attached to the captive line dragged the dead guard closer where they relieved him of his knife, sword, and the captive controlling cudgel as well as the whip every soldier in charge of the captives bore.

Father Thomas came up behind Larus as the second man fell, then watched as the sword in Larus' hand moved with incredible velocity as it struck the third one down.

"Come on," urged Larus as he raced across to the tent holding the stranger.

Soldiers shouted as scores raced toward the captive area.

Larus ran with all the speed he could muster. By the time he reached the tent, Father Thomas had fallen behind. The guard before the tent was quick to realize Larus was heading for him and braced for the attack. Before Larus could reach him, the soldier shouted a warning and another soldier emerged from within the tent with sword drawn.

He didn't even pause. Racing forward, Larus struck out at the guard and had his blow knocked to the side. The other man thrust at Larus' midsection and scored a long painful cut across Larus' stomach as he tried to dodge to the side.

Pain flared from the cut with great intensity though it was shallow. Striking out again, Larus' blow was again knocked to the side by the first soldier as the sword of the second sank into his right shoulder.

Crying out, Larus fell back as blood flowed from the wound. The two soldiers pressed forward. From behind him he could hear Father Thomas approaching, prayers issuing from him with great speed. All of a sudden, the pain began to diminish. Encouraged, he launched another attack.

This time his blow passed through the soldier's defenses and impaled him through the heart. When the second one stuck out at him, he was able to nimbly dodge to the side to avoid the blow. Using his left hand, he took hold of the soldier's wrist. Twisting, he heard bones snap as the sword fell.

Pointing to the tent, he shouted, "Get him!" as he ran the man through with his sword. Other soldiers were almost upon them. The pain in his shoulder was gone, as was the throbbing of the cut along his stomach. Almost laughing from the exhilaration of the fight, he turned toward the half dozen soldiers approaching. Raising his sword, he made ready to meet them.

Father Thomas finished a final prayer for Larus as he opened the tent flap. Inside he saw the stranger tied to a chair. "Hunter?" he said as he entered. Hunter's head lolled to the side. The man was unconscious and his body showed extensive evidence of brutality. His hair was matted with blood, clothes torn, dark bruises marred his skin.

"Lady help him," he prayed as he rushed to the stranger's side. "Let him still be alive." A quick check revealed that he still lived.

Outside the tent the sound of swordplay intruded upon the quiet inside. Next to the chair wherein Hunter sat was a table bearing an assortment of tools used in interrogation. One of them was a small knife.

Picking up the knife, Father Thomas quickly applied it to the ropes binding the unconscious man. First he cut the rope binding Hunter's legs to those of the chair, then he began freeing his wrists. Throughout it all he quietly voiced a steady stream of prayers. Once the last bond was cut, Hunter sagged in the chair.

"Hunter!" Father Thomas shouted, giving his face a slight slap. When that failed to revive him, he prayed to the Lady for forgiveness and then struck him forcefully across the face. Aside from leaving a red mark on his cheek, the blow had little effect.

"Give me strength," he prayed as he placed one of Hunter's arms across his shoulder and lifted him from the chair. Never one gifted with great strength, it was difficult for him to carry the unconscious man in his arms. Somehow, he made it to the tent flap where the sound of swords striking one another could still be heard. Then all of a sudden, it grew quiet.

Father Thomas stood before the tent flap, fearful to open it. What if Larus had been overcome? What then? But then the tent flap opened and Larus appeared.

"Is that him?" he asked.

Father Thomas nodded. "Yes," he replied.

"Give him to me," Larus said and then took the man. Almost as if he was handling a newborn babe, Larus easily placed him over his shoulder.

"Can you carry him?" Father Thomas asked.

"No problem," replied Larus. "We better get out of here while we can." Then he ducked back out of the tent.

Father Thomas followed and was shocked to find nine dead men littering the ground on the other side. He turned his gaze to Larus, astounded by such a display of martial skill.

"This way," Larus said, and began moving off.

As Father Thomas moved to follow, the sound of men and women shouting came from the captive area. Pausing, he turned to look back at the people he was leaving behind.

Soldiers were converging on the area from all over. Three of the captives, one being a young man, fought with swords while a dozen others wielded manacles as weapons, another four wielded cudgels. Others could be seen busily using knives appropriated from the soldiers Larus had killed to free others.

A hand settled on his shoulder. "There's nothing we can do for them," Larus said.

"I know," he replied. His people didn't have a chance. Soldiers began engaging the men and one fell, then another. The young man was screaming as he fought the soldiers, what he lacked in skill he made up for in pure rage. One soldier fell, then another. The last Father Thomas saw of him before he disappeared in the melee was a double handed downward hack that completely impaled a soldier.

"Now is our chance," Larus told him. "We must escape while the soldiers are being distracted." The attention of the soldiers seemed directed solely toward the captive revolt. What had transpired before the tent appeared to have gone unnoticed so far. Where Larus and Father Thomas stood was currently free of soldiers, as was the space from there to the camp's edge and freedom. But how long would that last? "Don't let their sacrifice be in vain," he urged.

Nodding with tear filled eyes, Father Thomas turned his back on his people. Unable to speak due to intense emotional feelings, he indicated for Larus to lead the way.

Larus turned and headed for the camp's edge. Once past the tent area, they had to cross an area of relative openness illuminated by campfires. Moving quickly, they made their way through the lit area and melded into the darkness.

Glances back revealed that none of the soldiers had noticed of their escape. With the cries of his people sending red hot daggers of guilt and regret into his soul, Father Thomas followed Larus as they pressed deeper into the darkness.

Chapter 8

By the time the sun rose the following morning, Father Thomas was exhausted. The man who rescued him had set a furious pace in their flight from captivity. Time and again fatigue would force Father Thomas to pause and recuperate his strength only to be reminded that pursuit could be right behind. Each time Larus allowed him only a short break before setting off again into the night.

Hunter passed sporadically in and out of consciousness as he lay across Larus' shoulder. During those semi-lucid times he would mumble and speak incoherently before lapsing back into unconsciousness.

When the eastern sky began to finally lighten with the coming of day, they reached a small stream running through a narrow break between two hills. Larus immediately turned them into the break to follow the stream for a short distance until they encountered a sheltered area in which to rest before setting out again.

It was a small stretch of dry ground with several trees which afforded them some degree of protection from searchers. "We'll stop here," Larus told the wearied priest. He moved within the trees and laid the stranger next to one of their trunks. Father Thomas collapsed on the ground next to him.

"Now Father..." Larus began as he turned toward the priest, but stopped when he realized the priest had already fallen asleep. He then turned his gaze toward the other man, the one Father Thomas had been so insistent they bring with them.

He was rather nondescript, except for the extensive signs of torture and abuse he had recently undergone. His clothes were nothing more than bloodstained tatters, his face discolored with one black eye and multiple bruises. With the left cheek marred by an ugly two inch blister which had to have been caused by the application of red hot metal, he barely looked human.

Larus tried using his Qyaendri senses to sense the man's injuries, but his returning powers hadn't come back to that extent. And that was another thing on his mind besides the enigma of this man. Back at the camp, his Qyaendri abilities had seemed to be returning. The glow, the strength, and the skill at arms all seemed to point toward a possible return of his former self. But ever since leaving the camp, his abilities had plateaued.

He now had above average strength and endurance, but nothing compared to the average Qyaendri. Skill at arms was exceptional as well. The speed at which he dispatched his opponents back at the camp was a good indicator of that. But his other abilities, ones which would make life so much easier for them such as healing the others, acquiring a mental picture of his surroundings, and so much more were for the time being beyond him. The shackles of mortality were still very much with him despite his renewed abilities.

His body was exhausted from carrying the other man for so long. Also, his stomach was grumbling some and would soon begin to demand more earnestly to be satiated. He needed to acquire food for himself and the other two before they set out later that evening when the sun went down.

Larus thought that perhaps where they were was safe enough to allow Father Thomas sufficient time to perform the ritual marking him as a follower of Casdralla, but he dared not take the risk, at least not until they were further away. Besides, Father Thomas was exhausted. He felt obligated to allow the priest sufficient time to recover before restating his request.

Standing silent for a moment, he listened to the sounds around him. The melodic sound of the stream as it coursed through its bed, birds awakening to the start of another day, and the rustle of leaves as a soft breeze moved them to and fro. But of men making their way through the hills, there was no sound. Hoping it to be safe for the moment to leave the two sleeping men for a few minutes, he left the sheltered area adjacent to the stream. Moving upstream, he went in search of food.

Father Thomas was the first to awaken. He was startled to find himself alone with the stranger. Looking around, he sought their rescuer but didn't see him. The thought filtered through his mind that perhaps Larus had deserted them, but then he remembered Larus' desire to become one of Casdralla's followers. *Perhaps he is simply having a look around,* he thought to himself.

Turning toward Hunter, he found him sleeping peacefully on the ground. Now in the light of day, the man's wounds could better be seen. "Oh my son," Father Thomas breathed as he came closer. He offered a prayer up for Hunter's recovery and for the Lady to ease the suffering he must be going through. A moment later, he felt the peace he hadn't felt since first being captured settle over him like a warm blanket and he somehow knew things were better.

A compelling need to rid Hunter's face of the blood, sweat, and dirt adhering to it came over him. Coming to his feet, he crossed over to the edge of the stream where he dipped a section of his robe into the water. Once it had become sufficiently soaked, he returned to the stranger and began using the dampened section to clean Hunter's face.

After a few minutes, the worst of it had been cleared away and the man almost looked normal again. He took extra care when cleaning the area around the blister on Hunter's cheek, as he did near the other injuries the man had sustained. When his face was as clean as Father Thomas could make it, he turned his attention to the rest of his body. Several times he returned to the stream to rinse out the blood and grime from the hem of his robe only to return and continue.

He had completed the job and was considering their situation when the sound of someone approaching could be heard drawing nearer from upstream. Fear that their captors had found them practically paralyzed him into immobility. Then, he saw Larus appear with three rabbits hanging limply from his hand. "Thank you Lady," he breathed as he came to his feet.

"I thought you were the Ullentites," he stated.

Larus gave him a grin and held up the rabbits. "Sorry to disappoint you," he replied. "But I thought you may be hungry. Gruel does little to satisfy one's hunger."

Before he could reply, a growling split the silence and Father Thomas grinned. "Considerate of you," he said, slightly embarrassed by the noise his empty stomach had made.

Splashing through the water, Larus came onto the dry area and tossed the three rabbits to the ground. "Let's get a fire going."

"Are you sure that is wise?" asked Father Thomas. "The smoke may reveal our presence."

"I wouldn't worry too much about that," replied Larus. "I scouted the area after we arrived and there isn't anyone nearby."

"What about pursuit?" Father Thomas asked. "Aren't you worried about that?"

Larus shrugged. Moving over to where several fallen limbs lay, he said, "Either we lost them or they are not hunting for us in this area." Picking up several of the pieces, he returned to a spot near the rabbits and began constructing the beginnings of a campfire.

Once the wood had caught and was burning on its own, Larus used the sword he appropriated from the guard to ready the rabbits for roasting. In fairly short order, the three rabbits were over the fire and a mouthwatering aroma began filling the air.

Larus had charge of two sticks bearing roasting rabbits while Father Thomas held the third. Rather than constructing a spit, they held the rabbits over the fire while they cooked, turning them as needed. It was after one such turn and a brief inspecting of the roasting progress that Larus noticed Father Thomas gazing at him.

"Something on your mind?" he asked.

"Actually, yes," the priest replied. "Just who are you?"

"What do you mean?" questioned Larus.

"I mean, you are obviously not from around here," he explained. "With just your bare hands you are able to part metal, and your skill as a fighter is impressive." Not seeing any reaction to his words from Larus, he continued. "Also, you failed to recognize the fact I was a priest of Casdralla, even though you were seeking one."

"I take it there are many in this area?" Larus asked.

Father Thomas nodded. "Just to the north is the kingdom of Casdra," he said. "Therein you will find the High Temple to Casdralla."

Larus thought in silence for a minute or so before answering. It was a fact that he couldn't tell Father Thomas the truth, and he didn't want to make the mistake of lying again. "I'm a stranger to these parts who had heard of the goddess," he explained. "And find that I wish to dedicate my life to her and be one of her followers." Basically the truth, though not in the way Father Thomas would take it.

"I see," said Father Thomas. He still bore a questioning look for Larus' answer had been a bit evasive. He hadn't even touched on how he had parted the metal of the manacles.

Larus returned his attention to the two rabbits cooking and watched fat as it dripped from the carcasses only to sizzle when it came into contact with the fire. The skin of each was beginning to brown and it wouldn't take much longer before they would be ready. In an attempt to turn the focus off of himself, he gestured over to where Hunter lay and asked, "What's his story? Why was it so important for us to take him when we fled?"

Continuing to direct his gaze toward Larus, Father Thomas replied, "He was entrusted to my care." At that, the memory of those he abandoned when the three of them fled the soldier's camp returned. The cries of his people as he fled in the night brought pain and no little amount of shame. Lowering his gaze to the fire, he absentmindedly turned the stick to which the rabbit was attached as visions of his people's fate coursed through his mind.

"He must hold some importance," stated Larus.

Bringing his eyes up from the fire, he met Larus' gaze again and asked, "Why do you say that?"

"He was separated from the rest of the captives, and from the looks of the wounds he bears, must have been tortured," he replied. "Perhaps for information?"

"I would not know," admitted Father Thomas. "He and I traveled only a short time together after the soldiers burned my village and captured its people."

"I'm sorry," Larus offered after a few moment's silence. "I know you have been through a rough time."

"Rough?" he exclaimed with a grimace. "Everything I have is gone."

"No," replied Larus, "not everything." When Father Thomas failed to speak, he added, "You still have your goddess."

In a barely audible voice, Father Thomas said as he slowly nodded, "I know. It is all that is left to me."

"But that is everything," Larus said. Almost out of habit, he slipped back into the mode of a Qyaendri sent to help a human in crisis. "As long as you have your faith in your goddess, everything will turn out alright."

"How...?" he began to ask before stopping.

Larus remained quiet as the priest worked out the turmoil of emotions afflicting him.

"How can she allow such a fate to befall her people?" Father Thomas finally asked. "Why did she not do something to prevent all this?" Pain and grief filled the gaze being directed toward Larus. "My people are suffering!" Silently he added, *and dying*.

Just then, a groan emanated from their companion. Two sets of eyes turned toward where Hunter lay and saw that his eyes were opened and looking at them.

"My son!" exclaimed Father Thomas. Elated that he had regained consciousness, Father Thomas laid the rabbit in his care on the ground near the fire then rushed to Hunter's side.

Hunter looked around with fear and trepidation in his eyes. When he saw that the three of them were the only ones in the vicinity, and that he wasn't in the camp of soldiers, he relaxed somewhat.

"Come," Father Thomas said as he indicated for him to join them at the fire, "we have food." Making motions mimicking eating, he tried to convey his meaning.

"Food?" Hunter asked.

"That's right," replied Larus. "We have three rabbits here that should be almost ready." He turned the rabbits again as the side closest to the fire was beginning to blacken. When he turned his gaze back, he saw two faces staring at him.

"You understand him?" Father Thomas asked with surprise while at the exact same time, Hunter asked, "You can understand me?" The expression on Hunter's face was the look of one who was hoping a hope he dared not believe to be true.

Larus looked from one to the other and realized that both men were speaking different languages. Nodding, he replied in the language Hunter was speaking, "Yes."

"Thank god!" exclaimed Hunter. Ignoring the pain his movements caused, he lurched from the ground and came quickly to Larus' side. "Where am I? Can you tell me how to get home?"

"Just calm down," cautioned Larus. "You may do yourself an injury."

"Tell me!" shouted Hunter, voice rife with desperation.

"Just a moment," Larus said as he turned his gaze to Father Thomas. In the priest's language he asked, "What is going on?"

Instead of replying, Father Thomas looked in awe at Larus, a look that made Larus decidedly uncomfortable. "Casdralla must have sent you to us," he breathed in wonder.

"What?" he asked then felt Hunter grab his shoulder, demanding his attention.

"You have to help me," he exclaimed. "These people are crazy and homicidal!" Pointing with his free hand to his blistered face, he shouted, "Look what they did to me!"

Turning toward the frantic man, Larus said, "I will do what I can. But first," removing Hunter's hand from his shoulder, he nodded over to Father Thomas, "I need to discover what happened."

Hunter calmed somewhat at Larus' assurance of help. "He's in on it," he said in a whisper with a nod over to Father Thomas.

"Let me talk to him and find out what's going on," he replied.

"Thank you," Hunter said.

"Now," Larus said, switching to Father Thomas' language, "would you care to tell me what is going on?"

"Yes," said Father Thomas. "Perhaps I should."

"Then please do so," Larus told him.

Father Thomas sat back down before the fire and retrieved the stick bearing the half cooked rabbit. Brushing off the dirt that was now adhering to the meat, he positioned it once again over the fire.

He remained silent for a moment to gather his thoughts as he glanced from Larus to Hunter then back again. "It was after my return from the High Temple that I discovered the ruination of my village," he began. "I prayed for Casdralla to help my people." He grew silent as his gaze turned toward Hunter.

"And..." prompted Larus.

"And, that was when he arrived," Father Thomas explained. Lowering his voice, he said, "A Qyaendri appeared before me with him at his side."

Larus' tongue went dry at the priest's words and a shiver crawled its way along his spine. "A...a Qyaendri?" he asked. His eyes flitted over to Hunter for the briefest moment before returning to Father Thomas.

"Yes," he affirmed, returning his gaze once more to Larus. "In the charred remains of my once beautiful temple the Qyaendri appeared with this man. *'There is a task which this man must complete'* the Qyaendri told me. Then he said I must aid him in whatever way possible."

Larus nodded slowly and turned his attention back to Hunter. "What," he asked then realized he was still speaking in Father Thomas' language. Changing back to the man's language he asked in a tone that was a bit strained, "What was the last thing you remember before coming here?"

"I had just bought a large popcorn and pop at the concession stand," he recalled. "You see I was at an all night Three Stooges' marathon and was on my way back to my seat when..." Hunter came to a stop when he realized Larus was no longer paying him any attention. "Sir?" Hunter asked, worried.

But Larus wasn't paying him any attention. His mind was reeling from the revelations these two men had laid upon him. *The Chosen One!* This had to be the one he gave up to Daeson as the one selected to save Casdralla's people. But how?

Thinking back, he recalled the final words Daeson had spoken before he came to be upon this world. *'May you suffer as those whom you have condemned will suffer!'* Daeson had put him before the soldiers who had taken Casdralla's people captive. And by making him mortal, he had undergone the same suffering as now plagued Casdralla's people.

Coming back to the here and now, Larus looked to Hunter and saw desperation in his eyes. Their gazes locked briefly before he said, "I don't think you are on your world any longer."

Hunter visibly sagged at his words. "I thought that might be the case," he said without emotion. "The clothes, the weapons, not even the language were anything like back home. I thought I had gone mad." After a quick glance to Father Thomas, he asked, "But how could this be? Did he bring me here?"

Larus shook his head. "No," he replied. "From what the good Father has said, you were brought here by a Qyaendri, a servant of the goddess Casdralla. You might refer to it as an angel."

A look of incredulity appeared on his face. "An angel? You're kidding, right?" he asked. His face turned slightly ashen when Larus shook his head and replied, "No."

"But how do I get back?" he asked. "I don't belong here!"

"As to that," Larus said, "I don't have an answer."

Father Thomas interrupted the conversation by asking, "Is he here to save my people?"

Larus turned to the priest and said, "He has no idea."

"Then why did the Qyaendri bring him to me?" Father Thomas asked.

While Hunter came to grips with the knowledge that he was a long way from home, Larus considered the priest's question. *Why indeed? To save Casdralla's people for sure. After all, that's what Xi told him when he first went to Earth to find him. But how? In what manner?* Xi hadn't given him that information. Looking at Hunter it was clear the man had no fighting ability. *A general perhaps?* Again doubtful, but maybe.

"I don't know," Larus finally replied. "Whatever he is supposed to do remains a mystery."

Father Thomas grew grim as he thought upon Larus' words. "Then we must bring him to the High Temple!" Father Thomas suddenly exclaimed. "Assuredly High Priestess Trystia will know. There is none other closer to the goddess than the High Priestess."

Larus slowly nodded. *That may be what we need to do,* he thought silently. Then the thought occurred to him that there may be a way for him to atone for his mistake. What if he were to see that Hunter completed that which he was there to do? If he were to make things right, he might be able to be fully restored and once again join the ranks of Casdralla's Qyaendri.

Go to the High Temple, find out what Hunter's task was, see it fulfilled, then everything would return to normal for him. Or at lest he hoped so. This could work out even better than his plan to become a follower of Casdralla and join her in the afterlife.

"Yes," agreed Larus. "That may be the wisest course to take." He glanced to Hunter who was looking very confused, and feeling left out. Returning his gaze to Father Thomas, he asked, "How far is it to the High Temple."

"On foot, many days," he replied. "The High Temple is deep in the mountains."

"Very well," Larus said. A smell of char reached him and he realized he had allowed the two rabbits he held to remain overlong above the flames. Turning them over, he saw that their flesh had been seriously blackened. Handing one to Hunter he said, "Here, I think it is ready."

Hunter looked dubiously at the charred carcass. But when his stomach let out with a growl he reached out and took hold of the stick. "Thank you," he said.

Larus nodded. Taking a bite from the other rabbit, he explained their plan to bring Hunter to the High Temple.

He sat there quietly while Larus explained that he was brought to this world for a reason and that they must figure out what that reason was. When Larus finally came to a stop, Hunter asked, "Why me?"

"What do you mean?" Larus asked.

"I mean, I'm not anything special," explained Hunter. "Why in the world would someone choose me?"

Guilt riddled Larus, for he knew exactly why Hunter had been chosen. Larus had panicked and in so doing, doomed this man to pain, torture, and who knew what else before all this would be over. "Such questions are often times meaningless," Larus explained. "When one is chosen, there is always a reason." *Even if it has nothing to do with you*, Larus finished silently.

They ate in silence for a bit before Hunter asked, "If I do this, do you think I will be able to go home?"

"I honestly don't know," admitted Larus. "There is always the possibility." And as far as he knew, that was the truth.

"But I could be stuck here for the rest of my life," he reasoned.

"Perhaps," Larus agreed. He wished he could offer him a more optimistic outlook, but wasn't about to raise false hopes.

Hunter ate the rest of his meal in silence. It was true that earlier in his life he had entertained daydreams about being taken from Earth and brought to another world. Only, during such times, he had never visualized the actual events as being so bad. A hero mayhap, not someone without control of his destiny and pushed along by events. Painful events.

While he contemplated this new reality he found himself in, Larus and Father Thomas spoke in their language. Occasionally one would cast a glance in his direction and their conversation would grow quiet. As if he could understand any of what they were saying!

He was deep in self deprecating misery when Larus stood up and announced it was time to leave. "Do you think you can make it on your own?" Larus asked him. "Or do you require me to carry you once more."

Hunter climbed to his feet and found his legs a bit shaky but didn't wish to be carried like a child. "I'll be alright," he assured them.

"Then let's go," Larus said. "From what Father Thomas says, the High Temple is quite a ways away."

Shrugging, Hunter waited for Father Thomas to head out then fell in behind. The way he felt right that moment, he didn't care if he lived or died. All that he knew was gone. Putting one foot in front of the other, he followed the other two as they left the trees and began making their way upstream.

Chapter 9

They worked their way between the hills as the sun arced across the sky overhead. First keeping to the stream, they eventually were forced to leave when it turned and began moving off toward the east. The hills were sparsely dotted with trees which afforded them some benefit of protective cover.

During each of the rest breaks Hunter's weakened condition necessitated, Larus left the other two to scout the vicinity for the presence of searching Ullentite soldiers. Moving to the tops of neighboring hills, he scanned the horizon for any signs of the army from which they had fled. It wasn't until the end of the day when during one such scouting excursion, that he saw a pillar of smoke rising in the west. Too far to see the source of the smoke, the size of the plume indicated that whatever was burning had to be sizeable.

He quickly returned to the others and told them what he had seen. Father Thomas immediately climbed the hill to see for himself. "It is Sterrom," he stated when he saw the column of smoke.

"Sterrom?" asked Larus.

Father Thomas nodded. "A city to the south of Xith," he explained without taking his eyes from the rising black column of smoke. "I believe they mean to invade Casdra."

After receiving the translation, Hunter asked, "You have an army too, right?"

"Not much of one I am afraid," he explained. "We have enjoyed a century of peaceful relations with our neighbors and such has not been needed for quite some time."

"You mean you have no soldiers whatsoever?" Hunter asked incredulously.

"I did not say that," argued Father Thomas. "We have soldiers, just not in any great numbers. Up until now their job was primarily to keep the peace and track down bandits and such." He glanced to Hunter while Larus translated what he had to say. "Despite our few numbers, no invading army has ever taken Xith." Again he waited while his words were being translated.

"Xith guards the sole pass leading into the heart of Casdra," he explained. "Its walls are very thick and tall with catapults arrayed atop the wall's towers. Before Casdra can fall, Xith must fall and I do not believe the force we were held captive by is strong enough to succeed."

"That's good to know," replied Hunter.

They watched the rising smoke a few more minutes before getting underway. All through the afternoon, the hills would periodically open up to reveal a good view of the rising smoke. Above the conflagration of what must have been Sterrom, a great cloud was forming. Winds worked to blow it out of shape toward the east, but despite the wind's efforts, it grew ever darker as the day wore on.

Steadily they made their way north. When the sun went down, still they continued. For if the Ullentites meant to invade Casdra, they would need to reach the pass before the way was blocked by the enemy.

To their right rose an imposing range of mountains and according to Father Thomas, to their left lay Xith which could very well be besieged by this time. "If this pass is the only way into the heart of Casdra," reasoned Hunter at one point, "wouldn't that also mean it's the only way for supplies to reach Xith?"

"No," replied Father Thomas. "Xith sits on a lake and can be supplied by ship. Those who constructed the great city would not have relied on but one way for supplies to reach its defenders."

"But still, wouldn't the Ullentites seek to shut off that avenue of resupply?" he asked.

"That would be reasonable," agreed Larus after translating for Father Thomas.

"Then…that would mean time is working against us if we wish to reach the pass quickly," he said.

Father Thomas nodded with a grim look. "Such had already occurred to me," he replied. "Unfortunately, we are still over a day away. It has been my hope that the enemy would spend an overlong time testing Xith's defenses before sending forces to the pass."

"I wouldn't trust to that," argued Larus. "I'm sure the commander of the attacking force has had spies here for some time, gathering intelligence. He'll know the route to the pass must be closed to reduce the amount of supplies and reinforcements that reach the city."

Hunter stopped next to a tree to catch his breath. Leaning upon its trunk, he gazed northward through the dark toward the mountains in which the pass was located. "We're not going to make it are we?" he asked.

Larus and Father Thomas came to him. "Not if I have anything to say about it," Larus assured him.

"The goddess is with us," added Father Thomas.

After translating Father Thomas' assurance, Larus said, "She sent you to her people and we are in her lands." He turned a serious look upon Hunter. "We will make it to the pass!"

Such was the matter-of-fact way he said it that much of Hunter's worry melted away. Left with only an uneasiness and mild fear for his well being, he said, "I hope you're right."

"If we only had some horses," Father Thomas said longingly.

From anyone else, such a desire would not be taken to Casdralla's High Temple on the plane in which she exists. But from one of her priests, even wishes such as what Father Thomas had uttered bore the power of prayer.

Immediately, Father Thomas' desire for horses was taken by a Qyaendri and whisked away to those whose job it was to determine if prayers were to be answered. In two beats of a mortal's heart, the answer was given and the Qyaendri had returned to the trio as they made their way through the dark.

The moon overhead gave off sufficient light for them to maintain their bearings. Off to the east the mountain peaks were a dark contrast against the multitudes of stars in the heavens.

Hunter was no longer the only one growing exhausted by their continued push for the pass. Father Thomas was beginning to feel the strain as well. Larus though, still felt fresh and full of vigor, something he attributed to the abilities that had returned to him.

He pushed the other two as fast as he dared, all the while knowing the frailty of the human body. Larus knew they needed rest, especially Hunter, yet they could ill afford such a luxury. Casdralla could only slow the invading forces so much. If they lolled away the time resting, all they hoped for may never come to pass.

Glancing over his shoulder, he saw the two of them working to keep up. After the sun had gone down, he discovered that he could see in the dark fairly well. It was by no means like seeing in the sunlight, but he could make out the outlines of hills and trees better than his two fellows could. With his partial night vision, he ranged ahead to scout for enemies and to make sure the way was clear. Behind him, Father Thomas led Hunter ever northward. Even with his limited vision, he could still discern the mountain range against the star-lit backdrop and keep the two of them on track.

The terrain continued to be hilly with sparse growths of trees. An occasional stream would be found working its way through the gullies between the hills. Larus for the most part spent time moving across the crests of hills while Father Thomas and Hunter made their way between.

During the passage from one hill to another, movement off to the northwest caught his eye. Altering course to investigate, he discovered several riders. There were at least four or five, though due to the darkness it was hard for him to tell for sure. He glanced back to make sure his two companions were still working their way between the hills before returning his attention to the riders.

He watched them ride in the moonlight. They could sure use those horses. It didn't take him long to reach a decision. Leaving the top of the hill, he began running toward the riders. Quiet and swift, he soon drew near.

"There ain't no one here," one rider complained.

A voice with an air of command said, "Our orders were to search this area, and search it we will. Now be quiet!" Riding in single file, the riders made their way silently eastward through the hills.

As he came closer he made out five distinct riders. Their armor marked them as Ullentites. Moving at little more than a fast walk as they were, Larus was able to quickly overtake them. As he drew near, he slowed and maneuvered to come up behind the one in the rear.

"Did you hear that?" the rear rider whispered to the others.

"What?" the leader asked. Coming to a halt, he turned his horse so it faced back toward the rear rider. The others came to a halt too.

"I thought I heard something moving out there," the rider explained.

"I heard it too," offered another.

Larus was mere yards away from the men and standing motionless. He could feel five pairs of eyes cross his position as they sought the source of the noise the men had heard. But since he was holding still, he was simply another shadow in a landscape of shadows.

After a few moments, the leader said, "Must have been an animal."

"This is stupid," said the rider who had originally complained. "Who are we supposed to find anyway? Can't see anything in the dark."

"Shut your mouth," the leader commanded. A moment later, he turned his horse back to the direction they had originally been heading and moved out. The other four riders fell in behind and followed.

Larus moved to follow as well. Keeping behind the man in the rear, he slowly closed the distance until only feet separated him from the horse. Then springing from the ground, he leaped atop the horse and grabbed the rider. One hand closed around the man's mouth while the other arm wrapped around his throat. He then pulled the rider off the horse and with a quick jerk, the man's neck snapped.

He immediately looked up to the next rider in line to see if he had noticed. With relief, Larus saw the man's attention was still focused ahead. Leaving the riderless horse to mill about where its dead rider lay, he raced after the fourth man. Then just as before, he moved into position, leaped, and dragged the man to the ground. Another quick jerk and the man's struggles ceased.

Usually Larus didn't like killing mortals. After all Qyaendris tended to take care of mortals, not dispose of them. But seeing as how these men were part of the force bringing misery and death to Casdralla's people, he held little remorse about what he was doing. Leaving the second dead man behind, he moved up unnoticed to behind the third rider in line. Luck was still with him, or was it perhaps the hand of the Lady?

But other forces were at work in the world. Forces that turned good luck bad or sought to counter one deity's power with another. Either way, those forces must have gained mastery for just as Larus was about to take out the third, a voice came out of the darkened night.

"Larus!"

Immediately, the three remaining riders came to a halt. Heads turned eastward toward the source of the cry.

Larus recognized the voice as that of Father Thomas. It didn't sound as if the good Father was imperiled, merely seeking to find him. He must have been away from them too long and they had grown worried. Returning his attention back to the third rider, he was startled to find the man looking down at him in shocked surprise.

"Captain!" was all the warning the man gave before Larus attacked. No longer worried about remaining undiscovered, Larus struck out with his fist as the man attempted to draw his sword. The blow hit the man in the kidneys which elicited an exclamation of pain from the rider. Grabbing one of the straps of the man's armor, Larus yanked him from the saddle.

Two swords left their sheathes as he leaped into the saddle. Taking the reins, he drew his sword just as the other two riders closed in. "He killed Arn!" one rider shouted. Closing with his horse, the man thrust at Larus' unprotected side. A clash of metal rang out as Larus struck aside the blow.

The captain moved around to Larus' other side while his man engaged him. Larus was aware of the captain moving to flank him, but couldn't readily disengage from the man before him to deal with it. Blocking another blow, he thrust toward the rider's midsection and felt the tip of his sword pierce flesh as it slid its way between interlocking folds of armor.

As he pulled his sword from the injured man, Larus kicked the sides of his horse and bolted forward, narrowly avoiding a downward hack by the captain. Turning around, he saw that the captain had bolted forward after him. With a cry, the captain struck out with his sword.

Twisting precariously in the saddle to avoid the blade, Larus felt the sword's passage through the air as it missed him by a fraction of an inch. Then his horse cried out in pain as the captain's sword followed through and connected with the beast's head. The horse reared.

Already in a less than secure position from avoiding the captain's blow, the rearing of the horse caused him to lose his balance altogether and was thrown to the ground. Immediately, he rolled away from the beast then came to his feet.

The thunder of hooves announced the captain meant to ride him down. He had barely reached his feet before leaping to the side to prevent being trampled. Once past, the captain turned his horse back toward Larus and kicked it hard in the sides. With another cry, the captain raised his sword as he thundered once again toward Larus.

This time, Larus met the charge. Since the captain held his sword in his right hand, Larus sidestepped to the captain's left. Then as the horse rode by, struck a mighty blow to the horse's foreleg, nearly severing it just above the knee. Both horse and rider went down.

Larus rushed forward all the while keeping away from the flailing of the horse as he sought the captain who was still pinned by the thrashing animal. When he found him, he saw that the man was struggling to extricate himself. One leg was trapped beneath the horse's side.

With sword held at the ready, Larus moved to finish the man off. "For Casdralla and her people!" he cried as he raised his sword to strike. The world seemed to freeze for the briefest of moments. The captain ceased his struggles and turned his eyes upward toward the sword that was about to end his life. Then the sword fell and the captain's eyes saw no more. A second blow ended the creature's thrashing and soon, the world grew still.

Larus scanned the darkness for any movement which might indicate the whereabouts of the man he pulled from the horse. The man still posed a threat since the blow to his kidney would not have crippled him severely. But the shadows in the night were still. The man must have fled.

"Where is he?" Father Thomas asked Hunter for the hundredth time. Even though he knew his words would not be understood, still he couldn't help but voice his frustration. It had been over an hour since Larus had last checked in and Father Thomas was growing worried.

"Larus!" he shouted again, though not with all his might. He wanted his voice to carry a little ways, but not so far as to alert anyone of their presence. Father Thomas was very much aware they may not be alone in the hills this night.

Hunter spoke to him and made a shushing gesture. Obviously he too was worried about others being about.

They kept close together as they passed between the hills. Neither one able to understand the other, yet were bound in common purpose: make it to the pass before enemy soldiers encountered them. If only Larus would return.

Then a noise came from the darkness ahead. Father Thomas froze when he recognized it as the sound of several horses making their way through the hills. Panic set in and he dragged Hunter back the way they had come. They had been found!

Fear began consuming him. Fear of being returned to the captive line, fear of other retribution. With one of the tattered remnants of Hunter's shirt gripped in his hand, he pulled him along as he broke into a run.

"It's me!" a voice shouted behind them.

Hunter abruptly came to a halt, the resulting cessation of forward momentum caused Father Thomas to tear the strip of shirt he held completely off. "Larus?" Hunter asked.

"Yes," came Larus' response as he rode closer.

"Where did you get those?" Father Thomas asked when the he saw Larus riding one horse and leading two others.

"Came across several of the enemy," he explained. "They were nice enough to allow us the use of their horses."

"I doubt that," the priest replied.

"Let us say that they no longer needed them," clarified Larus.

"You killed them then?" asked Father Thomas.

Larus nodded. "We are at war Father," he replied. Then he handed the reins of one to Father Thomas and the other to Hunter.

"I've never mounted a horse in my life," Hunter admitted a little abashedly.

"It's really quite simple," Larus said. He explained Hunter's problem to Father Thomas then dismounted to assist him. Indicating the saddle horn, he said, "First, take a good hold here." When Hunter had a firm grip on the saddle horn, Larus pointed to the stirrup. "Next, place your foot there and swing up into the saddle."

Hunter set his foot in the stirrup then attempted to mount. All he managed to do was turn himself askew. It took another two attempts and no little assistance from Larus before he made it.

If it had been light, they probably would have seen the look of fright come over Hunter from being atop the horse.

"Do you think you will be able to stay in the saddle while we ride?" asked Larus.

In the dark, Larus saw the shadowy head nod affirmative. "Very well then," he said. "We will take it slow at first so you can get familiar with being on a horse."

"Thank you," said a relieved Hunter. He had fearful visions of the three of them galloping through the night with him tipping precariously to the side the whole way and ultimately falling off.

"Will he be okay?" Father Thomas asked when Larus mounted his horse again.

"I hope so," he said. "We'll ride for a few more hours then take a short rest until dawn." Nudging the side of his horse, he got underway.

"We could all use a little bit of rest," Father Thomas replied. He was unbelievably fatigued from the ordeal of the last few days. Fortune was with them it seemed for they found travel provisions in the soldier's packs attached to the saddles. The dried beef and stale bread, though having seen better days, tasted like a banquet.

Over the next two hours, they continued working their way through the hills, at one point crossing a road that Father Thomas informed them led to his village of Billin. The memory of the devastation the invaders had wrought came back and with it great sorrow. Not so much for the village itself, but for its people. He still held great regret in his abandoning of those entrusted to him, though he knew his decision to leave was the right thing to do.

When at last Larus called a halt and told them they could rest until dawn, Hunter practically fell from the horse. His legs had begun to ache even from so short a stint on horseback. He was so tired, he promptly laid down in the grass and passed out.

Father Thomas was soon to follow. Larus didn't feel the need for sleep, though he did lie down to relax his body. And when the sun rose the following morning, discovered to his amazement that he had fallen asleep. Apparently, the mortal coil still held him in its grip.

Chapter 10

The smoke rising from the town of Sterrom was but a faint wisp of its former strength with the coming of dawn. Overhead the sky was a beautiful crystal blue across which traces of featherlike clouds drifted gracefully along in the upper atmosphere.

As the sun rose above the horizon to the east, three riders made their way northward through hills sparsely forested. Two rode with the finesse only years could teach. The third hung on for dear life, every jarring trod of his horse feeling as if it would thrust him from his precarious perch so far from the ground. His knuckles were white and the look of fear was etched firmly upon his face.

Hunter had always thought it would be great to ride a horse. He could even remember how as a small child his parents would take him to petting zoos where they would place him upon a pony's back. Saturday afternoon movies of cowboys watched with his grandfather filled him with thoughts of high adventure. Somewhere between those times of his youth and the present, he had developed an unreasoning fear of the beasts. It was a fear he didn't even realize he held until the prospect of riding one came about. Now, he clung on for dear life.

Not far ahead of him rode Father Thomas and Larus. They maintained as fast a pace as they dared. If it weren't for Hunter's ineptitude on horseback, they would have traveled much faster. But as it was they dared not risk the chance of him taking a tumble.

Riding beside Larus, Father Thomas glanced back to their companion. "I have never encountered anyone with such a fear of riding," he stated.

"I know," replied Larus. "I'm sure the fact that he has been taken from the life he knew plays no small part in it." When Father Thomas turned his attention to him, he added, "I doubt if anyone would do well should they suddenly be thrust into an unknown place so at odds to what they knew."

"You could be right," agreed Father Thomas.

Scanning the horizon to the west, they continuously sought movement that would indicate the enemy had pushed further northward. Thus far fortune had been with them. "Xith should be due west of us now," Father Thomas announced after several minutes of quiet riding. "Perhaps even a little to the south." The rising smoke from Sterrom was now more to the southwest. Since it was south of Xith, that should place the walled city almost due west of their position.

"How much further is it to the pass?" Larus inquired.

"If we keep this pace…," began Father Thomas then turned his attention to the mountains on their right before looking northward. Gauging the distance to the mountain range far in the distance ahead of them, he concluded, "Should be there by nightfall."

"Good." Larus was pleased. There was no enemy in sight and less than a day to the pass. After that they would make their way to Casdralla's High Temple on this world, find out what Hunter was here to do, then see it done. If all went well, he should be returned to the ranks of Casdralla's Qyaendri before too long.

He had to admit though, that the time spent as a mortal among mortals, was giving him an insight into them he hadn't appreciated before. Larus was sure that never again would he be so blasé about their suffering. For a brief moment he thought if that would be a good thing.

"Can we stop?"

Hunter's question interrupted his reverie. Glancing back, Larus saw him sitting slightly askew in the saddle. Nodding, he began to slow. "A short break," he announced.

"Thank you," breathed Hunter with relief. Bringing his horse to a stop, he quickly slid off and to the ground. Whether he lost his balance or his legs simply would no longer hold him, he stumbled after dismounting and fell to the ground.

"Hunter!" exclaimed Father Thomas. Dismounting quickly, he raced over to Hunter's side. "Are you okay?" he asked.

"No," Hunter replied. Lying on the ground with no desire to move, he turned his face toward the priest. "I am not okay. I hurt everywhere and it's not just from riding either."

Father Thomas understood. The wounds inflicted upon him in the soldier's camp had had little time to heal. With their initial forced march as a captive and now the hours of unaccustomed riding, healing had been slow if it had happened at all. "Rest yourself while you can," he finally said.

Larus appeared with two strips of dried beef and some of the stale bread. "Here," he said, offering it to Hunter. "Eat this. You will need your strength."

Hunter didn't reach out for the proffered food. He simply laid there with eyes closed. "I'll see that he eats," Father Thomas assured Larus and took the proffered food.

Indicating a nearby rise to the west, Larus announced, "I'm going to scout around a bit." Returning to his horse, he added, "Try to get what rest you can until I return."

"We will," replied Father Thomas. "Be careful."

"Plan to," he said. Then speaking in Hunter's language, he told him the same with an added urging to eat the food. "Your body won't heal if you don't eat," he told him.

Cracking open an eye, he looked up at Larus. "I'll try," he said.

Larus saw Hunter reach out and take one of the two strips of beef from Father Thomas, then mounted. Before he left, he gave Father Thomas one final warning. "I will be back shortly," he said. "Whatever you do, keep quiet."

Father Thomas understood the unspoken message. There was to be no more calling out Larus' name and possibly attracting the attention of an Ullentite patrol. "I promise," he assured him. Then as Larus turned to leave, Father Thomas offered up a prayer for his safe return.

Riding away from the pair, Larus turned his attention to the surrounding hills. For the most part, the hills rolled on for miles in every direction. From what he had been told by Father Thomas, to the west the hills gave way to plains before reaching the city of Xith. Xith itself sat upon the eastern shore of a large lake which had a major river feeding it from the north.

Upon reaching the crest of the neighboring hill, he surveyed the land in all directions. Far to the west he could see movement. Who they were or exactly how many, he couldn't be sure. Only that there were a lot. To the north there was little in the way of movement to indicate the presence of people. Just a few lone groups spread out among the hills, refugees escaping north toward the pass. East and south were quiet.

Returning his gaze westward, he strained to make out what was going on but was simply too far away. At least whatever was going on over there, it was far enough away that it was unlikely to impact him and the others.

The way north looked clear, at least of soldiers. Those pockets of refugees would hardly cause them any problems. Satisfied that they would face little interference on their ride north, he turned his horse about and returned to the others.

When he returned, he found Hunter fast asleep with Father Thomas sitting nearby. "Do we need to leave now?" Father Thomas asked.

Larus glanced at the sleeping form of Hunter. "I think we could give him a few more minutes," he said. Dismounting, he came over and sat next to Father Thomas.

"He has been through a lot," Father Thomas stated. He moved an errant strand of Hunter's hair from out of the sleeping man's face before moving his finger to the burned section on Hunter's cheek, "His time with the Ullentites must have been terrible. He is in a very bad way."

"I know," replied Larus. He gave Father Thomas a rundown on what was going on in the hills and plains around them. The priest's face grew grave when he was told of the groups of refugees making their way north.

"I wish we could help them," he said, then offered a brief prayer for the refugees.

"From what I saw, it looks as if they will most likely make the pass before the Ullentites reach this area," offered Larus.

"I pray that you are correct," Father Thomas said sadly.

They allowed Hunter to sleep for another half hour before waking him to continue their trek north. He was less than enthused about being awakened, and was even less so about the prospect of getting back up on the horse. But through the encouraging help of Larus and Father Thomas, he somehow made it.

Larus took the lead as they headed out. Keeping the mountains to their right, they wended their way northward through the hills.

Hunter for his part seemed better able to sit his horse. The feeling of being on the brink of tumbling off and being dashed to the ground wasn't nearly as strong as it had been earlier. Still fearful, or rather cautiously nervous as he preferred to call it, of the great beast, he thought he might be getting the hang of this riding business.

Hours went by as hill after hill fell behind. The sparse thicket of trees that adorned the hills gradually grew thicker the further north they went. From the midst of one rather thick copse of trees, two people unexpectedly lurched out as Father Thomas rode near. Larus had his sword out and ready for a fight before he realized they were part of the refugees. A man and a woman, their clothes showed signs of having been slept in and about each was an air of desperation.

"Father!" the woman cried, rushing forward with her man lending an arm for support.

Slowing to a stop, Father Thomas soon had a weeping woman gripping his leg. "Help us!" she cried. Pressing her face against his leg, sobs wracked her.

"What is the problem my child?" he asked. He could see the man was equally distraught though was trying to keep it together for the sake of the woman.

"It's our daughter," she replied. "I...I think she may be dying."

Father Thomas gently disengaged the woman from his leg and slipped off his horse. "Take me to her," he said. As he moved away, he caught the disapproving gaze Larus shot him as he headed toward the copse. Ignoring him, Father Thomas followed the couple.

"She was hurt when the soldiers attacked," the man said. "She's lost a lot of blood."

Fearing for the child, Father Thomas silently prayed for her well being as he followed the couple into the copse. He didn't recognize the couple so asked, "Are you from Rie?"

"Yes," the woman replied.

"How did you know?" The man asked.

"My companions and I passed through there a few days ago," he replied. The man looked questioningly at him in silence, and Father Thomas shook his head. "Everything was burnt to the ground and none of her people remained." True enough. He didn't have the heart to inform the couple that their friends and neighbors most likely had been taken captive by the soldiers. Though from the way they reacted to his words, they may already have known.

"She's right in here," the woman said as she hurried forward.

Following close, Father Thomas soon saw the feet of a small child sticking out from behind a tree trunk. Moving around the tree, he found a girl of about seven lying motionless on the ground. Her flaxen hair was arranged lovingly on either side of a face that was calm and peaceful. His eyes were drawn to the large red stain that had formed on the front of what had once been a beautiful blue dress, then returned to the child's face.

The mother knelt by the child's side, tears running down her face. "Momma's here," she said to the girl. Using her hand, she began to tenderly stroke the child's hair.

Sadness gripped him as Father Thomas watched the mother lovingly caress her child. This was the part of being a priest that he had never liked. How do you tell a parent that their child was dead?

Father Thomas glanced to the girl's father and saw in the man's eyes that he already knew the truth. "I'm sorry," he said.

The man nodded. Coming to his wife, he knelt down beside her and laid a comforting hand upon her shoulder.

"Momma brought a priest," the woman said soothingly to her child. "Everything will be alright."

"Dear..." the man started to say to his wife but then grief overcame him and was unable to continue.

"I am terribly sorry my child," Father Thomas said softly to the woman. "Your daughter has gone to be with the Lady." His words fell on deaf ears as she continued to lovingly caress her daughter's hair, saying that everything would be alright. Reaching out, he took the hand that had been caressing her daughter's hair and held it in both of his.

The woman's eyes turned to his. "She likes puppies," she began. "Our Miesha is due any day now. Soon, she will have many to play with." Giving Father Thomas a grin, she attempted to free her hand from his grip, but he held firm.

"She is gone," he said to her. "There is nothing that can be done for her."

"I think I will make her some sweetbread when we return home," she said. "It was always her favorite."

Father Thomas glanced to the woman's husband. "Thank you for coming Father," he said. Then as the woman pulled her hand free of Father Thomas' grip and began stroking her daughter's hair once more, the man motioned for him to step away with him.

"Let her have a few more minutes of happiness," the man said, choking back tears threatening to overwhelm him. Glancing back to his wife, he saw her smoothing their daughter's hair, just as she had done since the day their daughter was born.

"I am truly sorry for your loss," Father Thomas said, "but you cannot afford to stay here very much longer. The enemy will soon be coming this way, very soon."

Turning from gazing at his wife, the man nodded. "I know," he said sadly. After a brief silence, he said, "You should get out of here now Father. I'll stay and take care of my daughter."

"I shall pray for her," Father Thomas said. "And for you and your wife."

"Thank you," the man said.

"I wish I could do more."

The man simply nodded. Then leaving Father Thomas' side, he returned to his wife and daughter.

He stood there for a moment in sadness as he watched the man embrace his wife, then turned and left the copse of trees. Outside he found Hunter and Larus still sitting upon their horses, waiting.

"Is the little girl alright?" Larus asked. Father Thomas' silence was all the answer he needed.

"They will remain here a little longer," he told them.

"Didn't you tell them the enemy may come this way at any time?" Larus asked.

Father Thomas nodded. "I told them," he said. Coming to his horse, he mounted and turned one last sad look to the copse of trees and the family it held. As they left the copse behind, he prayed prayer after prayer for the little girl, the parents, and everyone else caught in this terrible situation.

From that point on, they began encountering more and more displaced people. Father Thomas offered blessing and prayers to all he met, as well as encouraging them to make for the pass with all speed.

Hours flew by as they raced for the pass. The mountains to their left gradually grew closer, rising majestically to the sky. Ahead, they watched as the mountains curved to form a range that encompassed the northern edge of the valley. There they would find the massive gate which spanned the breadth of the pass. It was Casdra's last line of defense should Xith fall.

Off to their left, the road from Xith leading to the pass came into view. It was swarming with slow moving refugees, mules, hand drawn carts, and wagons filled to capacity.

Father Thomas looked with sadness upon the displaced people. Though not directly under his charge, they were still Casdralla's people whose lives had been torn asunder. "Sad," he commented with emotion.

Larus nodded and began maneuvering more toward the road. Despite the number of people moving along its length, it would still be faster than making their way through the hills.

When their presence was first noticed by the refugees, many started to flee, believing them to be the enemy. But it was soon realized they were not and many called to Father Thomas for help, blessings, and news.

He did his best to assure them that everything would be alright, and to encourage them to move faster toward the pass. "The enemy is being delayed at Xith," he explained to them. "But they still may send riders this way so you must make haste."

Moving on, he knew his words of warning would do little to ease their fear, but better a little fear than to take one's time and be overtaken. As Larus led them alongside the road, Father Thomas repeated his prayers and words of warning to each new group they encountered. Afterward, he would glance back and see that they were moving much faster than before.

The sun arced across the sky and was halfway down to the western horizon when the road entered the canyon through which it would make its way up to the pass. At the canyon's mouth, they found a score of Casdra soldiers. Their primary concern was the flow of refugees, helping where they could. Of secondary concern was the enemy. Larus asked one in passing who said that should the enemy be sighted, they were to hold them off for as long as possible to allow as many of their people to escape as they could.

Larus didn't have to be told that should that event come to pass, these soldiers probably would not survive. Father Thomas offered a prayer for the success of their mission and for the safety of those on the road. Then they were in the canyon.

The way was gentle at first, a moderate incline that curved back and forth. Alongside the road flowed a river coming out of the mountains. Though deep, it had moments of cataracts and cascades that would roar to drown out all but the loudest shouts.

They reached the beginning of the climb a mile in. There the refugees began to bog down as carts weighted with mounds of belongings were being pushed and pulled by both men and women. In some instances children were forced to add their limited strength in order for the carts to continue up the pass. Those with mules or horses fared better, but they were definitely in the minority.

Fortunately the blockages were intermittent and they were still able to make decent time as the road continued its ascent up the side of the canyon. Threading their way through the gaggle of refugees they had climbed several hundred feet from the valley floor when they rounded one of the numerous bends in the road and came to a sudden standstill. For before them was a veritable logjam of people, carts, and animals. Up ahead where the people were the most compact, angry shouts and screams could be heard.

Larus noticed how the road narrowed to half its size where the commotion was hottest. It appeared that sometime in the past the mountainside had given way, taking a section of the road with it. Larus was quick to see that it wasn't the narrowness of the road that was the source of the congestion. Rather, it was a cart tilted askew. An angry crowd was gathered around the cart. It was from those people that the most heated exchanges were coming.

"Trouble," Larus told the other two. "Stay here," he said. Dismounting, he handed his reins to Father Thomas then began making his way through the people.

"Push it over the side!"

"We have to get through!"

Shouts of anger were being directed toward the cart and its owner. When Larus finally managed to elbow his way through the crowd to the cart, he saw that one of the cart's wheels had broken. It had already been removed and was lying on the ground nearby. The poor owner was attempting to use a large branch as a lever to raise the cart's axle. Standing with another wheel in hand, a boy of about twelve was waiting for the axle to rise sufficiently so he could place it on. Unfortunately, an otherwise simple task was being hindered by the angry people who wanted past. Several men were near the cart's owner, shouting at him while he tried to fix the problem.

The owner was red faced with effort as the thick branch he used as a lever raised the axel a little bit higher. That the man hadn't unloaded the cart first didn't make any sense to Larus. Perhaps the man had felt the people around him weren't going to afford him the time to do that. Then just as the axel was about to be level with the new wheel, there was a loud crack and the branch broke. Without the support, the axel fell back to the ground.

"Over the side!" one of the men shouted.

"No!" the man pleaded. "It's all we have!"

"Look," another shouted, getting into the man's face. "Your busted cart is keeping the rest of us from getting to safety. We have our own families to worry about!"

Larus could see the situation was quickly getting out of hand. The cart's owner reached down and placed the remaining section of the branch beneath the axel in another attempt at raising it. He was about to being raising it when a foot came out of nowhere and kicked it out of the cart owner's hand. It bounced once then slipped over the edge and was gone.

"Now!" the angry man yelled. "Over the edge!"

As four sets of hands gripped the cart, the owner was pushed out of the way. "No!" he shouted.

"Over the side boys!" the angry man shouted again. Taking hold of it, he and the others began edging the cart toward the side. They managed to come to within a foot of the cliff's edge when the cart's sideward momentum came to an abrupt halt.

Four heads turned to find Larus with both hands gripping the cart. "Stop this madness!" he scolded.

"Let go stranger," the angry man warned.

"No," replied Larus. "This is not the way people of Casdralla treat one another." Seeing that the men were at the moment no longer working to push the cart over the edge, he let go. Stepping around the cart, he glanced to the owner and saw relief wash over him. He then glanced to the lad with the wheel.

"Come here boy," he said, stepping toward the cart's axel.

The four men saw the sword hanging at his hip and the determined look on his face. As Larus moved toward them, he said, "Back off." Unwilling to bar the way of a determined, sword totting man, they backed off.

He came and stood next to the axel then turned toward the boy holding the wheel. "Put it on when I raise it," he said.

"But mister," the boy said, "you can't lift that all by yourself!" Indeed, with the cart loaded as it was, it would be a challenge even for several men to raise.

"Just be ready," Larus told him. He then positioned his back against the side of the cart and took hold of the wagon bed. Then after finding good purchase for his feet, he lifted.

At first the cart didn't budge and for a moment he thought his strength hadn't returned sufficiently for him to be able to raise it. Straining mightily, muscles working to their utmost, he managed to raise the side of the cart from off the ground.

Around him, the onlookers had turned from an angry mob to one of curiosity, then curiosity gave way to wonder as the cart began to rise still further. The men who had so recently tried to push the cart over the side now came to help him. Larus couldn't help but think that if they had helped the cart owner in the first place, all of them would even now be further up toward the pass.

With the men's help, the axle was raised sufficiently for the boy to slide the wheel on. Then the cart owner came forward, and with a few well placed blows from a hammer, drove in the pin and secured the wheel in place. A cheer went up as the cart was lowered and the new wheel rested on the ground.

The owner clapped Larus on the back and exclaimed, "Thank you!" The boy came to the man's side as well as another older woman who had to be the man's wife. "How can we ever repay you?" she asked.

With a glance back to those waiting to proceed toward the pass, he gave them a grin and said, "Don't worry about it."

"Come on!" a voice hollered. "Get going!" Turning, they found it to be that of the angry man. Larus cast him a glowering look and the man grew silent.

Larus waited until the man and woman each took hold of the drawbar of the cart and began pulling before heading back down to where Hunter and Father Thomas waited. The boy moved in behind the cart to add his strength and slowly, the cart began to move.

Father Thomas was grinning at him when he returned. "That was very nice," he said.

Swinging up into the saddle, Larus shrugged, "Couldn't let those poor people's belongings be thrown over the edge."

Hunter had watched the proceedings with great interest. The fact that Larus had begun to right the cart by himself wasn't lost on him. When the crowd began to move and they were able to continue, he took a good long look at the contents of the cart when they rode past. While Larus and the man exchanged another round of 'thank you' and 'take care' he saw that the cart held several pieces of furniture. Most notably was a thick oaken dresser that must have weighed a hundred pounds. Ornate and obviously an antique, he could understand why the family had brought it. But the weight! No wonder the original wheel had broken. In fact, considering the looks on the faces of the man and woman as they struggled to pull the heavily laden cart up the pass, he wondered if the chest would still be with them when they reached the top.

From that point on, the number of refugees thinned out and it wasn't long before they saw the massive gate blocking the pass ahead. Made of stone, the wall rose fifty feet beginning at the lip of the precipice overlooking the river, all the way to the side of the mountain. The gate itself was wide enough to allow the simultaneous passage of three wagons and was made of heavy wood with iron bindings. A guard tower sat on either side of the gate with an additional platform for archers built into the canyon wall above.

"Impressive," Hunter said.

"Indeed," replied Father Thomas after receiving the translation from Larus. "Once we pass through, we shall be in the heart of Casdra."

"How far is it to the temple from here?" asked Larus.

"A little over a day," he replied.

"Good," grunted Hunter when Larus translated. He was anxious to discover why he was brought here. Certainly it couldn't be for his military or tactical knowledge, he didn't have any. And with a war in the offing, he didn't know what else would save these people.

Before encountering the refugees in the pass and back on the road leading to it, he hadn't really cared one way or another for these people. After all, hadn't he been kidnapped? True, it was to help them but that hardly made it excusable. But after seeing the plight of these people, the hopeless looks on their faces, he had begun to wish there was some way he could be of help. Also, if helping these people put a monkey wrench in the plans of those who had tortured him, all the better.

"Father Thomas!" a voice cried out as they passed through the gate.

Turning toward the source of the salutation, they found a man dressed in robes similar to those worn by Father Thomas. "Brother Frey!" exclaimed Father Thomas delightedly. Brother Frey had been one of the junior priests assigned to the temple at Rie.

The other priest was somewhat younger than Father Thomas and his robe was cut slightly different, perhaps designating a difference in their standing within the temple. "When news came that Billin and Rie had fallen, I feared you had been taken."

"I was," affirmed Father Thomas. "But through the will of the Lady, I and my companions escaped."

"Then you must speak with the commander," Brother Frey insisted. "He will wish to hear of this."

The day was getting late and all three had been on the go for some time. He glanced over to Larus and received a nod. Turning back to Brother Frey, he said, "Very well. Take us to him."

"Excellent," said Brother Frey satisfactorily. "This way."

Father Thomas followed after as Brother Frey began leading them over to where three buildings sat some distance back from the wall and the gate. A number of soldiers were loitering nearby, and one was just emerging from the largest of the three buildings. It was to that one which Brother Frey led them.

"When word arrived at the Temple of what happened," explained Brother Frey, "I came here straight away to offer what aid I could."

"It was fortunate that you were not in Rie," said Father Thomas.

"I suppose I should consider myself fortunate," replied Brother Frey. "But still I wish I had been there with my people."

Father Thomas could well understand how he felt, for he too wished he had not been absent when the Ullentites had attacked Billin. "Have many of your people made it to the pass?" he asked.

"Only three," he replied sadly. "I heard two from Billin made it though I am not sure who they were."

"Two?" asked Father Thomas sadly.

"So I heard," affirmed Brother Frey.

Upon reaching the front of the building, soldiers came and took charge of their mounts as they dismounted. Following Brother Frey inside, they found an older soldier standing behind a table staring at a map lying upon its surface. On another table abutting the one with the map, sat a pile of dispatches awaiting the commander's attention.

"Pardon the intrusion commander," Brother Frey said as they entered.

Looking up at the Brother and those accompanying him, the commander didn't appear too pleased by the interruption. "Yes Brother Frey?" he asked with a tinge of impatience.

"I thought you would wish to speak to my fellow servant of Casdralla," replied Brother Frey. "May I introduce Father Thomas, priest of the temple in Billin."

That piqued the commander's attention. "Billin you say?" he queried.

"Yes Commander," Father Thomas replied, nodding.

Before anyone could say anything else, Brother Frey interjected, "They were held captive by the Ullentites!"

The commander's eyes widened. "The devil you say," he replied. Turning to a soldier standing nearby, he said, "Bring Sergeant Wills."

"Yes sir," the soldier replied. Then after a smart salute, he hurried from the building.

"It was fortunate you were able to escape from their clutches, Father," the commander said. "That you could do so is no less than miraculous."

"So it was," agreed Father Thomas. Casting Larus a barely perceptible sidelong glance, he repeated softly, "So it was."

Chapter 11

For the next several hours, Father Thomas and Larus were debriefed as to the size and compliment of those who had held them captive. The commander and Sergeant Wills were most distressed when told the number of catapults the enemy brought with them. The fall of Sterrom was old news to them and explained that Xith was already under siege.

"We have orders to keep the gate open until the enemy has been sighted at the base of the pass," he stated. "Once that happens, we close it tight and pray."

"I am certain our Lady will not allow her people to come to ruination," Father Thomas assured him.

"I pray you are right Father," replied the Commander. He then cast a look toward Hunter. He didn't like the fact that here behind the wall was a stranger of unknown origins. When he learned of Hunter's inability to understand their language, he had questioned Father Thomas about him. All he received in reply were vague assurances that he was no enemy and may possibly prove of worth against the Ullentites. He briefly entertained the thought of detaining him, but had quickly been informed that he was under the protection of Father Thomas and was being taken to the High Temple. He didn't like it, but wasn't about to gainsay one of Casdralla's priests.

Finally an hour or so later, Sergeant Wills and the commander concluded their questioning. Having gleaned every pertinent piece of information concerning the enemy that Father Thomas and Larus knew, they allowed them to leave.

Hunter was slumped fast asleep in a chair against the wall when Larus turned toward the door. Crossing over to him, Larus shook his shoulder. "Time to go," he said. Bloodshot eyes looked up at Larus then took in their surroundings. Nodding, Hunter came to his feet and accompanied them through the door.

Outside, refugees almost entirely packed the area this side of the gate, and the area abutting the road continuing on up toward the summit looked no better. Off to one side they saw the family Larus had aided earlier that evening. Now that the imminent threat of seizure or attack by the Ullentites was past, reaction had set in. Listless and looking without hope, the three of them sat around a small fire with another family, sharing a pot of stew.

Larus looked around for a decent place to camp but quickly concluded that the throng had taken all but the center of the road for their own. "Perhaps we should move further toward the summit before making camp," he suggested.

Father Thomas nodded in agreement. "But not too far," he replied wearily.

They were forced to travel for two miles or more before the throng of refugees thinned out sufficiently. When they came across a relatively vacant area backdropped by a small waterfall cascading down the side of the canyon, Larus brought them to a halt.

Hunter quickly staked out a place near the stream flowing from the base of the falls and was asleep in no time. Once a fire had been built and Father Thomas opened a saddle bag contained travel rations, he nodded over to Hunter who was fast asleep and asked, "Should we wake him?"

"You would know better than I," replied Larus.

Father Thomas handed Larus a strip of dried beef and a hard chunk of extremely stale bread. It was so hard in fact that he had to dip it in water to soften it up sufficiently so he wouldn't run the risk of breaking off his teeth. Glancing over to their sleeping comrade, he ripped off a section of the dried beef and began chewing.

"Sleep may be the best thing for him right now," he replied. "His body most likely needs him quiet while it works to heal." Returning his attention to Larus he added, "Though I am sure he will be quite hungry upon wakening."

Larus nodded. Then chewing off another piece of the shoe leather tough beef he asked, "What are we going to do once we reach the Temple?"

Father Thomas remained silent for a minute then replied, "First we will consult with High Priestess Trystia. If anyone would know what to do, it would be she." Taking another bite, he chewed in silent contemplation before saying, "After that? Who knows? We shall have to see what the High Priestess has to say on this matter before any further plans can be made."

The crackle of the fire played descant to the melody of the falls as it crashed upon the rocks. Father Thomas gazed around to the other fires lining the road in both directions. Around each were people, families whose lives had been ripped apart by the advancing Ullentite army. He said a prayer of thankfulness for their deliverance. He also prayed that each of them including himself would have the strength and fortitude for what may come.

His attention was drawn time and again over to Hunter's sleeping form. "Where does he come from?" he asked Larus after several moments of quiet. Turning his attention back to his companion, he cast him a questioning look.

"Why do you ask?" His gaze remained directed at the fire, this was not a subject he desired to discuss at any length.

"You speak his language," explained Father Thomas. "You must know something about him."

Larus remained quiet while he considered his response. Finally, he looked up at the priest. "His people live very far away," he said. "I spent some time among them during one of my numerous journeys."

"What kind of people were they?" he asked.

"Oh, I suppose you could say they are very much like those here," explained Larus. "Some are good, others are bad. Most just want to make it from one day to the next without complications."

"Like being invaded by hostile soldiers?"

Larus nodded and grinned. "You might say that," he chuckled.

"What do you think the goddess has in store for him?" Father Thomas asked.

Shrugging, Larus said, "If I knew, we wouldn't be traveling to the High Temple to find out." Changing the subject so as not to dwell overlong on the details concerning Hunter's world, Larus said, "Perhaps we should get some sleep."

A yawn escaped Father Thomas and he nodded. "If we get an early enough start in the morning, we might be able to make the Temple before sundown."

Larus stretched and was surprised when a yawn unexpectedly escaped him. "Then I bid you good night," he said. Lying by the fire, he watched as Father Thomas covered Hunter with a blanket to ward off the mountain's chill. Then the priest took another for himself and came to rest near the fire.

No further words were spoken as each slowly allowed sleep to overtake them.

The following morning they woke to find the sky slightly overcast. Yesterday it had been clear and sunny. But sometime during the night clouds had moved in, though Father Thomas assured the other two that rain was unlikely.

Sleeping throughout the night had refreshed Hunter immensely. Though pain still throbbed here and there, the burn on his cheek had lost much of its redness and he felt better able to take on the world.

Larus watched him as he went to the falls for a morning drink. On his return, Hunter gave him a smile. "Feeling better are we?" Larus asked.

"Oh man yes," replied Hunter. "I feel better than I have since coming to this crazy world." His gait was a bit off, probably his inner thighs were sore due to time spent in the saddle. But it didn't look as if it bothered him all that much.

The road was beginning to fill with refugees on their way to the summit. Father Thomas distributed the last of the rations the soldiers had carried in their saddle pouches. It wasn't much, and though it seemed unlikely, harder to chew than the day before.

"We best be getting out of here," Larus announced through a bite of beef. From the amount of people, carts, and wagons they had passed after taking their leave of the commander, he knew the road would be a veritable madhouse before long. Even now the road continuing up to the summit was anything but deserted.

"I think you are correct my son," Father Thomas replied.

By the time they were in the saddle and heading up the last bit to the summit, the road had congested to such an extent they were forced to travel at a walk. It took some time before they finally threaded their way past the press of refugees and were able to proceed more rapidly.

After an hour of faster travel, Father Thomas announced they had reached the summit. Other than a barely perceptible downward slant on the other side, there was no indication that this was the top. The mountains still rose tall on either side, and the road continued to look as if it was continuing up. Father Thomas explained that this area played a trick with the eyes, making one feel as if they were still going up when in actuality they were heading down.

Frankly, Larus didn't care. All he was concerned with was reaching the High Temple and hopefully returning to the ranks of Qyaendri. Being mortal had been anything but enjoyable, and he was definitely ready to put it behind him.

From that point on in ever increasing degrees, the ground began sloping downward more noticeably. When the mountains opened up and revealed a tree covered valley of rolling hills Father Thomas explained that not too much further ahead they would come to where the road forked. The main road would continue down to the rolling valley while the other would continue north along the rolling foothills of the mountain's slope.

"The northern branch will ultimately take us to the High Temple," Father Thomas explained.

"Where does the main road go?" Hunter asked after receiving the translation.

"To the heart of Casdra," Father Thomas told him.

"Ah," Hunter said.

Continuing down from the summit, the number of refugees continued to thin until they were only an intermittent obstacle. Before they reached the branching Father Thomas had spoken of, a company of cavalry was seen approaching along the west road further down in the valley.

"Reinforcements," commented Larus.

"May the Lady give them strength and see them victorious," prayed Father Thomas.

There were a hundred riders, each armed in mail made of interlocking rings. With long spears and shields, Hunter thought they looked like something out of Camelot.

They reached the junction a fraction before the riders and quickly moved down the northern branch to get out of their way. It was quite an impressive sight to see the hundred riders thunder by.

Father Thomas' lips moved in silent prayer as he watched the riders make their way past. Once the thundering roar of their passing diminished, the three comrades left the junction behind and resumed their trek to the High Temple.

From the junction the road continued through tree covered hills. In places the trees became so dense that the sky was completely blotted out by the interlocking branches overhead. They came to another junction two hours later where their road forked yet again. Father Thomas directed them to continue straight and disregard the other road.

"We are heading east now," Father Thomas explained. He was about to expand further when the sound of a fast moving rider came to them from up ahead. A moment later, the rider appeared, moving at a fast gallop. Barely even acknowledging their presence, he shot past them and disappeared on his way to the junction where they had encountered the cavalry.

"Courier from the High Temple," stated Father Thomas. He glanced to Larus and asked, "Did you see the small red sash he wore?"

Larus nodded.

"That marks him as being on Temple business. Anyone bearing such a sash must be aided in any way possible." Father Thomas turned his gaze toward where the courier had disappeared.

"Heading to the fighting do you suppose?" asked Hunter after receiving Larus' translation.

Father Thomas shrugged. "Perhaps," he replied. Turning his horse back to follow the eastern road, he indicated for the others to follow. He gauged the light coming through the trees and figured it to still be early afternoon. "We should reach Veradin before dark."

"Is the High Temple in Veradin?" asked Larus.

"No," answered Father Thomas. "It is a small village sitting at the base of the trail leading to the High Temple." A grin came to him as he said, "Most people call it 'Temple Town', but the use of that name is frowned upon."

"Especially by the priests I would think," guessed Larus.

Father Thomas nodded and chuckled. "Those high in the Temple's hierarchy do consider its use less than proper," he agreed. Though from his amusement, it appeared to Larus that Father Thomas may have used the name on occasion.

Hunter followed their conversation as best he could. Having to wait for Larus to translate was growing annoying. "You said there was a trail leading from Veradin to the High Temple?" he asked.

"Yes," replied Father Thomas. "It is narrow, barely wide enough in places for even a single cart to pass."

"Then, shouldn't we wait until morning so we don't get caught on the trail when the sun goes down?" he asked.

"Worry not Hunter," Father Thomas assured him. "There will be adequate light for us to make the journey."

"I hope so," Hunter mumbled.

The trees began to thin as the road started its climb toward the upper elevations. Twice they crossed wooden bridges spanning small streams and another that was a good deal larger which spanned a narrow, but very deep gorge. By the time the first building of Veradin came into view, they had climbed almost a thousand feet.

Veradin was your typical backwater village, despite the fact that the High Temple was nearby. Most of the buildings were single story and situated throughout the neighboring hills. Plain and unadorned, they looked for all intent and purposes as your run-of-the-mill country homes. The only thing that set it apart from other similar villages was the number of inns found at the village center.

The typical village of this size may be able to support one inn, or perhaps two if it sat on one of the main roads. But this one had five. Three were two storied structures, another boasted three, while the last had an amazing five. When Larus first saw it he thought it must be something of importance, but Father Thomas explained that it was simply another inn.

"But how do they stay in business?" Larus asked. "Surely there couldn't be enough traffic along this road to fill this many." In fact, other than the courier, they hadn't encountered another soul since turning off the main road.

"Every once in a while the Temple has more visiting priests in attendance than they can adequately house," Father Thomas explained. "Needing extra space to put them, the Temple built these inns. Priests stay free of course, everyone else pays the going rate."

"You have that many priests?" he asked, surprised. From what he had seen of Casdra thus far, it didn't look like it would have all that many.

"It is not just the priests," Father Thomas explained. "Many bring their families with them."

That surprised Larus. In most worlds where he had interacted with mortals, priests were celibate. It wasn't a dictate of the Lady, just one of the mores that humans tend to associate with priests.

Hunter was gazing at the five story building. "Which is the best?" he asked.

"I have never had a bad experience staying at The Felled Tree," Father Thomas replied, indicating one of the two storied inns. "I always stay there when I visit the Temple."

Turning a surprised gaze toward Father Thomas, Larus asked, "You don't stay at the Temple?"

Father Thomas shook his head. "No, not even if there is room. I enjoy being around our Lady's people," he explained. "Besides, the Temple can be a bit, uh, formal if you know what I mean?"

Larus laughed. Oh yes, he knew exactly what he meant. One couldn't let their hair down as it were at the Temple. Plus, most of the minstrels performing within the High Temple would most likely choose uplifting, and morally correct selections of music. *The fun stuff would only happen here in 'Temple Town'*, he thought with a grin.

As they made their way toward The Felled Tree, Larus took a good look at the people. Most were what you would expect to find in a village. Others drew his attention. Several priests were making their way from one building to another. He saw two heading toward the eastern end of town. Father Thomas explained they were probably on their way to the trail leading up to the High Temple. There was also a group of six soldiers standing in front of the five storied inn. Another pair was practicing their fencing around the side.

The priests were intent with their own concerns and paid the trio little heed. One did offer a salutation to Father Thomas as he went by, but barely slowed enough to receive one in return. Larus thought it seemed out of character for priests, but gauging the way Father Thomas reacted, or rather failed to react to his fellow priest, figured such was the norm.

Coming up to The Felled Tree, Father Thomas said, "Ah, here we are." Dismounting, he turned to the pair. "They have some of the best food here that it has ever been my pleasure to eat."

Indeed, the aroma coming from within corroborated his statement very well. Fresh baked bread with a hint of nuts, and if Larus wasn't mistaken, there was also a whiff of char indicating a shank of meat roasting on a spit. He glanced at Hunter and could see his salivary glands were working overtime. "Hungry?" he asked with a grin.

"You know it," replied Hunter enthusiastically. After the meager and barely chewable food they had ingested over the past several days, all three of them had stomachs aching to be fed.

Securing his horse to the rail, Father Thomas walked to the door and entered quickly followed by the other two. The common room was crowded but they did manage to find a small table wedged into the far corner where though it was a bit cramped, they could at least be by themselves.

The mood of the room was anything but happy. No minstrel was in attendance and the faces of everyone bore the looks of fear and worry. Apparently rumors of what was transpiring to the south had already begun circulating.

A girl with a semi-forced smile came to their table. When her eyes turned onto Father Thomas, they widened in recognition. "Oh Father!" she exclaimed. "I was so worried about you." She glanced to his two companions then returned her attention back to him. "They say the Ullentites destroyed your town of Billin!" Reaching out, she laid a hand on his shoulder.

"It is true my dear," he replied, giving her hand a pat. "My friends and I have just come from there."

Suddenly the whole room grew quiet. All conversation ceased as every eye turned toward them.

From a nearby table, one man said, "They say Rie has been destroyed too."

"I heard that Xith itself was under attack," another added.

Father Thomas gazed around the room to the worried faces directed toward him. "All true I am sorry to say," he finally said. Their server gasped and several muted curses came from the back of the room.

One man stood up and came forward. "Any word about Cuellyn?" he asked with a tremor to his voice. Cuellyn was one of the towns on the shores of the same lake upon which Xith sat.

"I believe we saw Sterrom afire during our flight from the Ullentite army," he said. "Billin had been destroyed before I was able to return and we passed through what was left of Rie. Of the other towns south of the pass..." he paused momentarily and saw many a head move closer to hear what he was about to say, "there has been no word. The Ullentite army is quite large, at least the portion we encountered." He paused for a moment then quietly said, "I fear for them."

"Damn!" cursed one man.

"Many of our people were able to flee before the Ullentites could cut off their retreat," he explained quickly. "Hundreds have made it safely through the gate guarding the pass, and I am sure more are even now on their way."

"Cursed Ullentites!" one man exclaimed.

Their server was on the verge of tears. Father Thomas realized the effect his words were having on her. Patting the hand on his shoulder yet again, he gave her a reassuring smile. "I am sure they will not be able to breach the defenses at Xith," he told her. "We will be safe here."

Lower lip trembling, she quietly said, "My brother and his family had moved to Sterrom last year."

Coming to his feet, he reached out and she came forward into his embrace. "I am sorry child," he said. Even though her face was pressed into the folds of his robes, they did little to muffle her sobs. Father Thomas held her comfortingly until she quieted down, all the while stroking her hair and assuring her things would work out.

By the time her sobs subsided, the other guests were talking among themselves about the news. A few outbursts and condemnations rose above the din and several hurriedly left the inn on their way to the pass to inquire about loved ones.

The nape of his robe was a little moist when the girl finally pulled away. "I'm sorry Father," she said, wiping the last few errant tears from her eyes.

He gave her another reassuring smile. "I shall pray for your brother and his family," he said to her.

"Oh thank you," she said in relief.

"If they made it through the pass," Larus interjected, "would they come here?"

She thought for a moment. "Perhaps," she said as if she hadn't even thought about such a possibility. "Or he may go to Ascet. Our mother lives there with her sister."

She thought about that for several seconds before coming to the realization that she hadn't yet taken their order. "I'm sorry gentlemen, Father," she said apologetically. "You must be hungry."

"It is quite alright," Father Thomas assured her. "We understand."

Larus gave her a reassuring nod of agreement as well.

"What can I get for you?" she asked.

"A double portion of whatever is causing that wonderful aroma," Larus told her. "Ale and a full loaf of bread for each of us."

"Right away," she said, then turned to return to the kitchen.

Father Thomas laid a hand on her arm before she could depart. "I am certain the Lady has looked after your brother and his family," he told her. "They will find you before too long."

She paused and gazed into his eyes for a second. Then with a "Thank you Father," she hurried toward the kitchen.

Father Thomas watched her until she passed through the doorway and then turned to find Larus staring at him.

"How can you say that?" Larus asked him. "You don't know whether they are safe or not!"

"He and his family are safe," Father Thomas said matter-of-factly.

"How can you know?" asked Larus.

"I know," was the reply.

Larus started to argue but then realized that perhaps Father Thomas did know. Qyaendri! Of course they could have given him that knowledge and the surety that it was true. He had done it himself numerous times when he had been one of them.

A priest such as Father Thomas had to have several Qyaendri in attendance just to handle the multitude of prayers the man exuded. Even for a priest he tended to pray more than most. The man prayed about everything. For a brief moment he wondered if any of the Qyaendri in attendance were ones he knew. If they didn't know him personally, by this time they must have heard of his disgrace and all that transpired within the temple. He couldn't help but glance around the common room and feel a little bit ashamed.

But he was making things right wasn't he? Everything will be as it was once Hunter completes whatever he had been brought to this world to accomplish. More than once Larus had thought back to the information Xi had directed him to impart to the one to be chosen. And not one piece of it told him anything about what Hunter was supposed to do. Or how to do it. Nothing! Perhaps Hunter was meant to make the journey to the Temple in any event. They would find out soon enough.

When the meal came it was the finest feast any of them could ever recall having. The meat was charred but not too black with every bite causing juice to dribble down their chins. Bread with a smattering of nuts sprinkled across the top, the outside crisp and the inside was like biting into a cloud. They set in with gusto.

Hunter found the fruity preserves to be quite tasty and slathered a healthy helping on every bite of bread. Never before could he recall ever eating so much at one time. Not even during Thanksgiving at his grandparent's house.

Once the meat disappeared and Larus was pushing the remaining section of his loaf around in the juice coating the bottom of the platter, a priest from a neighboring table approached.

"Excuse me," the priest said as he came to them.

"Yes?" asked Father Thomas.

"I am Father Kyren," the priest introduced himself.

"And I am Father Thomas," he replied.

"Yes I know," Father Kyren said. "I was in attendance during your talk on the 'Ramifications of Faith' with Father Young."

"Oh, uh, yes?" recalled Father Thomas. Though what he remembered about the only talk he had held with Father Young had been more of a shouting match over a finer point of doctrine, than a 'talk'. And where did Father Kyren get the title 'Ramifications of Faith'? According to his recollection, he and Father Young had begun discussing some matter or another that ultimately degenerated into a shouting match. It was true that by the time their 'talk' had come to a close, they had drawn quite a crowd. Apparently this Father Kyren had been one of them. Father Thomas was still a bit embarrassed by the fact that he had allowed his emotions to get out of control in such a way.

"You said you went through the town of Rie?" Father Kyren asked, snapping him out of his reverie.

"That is correct," affirmed Father Thomas. The worried look behind the priest's eyes gave Father Thomas a foreshadowing glimpse of what the priest was about to ask.

"Did you by chance meet an elderly man there?" he asked. "He would have had slate gray hair and walked with a limp. Goes by the name of Danner?"

"Your father?" guessed Father Thomas.

Silently, the priest nodded.

"I am sorry to say that I did not," he replied. Given the fact that the town was destroyed and Ullentite soldiers had encompassed the entire area, it was unlikely this Danner would turn up. But he wasn't about to offer such disheartening information unless asked directly.

Father Thomas stood and placed a hand on the priest's shoulder. "I am truly sorry."

"I was planning to leave in the morning to visit him," the priest said quietly.

"There is still the possibility that he made it to the pass," offered Larus. Both priests turned their heads and focused their attention on him. "There were hundreds fleeing through the pass, it's possible he could have been one of them."

A glimmer of hope sprung to the priest's eyes. "Yes," he said. "He would have fled with the others." A pause then…"I should hurry to the pass."

Father Thomas wished him good fortune as the priest hurriedly returned to his table to collect his belongings. That was when he realized the common room was much emptier than it had been.

"It seems there are many anxious to discover the fate of loved ones," Larus observed. At least half the tables showed signs of having been hastily deserted. For those who remained, the mood had turned much more frantic.

"I pray they find their family and friends," Father Thomas said sadly as he returned to his seat. Tearing off a small piece from his loaf of bread, he quietly ate until the sound of their server emerging from the kitchen drew his attention. Father Thomas saw her pause with a platter of food and looking perplexed at all the newly emptied tables. Then she noticed him gazing toward her and made her way over to him.

Before she could ask, he said, "I am afraid I scared your patrons away."

"What?" she asked. "How?"

He gave her a brief recap of what he had said and she nodded. "It's just as well," she replied. "I'm not really in the mood for a crowd just now." Sighing, she then moved over to another table around which sat four men, traders by the looks of them. There she deposited the tray of food.

A glance outside showed that night was fast approaching. "Perhaps we should make our way to the temple before the light completely fades?" Hunter suggested.

With their meal consumed, there was no reason for them to tarry any longer. Their server waved a goodbye as they made their way to the door. She attempted to grin but it didn't quite manifest properly.

"Take care my child," Father Thomas said to her. "May you find your brother and his family safe and well."

She nodded then turned and carried four mugs of ale over to the four men.

Once out the door, Hunter's gaze followed the road toward the east. Before it disappeared into the surrounding forest, he saw where it narrowed to half its size as it began its ascent up to the High Temple.

Pausing next to his horse, Father Thomas announced, "The Temple sits on a wide plateau further up the mountain."

"How far?" asked a concerned Hunter.

"A couple of hours," came the reply.

Hunter didn't like the sound of that. From the way the light was beginning to wane, he had grave concerns as to their ability to reach the plateau before the light faded altogether.

Father Thomas noticed his worried expression. "I assure you Hunter," he said. "There will be sufficient light for us to reach the Temple."

After Larus gave him the translation, Hunter mumbled quietly to himself, "I hope so."

Giving them both an assuring smile, Father Thomas swung up into the saddle and led them toward the trailhead.

Chapter 12

The trail wasn't as steep as Larus had anticipated, not initially anyway. Once past the edge of town, it began a gradual rise. Father Thomas led the way with Larus and Hunter close behind.

Rising alongside the mountain's slope, the trail entered a narrow gorge not long after leaving the village. A small river cut its way through from out of the mountains. As they climbed further above the gorge's floor, the water below was soon to be hidden in the deepening shadows of early evening.

"How far is it again?" asked Hunter and not for the first time.

"Oh, a couple hours," replied Father Thomas.

Already the sun's light was blocked by the mountains, with only the highest peaks on the eastern side still lit with the sun's rays. Hunter gauged the approach of darkness and was certain they wouldn't be able to reach the Temple in time.

"I don't suppose anyone has a flashlight?" he asked.

Larus shook his head and replied, "No."

"A lantern perhaps?"

Father Thomas glanced over his shoulder back to where Hunter rode. Though he couldn't understand the words, he understood the meaning. Giving him a reassuring smile, he said, "Do not fear. We are in no danger."

Hunter thought the priest's lack of concern for their safety rather ignorant. There they were, riding on a trail that was gradually narrowing as it rose ever steeper, where a single misstep would plunge them down the rocky slope to the bottom below, and he thought they were in no danger. Snorting to say he didn't believe it, Hunter kept as close to the inner side of the trail as he could.

Cool air coming down off the mountain soon began battling the residual warmth left over from the day for supremacy. Gradually, the cooler air won out and the temperature began to drop. Shivers would at times riffle their way through Hunter whenever the breeze struck him head on. Bending low over his horse helped to keep the worst of the cold at bay. He envied Father Thomas his robe right about then, and the fact that Larus didn't seem to be affected by the wind really bothered him.

The sunlight on the eastern peaks finally disappeared and the world began its descent into darkness with a vengeance. It wasn't long afterward that the trail became increasingly hard to see.

Hunter edged his horse even closer to the side of the mountain, close enough in fact that he could reach out and touch it if he had a mind to. He was about to voice his objection to their continued advance along the trail in such conditions when light suddenly sprang to life on his right.

"Ah," Father Thomas said. "There we go." Glancing over his shoulder toward Hunter, he saw the startled look upon his face. "I told you there would be light."

Glancing first to meet Father Thomas's gaze, Hunter then turned his attention toward the outer edge of the trail which was where the light originated. Lying amidst the rocks and rubble of the trail was a glowing, oval shaped rock about the size of a man's hand. Another glowed a few yards further up the trail while yet a third shone a little ways back down the trail.

"They are called Priest Stones," Father Thomas explained.

"Priest Stones?" asked Larus. In truth, he had never encountered such a thing before.

Father Thomas nodded. "They are called Priest Stones because they only shine when a priest is near," he explained. "They have been here for a very long time."

Hunter dismounted and picked up the oval shaped Priest Stone. The light coming from it was not overly bright, yet was sufficient to illuminate its immediate surroundings. It and the other two currently glowing lit the trail's edge well enough that a misstep was unlikely.

"Have him replace the Stone," Father Thomas said to Larus.

"Put it back Hunter," Larus said. "You're bothering Father Thomas."

"Oh sure," he replied then bent over and set it down in the exact spot from which he took it. Standing up, he turned toward Father Thomas. As a cold breeze sent another shiver through him he asked, "It only lights when a Priest is near?"

"That is correct," answered Father Thomas.

"No one else?" he asked.

Father Thomas shook his head. "No one else," he replied. "The story goes that a High Priest of Casdralla was caught on this trail during a bad storm centuries ago. Alone in the dark, he closed his eyes and prayed for deliverance."

Waiting for Larus to translate for Hunter, Father Thomas gazed further up the trail. Another area of light could be seen, and as he watched, he observed it moving further toward the summit. Obviously he was not the only priest on their way to the High Temple this night. When Larus completed the translation, he continued.

"When he opened his eyes, the High Priest saw a glow coming from a stone. Saying a prayer of thankfulness, he continued on his way. From that time on, no priest has ever been caught in the dark upon this trail."

Hunter had swung back up into the saddle while Father Thomas spoke. When he finished, Hunter asked, "How many stones are there?"

"Seven hundred and forty three," he stated.

"Interesting," murmured Hunter. "Has anyone ever taken one?"

"Why would they?" Father Thomas asked in return. "They only come to life for Priests of Casdralla, and none of us would do so." A bit put off that Hunter would suggest such a thing, Father Thomas abruptly turned his horse toward the summit and began moving. After traveling a sufficient distance from the Stone furthest down the trail, it winked out only to be replaced a moment later by the next one up the trail.

Hunter was intrigued by the Stones. He wondered if they could be motion sensitive or perhaps detected the heat of their bodies. What Father Thomas said about it only working for priests seemed a bit superstitious to him so he thought he would put it to the test. Unobtrusively slowing his horse, he began falling behind.

When he had fallen behind sufficiently that he was next to the last lit Stone, he slowed to a stop and waited. He didn't have long to wait until Father Thomas and Larus had moved further up the trail, far enough that the Stone should have winked out by now. He was about to smile in triumph when the Stone suddenly went dark.

"It really does work that way," he said to himself in surprise. Nudging his horse into motion, he hurried to catch up with the others half expecting the Stone to light with his movement, but was disappointed.

Night had settled in with a vengeance by the time they reached the plateau upon which sat the High Temple. Rising to either side of the plateau, silhouettes of tall peaks were outlined against the blanket of stars overhead. Father Thomas explained that the plateau left the gorge and continued through the mountains for well over a mile.

Once they left the gorge behind and began heading across the plateau, so too did they leave the Stones. The glow from the last Stone vanished once they were safely upon the plateau and heading toward the High Temple. Darkness enveloped them, but there was no fear of taking a misstep now. Losing their way wasn't a possibility either since a glow could be seen far across the plateau.

"There sits the High Temple," Father Thomas explained, looking toward the light in the distance.

"Why is it in such a desolate and hard to reach location?" asked Hunter.

"The original location of the High Temple was far to the north," Father Thomas explained. "Centuries ago, the then High Priest Olayni announced a revelation had been bestowed upon him. The High Temple must be rebuilt in a new location."

"Rebuilt?" asked Larus. "Just like that?"

Father Thomas nodded. "And it could not be just any location. But a specific locale revealed to him in a dream of urgent import."

"They searched these mountains for over five years before finding the plateau in his dream. After that it took two decades of hard labor before the

Temple's construction was completed. A testament to the faith of her people that it was done so quickly, and in such a remote area."

"I would guess so," replied Larus.

Father Thomas rode quietly for a moment as he gazed across the plateau toward the glow in the distance. "Sixty five years after the new Temple was constructed and consecrated by Her priests, Casdra was invaded."

"Ullen?" questioned Larus.

Father Thomas shook his head. "No," he replied. "The attack did not come from the south, but out of the mountains along our northern border." Again, he went silent as he gathered his thoughts. "Wild men boiled from the mountains and set about destroying many towns before being driven back and their people destroyed. When the fires subsided, the previous Temple was gone, a charred husk of its former glory."

Larus understood the significance of the destruction of that temple better than anyone else on this world. The first temple, or Temple Prime as the Qyaendri considered it, held special significance. It was a bastion of faith upon the world allowing the god's followers room to breath in order to establish themselves.

Unbeknownst to mortals, it wasn't their blood and sweat alone that went into such a construction, but that of Qyaendri as well. It was considered an honor without peer among the Qyaendri to be one of those selected to give part of their being for the Temple Prime.

Such would enable the Temple to shield the followers and ward off rival Qyaendri of another god who might seek to thwart the establishing of another god's presence within their zone of control. Planting believers on other worlds was risky, and without the Temple Prime, the risks increased tenfold.

Fortunately, the number of Casdralla's believers upon this world had grown to such an extent that the Temple Prime was no longer needed in that respect. For now that their numbers had reached a certain point, their faith alone would create a Sphere of Control that would keep rival Qyaendri from doing too much harm.

As they crossed the darkened plateau, they began to better make out the High Temple. It was an impressive structure, easily the largest building Hunter had come across since arriving on this world. It was soon apparent that along with the High Temple, a large complex of buildings had sprung up as well. The trail upon which they rode led straight toward a courtyard in front of the Temple.

A large arch framed the entrance to the courtyard, beyond which ran an open thoroughfare lined with stately columns. Midway from the arch to the temple stood a statue depicting the goddess. Thirty feet tall, it dwarfed everything else but the Temple which rose majestically behind it.

The High Temple itself was reminiscent of a great gothic cathedral with minarets and towers. The front of the Temple glowed with light shining through many windows, giving it an ethereal aspect.

"Impressive," breathed Hunter. He was clearly awed by what he saw.

"I would agree," said Father Thomas with a grin. He knew the effect of first seeing the temple at night and that had been part of the reason he urged them to push on after Veradin.

Movement was observed within the courtyard and among the buildings radiating outward from the Temple. Most were dressed in similar fashion as Father Thomas, priests of Casdralla going about their business. One such stood near the arch through which all must pass before entering the courtyard. He was a younger priest and the plainness of his robe suggested he was a relatively new one.

The young priest took note of their arrival and stood a little bit straighter as he stepped forward to greet them.

"Welcome travelers," he said with a smile that was a touched forced.

"Still have the duty Arren?" Father Thomas asked, amused.

Arren squinted to make out who it was that spoke to him. When they had approached enough to be fully illuminated by the lights burning in the courtyard, his eyes widened. "Father Thomas!" he exclaimed. "Praise be!" Coming forward, he looked up and said, "When news came that Billin had fallen to the Ullentites, we assumed you were lost."

"The Lady looked after me," replied Father Thomas.

Now with a smile as genuine as it could be, Arren said, "I'm glad you are alright."

"As am I," Father Thomas assured him with a grin. "While I would love to remain and speak with you, I am afraid we have urgent business with High Priestess Trystia."

At that, Arren's smile disappeared in a flash. "She is not here," he stated.

"Not here?" asked Father Thomas, surprised. Rarely does a High Priest or Priestess leave the High Temple.

Arren nodded grimly. "She has gone to Xith," he explained.

"Xith!" Larus practically shouted. "Doesn't she know what is going on out there?"

Again, Arren nodded. "Shortly after word reached the High Temple of the Ullentites advance upon our cities, she immediately left and took most of The Fathers with her." He wasn't talking about priests in general, but of a quasi-council whose dozen members were called The Fathers. They aided the High Priest or Priestess with all matters concerning the faith. And when the current High Priestess passed away, they would be the ones to choose her successor.

"That is grim news," Father Thomas said. "We heard Xith is already besieged."

"A messenger came through earlier today and said that an army of over ten thousand has Xith cut off," he explained.

"What about by river?" asked a worried Father Thomas.

"That is still open for them…," he began then grew quiet.

Larus picked up that the young man hadn't said everything he knew. "But?" he prompted.

Arren turned his gaze toward Larus and looked him over, then returned his gaze back to Father Thomas. "Cuellyn has fallen too," he said.

"So?" asked Larus.

"Cuellyn has two shipyards that make fishing and pleasure craft," he explained. "The messenger said that they believe the Ullentites have captured several ships and are building more in order to attack those bringing aid to Xith by water."

Larus was about to ask another question when Father Thomas held up his hand. "Thank you Arren," he said with a sidelong glance to Larus. "I am sure the Lady will look after her children."

"So do I Father," he replied.

"I shall pray your duty at the Arch will be short," he offered.

Arren gave him a grin as Father Thomas nudged his horse into motion.

Once they were past the Arch and into the thoroughfare, Father Thomas quickened their speed.

Larus could see the priest was troubled by the news young Arren had given them. "Why would she go to Xith?" he asked. "I can't see that being a good strategic move."

Father Thomas continued riding in silence until the path they were on turned to make its way around the statue of the goddess. "I would not think so either," he replied. Then he slowed his horse as he gazed up toward the face of the statue. "Unless she was told to be there."

"Perhaps," agreed Larus. If the situation was desperate, having the High Priestess within the walls of Xith would bolster the moral of Casdra's soldiers. Of course if Xith fell and High Priestess Trystia were taken captive or killed, Casdra would suffer a serious blow. He followed Father Thomas' gaze up to the visage of the goddess and realized that this statue was very similar to the one standing in the Rotunda of the High Temple located on a different plane of existence.

"What's going on?" Hunter asked.

Larus quickly filled him in.

"So we came all this way for nothing?" he asked. "How can she help us if she's back in Xith?" Then his face turned ashen as he asked, "We aren't going back there to find her are we?"

Shrugging, Larus replied, "I don't know. We'll have to see."

Following the path around the statue, they quickly crossed the remainder of the way to the entrance of the High Temple. Before reaching the entrance, two boys of eight and ten came forward and took charge of their mounts. As the lads took the horses over to the nearby stable, Father Thomas led Hunter and Larus into the Temple.

Just within the entrance was a large hall, two stories high and would have safely housed the inn in which they had recently broken their fast. Larus was little surprised to discover the interior was almost an exact duplicate of the Rotunda within the High Temple on the Casdralla's plane of residence. It too had the large statue of the goddess standing in preeminence with the ring of lesser ones encompassing it.

Within the hall they found several groups of robed individuals in deep discussion. One group of three stood closest to the entrance. When Father Thomas entered, the younger man of the group turned at his appearance and grew quiet. Talk ceased within his group as the other two looked to see what had drawn his attention.

"Thomas!" the young man exclaimed and moved to intercept him.

Father Thomas gave the younger man a grin and altered course to meet him halfway. "Gerhardt," he said. "It is good to see you."

Gerhardt came and gave Father Thomas a hug. "We thought you lost," he said once the embrace had ended.

"So young Arren told us," he replied.

The other two men, priests much older than Gerhardt came forward and added their thanksgivings.

Father Thomas introduced Larus and Hunter to the three priests. In turn, Thomas introduced them to Fathers Jerome and Kren.

Turning to his companions, Father Thomas said, "Gerhardt and I grew up together."

Larus translated for Hunter which drew curious looks from the three priests.

Father Thomas noticed the looks and said, "It is because of him that I have returned." When the three priests turned their gazes upon him, he added, "It was my hope to discuss the matter with High Priestess Trystia."

"She has gone to Xith," explained Gerhardt.

Nodding, Father Thomas replied, "So Arren informed us." He paused a moment then turned to the elder of Gerhardt's fellows. "Father Jerome, Arren also said that she had taken The Fathers with her."

"Most of them," he replied. "Father Kippen and Father Biern remained behind. Father Kippen because he is much too old to survive the journey, and Father Biern because he broke his leg the day before she was to depart." All the while he spoke, he kept glancing toward Hunter. Curiosity was getting the better of him.

"I would think Father Kippen would already be in bed for the night," stated Father Thomas and received a nod from Father Kren.

"Father Biern may still be in the refectory," offered Father Jerome. "He came late to dinner."

"Thank you," Father Thomas replied. "I must see him at once."

Neither Gerhardt nor his two companions asked why Father Thomas had to see Father Biern at once, though each greatly desired to know.

Before Father Thomas could get away, Gerhardt gave him another, brief hug. "I hope you will have some time later?" he asked.

"Possibly," Father Thomas told him. "Though first we must speak with Father Biern."

"I understand," he said then cast Hunter a look.

Father Thomas said a brief goodbye to the three priests. Even as they were returning his farewell, he headed off across the hall to a door on the left. Once they past from the hall and into the hallway, the aroma coming from the kitchens was detected.

They encountered another priest approaching in the opposite direction, an older priest with hair all but gray. Father Thomas offered him a friendly greeting but hurried on past to avoid the possibility of a protracted conversation.

Upon reaching the refectory, Father Thomas rushed in and paused as he glanced around at the few remaining priests still sitting at the tables. One offered him a wave which he returned. "He is not here," he said after a minute's examination. Before Larus had a chance to respond, Father Thomas flagged down one of the servers moving among the tables. The server quickly made his way over to them.

"You are just in time Father," the server stated. "We were about to close but I'm sure there is still enough left for you and your two companions."

"That is all right my son," he replied. "We were told Father Biern was here."

"He left but a moment ago," the server said as he turned to indicate a door across the room. "I believe he was returning to his rooms."

Father said a quick 'thank you' and made a beeline for the door. On the way he fielded two more greetings and was soon through the door. Once through they saw a figure hobbling along with a crutch.

"That is him," Father Thomas said to his companions. Hurrying along, he hollered, "Father Biern!"

The figure paused in the hallway and glanced over his shoulder at the three of them moving toward him. "Father Thomas?" he asked, surprised.

"Yes Father," Father Thomas replied.

"Well, this is certainly unexpected," he said with a grin. "I thought you had returned to your village some time ago?"

"I had Father," he replied. Lowering his voice, he added, "By the time I arrived, my village had already been attacked and burned to the ground by the Ullentites."

Sadness creased the Father Biern's face. "Oh, I am sorry," he replied. "Praise the Lady you are safe."

Father Thomas nodded. "Yes, but that is not what has brought me back to the High Temple."

The priest silently gazed questioningly at Father Thomas.

Lowering his voice still further, he said with a slight tremor, "A Qyaendri came to me."

Father Biern's eyes widened. "A Qyaendri? Are you sure?" he asked. When he received Father Thomas' affirmation, he said, "Such a thing has not happened for a century or more."

"Father," Father Thomas said, "I prayed for the goddess to aid those of my village who had been taken. And right after was when the Qyaendri appeared."

"And?" prompted Father Biern.

"And the Qyaendri gave me something." When Father Biern looked questioningly at him, Father Thomas turned and pointed to Hunter. "Him. The Qyaendri gave me him."

Chapter 13

"Incredible!" Father Biern exclaimed.

Sitting in the warmth issuing forth from his fireplace, Father Biern looked at the three companions with amazement. Having just heard the full account of everything which had transpired from the moment the Qyaendri appeared with Hunter to the present, he sat back with his leg resting on a padded stool, and was simply astonished.

Larus had added his input as well, but left out certain details which were better left unsaid. Such as how he had once been a Qyaendri. Though when Father Thomas explained to Father Biern how Larus had broken through the manacles and freed them from the captive line, he silently studied the former Qyaendri for a length of time leaving Larus feeling most uncomfortable.

Father Thomas raised his glass to his lips and took a small sip of wine. "All that was told to me by the Qyaendri was that Hunter had something to do and I was to help him."

"No further explanation than that?" questioned Father Biern.

"Nothing," replied Father Thomas. "From what Hunter has told us, he has no military experience, no skills with which to aid us in the fight against the Ullentites."

Just then a servant entered with a tray of pastries and another bottle of wine. The one Father Biern had on hand when they arrived in his rooms had been all but empty. Barely sufficient to offer even a small quantity to his guests.

As the servant placed the tray on the table, Father Biern said, "Thank you Edward. That will be all."

"Yes Father," the servant replied. Then with a bow, the young man turned and left the room.

"Please," Father Biern said to his guests as he gestured to the pastries, "help yourselves."

"Thank you," Hunter said after receiving the translation. Selecting one that was filled with a dark red jelly, he bit off a corner. Sweet and full of berry flavor, it melted in his mouth. "This is wonderful." Indeed, it was the first of what his grandmother used to call 'comfort food' he had tasted since coming to this world.

Father Thomas forwent having any of the pastries while Larus grabbed two. As Father Biern took up a pastry and began nibbling, Father Thomas asked, "What do we do now? There must be a reason why Hunter was brought to us."

"Not us," Father Biern replied. "Rather he was brought to you." While nibbling off another small section he gazed to Father Thomas for a moment in quiet contemplation. "The Qyaendri came to you and said for you to aid him."

"But what am I, or we, to do?" he asked. "I do not have a clue as to where to go from here."

"Pray," offered Father Biern. "There is no where else in the world where prayers are more likely to be answered than within the High Temple."

"I have been," asserted Father Thomas.

Turning his eyes to Larus, Father Biern asked, "Have you?"

Surprised by the question, Larus was about to answer then stopped. Finally, he replied, "I am not one of Casdralla's followers."

"You said you wished to be," Father Thomas said.

"That is true," he affirmed.

"If you still wish," continued Father Thomas, "we could perform the ceremony right now."

Father Biern looked from Larus, to Father Thomas, then back again. "I do not think that will be necessary," the priest said. "Ceremony or no, what is in your heart is what matters. If it is directed toward the Lady, She will hear."

Larus met the priest's gaze. *Or at least those Qyaendri in attendance would*, he added silently. *Would they take charge of a prayer by one such as me?* He wondered. Then he saw a strange look in Father Biern's eyes, a look that he couldn't quite figure out.

"It is entirely up to you of course," Father Biern said. "Should you desire to, perhaps the Silver Leaf Room would prove a suitable location. It is out of the way and seldom does anyone go there." He cast a questioning look toward Father Thomas. "It would prove an ideal place to find quiet, and solace."

"I know where it is," he assured him.

"Very good," the Father replied. Reaching to the wall behind him, he pulled on a long, decoratively embroidered rope. A moment later the servant who had earlier brought in the pastries appeared.

Hunter noticed the appearance of the servant and asked, "Are we leaving now?"

"It looks that way," replied Larus.

"Edward will show you to your rooms," said Father Biern. "I will study upon your situation. And with guidance from the Lady, perhaps together we can devise a course of action."

"I sincerely pray you are correct," Father Thomas said as he came to his feet.

"Excuse me for not seeing you to the door," Father Biern said, indicated his broken leg.

"We understand," Father Thomas assured him. "Thank you Father."

Larus nodded and again, he received what felt like a penetrating stare from the priest. Feeling slightly unnerved, he hurriedly followed Edward from the room.

"This way if you will," Edward said as he turned and headed down the hallway.

"Not much...," began Larus when Father Thomas silenced him with a shake of his head.

"Not here," he said in a barely audible whisper.

Larus kept silent and nodded that he understood.

The room to which Edward brought them was not very far from those of Father Biern. Down the hall a short distance then a hundred feet along a side passage and they were there. Edward opened the door and preceded them into the room.

"These are for you during your time with us," he said.

As it turned out, they had been given a suite of rooms. On the other side of the door was a large sitting room with two short hallways extending to the right and left, each with two connecting bedrooms.

Edward indicated an embroidered bell rope similar to the one Father Biern had used, though much plainer. "Should you require anything, simply ring and one of the servants will come."

"Thank you Edward," Father Thomas said.

Giving them a bow, Edward turned about and passed back through the doorway, closing it behind him.

Hunter looked around the room. There were three separate couches and two tables, each with a pair of plush chairs. Adorning the walls were several pictures, and even one statue depicting the goddess. "Nice," he said. "I could learn to like this."

Father Thomas grinned at him after Larus translated. "Guests are treated very well here," he explained.

"I can believe it." Then a yawn escaped him and fatigue suddenly reared its ugly head.

Gesturing to the branching hallways, Father Thomas said, "Go ahead and rest if you like. We will be here for some time."

"How long?" asked Hunter.

"I really do not know," he replied. "Throughout the night at the very least."

Another yawn and Hunter nodded. "That might not be such a bad idea," he said. Heading for one of the short hallways, he entered and saw two doors, one to the right and another at the end. Opening the one on the right, he found a bedroom with a large bed containing thick, downy covers.

"Oh man," he said as he hurried over and sat down, sinking several inches before coming to a stop. Quickly removing his boots and outer clothes, he was soon snuggled beneath the softest covers he had ever encountered. The unintelligible sound of conversation drifted in from the outer room as sleep quickly overcame him.

"What now?" asked Larus. Crossing the room, he took a seat on one of the couches.

Father Thomas came over and sat in a chair opposite him. "I think we should heed Father Biern's advice," he replied.

"What, go and pray in the 'Silver Leaf Room'?" Larus looked skeptical about such a course of action. "Why shouldn't a prayer be just as affective in here as opposed to there?"

"Ordinarily I would say that it would not matter where one prayed," he replied. He paused a moment then added, "But we did come here looking for guidance in what to do with Hunter."

Larus nodded as he thought of the matter. Finally, he said, "You told Father Biern that you knew where it was."

"That is correct," asserted Father Thomas and then grew quiet as he waited for Larus' decision.

Having been on the other side, Larus knew that where a prayer was said had no bearing on anything. If there was a Qyaendri present, it would be taken to the Chamber of Decision where its merit would be judged and decided upon. Though he couldn't see any, he knew that this place of all places on this world would have the greatest concentration of Qyaendri in attendance. And once a prayer was started, it would draw the nearest Qyaendri just as light does a moth. So, why would praying in one room be preferable over another?

"It wouldn't," mumbled Larus.

"What?" queried Father Thomas.

"Hm?" Larus asked. Then he realized that he had spoken aloud. "I was just thinking that this room is quiet and would be perfect for the saying of a prayer."

Father Thomas gave him a slight grin as he met Larus' gaze. "It may be prudent to remember that had Father Biern not broken his leg, then he would even now be accompanying the High Priestess on her way to Xith."

"Meaning?" Larus asked.

"Just that...," Father Thomas paused a moment as he gathered his thoughts. "Just that maybe the breaking of his leg was not entirely... accidental."

"The goddess broke his leg so he would remain behind and thus be available to guide us to the Silver Leaf Room?" concluded Larus.

Father Thomas shrugged. "It was a thought."

Larus grew quiet again as he considered that idea. "Is there anything special about the room?" he asked.

"Not that I am aware of," replied Father Thomas. "It's a small room on the second floor set all the way in the back." Growing silent for a moment, he drew on his memory for any and all details of the room. "The only time I had occasion to enter the room was during my time as a novice. One of the venerable Fathers requested for me to meet him there for some reason, though exactly why escapes me."

He glanced surreptitiously out of the corner of his eye to Larus before continuing. "I recall there being but a single small bench set against one wall, and when the door shut, it was absolutely silent. I remember feeling that it would be a great place to commune with our Lady." After Father Thomas grew quiet, he remained thoughtful until finally shaking his head. "That is all I recall," he said.

From the room where Hunter slept, the sound of his snoring drifted out to where they sat. "What about him?" asked Larus, meaning Hunter.

"Oh, I doubt if he will awaken before morning," Father Thomas assured him. "Even if he did, where would he go?" Then the significance of Larus' question came to him. "You mean to go then?" he asked.

Larus nodded. "It isn't like we have anything else to do right now," he replied.

Father Thomas gave him a grin. "Excellent," he said, coming to his feet. "We best be on our way before Hunter awakens."

Rising from the couch, Larus concurred. Following Father Thomas from the room, Larus shut the door after them and they proceeded down the hallway back the way they had come. They eventually came to the stairs leading up and were soon traversing another hallway on the second level that appeared to run the length of the Temple. Candles burning in individual holders at ten foot intervals provided ample light with which to see.

As they made their way through the Temple, they encountered several servants scurrying about on various errands, and one priest. The priest was so engrossed with his own inner thoughts that he didn't appear to take notice of them as they passed.

The Silver Leaf Room was situated at the very end of the long hallway. In fact, the door leading to it was the only egress from the hallway during its last twenty feet. When they came to the doorway, Larus immediately understood why it was called the Silver Leaf Room. The door was embossed with a wreath of leaves worked in delicate silver filigree.

"It is quiet down here," observed Larus. Reaching for the handle, he gripped it and opened the door.

Inside was dark. Father Thomas retraced his steps down the hallway to the last candle they had passed. Picking up the candle holder, he returned with it to where Larus still waited in the hallway. "I shall wait here until you are finished," he said as he handed him the candle holder.

Larus took the candle holder and nodded. Turning back to the room, he could see where the candle's light revealed the bench Father Thomas had mentioned earlier. As he entered the room, he discovered the walls and ceiling to be painted in meticulous detail showing various aspects of a priest's life. Closing the door, he crossed over to the bench.

It was small as benches go, barely wide enough for two men to sit side by side. The top was padded and looked to have been made of the finest velvet, but use over the years had worn the material. To one side of the bench was a small wall niche, large enough for the candle holder he carried to fit comfortably. From the soot scoring the top of the alcove, Larus knew the niche had held many candles over the years. Crossing over to the alcove, he set the candle holder inside.

"It really is quiet," he said to himself. Try as he might, the only sounds to be heard were those of his own making.

"Okay," he said. "I'm here."

Looking around the small room, he halfway expected someone or something to materialize or otherwise make itself known. He was surprised at the relief he felt when nothing did.

Perhaps he would have to pray first. It felt odd for him to be on this end. Throughout his existence, ever since first joining the ranks of Casdralla's Qyaendri, he had been one of those who either took charge of a faithful's prayer, or saw to its implementation.

"My Lady," he said in the most reverent tone he could muster. "I have great need of your aid. I know I have made grievous errors, but I beseech you now to allow me to atone for them. The Chosen One has come and I fully accept complete responsibility for his lack of preparedness."

Nothing.

"I wish to see him through in his mission, whatever that may be. Your people are in dire need. Great Casdralla, help us!"

He grew silent as he slowly rotated in the middle of the room. Eyes scanned for the hint of anything which might reveal the presence of a Qyaendri. He then turned internally for the sense of peace that comes over those whose prayers have been answered. Just like the Qyaendri, it too failed to materialize.

"Come on!" he said to the air around him. "I know you are there!" There had to be at least one Qyaendri in attendance within the room. There had to be! "Tell Daeson that I am sorry and that I am working to see the Chosen One fulfill that which he must do. But I need help! We don't understand his purpose."

Still, there was only silence and no sense of peace came to settle over him. His prayer was not being answered. The thought occurred to him that he may be currently incapable of having his prayers answered since he was not technically a follower of Casdralla's. Or it could be that such was the contempt her Qyaendri held for him that they would allow his prayers to wither and die before taking charge of them. All too well did he remember the looks cast his way by those Qyaendri in attendance when Daeson pronounced judgment upon him.

Downcast and forlorn, Larus went over to the bench and sat. He hoped things would be better. Raising his head, he looked heavenward and cried in anguish, "I'm sorry!" Then he dropped his head into his hands and sobbed.

All the pain, weariness, and loss overcame him as emotions long held in check rose uncontrollably. He didn't know how long he sat there, wracked with uncontrollable sobbing, before they finally began settling down.

Unwilling to leave the room and face Father Thomas with red rimmed and puffy eyes, he remained within the room for some time to allow them to return to normal. While he waited, he turned his gaze to the paintings adorning the walls.

Directly in front of him a priest was walking among numerous people, each with joy radiating from their faces. As his gaze moved around the walls, the scene changed to one of a priest aiding the injured, another of a priest traveling upon horseback, and still another of a priest facing death at the hands of an enemy.

His gaze lingered on the grisly scene for a moment. Standing straight with the look of acceptance and determination, the priest was shown exhibiting great courage. Around him were a dozen soldiers, one of which had his sword drawn and looked to be about to strike the priest's head off.

"Strength in belief," he said to himself. "That must be what it is trying to say." His gazed remained on the priest about to meet his fate for another minute or so before his head tilted upward to gaze on the scenes depicted across the ceiling.

The scene upon the ceiling depicted one army storming the stronghold of another. The attacking side appeared to be the stronger of the two, so had to have been forces of Casdra. For the artist would hardly have painted a scene showing Casdra's soldiers suffering a defeat.

Intrigued, he panned across the battle until he reached those defending the stronghold, or now that he was giving it more attention, it looked more like a very formidable temple. There were definite lines in the architecture that were common to that type of building.

The faces of the defenders seemed not quite right but in the poor light of the single candle, he couldn't make them out clearly. So removing the candle holder from the alcove he stepped up onto the bench and raised the candle for a closer look. With the burning candle now much closer to the mural, he could see that the men defending the temple bore the aspects of demons. Slit eyes, fangs and pointed ears with a slight loop, the artist had done a masterful job in demonizing Casdralla's foes. Such demonization of ones enemies was quite common. Larus had seen it before on other worlds, in other temples.

The temple wall had been breached and what had to be the leader of the attackers was wielding a mighty sword with which he had just cut a foe in two at the midsection. Moving his gaze to the face of the leader, he could barely make it out beneath the helm. There was something about that face...

Raising the candle higher, he strained to make out the leader's visage more clearly. When recognition came, Larus was so startled that he lost his balance and stumbled from the bench onto the floor. He barely avoided dropping the candle holder as he came to rest against the side of the room.

"It can't be!" he exclaimed to himself as he hopped back onto the bench. Once again moving the candle closer, he confirmed what he had originally discovered. The leader was Xi!

Larus was amazed at the likeness of Casdralla's supreme Qyaendri. How could the artist have known? The answer was quite simple, 'Divine Guidance'. During its creation, the painter had been 'inspired'.

If the leader was Xi, then what was being depicted was a Qyaendri assault on a rival's stronghold. Such an action was rare in the extreme, but if such was the case, then Xi would have been the one to lead it. With that thought still fresh in his mind, he turned his attention to the rest of Xi's Qyaendri. Maybe the artist had captured the likenesses of others, others Larus would know.

As his gaze went from one face to the next, he failed to recognize any of the Qyaendri in Xi's assault. It wasn't until he had searched everyone in the main assault and had reached the outer edge of the battle scene that he finally recognized another face.

The face belonged to a Qyaendri at the furthest edge of the battle scene. He stood apart from the others as if he was part of the attack force, yet at the same time wasn't. No armor or helm did he wear and in his hand the Qyaendri held the hilt of a broken sword. His eyes widened and lungs froze as he looked upon the sad and dejected figure standing at the edge of battle. For the pathetic figure was him.

Father Thomas stood in the darkened end of the hallway for what seemed like a long time before the door to the Silver Leaf Room opened. About to question Larus as to whether anything came of it, he stopped when he saw Larus' face.

Larus bore a most peculiar expression, one that Father Thomas couldn't figure out. "Is everything okay?" Father Thomas asked.

Nodding, Larus handed the candle holder back to him. "I...I don't know," he replied.

Taking the candle holder from him, Father Thomas laid his other hand on Larus' shoulder. "Did you pray as Father Biern suggested?" he asked.

"Yes," he replied. "I did."

"And?" prompted Father Thomas. Something was definitely bothering Larus.

"And nothing," he said, turning his eyes to Father Thomas. "I don't think my praying did any good."

What happened in there? Father Thomas asked himself. He could see that something had altered Larus' mood. And he didn't think it was because his prayer went unanswered.

Larus suddenly gripped his arm and said, "I need to see Father Biern again."

"He has most likely gone to bed by now," he replied. "Perhaps in the mor..."

"No," argued Larus, cutting him off a bit forcefully. "Now!"

Father Thomas could see the look in his eye, the need to do this. "As you wish," he said. Turning about, he silently proceeded down the hallway, wondering all the while about what had happened.

Chapter 14

The city was deserted as he walked down the middle of a boulevard bordered by gray shadows of buildings rising high on either side. Such was unusual as there was always the roar of an engine to be heard, or the shadowy heap of some homeless person lying upon the sidewalk. Even at this late hour one would expect some disturbance in the silence other than the tap-tap of his shoes upon pavement as he walked along. Instead, there was naught but eerie silence.

Darkness enveloped the streets. The light filtering down from the moon overhead seemed diffused, almost as if it had to fight its way through interference in order to reach the ground.

Tap-tap. Tap-tap.

He had to reach his destination and timing was crucial. Glancing overhead to the moon, he saw in growing panic that it had progressed even further across the sky. Time was running out! Quickening his step, he hurried through the streets.

Tap-tap-tap. Tap-tap-tap.

Streetlights were dark, windows in the buildings he passed gaped open like the maws of hungry beasts. Fear rose as he glanced again to the moon and saw that it had moved still further. Now it had apexed and was making its way to the horizon.

Hurrying along, he reached a point where the street ended at an intersection. To the right was nothing but darkness. To the left, a barely perceptible glow. Hope sprung to banish the fear at sight of the glow. Turning to the left, he broke into a run.

Out of the corner of his eye, he caught sight of movement in the shadows, and fear returned. A shadow among the deeper shadows was following his movement, pacing him as he raced along the street.

Before him, the glow didn't seem to be drawing any nearer and the moon was rapidly closing with the horizon. He knew he had to reach the glow before the moon hit the horizon or all would be lost.

A hissing noise began to be discernible coming from the darkness surrounding him. More of the shadows had joined with the first, how many he couldn't be sure. As he ran, the hissing grew in volume and the ranks of the unknown within the darkness swelled.

Fear drove his feet with greater and greater speed. Somehow he knew that the destination of the shadows was the glow in the distance. If he didn't reach it first, all was lost. Giving it everything he had, he soon left the tall buildings behind and entered the countryside.

The road began altering beneath him. No longer was it smooth and paved with asphalt. Rather, the road had changed to one of dirt and was uneven. He faced the very real threat of taking a misstep but he couldn't slow. He had to beat the shadows to the city.

A city! That's where he was headed. A great walled city. He had to reach it before the shadows in order to save those inside! Not for himself was he racing across the countryside, but for others. They needed his help!

He began to make out shapes within the glow ahead, or rather one large shape, that of a giant wall. It rose impossibly high and as he drew closer, threatened to blot out the starlit sky. A gate stood where the road and the wall met. It was open and a soothing glow issued from it. Standing before the gate was a single guard bearing a halberd.

"Halt!" the guard commanded. Lowering the halberd, the guard blocked his way into the city.

Coming to a halt, he glanced behind him to the roiling mass of darkness coming straight for them. "Let me in!" he yelled.

"Do you have it?" the guard asked.

"What?" he asked.

"Do you have it?" the guard asked again.

"I..." Glancing back, he saw the darkness was almost upon them. Turning back to the guard, he shouted, "There is no time!"

"Then all is lost."

Hunter tried to force his way past the guard only to be pushed unmercifully back. Stumbling, Hunter's foot tripped on a rut in the road, and he fell. The world seemed to slow as he hit the ground. The moon reached the horizon. Darkness enveloped him as the shadowy darkness consumed the guard and flowed into the city.

"Nooooooooooo!"

A scream tore from Hunter's throat as he sat bolt upright in bed. Trembling with fear and covered in a cold sweat, he looked for the shadows. But there was only ordinary darkness. Then he felt the covers and realized he was still in bed.

"It was just a dream," he told himself shakily. Taking a few deep breaths in an attempt to calm his rattled nerves, he laid his head back down on the pillow. He had to turn the pillow over as the side he had been laying on was moistened with his sweat and uncomfortable.

"Man what a dream," he said after the pillow had been turned. It was still vivid in his mind; the city, the sense of urgency, and most of all the shadowy darkness. Or rather the fear that had resulted because of the shadowy darkness.

A small sliver of light could be seen coming through the cracks around the door. "I'm not going to be able to fall back to sleep any time soon," he told himself. Indeed, he was about as far from being sleepy as one could get. Hoping the others were still awake, he sat up on his bed and pulled on his outer clothes.

The stone floor was cold to his bare feet but he didn't care. Crossing to the door, he opened it and went out to the front room. There he found a candle all but burnt to a nub. Larus and Father Thomas were not there. The doors to the other rooms were cracked open and he went to check them. He knew Larus never seemed to sleep very much and hoped he would still be awake. But after checking the other rooms, he discovered that he was alone.

Fear from the dream rose up again and he realized that he didn't want to remain by himself. Moving to the door leading from the suite of rooms, he opened it and glanced down the hallway passing just outside. Not seeing anyone, he hollered, "Larus! Father Thomas!" When no answer was forthcoming, he stepped from the room and closed the door.

From earlier discussion with Father Thomas, Hunter knew this was the main temple for the priest's faith. More than likely, he and Larus were visiting with one of the priests. He was a bit put out that they had left him alone with no word as to where they were going.

Hunter realized this place was big and that there was a language barrier that prevented him from affectively conversing with anyone he met. Despite such obstacles, he simply couldn't remain within the suite by himself, he was still much too rattled by the dream.

Unable to remember which way they had come, he headed down the hallway to the left and hoped to find them soon.

The Father was reading the ancient text written upon the pages of one of five very old tomes that were laid out upon the table before him. He had Edward and other servants scrambling to gather them once Edward had returned from seeing Father Thomas and the other two to their rooms.

There was something, a long forgotten memory that their appearance had brought to mind, unfortunately not in its entirety. That was why these specific tomes had been gathered. If he had been right about Father Thomas' companion…

Flipping the pages hurriedly, he sought the fragment of an old prophecy, perhaps the oldest one ever prophesized by a High Priest of Casdralla. At least he thought it had been given by one of them. The books laid out before him detailed every prophecy ever uttered and the related meanings those at the time thought were pertinent.

One of the prophecies held but one line, '*Two will give three when the red house blossoms*'. Such was the dross he had to sift through before he found the one he partially recalled.

He was halfway through the third tome when he came across a dissertation by High Priestess Lymma on Qyaendri and their relations with

Casdralla's faithful. Reading a few lines sparked recognition and he knew he was close. This was the book. He remembered because during his early years as a novice priest, a former mentor had requested that he read High Priestess Lymma's dissertation. True, it held much of value, but it was written in such dry, uninteresting prose that it was hard to read all at once. Many times he had put off reading the dissertation by flipping through the rest of the pages to see what else the book held.

A smile came to him at the many memories of his early years in the priesthood this book brought back. Then the smile faded and he returned to the matter at hand. This was no time for woolgathering! Somewhere among these pages was the prophecy he sought.

Page after page he turned until coming across a full-paged illustration. "Yes!" he said triumphantly. On the page opposite the illustration was the prophecy:

> *When the mighty is shunned, when the mighty is scorned,*
> *And doomed to walk the land,*
> *Thy days will be numbered, thy nation soon sundered,*
> *For Days of Darkness are at hand.*

A shiver went through him as he read the prophecy again after all these years and he prayed that he was not right. "Days of Darkness," he mumbled to himself as he reread the prophecy yet again.

Thy days will be numbered, thy nation soon sundered. "Please Lady," he prayed, "let me be wrong!" A creaking sound broke his concentration and he looked up to find the door cracked open and Father Thomas' companion, the one called Larus, stood peering in.

"Yes?" he asked as he closed the tome, first marking the page of the prophecy with a piece of parchment. The man passed through the door silently. Father Biern could see Father Thomas standing out in the hallway bearing an anxious look. He laid a hand on the closed tome as he watched Larus shut the door and cross over to the chair sitting on the other side of his desk.

Father Biern remained quiet as he studied the young man.

Finally, Larus asked, "Why did you have me go to the Silver Leaf Room to pray?"

Shrugging, Father Biern replied, "It has always been a place that I myself have found to be perfect for quiet contemplation."

Larus' face grew into a frown. Obviously that was not the response he was looking for and Father Biern wasn't about to elucidate further. After another elongated silence, Father Biern asked, "Did you find it conducive to prayer?"

"Oh yes," replied Larus.

"I am glad," said Father Biern. He could see that the man had something he direly wished to ask but was having a hard time coming up with the appropriate words. And if Father Biern's hunch about this young man was correct, he could well understand his dilemma.

The two men's eyes locked for several seconds, each trying to bore into the mind of the other with unsatisfactory results. Finally, Larus came to a decision and said, "I saw the mural."

"Oh?" questioned Father Biern.

Larus nodded. "Is that why you suggested I go there?" he asked.

"I am afraid you will have to be more specific than that," replied Father Biern.

A look of annoyance flashed across Larus' face. Coming to his feet, he put both hands on the desk and said with much more forcefulness than he intended, "The lone man standing at the edge of the battle painted across the ceiling! The one with the broken sword."

Father Biern stared into the eyes of the young man and thought to deny it. But then he sighed and nodded. "Yes," he said. "But the lone figure with the broken sword isn't a man. He is a Qyaendri, one of the *mighty* servants of our Good Lady." *And he bears a striking resemblance to you.*

Larus could see the Father watching his reaction as he spoke. He knew that the Father knew, or at least suspected. There was an unspoken question burning behind the Father's eyes and Larus was loath to answer it.

The first rule of being a Qyaendri was never to reveal yourself as such to any mortal. But if Father Thomas' theory that Father Biern's leg had been broken so he could remain there to aid them was true, then that would seem to suggest he was worthy of Larus' trust. That Father Biern had recognized the resemblance between him and the figure in the mural was obvious. And after everything that they had told him about their escape, especially the way he had dealt with the manacles, it was plain what conclusion Father Biern had reached.

"Do you think that I am a Qyaendri?" Larus came out and asked.

"Are you?" asked Father Biern.

Larus hesitated before saying, "Not any more."

"Amazing," Father Biern said. Then he glanced toward the door. "Does Father Thomas know?"

"Not that I am aware of," Larus replied. "Though he may suspect something is out of the ordinary about me."

Father Biern nodded. "He has always been exceptionally intelligent."

"So I have gathered," Larus agreed. Sitting back in his chair, he said, "I would rather only the two of us know of my origins."

"I quite agree," replied Father Biern. "Though having actual proof of the validity of our belief in our midst would be a great boon to our efforts."

Larus grew grim. "That is not why I am here," he stated.

Father Biern sighed. "I know."

Surprised, Larus asked, "You do?"

"Not exactly, no." He grew quiet for a moment as each gazed across the desk at the other. "But I am quite sure one such as yourself would not have been sent here to be put on display for our benefit."

Larus grinned and shook his head, then grew solemn once again as he recalled the events that immediately preceded his appearance on this world. "In truth I thought my time upon this world was a penance of some kind."

"Oh?" queried Father Biern.

"Humans are not alone in their imperfections," he said. "I made a mistake which culminated in being made mortal and deposited on this world."

Father Biern looked skeptical about such a possibility. He doubted if that was truly the entirety of the reasoning behind Larus being sent there. Unconsciously working a fingertip along the raised design upon the tome before him, he cast a quick glance toward it before returning his attention to Larus. "I wonder," he said.

"It was, and is, my hope that by aiding Father Thomas and Hunter in what they must do, I can make atonement," explained Larus.

"So you truly do not know why a Qyaendri appeared before Father Thomas and gave Hunter into his charge?" Father Biern asked.

Larus paused a moment to consider the question before answering. Shaking his head, he replied, "Not for sure, no."

Pursing his lips, Father Biern adjusted his broken leg where it sat atop a stool as he leaned forward ever so slightly. "Too bad," he said. "For I believe my people are at crux that could well mean their annihilation."

"What leads you to believe such a thing?" he asked.

Father Biern rotated the tome laying before him toward Larus. Opening it up to the section marked by the piece of parchment, he pointed to the prophecy.

Larus leaned forward and read the words:

> *When the mighty is shunned, when the mighty is scorned,*
> *And doomed to walk the land,*
> *Thy days will be numbered, thy nation soon sundered,*
> *For Days of Darkness are at hand.*

"At the time this was written, Qyaendri were often referred to as the 'Mighty'," explained Father Biern. Having watched Larus as he read the passage, Father Biern noticed only a small alteration of his expression. "You made a mistake that doomed you into mortality. You are now walking this land." When Larus looked up from the book and met his gaze, he added, "And Casdra now stands on the brink of a war it may not be able to win." A pause, then, "Days of Darkness are at hand."

"But," argued Larus, "this prophecy could have applied to numerous people and circumstances throughout the ages. What makes you believe this prophecy is specifically referring to me?"

"This," replied Father Biern. Removing the piece of parchment from where it covered the opposite page, he revealed an illustration.

Larus sat back in his chair in shock when he saw that the illustration was of the lone man standing at the edge of the battle painted across the ceiling of the Silver Leaf Room. The one with the broken sword. There was no mistaking that the face he looked upon was his own.

His mind reeled with the implications. This had to have been done centuries ago, yet how could they have possibly known he would have been there, at this specific time. He knew that certain, rare Qyaendri had the gift of foresight, as did the gods, but this was almost beyond belief.

"My people stand on the brink of annihilation," Father Biern stated. "Most prophecies are far vaguer than this one."

"What do you mean?" asked Larus. He was still trying to get a handle on this new revelation and his mind was finding it hard to function.

"'*Thy days will be numbered, thy nation soon sundered,*'" said Father Biern. "To me that seems to infer the Ullentites will not be overlong in their siege of Xith. And once it falls…"

Larus' eyes were filled with pain. This was the doom to which Xi had inferred when he first set Larus' feet upon the road to find the Chosen One.

"*Our Lady's people are faced with great difficulties in the times ahead,*" Xi had said. "*Her presence on their world may come to an end.*"

"*What does our Lady want of me?*" Larus asked.

"*Why,*" replied Xi, "*she wants you to save her people.*"

"Save her people," mumbled Larus in despair. "But I don't know what to do!" Eyes full of agony turned toward Father Biern. Larus felt woefully inadequate. He was not the one for this job!

"Then you must discover what must be done, and quickly," Father Biern said.

"How?" asked Larus.

Just then, the door burst open and Father Thomas rushed in. "Hunter is gone!" he exclaimed.

"What?" asked Larus as he quickly came to his feet.

Father Biern quickly closed the tome, concealing Larus' picture from his fellow priest.

"You were overlong in your talk with Father Biern," he explained, "so I went to check on him only to find his bed empty."

Larus turned toward Father Biern, "We have to find him."

Already having pulled the embroidered bell rope, he nodded. "I quite agree." A moment later another figure entered the room through the open door behind Father Thomas. "Edward," he said as the young man moved around Father Thomas and came closer, "their companion has left their rooms and may be lost within the Temple."

Edward gave a slight bow and nodded. "We shall find him," he assured them and then turned about to head for the door.

Larus stopped him and said, "He is a stranger and cannot speak the language."

"I understand," replied Edward then hurried from the room.

"They will find your friend," said Father Biern. "I would suggest returning to your rooms to wait."

Larus shook his head. "I can't just sit still while he's lost," he asserted. Turning to Father Thomas he asked, "You know this place well enough?" When he received a nod in reply, he grabbed Father Thomas' arm and began dragging him toward the door. "Then let's go find him."

Before they left, Father Biern said, "I shall continue searching for the answer we both seek."

Pausing by the door, Larus turned back and gave him a brief nod. Then he and Father Thomas were out in the hallway.

Headed back to their rooms at a fast walk, Father Thomas asked, "What answer?"

Larus ignored the question as they reached their rooms and begun the search for Hunter. He didn't fear for Hunter's safety, not here in the High Temple. Still, it would be best if they were to find him as quickly as possible.

Two hours later, Hunter still had not turned up. Edward and every other servant serving in the High Temple had combed the halls and rooms on every level to no avail. Word began to circulate among the priests and they began to aid the endeavor.

After the third hour of searching came and went, it was soon clear that Hunter was not within the temple. "How could he have managed to leave?" demanded an irate Larus. Everything hinged on Hunter. He had to be found!

"It is an open building," stated Father Thomas. "Not one designed to keep people in."

They stood out in the courtyard before the entrance, a cool breeze was blowing through the columns. Coming from all around them, they heard the voices of priests, servants, and anyone else they could wrangle in joining the search as they went from building to building, calling Hunter's name.

"You know him best," said Father Thomas. "Where do you think he would go?"

Glancing around at the darkened buildings radiating outward from the High Temple, he shook his head. "I couldn't even hazard a guess," he said. "To be honest, I'm surprised he would even leave the Temple."

"Father Thomas!"

They both turned to find Arren, the young priest they had met upon first arriving, running toward them. "Father Thomas!" he again hollered as he quickly approached.

Coming to a stop, he announced, "Your friend has been found!"

"Where?" Larus demanded.

Pointing toward the northeast, he said, "In the Caves!"

Larus turned toward Father Thomas and could see surprise registered there. "Caves?" he asked.

Ignoring Larus' question, Father Thomas asked Arren, "Are they sure?"

Arren nodded vigorously. "Yes Father," he replied. "Father Greal saw tracks leading toward the entrance." Lowering his voice, he added, "He was found in the Artifact Grotto."

Father Thomas gasped. "Is he still there?" Hunter's presence within the Caves couldn't have made Father Greal very happy. He was the one in charge of the Caves and Hunter's presence was a grievous violation of Temple Law.

"As far as I know," Arren told him. "They sent me in search of you as soon as they were sure he was in there."

"Thank you Arren," he said. Without so much as a glance toward Larus, Father Thomas started across the courtyard in the direction the young priest had indicated. Larus hurried to catch him.

"What is this place?" he asked once he had caught up with him.

"It is a place where we maintain the history of our people and our faith," he explained. "Within the Caves are many grottoes, the one our friend has managed to enter is called the Grotto of Artifacts."

"Grotto of Artifacts?" questioned Larus.

Now that they were out of the Temple's courtyard, the darkness grew deeper as only the occasional lights coming from within the nearby buildings were present. They made their way through numerous smaller buildings, most were housing for priests and their families while others held more of a utility capacity.

"The Grotto of Artifacts holds many items that we have accumulated over the years from faiths other than our own," he explained. "Some hold to the belief that these items may have supernatural powers, though I have yet to witness any evidence to support such a view."

"How did he get there?" wondered Larus.

"I do not know," Father Thomas replied worriedly.

Once past the last building, they saw a light some distance away. As they drew closer, they could see two torches lighting an opening at the base of a sizeable cliff. "That's the Caves?" asked Larus.

Father Thomas nodded. "It was shortly after they began constructing the Temple that the Caves were found," he explained. "Within are nine Grottoes, each containing various items."

Movement was detected just within the entrance. Five priests with their attention directed inward were standing together in a group. As Larus and Father Thomas drew closer, they could hear whispered conversation passing between the five priests.

Before they reached the entrance, one of the five turned and noticed their approach. "Father Thomas," greeted a priest with a less than happy expression. "I am told he is your charge?"

Father Thomas nodded. "Yes Father Greal," Father Thomas replied. "He somehow wandered away from the Temple."

Father Greal didn't look pleased. "You know that only the priests of Casdralla are permitted within the Caves," he stated. In fact, for a non-priest to enter the Caves was a grave infraction.

"I am well aware of this," he replied. The faces of the five priests looked upon Father Thomas with disapproval as he moved to pass by and enter.

Larus moved to follow him deeper into the Caves when another of the five priests stepped before him and blocked his path. "You cannot enter," he stated.

Coming to a stop, Father Thomas glanced back as two other priests moved before Larus to prevent him from continuing further. "He must accompany me," Father Thomas explained. "He is the only one who can speak the language of the man."

"You have my word that I shall harm nothing," Larus assured him.

Father Greal's displeasure at the situation deepened. "He cannot enter," he reiterated.

"He must!" argued Father Thomas. Though Father Greal outranked him in the Temple hierarchy, he stood his ground. "I shall take full responsibility for his actions while he is within the Caves."

One of the other priests turned to Father Greal and said, "If this will quicken the removal of the trespasser, then it needs to be allowed."

"What if we have to remove him by force?" another priest asked. "What may happen to the contents of the Grotto should that come to pass? We need to allow this."

Father Greal remained steadfast, barring Larus' path for a full minute as he considered the arguments of his fellow priests. Finally, he stepped aside. "Be quick and touch nothing!" he warned.

"Thank you," Father Thomas said as Larus moved to join him.

"Father Thomas," Father Greal said, turning his gaze toward him.

"Yes?" he asked.

"If anything is so much as out of place..." he warned, leaving the threat unvoiced.

"I understand," Father Thomas replied. Then to Larus he said, "Come on." Turning his back on Father Greal and the other four priests, he led Larus deeper into the Caves.

"Are you going to be in trouble over this?" Larus asked once they were far enough from the entrance not to be overheard.

"Probably," answered Father Thomas. "Though with everything else that is going on, it is unlikely anything will come of it."

"I hope you are right," replied Larus. Then in the dim light of sparsely spaced torches, they continued deeper into the Caves.

Chapter 15

The Caves extended deep into the mountainside. The main passage through which they walked was wide enough for five men to walk abreast without rubbing shoulders, and high enough for even the tallest to have little fear of scraping.

When they reached the first of the torches burning along the main passage, Larus saw a dark opening to their right.

"That passage will take you to the Grotto of Light," he said. "There you will find many items sacred to Casdralla." Father Thomas glanced to him and added, "It is the largest Grotto within the Caves."

Larus peered into the dark opening as they passed but was unable to see anything other than a passage much smaller and narrower than theirs moving deeper into the mountainside. "Why do they keep all this in such a place?" he asked. Once past the entrance to the Grotto of Light, the light grew fainter as they moved away from the torch burning behind them. They then entered a darker area through which they had to pass before reaching the next burning brand further down the passage.

Father Thomas replied with a shrug. Indicating the burning brand coming up ahead he said, "The passage leading to the Grotto of Artifacts lies there."

"It's amazing that Hunter made it this far," Larus commented.

"I doubt if it was by chance," stated Father Thomas. A glance to Larus revealed that he had been thinking the same thing. "There is always a priest watching the entrance to the Caves and he would have assuredly prevented Hunter from entering."

As they neared where the burning torch sat in a wall sconce, Larus saw the opening of the passage leading to the Grotto of Artifacts. When they reached it, Father Thomas removed the torch from the wall sconce and took it with him as he entered the smaller passage.

Following close behind, Larus could see how the passage they were now in had been widened in places from its natural shape to allow sufficient room for men to pass. It curved back and forth almost continuously, at times entering areas where it widened and rock untouched by the tools of men could still be seen.

"Must have been an old waterway," guessed Larus.

"So they say," agreed Father Thomas.

Spaced along the passage walls were a total of four wall sconces where further torches could be placed to light the way. Currently, each was empty except for the fourth which held an unlit torch.

Before he came to the unlit torch, Father Thomas turned his head toward Larus and said "We are almost there."

Larus nodded. Then in a voice that seemed much louder due to the closeness of the passage walls, he shouted, "Hunter!" Continuing pass the unlit torch, they each strained to hear a reply.

When none came, Father Thomas shouted, "Hunter."

Not far past the unlit torch, the light from the torch Father Thomas held revealed where the passage entered a much larger area. Larus glanced to Father Thomas who nodded. "That is the Grotto."

It wasn't what he had expected. Instead of being an underground cave, it was instead a room one might find in any stone building. The walls of the Grotto were not natural stone, rather they were made of stone blocks set one upon the other. Even the ceiling was of manmade construction. The only thing that looked like it may still be the original cave was the floor.

Several items were displayed upon the walls while still more sat upon tables spaced around the room. The artifacts in this room were rather plain. A cloak of blue with ribbons of dark purple attached along the neckline, three knives identical to each other lay by themselves in a uniform row upon a table, and four vases along with two statues sat upon another.

Father Thomas paused at the entrance as he gazed into the Grotto. When he failed to find Hunter, he stepped into the room and made his way further toward the back.

Moving past the artifacts, he went to the rear of the room where a small archway was located. Passing through the archway, he entered a short, narrow passage that quickly ended at another room.

This room was smaller than the first. The walls on the left and right of the room each held a single niche. One held a small statue of a gnarled, evil looking creature while the other held what looked to be a knife.

The space between two large tables formed an aisle which led from where they stood to the archway leading from the opposite side of the room. On the table to their left were arrayed five oval stones the size of a man's hand that looked plain and rather unimposing. The table on their right held a long, thick staff with part of a human skull at its apex. At first Larus had thought the staff was made of wood, but as they crossed through toward the other archway, he saw that it was made instead of human femurs wrapped in dried skin. The sight of it made his skin crawl.

"Where did you get that?" he asked.

"I do not know," replied Father Thomas. "Most of what this Grotto contains has been with the Temple for a very long time. I would think it came from another god's follower, one that was at odds with the Lady."

"Any priest who would construct a staff like that would have to be no friend of the Lady," agreed Larus. As they passed the staff and neared the archway, he asked, "How many rooms does this particular Grotto hold?"

"Six I believe," replied Father Thomas. "Previously, I have only had occasion to enter the first four."

"What is held in the last two?" he asked.

"More of the same I would suppose," came the reply.

This time the archway opened onto an adjacent room rather than another passage. Father Thomas again went first with torch held aloft. His eyes scanned the small room for any sign of Hunter. Two other arches led deeper into the Grotto, one in the right wall and the other in the left.

Entering behind him, Larus saw six pedestals standing in a hexagonal formation in the center of the room. It was clear what had once sat upon the pedestals, for what once had been highly detailed, decorated crockery lay in shattered remains around their bases.

Stepping through the debris, Father Thomas commented, "Father Greal is not going to be happy about this." Aside from the shattered crockery, there was nothing else of note within the room. He paused a moment to determine which of the two archways they should pass through first.

Larus went to stand in the center of the hexagonal pattern of pedestals and grew motionless.

"What..." began Father Thomas when Larus motioned for him to remain silent.

After several seconds had passed, he pointed toward the left hand arch. "He's that way," he stated.

"Are you sure?" asked Father Thomas.

Nodding, Larus replied, "Absolutely." Not waiting for the priest to lead the way, he hurried toward the archway and passed through into another small, connecting passageway. At the other end, it opened up onto a room, twice as large as the one they had just left.

This one held a curious apparatus. A square box with several rods emerging from it at all angles. The box was constructed of wood while each of the rods were made of a different metal. As curious as it was, Larus paid it little heed. Instead, his attention was focused on the man sitting in the corner of the room. His hands were held together in his lap and his head lolled forward so his chin rested on his chest.

"Hunter?" he said softly, afraid the man may be dead. When he didn't immediately react to Larus' call, Larus crossed over to within a couple feet. Behind him, Father Thomas held the torch high as he followed.

Coming to a stop, Larus asked, "Are you okay Hunter?"

Slowly, Hunter's head came up but he didn't look at the two men standing before him. His eyes didn't look as if they were looking at anything at all, remaining unfocused and staring off into nothingness.

"What is wrong with him?" questioned Father Thomas after quietly saying a brief prayer.

Larus shook his head. Moving forward, he knelt next to him so his face would come into Hunter's line of sight. Reaching out, he laid a hand on Hunter's shoulder. "Hunter," he said, giving him a gentle shake.

Quite suddenly, Hunter's head twisted to the left and right as panic came to his eyes. Then he seemed to notice for the first time Larus standing before him and just as quickly grew calm. "Hey Larus," he said.

"Are you okay my son?" asked Father Thomas.

After Larus repeated the question in Hunter's language, Hunter gave them a small smile of assurance then said, "I feel fine." His grin quickly faded when his eyes began flicking around the room. Returning them to Larus, he asked, "How did I get here?"

"You don't remember?" Larus asked.

Looking confused, Hunter shook his head. "No," he replied.

"What was the last thing you remember?" asked Father Thomas.

Hunter grew quiet as he considered the question. "I had just awoken from a bad dream," he said. "I didn't feel like I could go back to sleep so I left my room to see if you two were still awake. When I found you gone..." He grew quiet as he struggled to remember.

"Yes?" asked Larus. "Go on."

"I...I left the room in search of you," he continued. "Thought maybe to find Edward or one of the other servants who could then aid me in finding you."

"Did you find someone?" Larus asked.

"I..." his eyes got a far away look as he sought the elusive memory. "I...don't remember anything after leaving our rooms." He glanced from Larus to Father Thomas then back. Nervousness and a little bit of fear was evident in his voice when he said, "I don't know!"

Larus searched Hunter's eyes and determined he really didn't know. Nodding, he laid a hand on his shoulder and said, "Let's get you back to the Temple."

Hunter's eyes widened. "I'm not even in the Temple?" he cried.

"No," replied Larus with a shake of his head. "In fact, somehow you made it quite a distance across the dark plateau to reach this place." Coming to his feet, he offered Hunter a hand up.

Reaching out with his right hand, Hunter grasped Larus' and with his help, came to his feet. "Thanks," he said and started to say something else when he saw a flash of something red that was clutched in his left hand. Moving his hand closer so he could see better, he opened his fingers.

"Ahhhh!" he cried when the crystalline arachnid sitting upon his palm was exposed. With a startled jerk, he hurled the arachnid away from him.

Larus saw the crystalline arachnid leave his hand and sail through the air. Without thought, he leapt and caught it before it could hit the ground. Coming to a stop, he gestured for Father Thomas to bring the torch closer so he could better see it.

"What is that thing?" Hunter asked as a shiver went through him. Backing several steps away from Larus, he eyed the crystalline arachnid with apprehension.

It had eight crystal legs and was slightly reminiscent of a tarantula. The head was of a darker crystal as was the main body though it appeared the entire piece had been carved from but a single crystal.

"Amazing," Father Thomas breathed.

Larus glanced to the Father. "Any idea what it is?" he asked.

"Looks like some sort of spider," replied Father Thomas.

"No," said Larus, "I mean, why is it here in the Grotto of Artifacts?"

Gazing at the spider resting on Larus' palm, Father Thomas shook his head. "I have never heard of anything like this before," he stated. "I'm sure Father Greal would know, though seeking his counsel may not be the wisest course."

Larus nodded. "I would agree." He recalled how vehemently Father Greal had voiced his objection to his entrance into the Grotto. He could very well imagine his reaction to their possession of the crystalline spider.

"How did it come to be in my hand?" question Hunter.

The two of them turned toward him and saw the beginnings of fear appear on his face. "We don't know," Larus told him. He paused as he gathered his thoughts then said, "But I would think it has something to do with your being here."

"What?" asked Hunter. "How?"

"That is something we have yet to figure out," explained Larus. "The mere fact that you are here in the Grotto with no memory of how you arrived seems to indicate it was by no mere coincidence." Holding forth the crystalline spider, he added, "You were brought here for this."

"You mean, by a god?" he asked.

Larus grinned and shook his head. "Nothing so grandiose I'm sure. But rather by one of Her Qyaendri I would guess."

"He could have been under a compulsion to come here," suggested Father Thomas. "Ask him if there was anything unusual about that last person he met after leaving our rooms."

Nodding, Larus turned to Hunter and asked.

"No," replied Hunter with a shake of his head.

Raising the crystalline arachnid to draw their attention to it, Larus said, "This is important some how." The crystal body of the arachnid caught the light of the torch and refracted it in a dazzling display.

"Desecration!"

Turning toward the room of the hexagonal formation of pedestals, they saw Father Greal standing amidst the broken shards of pottery with the other priests who had been with him at the entrance. He stood amidst the shards of shattered pottery. Even from where Larus stood in the adjoining room, he could see Father Greal's hands trembling as he assessed the destruction. Then the priest turned a gaze bordering on rage through the arch at Father Thomas.

"Oh my," said Father Thomas.

Larus immediately moved the hand holding the crystalline arachnid behind his back to shield it from the enraged priest's view. Ever so carefully, he slipped it beneath his jacket and wedged it into the waistband of his trousers.

"Father Thomas!" Father Greal shouted as his feet carried him through the shards toward the arch. "What is the meaning of this?"

"I believe our comrade had broken those when he first arrived," he replied.

"This is a serious matter," Father Greal said as he passed through the arch. "Those vases were over five hundred years old."

"I am truly sorry," Father Thomas replied humbly. "But he was not himself at the time."

Father Greal seemed to pay little heed to his words. Turning his angry gaze upon Hunter, he said, "To enter the Grotto is a very serious matter young man. But to destroy that which was contained within! There can be but one punishment." Then he turned to Father Thomas. "He must be thrown from the plateau."

Out of the corner of his eye, Father Thomas saw Larus' face darken at the priest's words, and that his hand had moved ever so slightly toward the sword hanging at his hip. "I am sure such drastic action will not be warranted in this situation," he told the priest before him.

"That is the law of the Temple," asserted Father Greal, "set forth when the Caves was first constructed." He glared at Father Thomas and dared him to argue the point further.

Father Thomas' mind raced as he sought a solution to their predicament.

To the priests with him, Father Greal indicated Hunter and said, "Take him to the cliff."

"Wait!" shouted Father Thomas. Whether his cry was directed to the priests on their way to claim Hunter, or to Larus who had begun to draw his sword, he couldn't be certain. But the impending conflict was averted when the priests came to a stop and Larus' sword remained in its scabbard. "Hunter was brought here by a Qyaendri!"

A narrowing of the eyes was all the response his statement produced in Father Greal. "That is an easy thing to say," the priest replied, "but very hard to prove."

"I swear by the Lady that it is true," asserted Father Thomas.

One of the priests who accompanied Father Greal asked, "Did you see the Qyaendri?"

Taken aback by the fact that he was not immediately believed, Father Thomas grudgingly said, "No. But that does not mean it did not happen!"

"Nor does it do much to make us believe that it did," countered Father Greal.

"There must be some way in which this can be resolved?" asked Larus.

"The Fathers!" exclaimed Father Thomas in a rush.

Father Greal frowned. "They accompanied High Priestess Trystia when she left for Xith," he stated.

"Not all of them," corrected Father Thomas. "Fathers Kippen and Biern are still within the Temple and I demand that we lay this matter before them."

Father Greal looked from Father Thomas then to Larus and finally settled upon Hunter. His gaze lingered overlong on Hunter making him feel most uncomfortable. Then when his gaze came back to Father Thomas, he nodded. "So be it," he said. "I will bring this before them in the morning as the hour is late. But until then..." raising his hand he pointed toward Hunter, "he will be bound and guarded."

"I don't think we need to wait so long," Larus said with confidence. "I'm sure Father Biern may still be awake. Let's settle this matter now."

The priest's gaze turned toward Larus. "What would you know of Father Biern? Or even whether he is awake or not."

"But he may be," argued Father Thomas, bringing the attention of Father Greal back to himself.

Father Greal considered the matter for a moment then replied, "If he is still awake, then I will see if he would be willing to rule on this matter tonight."

"Excellent," said Father Thomas. Breathing a sigh of relief, he glanced to Larus who flashed him a grin. "You better explain to Hunter what is happening."

"You're right," he said, then proceeded to explain the situation. Hunter was none too pleased at having his hands bound behind his back, but with Larus' assurance that nothing would happen to him, he didn't put up a fight.

So with Father Greal leading the way, they left the room of the strange apparatus. Father Thomas walked just behind him while the other priests followed with Hunter between them. Larus brought up the rear.

Passing through the room with the shattered crockery, Larus skirted around the broken shards and glanced at the pieces, wondering if this had been where Hunter had found the arachnid which was now firmly ensconced in his waistband. If so, he doubted Father Greal had known of its existence or they never would have been allowed to leave the area until it was found.

Larus could feel the hand of Qyaendri in this. Hunter would never have come here of his own volition, not to mention the fact that Father Greal would have prevented him from ever setting foot within the Caves, let alone leave with the crystalline arachnid.

As they passed through the last of the Grotto and entered the main passage which would take them to the outside, his thoughts turned toward the crystalline arachnid. What part did it play in all this? None of the knowledge Xi had given him mentioned any of this. But such was a normal state of affairs when dealing with fate and destiny as he well knew. Premature knowledge often had the effect of diverting the timeline from its desired destination, often with disastrous repercussions.

Suppose upon Hunter's arrival Father Thomas had been instructed by the Qyaendri to bring him to the High Temple, enter the Grotto of Artifacts, and retrieve the crystalline arachnid. The result of that premature revelation would have been Father Thomas taking Hunter immediately toward the High Temple and their meeting with Larus in the enemy camp would never have taken place.

Larus was ruminating upon such things as they reached the torch burning near the entrance of the passage leading to the Grotto of Light. Just as he was passing by the grotto, he caught the sight of light some distance down the side passage. It was more of a glow than an actual light and the sight of it brought him to a sudden halt. The others hadn't noticed it, nor were they aware of his stopping. They were still making their way on to the end of the passage and outside.

Ducking into the passage, he hurried down it toward the waiting Qyaendri. When he drew near, he recognized it as Ftheril, one of the Qyaendris Daeson oversaw. Awe and a touch of fear entered him at the sight. A strange occurrence which he figured must be arising from the fact that he was in a mortal state.

"Larus," Ftheril said with a grin. It wasn't a scornful grin as one would expect directed at one shamed and reduced to mortality. Rather it was one that said he was glad to see him.

"Ftheril," Larus replied. Amidst the awe and fear rose a touch of shame. He knew the Qyaendri would know of what had happened, and of how he failed in his duty.

"You haven't much time," Ftheril told him.

"Time for what?" he asked. "Do you know what Hunter is supposed to do? Is that why you are here?"

Ftheril shook his head. "You know better than that Larus," he replied. "Even if I did know, I could not impart such knowledge to a mere mortal."

Shame again turned his face red at the utterance of his punishment.

"In fact," he replied, "I am not technically supposed to tell you even this much, but the situation is dire."

"What?" asked Larus. "What aren't you supposed to tell me?"

"I already have," Ftheril replied. "You're doing well Larus. Just remember the ways of the Qyaendri." And with that, he vanished.

"Ftheril!" he said with urgency. *He hadn't told him anything!* Upset with the less than satisfying encounter, Larus knew he wouldn't be given anything further. As he turned about to retrace his steps and rejoin the other, he went over the encounter in his mind.

'You haven't much time.'

That phrase more than any others stood out as important. Of course he didn't have much time, he knew that. Perhaps it meant they should not tarry overlong at the High Temple? He had already planned to leave as soon as possible. With the Ullentites already besieging Xith, he knew time was a precious commodity. Ftheril had also said he was doing well. At least he knew they were on the right track.

Once back in the main passage, he saw the others had already moved quite a distance from the mouth of the side passage. Moving quickly, Larus was able to resume his place at the end of the line without anyone being the wiser. Soon they were out of the Caves and making their way across the darkened plateau back to the High Temple.

Chapter 16

Upon their return to the High Temple, Father Greal had them sequestered in their rooms while he went to call on Father Biern.

"What do you think is going to happen to us?" asked Hunter. He was worried, more so than the others. For if the outcome was bad, he'd be tossed over the cliff.

Larus glanced to the door, on the other side of which stood two of the Temple's guards and one of the priests from the Caves. "I doubt if you have anything to worry about," he assured him.

"Neither do I," agreed Father Thomas. "We are doing the Lady's will."

Despite their assurances that things would work out, Hunter couldn't help but remain on edge. So when an hour later the door opened and Father Greal stepped within, he quickly came to his feet.

The look on Father Greal's face spoke volumes. He was not happy. "It would seem Father Biern agrees that your friend should not be held at fault for violating the sanctity of the Caves," he said to Father Thomas.

Hunter grinned when he received the translation. "That's good news," he replied.

Father Greal turned toward him. "I on the other hand do not." Eyes ablaze with less than uplifting emotions, he said, "So I have convinced him that you should be held until the return of High Priestess Trystia and the rest of The Fathers."

"What?" exclaimed Larus.

"Surely you cannot mean that!" shouted Father Thomas. "We are on the Lady's business and to hinder us would mean ill for our people."

Turning upon Father Thomas, Father Greal said, "If you are on the Lady's business as you suggest, then why would she have you violate her own laws?"

To that, Father Thomas had no answer.

"As I thought," he replied.

"But if Xith falls, she may never return," argued Larus.

Hunter's uneasiness grew as he watched the heated conversation unfolding before him. "What's going on?" he asked Larus.

Larus glanced at him and said, "They plan to hold us until the return of their High Priestess."

"But we don't have much time," he replied.

"Don't I know it," Larus said.

Father Thomas stalked toward the door. "I shall see about this!" Father Greal stood in his way and Father Thomas almost knocked him aside so angry was he. But at the last moment he simply stepped around the obstinate priest.

"Keep an eye on Hunter," he told Larus then strode through the doorway.

Father Greal watched him leave then turned back to the other two. "You are to stay within your rooms," he explained. "Any attempt to leave will be dealt with by the Temple Guard." Giving them one final glare, he turned about and left the room.

"Now what?" asked Hunter.

"I don't know," he said. Again the words of Ftheril came back to him: *'You haven't much time.'*

Not even bothering to knock, Father Thomas thrust opened the door to Father Biern's rooms. Inside he found Father Biern sitting at the same desk as he had been during Larus' visit. "Why are we being held?" he demanded.

Father Biern looked up as the priest barged into his room. "Shut the door," he said when Father Thomas failed to close it after him.

Pausing, Father Thomas turned back and closed the door. "Now," he said, rounding on the Father, "why are we being held?"

"I am afraid Father Greal is completely within his rights to hold you until High Priestess Trystia's return," he said.

"How can you allow this?" Father Thomas asked incredulously. "You know we are on the work of the Lady."

"Yes, I do know that," he replied. Indicating the seat across the desk from him, he gestured for Father Thomas to sit. "I was not about to allow the detention of you and your friends. But when they brought in Father Kippen, who by the time he arrived had already been convinced of your friend's guilt, there was no consensus."

He sat back and grew quiet for a moment while Father Tomas digested that, then added, "And as you know, when there is no consensus among The Fathers..."

"...then the ruling must come from the High Priestess," Father Thomas finished.

"Exactly," nodded Father Biern. "A point of Temple Law which until now has rarely been utilized."

"Then what can we do?" asked Father Thomas.

Father Biern grew silent for a moment. "What does your friend Larus think you should do?" he asked.

"He is impatient to leave the Temple," he replied. "Ever since we emerged from the Caves it seemed his impatience has only intensified."

"Understandable I would think," he agreed.

Father Thomas nodded.

"I have already heard Father Greal's account of what transpired within the Caves," Father Biern stated. "I would like to hear yours."

So Father Thomas explained in detail what happened, of the room with the shattered crockery and the subsequent finding of Hunter. "He did not know of how he came to be there." He paused before saying, "Larus believes it to be the work of Qyaendri."

"Do you?" Father Biern asked.

Nodding, Father Thomas said, "Yes. There can be no other explanation."

"You say Hunter destroyed Artifacts within the Grotto?"

"I do not know as if they were actual artifacts," explained Father Thomas. "It rather looked like vases that had been smashed."

"And they had been sitting upon six pedestals forming the points of a hexagon?" he asked.

"Yes," replied Father Thomas. "Why?"

Scanning the tomes lying on the desk, Father Biern selected one and laid it before him. "Father Greal would know more about the significance of the urns than I, though I somehow doubt he would be completely forthcoming with me seeing as how I tried to help those who, according to him 'desecrated' the Caves, avoid punishment."

Opening the tome, he began flipping through pages. "This tome contains a description of every item contained within the Caves," he explained. Turning a few more pages he finally nodded and showed the illustration to Father Thomas. It was of the pedestals and the urns that had once sat upon them.

Father Thomas leaned closer to better examine the urns. He hoped to see one that might have a picture of the crystalline arachnid depicted upon it, but was disappointed. "Where did they come from?" he asked.

Bringing the tome closer, Father Biern read the words upon the opposite page. "It would seem they were brought to the Grotto of Artifacts shortly after its construction," he said as he continued reading the archaic words. His eyes widened ever so slightly as they left the page and met Father Thomas'.

"Remember the wild men who caused so much trouble centuries ago?" he asked. When Father Thomas nodded, he continued. "During the final battles, our soldiers along with many priests cornered them in what was believed to be their point of origin. Though how they first came to be there is not mentioned."

"Where?" asked Father Thomas.

He returned to the tome and read more of the archaic words. "In the mountains north of Casdra," he explained after a moment. "There you can find a temple carved from rock encircled by a deep abyss."

"An abyss?" asked Father Thomas skeptically.

"That is what it says," Father Biern explained. "The wild men, or the Or'tux as they called themselves, worshiped an evil god." He glanced up from the tome. "It is mentioned in another tome which deals more specifically with them that the god of the Or'tux demanded sacrifices. Human sacrifices."

"That is an abomination!" exclaimed Father Thomas.

"So our Lady tells us," he replied. "The six urns were found within that temple and brought back to the Caves."

"Do you think Hunter's mission for our Lady has something to do with the Or'tux?" questioned Father Thomas.

Father Biern shrugged. "Hard to say for sure," he replied, then grew silent for a moment as both priests gazed upon the illustration of the urns. "It would seem odd for him to have shattered all six, even if he had been stumbling around in the dark."

Father Thomas looked to the senior priest quizzically.

"What I mean is," clarified Father Biern, "that for him to have knocked one or two off their pedestals would be reasonable. Maybe even three or four. But all six? I doubt such a thing to be the result of mere chance."

"Unless he was looking for something," suggested Father Thomas.

"What makes you say that?" asked Father Biern.

"When we found him, he was sitting against the wall dazed and confused," Father Thomas explained. "And in his hand he held what looked to be a spider made entirely of crystal." A pause, then... "He did not even realize he held it. Startled him when he did."

A faraway look came over Father Biern as he sought an elusive memory. "Seems I read something once where the god of the Or'tux was associated in some ways with spiders. Could have been their symbol though I am not sure. Does Father Greal know you are in possession of it?" he asked.

Father Thomas shook his head. "No," he replied. "Larus had the good sense to hide it."

"Good. In the morning I will search for any mention of that spider in the old tomes," he said. "Until then, I would suggest you and the others get some sleep."

"But what about Father Greal?" demanded Father Thomas. "Can he hold us here indefinitely?"

"According to Temple Law yes," replied Father Biern. "But I shall discuss this matter further with Father Kippen tomorrow morning and see if I can bring him around to our side."

Father Thomas knew he was being dismissed and came to his feet. "I thank you for all your help in this," he said, then gave the Father a brief bow.

"Tomorrow I hope to be able to do more," he assured him. As Father Thomas turned and made his way across the room to the door, he returned his attention to the tome and the words concerning the urns.

"What does it do?" asked Hunter.

Seated upon one of the couches within their rooms, Larus held the crystalline arachnid close and was examining it carefully. "Nothing," he replied. "It looks just like a small figurine." He ran a finger along one of the eight double jointed legs. "It appears stronger than regular crystal."

"Transparent aluminum?" Hunter asked. When Larus shifted his gaze from the crystalline arachnid to Hunter, he had a confused expression so Hunter explained. "Ever watch Star Trek?"

"The original?" he asked.

"Ha!"

"What?" asked Larus.

"You have been to Earth!" he shouted triumphantly. "How else would you know there was more than one?"

Larus sighed, realizing his mistake. So wrapped up was he in the question of the spider that he had completely dropped his guard. "A guess?" he asked.

"I don't think so," argued Hunter. "I thought you must have since you speak English."

He knew the next question Hunter was going to ask. "No," he said, cutting him off, "I cannot bring you home."

"Why not?" he demanded.

Sighing, Larus set the crystalline arachnid on the table next to him. "It is not within my power," he explained. Folding his hands, he set them in his lap. He was feeling decidedly uncomfortable with the direction this conversation was going.

"Then how did you get there and back?" he asked.

"I really can't talk about it," he replied. "Trust me when I say that I cannot take you back."

"You must know who can then?" asked Hunter desperately.

"I know of no one on this world that can do such a thing," he stated.

Hunter's eyes narrowed. "That's not a no," he said.

For a human, this Hunter was rather perceptive.

"Tell me," demanded Hunter once again.

"The gods could do such a thing," he said. "I am certain it was through one of them that you were brought here."

"Casdralla?" asked Hunter. "She's the one whose people I'm supposed to save."

"According to Father Thomas' account of your appearance upon this world, you were in the company of a Qyaendri," explained Larus. "It would therefore stand to reason that only another Qyaendri could bring you home."

"How does one go about finding one of these Qyaendri?" Hunter asked.

Larus gestured to the air around them. "They could be in this very room right now," he replied. "They are the emissaries of the gods and come and go as they will."

"You mean they could be here among us right now?" he asked.

"In a place such as the High Temple, there would have to be many," offered Larus. "Though since they brought you here for a reason, it's unlikely any would take you back before your task is completed."

"But I don't even know what that is!" cried Hunter. Looking around the room he searched in vain for one of the elusive Qyaendri. "Take me home!"

he demanded. "You had no right in bringing me here!" When the room remained still and quiet, Hunter cursed. "Damn you!"

"Cursing them will not help your situation," advised Larus. "Do what must be done and they may take you back."

"Do you really think so?" Hunter asked hopefully.

Shrugging, Larus said, "It's the only hope you have of going home." He could see the frustration Hunter felt playing across his face. Larus felt genuinely sorry for the man, due in no small part for his own role in Hunter being there. Taking up the crystalline arachnid once more, he quietly continued his examination of it while hoping the discussion had come to an end. Just then the door opened and Larus quickly stuffed the crystalline arachnid into his shirt. Then saw that it was just Father Thomas returning from his talk with Father Biern.

"So?" Larus asked.

"Tomorrow morning Father Biern is going to try and convince Father Kippen to change his mind about us," he explained. Then went into detail about what he had learned concerning the urns and of the Or'tux.

Once his narration concluded, Larus translated for Hunter then thought on what he had just heard. Glancing over to where Father Thomas now sat reclined on one of the couches, he asked, "Back on the trail to the High Temple, you mentioned that the first temple ever built to Casdralla was destroyed by marauders from the north."

Father Thomas nodded. "That is correct."

"It wouldn't have been the Or'tux would it?" he asked.

Again, Father Thomas nodded. "It would," he affirmed. "Do you believe it has some bearing on all this?"

Larus shrugged. "I don't know, maybe." He left the crystalline arachnid tucked in his shirt as he came to his feet and began pacing. Thoughts coursed through his mind as he walked to and fro:

...time is running out...

...Hunter found with the crystalline arachnid...

...urns having come form the Or'tux temple...

...time is running out...

...crystalline arachnid had to have some significance...

...Hunter's mission...

...time is running out!

Coming to a stop, he turned to the others. "We're leaving," he said.

"But they will not allow that," argued Father Thomas. "The Temple Guard will prevent us from leaving the Temple."

Larus turned to the priest. "Time is running out for your people Father Thomas," he stated. "The longer we sit here, our chances of effectively doing anything rapidly diminishes." When he saw the priest begin to protest, he added, "We must trust in Casdralla. If she wills for us to depart, we will. If not, we'll be stopped before we get very far."

Father Thomas frowned at such logic. "Such an argument has been used by many for the basest of actions," he responded.

"You were given the directive by one of Casdralla's Qyaendri to assist Hunter in the completion of his mission right?" he asked.

Father Thomas nodded.

Turning to Hunter, Larus asked, "Do you feel that remaining here is wrong?"

It didn't take more than a moment's consideration before Hunter nodded. "Absolutely," he asserted. "We need to get moving."

"Ah," said Father Thomas after Larus gave him the translation. "There is the crux of the matter. Just where do you propose we go?"

"North," he said. "To the place where the urns were found. The temple of the Or'tux."

"By all accounts, that placed is cursed," objected Father Thomas.

"Irregardless," Larus countered adamantly, "that is where we need to go." Pulling forth the crystalline arachnid from his shirt he held it before the priest. "Why else have Hunter find this if not as a clue directing us to where he needs to go."

When it looked like Father Thomas was still ready to balk at the suggestion, Larus said, "Pray."

Father Thomas looked surprised Larus would suggest such a course of action.

"You pray about everything else," he explained. "Pray about this."

"Of course," he said, rather ashamedly. *Why didn't I think of that? he asked himself silently.* Dropping to his knees, he knelt before the couch and rested his elbows on its cushions as he prayed. *Is this the right course of action? Must we go to the cursed temple of the Or'tux?* As he prayed, a feeling of peace settled over him and he knew this was the right thing to do, whether or not their premature leaving violated Temple Law. When he finished, he rose and turned back toward Larus and asked, "How do we get out of the Temple?"

Larus walked over to the embroidered bell rope and pulled. A moment later, the door was opened by a large member of the Temple Guard. He stuck his head in and saw that they were standing some distance away, then stepped back to allow Edward in. Larus was relieved when he saw Father Biern's servant walk in.

"How may I be of service?" Edward asked as he entered. Turning to close the door he was stopped by the guard.

"Leave it open," the guard told him.

Edward nodded and the door was left ajar.

Larus came forward and met him not far from the partially opened doorway. What he planned was risky, but may prove to be their only chance to avoid armed confrontation. He looked upon Edward and hoped he was right.

"Up kind of late aren't you?" Larus asked. A rather innocuous greeting, but whose reply could speak volumes.

"Father Biern asked if I would leave myself available should you need anything," the boy explained.

"Those were his exact words?" asked Father Thomas. Edward nodded.

Lowering his voice so as to be almost unheard, Larus said, "We need to leave the Temple tonight."

Edward did not so much as bat an eye. Turning slightly, he immediately went to the embroidered bell rope and yanked hard on it twice. Then he turned and walked back toward the door. As he passed next to Larus, he said, "I'll be back shortly." Without another word, he walked to the door and left the room.

The door had no sooner closed than Larus turned to Father Thomas. "Do you think he is going to help us?" he asked.

"We will know soon enough," he replied. "That was a big chance you took."

"Yes, I know," admitted Larus. "But when I saw him walk through that door, I couldn't help but think that he had been placed there to help us."

"I thought the same thing," agreed Father Thomas. "Edward is Father Biern's personal servant. The only reason why he would have answered the summons was if Father Biern had arranged it."

"And Father Biern believes we are acting on behalf of the Lady," added Larus. "Won't this cause him trouble?"

"Most likely," replied Father Thomas. "But if so, his reward will be all the greater when he stands before Her."

Larus filled Hunter in on what was going on. "So we just sit and wait?" he asked.

"That's right," said Larus. "Edward said he would be back shortly. We must be ready to go when he does."

"If he comes back at all," stated Hunter. He wasn't as trusting of Edward's intentions as the other two seemed to be. Either way, there was nothing he could do about anything right now so he went over and sat on the couch to wait. A yawn escaped him as he made himself comfortable. Sleep had been a rare commodity the last few days and as he listened to Father Thomas and Larus speaking together, he started nodding off...

Tall shadows of rectangular buildings rose to dizzying heights on either side. The streets were silent and empty. An uneasiness filled him as he walked swiftly down the darkened boulevard, the silence a foreboding presence.

'The city should not be so quiet,' he thought to himself. Scanning the darkness, he sought the comforting sight of another living being, but found he was alone. His uneasiness grew steadily with every step. The tap-tap of his footfalls echoed in the darkness.

Coming to an intersection, he paused only a moment as he tried to determine the best way to go. That was when he discovered he didn't really know where he was going. His fear grew as he came to realize he didn't know how he had come to be in such a lonely, deserted place. All he did know was that he had to get out, and get out fast. Time was short.

Then, down the street to his left, he detected a faint light. Hope overthrew the fear that had filled his heart at the prospect he may not be alone. Rushing forward toward the light, he ran.

"Wait!" he hollered when he saw the light moving away from him. When it didn't stop, he was about to shout again but the cry was never uttered. For in the darkness nearby, something moved. Fear that had been banished by hope, surged anew.

Far ahead of him, the light turned a corner and vanished. Hunter grew ever fearful of that which was in the darkness. Running for all he was worth, he raced for where the light had vanished from his sight. He didn't know how, but he knew that he had to reach it or all was lost. Just exactly what 'all' was he didn't know and frankly, didn't have the luxury right then to contemplate what it could be.

The presence in the darkness was after him, he felt that to be true down to his innermost being. If it reached him before he reached the light...well he didn't know exactly what it would do but he was sure it wouldn't be pleasant. A festering malignancy was what the presence felt like, something that had emerged from the darkest recesses.

At last, he reached the corner around which the light had disappeared. When he rounded it, he saw the light was much closer now. Behind him, he felt the presence had gained as well. With as much speed as he could muster, he fled toward the light. Leaving the city behind, he found himself entering an area of hills and trees.

Chtk-chtk. Chtk-chtk.

A strange noise was coming from the light. He could discern movement within the light when he drew closer. He realized the light was not just a light, but rather a creature moving along the ground, glowing with the light. The sound he was hearing came from the meeting of the creature's appendages with the ground.

Hunter ran. He was so focused on the creature he pursued, that he almost failed to notice the creature's destination. When his eyes fell upon the darker darkness that was the creature's destination, he knew that it was not the creature he needed to reach, but rather what lay ahead.

The instant he had that revelation, the malignancy which pursued him seemed to swell in size and increase its speed. It was trying to stop him from reaching the creature's home.

Running with every ounce of speed he had, he fled. Still gaining on the creature, he finally drew close enough to be able to discern parts of its body. Its legs were spindly and double jointed...

"Hunter."

A hand shaking his shoulder wrenched him into the waking world. He looked with wide eyes upon Larus who stood bent over him with a hand on his shoulder. "Hunter," Larus said again. "It's time to go." It took him a moment to realize where he was and what Larus was talking about. But when he saw Edward standing nearby, it all came back to him.

Nodding, Hunter said, "Alright," and then came to his feet.

"He almost had it," Ftheril said.

"Another dream or two and they'll have all the pieces," agreed Daeson. Turning his eyes toward the one-time Qyaendri he added, "Now, if Larus can just put them together in time."

Chapter 17

Indicating the other side of the closed door, Edward said, "Father Korell has been called away and one of the two guards is otherwise occupied elsewhere." The boy turned his gaze toward Larus. "You must subdue the remaining guard quickly."

Larus nodded and moved toward the door. Reaching for the handle, he was stopped by a hand on his shoulder. Turning he saw that it was Father Thomas. "Do not kill him," the priest cautioned.

"Didn't plan on it," he assured him. Then to Edward Larus asked, "On which side of the door is the guard standing."

"To the left," the boy said, gesturing in that direction.

"Alright," he said as he motioned Father Thomas to step further back from the doorway to allow him more room. Once the priest backed away several feet, he returned his attention to the door. Grasping the handle, he took a calming breath. With a mighty yank, he pulled open the door and raced through. Before the guard had time to realize what was happening, Larus struck him with a powerful blow to the side of the head, knocking him senseless.

Larus caught the guard before he could hit the floor and dragged him into the room. Glancing toward Father Thomas he said, "He's still alive."

"Thank you," replied the priest.

Hunter came forward and took the guard's feet. He and Larus then carried him over to the nearest couch where Larus proceeded to bind his hands and feet.

"The other guard will be back soon," warned Edward. "We must be quick."

Once the guard was securely bound, Larus removed the man's sword belt and buckled it around his own waist. He saw the disapproving look Father Thomas directed toward him. "We may need it," he told him. "Don't worry, I promise not to use it on anyone within the Temple." *Not the edge anyway*, he added silently to himself.

Father Thomas did not reply.

At the door, Edward waited impatiently. "You must hurry," he urged and when he saw Larus was ready, entered the hallway. He turned and led them in the opposite direction of where Father Biern's rooms were located. With only brief pauses at intersecting hallways to make sure they were clear, he led them on a roundabout route through the Temple.

Very soon, Father Thomas was in an area of the Temple that was unfamiliar to him. "Where are you taking us?" he asked the young servant.

"There are many ways in which to leave the Temple," Edward assured him. "Not far from here lies one of which few know."

"How is it that you know?" asked Larus. Edward failed to answer.

After turning into the tenth hallway since leaving their rooms, they came to where a smaller, side hallway joined theirs. When Edward paused to make sure it was clear, he held up his hand. Turning his head back toward Larus, he indicated someone was approaching. Not far back down the way they had come stood a closed door. Edward pointed toward it and indicated for them to hide.

While Edward remained in the hallway, the other three ran back to the doorway. Fortunately the door was unlocked and they rushed through into a storage closet. Filled with supplies and equipment which servants used to keep the Temple clean and orderly, it left little room for the three men. Wedged in amongst the barrels and boxes, Larus shut the door.

Mere seconds later they heard muffled voices coming through the door as Edward spoke with another person. The thickness of the door and the fact that the speakers were not directly on the other side prevented them from clearly hearing what was being said. But when the voices finally grew silent, the door opened and Edward gestured for them to come out.

"The Temple servants are beginning to ready the Temple for the day," he explained.

"Is it far?" questioned Larus.

Edward shook his head. "No." Without further ado, he returned to the branching smaller hallway, gazed down it, then motioned for them to follow. Turning into it, he quickly led them past three doors, coming to a halt before the fourth.

"It's in here," Edward explained. Producing a key, he inserted it into the lock and opened the door. Ushering them inside, he followed and locked the door once it was closed.

The room was pitch black with only a faint outline of light coming through the cracks around the door. "Stand still until I find it," he told them. When Hunter began asking a question, he said, "And be quiet!"

Larus advised Hunter of the need for silence and soon the only sound was that of Edward making his way through the room. It didn't take long before he found what he was looking for and a narrow crack of light began to be seen.

"Help me with this," he said.

Grabbing Hunter, Larus crossed over to where Edward was trying to open a hidden doorway. He was having trouble moving the opening aside. Once Larus and Hunter added their strength to the project, the opening was soon wide enough to allow a single man to squeeze through. A barely felt, cool breeze flowed through the opening.

"Once on the other side," whispered Edward, "you will need to help me close this. I didn't realize how obstinate it would prove. As far as I know, this way hasn't been used for a century or more." He then pointed toward an opening between two of the neighboring buildings. "Once this is closed, make your way down that street until you come to the last building. From there, proceed three hundred paces directly across the plateau. At that point whistle two short bursts. Not too loud, you wouldn't want to attract any unwanted attention."

"Why?" asked Father Thomas.

"Another servant loyal to Father Biern will be somewhere close to that point with your horses," he explained. "If no one appears, whistle again. Bringing the horses from the stable was the only part of this that was uncertain. If after the second round of whistles no one appears, make your way as best you can on foot."

Larus led the way through the opening with Hunter right behind.

"Thank you Edward," Father Thomas said.

"Anything for the Lady," he replied. "Good luck."

Father Thomas patted him on the shoulder then followed his two companions through. While Larus and Hunter worked quickly with Edward to close the opening, he glanced around in order to determine where they were. The roundabout route through the Temple had confused him.

Before the hidden opening stood two trees of similar breadth and height. As best he could figure they were on the north side of the Temple, far from the main entrance. Now that they were on the outside, the breeze they had earlier felt passing through the opening blew much stronger and felt quite a bit cooler. Father Thomas pulled his robe tighter about him and was thankful it was still summer and not the dead of winter.

"Okay," Larus said quietly when he and Hunter joined the priest. "Let's be quick and silent." Taking the lead, Larus scanned the nearby area for anyone who may be about. Not finding anyone, he led them across to the street Edward had indicated. From there it was an easy matter to traverse it all the way down to the last building. They only saw two other people out at this early hour and neither one had noticed them.

Upon reaching the last building, Larus made sure the coast was still clear then led them out onto the plateau. Next to him Father Thomas could hear him counting quietly to himself. By the time he reached two hundred, they were quite a distance from the Temple and completely shrouded in night.

Larus then whistled twice and grew quiet, listening for any sound indicating the approach of a servant with horses. He waited a minute then repeated the two short whistles. "At least they managed to get us out of the Temple," he said at last when it appeared no servant with horses was forthcoming.

"Won't being on foot prove a problem when they find us gone?" asked Hunter.

"Yes," replied Larus. "So we better get out of here fast." To Father Thomas he asked, "Which way to the trail leading down from the plateau?"

Above, the half moon was partially hidden by clouds but in the dim moonlight they could see Father Thomas pointing toward the trail. "It's that way," he whispered and started heading in that direction. The other two remained quiet as they followed.

Hunter didn't like riding horses, but he definitely preferred them to walking. He was cursing their bad luck at not being able to rendezvous with the servant bearing horses when from out of the dark two short, barely audible whistles split the silence.

All three froze and looked around, trying to penetrate the darkness. Then, the sound of a horse snorting was heard. Immediately, Larus gave two short whistling bursts which were answered by a single burst.

Shadows emerged from the greater darkness and quickly turned into flesh and blood. It was the servant with their horses. "Father Thomas?" the servant asked hesitantly.

"Yes my son," he replied.

An audible relieved sigh was heard as the lad came forward quickly. "With Father Biern's compliments," he said. Handing each of them a set of reins, the boy added, "You will find food, blankets and a woolen jacket for each of you in the packs behind the saddle."

"Thank you," Larus said.

The boy came up to Father Thomas and held out a rolled piece of parchment tied with a string. "Father Biern said you might need this," he said.

"What is it?" Father Thomas asked as he took it.

"I don't know," he replied. "I was also told to urge you not to stop in Veradin this night."

Father Thomas nodded "I understand."

"Good luck Father," the boy said.

"The Lady shall bless you for the aid you have given," the priest assured. Stepping into the stirrup, Father Thomas mounted his horse. "You best hurry and return before you are missed."

"Goodbye Father," the boy said, then turned and disappeared into the night. The sound of his rapidly retreating footsteps quickly faded into nothingness.

"Much better," Hunter said, as he sat in his saddle.

Larus couldn't help but grin. Hunter had earlier hated being on horseback so much, that the statement seemed rather comical now. He was glad the darkness hid his amusement.

"Let's go," he said. "Obviously there's a long road ahead before we can afford to stop."

"That is true," agreed Father Thomas. "Once past Veradin we will be beyond the reach of the Temple Guard. Father Greal will not send them far from the Temple, not with war on our doorstep."

"Good," stated Larus as they began heading toward the trail leading from the plateau.

After the initial rush of being free from the Temple and not having to face being thrown over the cliff, the darkness seemed to close in on Hunter. His last couple of dreams were still very much on his mind, especially the last one. Could the darkness of the plateau conceal the malignant presence present in his last dream? Though he knew it to be but a dream and not real, still he found himself constantly scanning the darkness for any sign of it. Not until they reached the trailhead and the first Priest Stone blossomed into life was he able to shake the feeling of dread that had accompanied him throughout their trek across the plateau. But now with the Stone's glow banishing the darkness, the fear was gone.

The light of morning found them encamped several miles west of Veradin in a secluded clearing some distance off the main road. Larus had stood watch throughout the night, worried that despite the assurances of Father Thomas, the Temple Guard would still be sent after them. A worry as it turned out that had been in vain for there had been no sign of the Temple Guard upon the road. In fact, there had been no traffic whatsoever.

At the moment he sat before a small fire, fueled with the driest wood he could find to reduce the quantity of smoke rising to the sky. In his hand he held the crystalline arachnid which he knew was important in some way though he didn't know exactly how.

On one side lay Father Thomas who had begun to stir, on the other lay Hunter who had tossed, turned, and moaned throughout the night. Not for the first time he felt pity for the man. Being on a world other than the one he was born was really wearing on him.

While he considered the crystalline arachnid, he thought about everything that had happened to him since he first came to this world. In the back of his mind he had begun to develop the theory that maybe his coming here hadn't completely been a punishment. The mural bearing his visage painted across the ceiling of the Silver Leaf Room, the prophecy Father Biern had revealed to him, it all seemed to indicate that his presence on this world at this time had been preordained long ago.

Glancing over to Hunter, another theory came to mind. If his presence was preordained, then so too must be Hunter's. Could it be possible that Hunter was meant to be the Chosen One all along? Larus would like to believe that, it would alleviate much of the guilt that had plagued him since that fateful day when his moment of panic at failing in the Goddess' mission had resulted in the selection of Hunter.

The ways of the gods were unfathomable, even by the greatest of Qyaendri.

"Ahhhh!" cried Hunter as he sat bolt upright. Spittle foam flecked the right side of his mouth and there was a wild look to his eyes.

His cry startled Father Thomas from a sound sleep.

Larus remained where he was though his gaze was fixed on Hunter. "Hunter?" he asked.

Father Thomas quickly realized something was wrong and started toward him.

"Stay where you are," Larus said, his gaze never leaving Hunter's face.

Pausing, Father Thomas glanced to Larus then turned back to Hunter.

Raising his arm, Hunter wiped the flecks of spittle from his face as his eyes lost their wildness. He saw the two of them staring at him. "Everything okay?" he asked.

"I think so," Larus replied, though there was a touch of uncertainty in his voice.

"Good," he said. "Any sign of Temple Guards?"

Larus shook his head. "No, it's been quiet," he assured him.

"That's welcomed news." Coming to his feet, he glanced around the small clearing then headed off toward the trees to take care of his morning business. All traces of the wildness he had exhibited upon awakening were gone.

Once Hunter had moved out of earshot, Larus turned toward Father Thomas. "I think he's not adjusting too well," he said.

Father Thomas nodded. "He has been through an awful lot since first arriving," he agreed. "Taken from home like he was, not to mention his mistreatment at the hands of the Ullentites, had to have taken their toll on him."

"True." Larus gazed over to where Hunter had disappeared into the trees. "He hasn't had any time to rest and acclimate to his new environment." Turning to Father Thomas, he added, "It seems that at every turn, something new comes at him."

Concern for their comrade could clearly be seen in the sad expression Father Thomas wore. "I thought he was handling it well," he said. "But now?" The wild look Hunter had upon first awakening said something was going on.

"What can we do?" Larus asked.

"Pray," replied Father Thomas.

Just then, Hunter appeared coming out from the trees. "Let's have a bite to eat then get going," Larus said in English. Turning to Father Thomas he asked, "Do you know where this temple of the Or'tux lies?"

"Somewhere to the north," he relied. "Exactly where eludes me."

Hunter came and sat down next to Father Thomas. "Good because I'm starved." Last night they had removed the packs that were secured behind their saddles for the blankets they contained. Within each they discovered quite a bit of food as the boy had indicated; a large loaf of bread, dried fruit and meat, and a flask of ale, enough to last for several days.

While they ate their meal, Father Thomas took a stick and drew a rough representation of Casdra in the dirt. Pointing to the upper left area of the drawing, he said, "The original High Temple which the wild men destroyed sat here. If memory serves, I believe they came from out of the mountains east of there, somewhere in this vicinity." Moving his stick to the right of the map, he tapped that area. Then he moved the end of the stick further up and indicated a rather large area. "Somewhere within this area is where we will find their temple."

"I take it that area is nothing but mountains?" asked Larus, remembering back to a conversation they had earlier about Casdra.

Father Thomas nodded. "Pretty much," he replied. "I had the opportunity to venture there in my youth," he explained. "Very rugged country."

Larus looked at the map and the area where the point of the stick still rested. "We don't have time to spend searching such a large area," he said. "The wolf is at the door so to speak."

"Indeed," agreed Father Thomas.

Hunter busied himself with eating while the other two talked. Every now and then Larus would pause and give him the gist of their conversation. He didn't like the sound of having to play Lewis and Clark in search of the Or'tux temple. What they needed was someone like Sacagawea to lead them there. Breaking into the other two's conversation, he said, "What we need is a guide."

Both grew silent and turned toward him. Larus relayed to Father Thomas Hunter's suggestion. "Just where do you suppose we go looking for one?" Larus asked.

Hunter shrugged. "Didn't you say that Father Biern thought the place was cursed?" he asked.

"That's right, he did," affirmed Larus.

"Seems to me a cursed place would be known by those living in the area," he suggested. "Let's go to the town nearest those mountains and ask around."

When Father Thomas received the translation, he agreed that Hunter's idea had merit. Using the stick yet again, he moved it back to just south of where he said the wild men had emerged from the mountains. Making a small circle, he said, "There is a settlement sitting along the shores of Lake Cuer. It isn't very big, not much more than a small fishing village that hunters and trappers use as a winter supply stopover. If anyone could guide us to the Or'tux's temple, we would find them in Sharstan." At that, he tapped a spot on the southern edge of the circle.

"How far is it?" Larus asked.

"Almost three days," he said. "Between here and Milltown we have good roads. We can make that by nightfall if we set a fast pace. After that there is nothing but a small trader's path cut through the wilderness. It is the same distance from Milltown to Sharstan as it is from here to Milltown, but the path is not kept up and…"

"Will slow us down," Larus finished.

"Exactly," affirmed Father Thomas.

"Then we had best get started," Larus announced. Coming to his feet, he grabbed his pack and crossed over to where his horse was secured to the branches of a tree. "How are you this fine morning?" he asked his horse while patting its neck. The horse just snorted in reply.

Larus chuckled as he secured his pack behind the saddle. Once it was in place, he stepped into the stirrup and mounted. Glancing over to Hunter, Larus saw that he was just finishing securing his pack and making ready to mount. Father Thomas on the other hand stood still beside his horse. He was examining something in his hand. Upon closer examination, Larus saw that it was a piece of parchment.

"What do you have there?" he asked.

Looking up from reading the words written upon the parchment, Father Thomas replied, "It is a note from Father Berin. The boy handed it to me last night when he met us with the horses. I had forgotten about it until just now."

Moving his horse closer, Larus asked, "What does it say?"

Father Thomas grinned and held it up for Larus to see. Among the other words written on the parchment, he readily made out the name Sharstan. "He was telling us to go to Sharstan?"

"That is correct," replied Father Thomas.

"We already figured that out for ourselves," Larus said.

Father Thomas nodded. "He also mentions a trapper by the name of Bellion Shank. Father Biern thinks that if he happens to be in Sharstan, he may be our best bet to find the temple."

"How did he know we were going there anyway?" asked Hunter after receiving the translation.

"Father Thomas and I spoke with him about what happened in the Caves," explained Larus. "He must have deduced that would be our destination, just as we did."

Rolling closed the parchment, Father Thomas tucked it within his robe. "From the looks of the way he wrote the message, he must have written it hastily," he commented. "May have come to the realization at the last minute." Taking hold of the saddle horn, he put his foot in the stirrup and swung up into the saddle.

"Either way, we have a long way to go and a short time to get there," said Larus. Heading his horse back toward the road, he led the others from the camp. He paused only a moment at the edge of the treeline to see if there was anyone else about. Not seeing anyone, especially Temple Guards, he emerged from the trees and turned west.

Not far after that they came to the road heading north toward Milltown. After turning onto the north road, Larus set a fast pace. By noon, they had yet to encounter anyone.

"Not much traffic on this road," observed Hunter.

"No," replied Father Thomas once Larus relayed the comment. "There isn't much up this way but small villages and a mine or two. The only village of any size is Milltown, but it would hardly qualify to be called a town. Doubt if we encounter anyone on the road other than a trader or two."

Father Thomas' words proved prophetic for by the time the sun was low on the horizon and Milltown's first outlying building appeared through the trees, they had yet to encounter anyone.

Milltown was pretty much as Father Thomas had described it, a large village. There were several inns along the road and one building larger than the rest which he explained was where this region's governing body resided. Comprised of five men, it basically made sure traders continued bringing in supplies, settled disputes, and saw to the safety of the people with a region garrison of twenty men. Hunter thought it looked a bit rustic as they came to a stop before the Stunted Pine, an inn that looked fairly reputable.

Later that evening while they were taking their ease in the common room, they enjoyed the efforts of a less than talented man strumming a lute-like instrument. It was clear that this was not the primary means with which he supported himself. He had the look of someone more suited to the outdoors than performing for others. As it turned out, they later learned that he was a local who would play at the local inns from time to time. In such an out of the way locale, it must be hard to attract any real talent. Most of the musicians who made a living performing spent their time in the common room of inns located further to the west where the bulk of Casdra's citizenry lived.

They made inquiries as to the whereabouts of the trapper Bellion Shank, but none of those they questioned knew the man. One patron said that most of those who trapped in the mountains rarely came as far south as Milltown. That they preferred the company of the wilds over that of people and only came out of the mountains when need arose.

After enduring several well intentioned but poorly executed selections by the lute player, they decided to turn in so as to get an early start in the morning.

Chapter 18

A harsh wind blew as he made his way along the trail, high upon the canyon wall. One misstep and he would plunge to the unseen depths of the gorge below. In the dim moonlight filtering down through the clouds, it was all he could do to keep his footing. The way was very narrow and the wind at times gusted so fiercely he thought it would surely knock him from the trail and to his death.

The fear which had been a constant companion for so long now had begun to diminish. The malignant presence haunting the dark had inexplicably vanished. He didn't know how or why, he was just glad that it no longer dogged his every move.

Hunter leaned against the wind as he fought his way further up the trail. He glanced back the way he came, wondering if he should turn back, but knowing that somewhere back there lay something evil. His eyes searched the dark, questing for the presence, all the while fearing that he may actually find it. Other than a few areas of the trail illuminated by stray beams of moonlight, there was nothing. Turning back, he resumed his progress.

Where was he? He didn't know. How exactly he came to be there? He didn't know that either. All he knew was that he had to keep going. That it was of dire importance for him to continue and not stop. For deep in his innermost being, he knew that to stop would cause the presence to find him once again. He didn't even know where this trail led, only that somehow he must go on.

Then suddenly, a gust of mammoth proportions struck him and knocked him off his feet. Sailing through the air, fear sprung anew as visions of being swept off the trail and plunging to his death flashed through his mind.

Oomph!

Landing on his back, he started rolling to the side and felt his leg slip over the edge. Panic erupted and he frantically grasped at anything he could get his hands on to save himself. One hand encountered a root and he held on with a death grip as his other leg went over the side.

Grasping the root with his other hand, he halted his downward plunge with both legs and half his body dangling over the side. He held still for a second as he fought the panic and brought his muscles back under control.

Chtk-chtk. Chtk-chtk.

As he hung there, half dangling precariously over certain death, an odd, yet strangely familiar sound came drifting upon the breeze. Then from up the trail, a barely perceptible glow appeared and slowly made its way down the trail toward him.

He froze, remaining as he was while the glow came closer and closer. Was it akin to the evil presence he had fled from? Or was it something else? The initial moment he saw the glow brought back the fear. But then as he continued watching its approach, the fear lessened. Whatever it was, it didn't have the same affect on him as had the malignant presence.

Chtk-chtk. Chtk-chtk.

The glow coming did little to banish the dark, only managing to illuminate a small radius. And as it grew closer, he began to make out features within the glow. Eight double jointed legs and a round, bulbous body. It was a spider! But unlike any spider he had ever seen for it was translucent and the glow seemed to emanate from its very core.

Hunter watched as it drew ever closer, fear gave way to amazement and wonder. When the glowing spider was within thirty feet of him, it paused in the middle of the trail. For a moment it felt almost as if the spider was looking at him.

Then it scurried to the rock face and began climbing diagonally up from the trail. The glow emanating from its body lit the rock face as it scurried across its surface. Five feet up from the trail, it ducked into a depression and disappeared from sight. A second later, a thin band of the rock face began to glow. The thin band glowed for several seconds before growing dark once again. A moment later, the spider reappeared on the side of the cliff face. It paused there for a moment. Again, Hunter felt as if the spider was looking at him. He was transfixed by the spider. Despite his precarious position, he remained motionless and watched.

The spider began moving again, this time scurrying horizontally across the cliff face down the trail in his direction. When it came to within five feet of where he hung, it slowed and then came to a stop. The glow coming from its body revealed a depression in the side of the cliff. It seemed to turn its head and Hunter almost felt it beckon for him to follow. Then moving into the depression, it passed out of sight. The glow coming from where it disappeared gradually faded until at last, it was gone.

Now no longer transfixed by the spider, Hunter's immobility vanished and the seriousness of his predicament returned. Using the root to support his weight, he began pulling himself up onto the trail. He was about to lift a leg up onto the trail when the ground covering the base of the root broke open causing the root to come several inches further from the ground.

The unexpected movement of the root caused Hunter to lose his balance. Keeping hold of the root, it brought his fall to a sudden halt when the root reached its full extension once more and grew taut. Now with everything from his shoulders down dangling over the edge of the cliff, he held on for his very life

When it appeared that the root might still be able to hold his weight, Hunter started pulling himself up very slowly. Hand over hand, he dragged his body inch by inch onto the cliff. Just when he thought he would make it, he saw the dirt around where the root entered the ground of the trail begin to crack and rise upward. The root was coming out again!

Swinging his leg up, he managed to hook his foot over the edge. Keeping a constant watch on the rising dirt covering the as yet unearthed portion of the root, he pulled ever so gently on the part he held in order to bring up the rest of his body. The leg of the foot that had made it up had just managed to place its knee above the edge of the drop-off when a section of the root popped out of the dirt.

Hunter was thrown off balance once more and his leg slipped from the edge, his full weight suddenly jerking upon the root. Twice more it popped out of the ground and each time he fell a little more until he was completely dangling over the edge of the cliff. A glance below revealed nothing but darkness.

Then he felt it. The malignant presence. It was coming. He had sat still too long and it had caught up with him. But where was it coming from? Out of the darkness below him? Or was it approaching down the trail?

Panic took him and he no longer sought to reach the top carefully. Pulling hard on the root, he began climbing up and over the top. Halfway over the top, he stopped when the presence from out of the darkness grew more intense. The fear started spiking. It was nearer. But where?

Then a cold sense of foreboding settled upon him and his eyes turned toward the section of the trail leading down. It was there! It was upon him! With a cry, he felt evil touch him. A searing sensation that felt as if the flesh from his arm was being seared from his bone.

Crying out in unbelievable pain, he lost his grip on the root and plummeted backward, off the cliff...

Larus sat bolt upright in bed as a blood curdling scream tore through the night. "Hunter!" he cried. Leaping from his bed, he grabbed his sword belt that was draped over the back of a chair and rushed through the door.

Father Thomas emerged from his room bearing a glowing candle a second after. "What was that?" he demanded.

"Hunter," was all he said as he crossed the hallway to Hunter's room. Not bothering to knock, he opened the door and barged within. The light from Father Thomas' candle fell upon a supine figure lying atop the covers of the bed. Coming to their friend, they saw that his hair was matted with sweat and he was panting hard.

Seeing no one else in the room, Larus tossed his sword belt onto a nearby chair before sitting down next to Hunter on the edge of the bed. Again he saw that Hunter had foam flecked about the sides of his mouth and a wild, feral look to his eyes. Laying a hand gently on Hunter's chest, Larus softly gave it a shake and said, "Hunter."

Father Thomas came near and then jumped back as Hunter exploded up from his bed at Larus' touch. Half naked and with a growl deep within his throat, he knocked Larus aside as he came to his feet.

"Shut the door!" Larus hollered to Father Thomas.

Turning to do as instructed, he drew the attention of Hunter who gave out with a primal scream and leaped toward him. Backing away, he was unable to avoid Hunter who tackled him, and with fingers curled into claws, began raking his face.

"Ahhhh!" screamed Father Thomas as he tried to ward off Hunter's attack. He received three sets of scratches before Larus struck Hunter in the side of his head with his fist and knocked him off the priest.

Leaping after him, Larus quickly had Hunter pinned beneath him. Snarling, he tried to escape Larus' grip but couldn't.

"Hunter!" shouted Larus. When Hunter continued snarling and struggling to escape, Larus struck again and this time, succeeded in knocking him out. When the man in his grip grew still and quiet, he turned to Father Thomas. "Are you okay Father?"

One set of scratches marred his right cheek, another had scored across his throat, while the final set had dug deep furrows along his left forearm that were beginning to well blood. "I shall live," he said. Grimacing, he indicated Hunter and asked, "What is happening to him?" He well remembered the wild look Hunter had earlier that morning when he first awoke.

Larus removed himself from the unconscious Hunter and shook his head. "I don't know," he replied. "Is he losing his mind?"

Father Thomas crossed the room to a table upon which sat a pitcher of water and a bowl. He took the pitcher and partially filled the bowl. Then with a cloth, began seeing to his wounds. "I do not know. Perhaps the strain of no longer being on his native world is affecting him worse than we thought," he supposed as he dabbed at the scrapes upon his face. None were too deep though more than one was welling blood.

Hunter lay quiet and unmoving, still unconscious from Larus' blow. Reaching down to pick him up, Larus said, "Probably shouldn't leave him on the floor." With one arm supporting Hunter's shoulders and the other beneath his knees, Larus lifted him off the floor and carried him over to the bed where he gently laid him down.

Larus sat next to him on the bed. He gazed at Hunter for a moment then looked over to Father Thomas. "He's getting worse."

"I know," replied the priest. "I had hoped what we saw when he first awoke yesterday might have been our imagination. But now?"

Nodding, Larus turned his gaze back to their comrade. "Yesterday morning he came out of it fast," he stated. "This time he grew violent." Now in his quiet repose, there was nothing in Hunter's visage that spoke of the madness which had taken hold of him earlier. "And only by rendering him unconscious did it stop."

"Has it?" questioned Father Thomas, as he came and sat on the opposite side of the bed from Larus. "Let us pray that when he again regains consciousness, the madness will be gone."

Larus only nodded.

An hour later when Hunter began stirring, they kept their distance just in case he proved violent. But when Hunter opened his eyes, they saw no trace of the madness that had been there earlier.

Father Thomas came forward and asked, "How do you feel my son?"

Once Larus gave the translation, Hunter looked perplexed. "Fine." A pause then... "Why?" Looking first to Larus, then to Father Thomas and that's when he saw the scratches along Father Thomas' face and throat. Alarmed, he sat up in bed and asked, "What happened to you?"

"He was attacked Hunter," explained Larus. "You attacked him."

"I did no such thing!" exclaimed Hunter. "I would never attack the good Father!"

Hunter's reaction was clear to Father Thomas, despite not having it translated for him. Coming closer, he sat on the bed next to him and said, "I am afraid it is true my son. We heard you shout and came in to see if you were alright. That is when you jumped from off the bed and attacked me."

Hunter's expression turned darker as the details of what he had done were laid out. As Larus was talking, Hunter lifted his right hand and looked at it. The nails were stained red and tracks of dried blood spider webbed their way past two knuckles. Bits of skin were still wedged beneath the nails of the forefinger and the middle one.

"It can't be," he said, voice soft and quavering. Moving his eyes from his hand to Father Thomas, he said, "I..."

Giving Hunter a reassuring grin, Father Thomas laid a hand upon his shoulder. "It is alright," he assured him. "I know you did not mean to harm me."

"We think you may be affected due to being on a world other than the one upon which you were born," explained Larus. "Ordinarily, such a juxtaposition would not have much of a negative affect. But, considering all you have gone through, as well as your lack of sleep, it may be proving too much." He allowed that to sink in for a minute then said, "We may need to stay here a day or two so you can rest."

"No!" shouted Hunter. His reaction was as much a surprise to him as it was to the other two. "I...I don't think we should tarry. I feel much better, and rested."

Larus translated Hunter's words for Father Thomas. When he was done he asked the priest "What do you think?"

With lips pursed, he gazed thoughtfully on Hunter. "It may be past," he stated. Looking deep into Hunter's eyes, he sought any hint of the madness they had witnessed earlier. "Let us see how he is when dawn arrives. If there is no sign of madness, then we can continue."

"Yes," agreed Hunter. "I'm sure whatever it was is over."

"Let's hope so," said Larus. Then to Father Thomas he added, "Morning is only three hours away. Why don't you return to your room and get what rest you can. I'll stay here with him."

A yawn escaped him as he nodded. "Let me know immediately if..." he said with a nod to Hunter.

"I will," agreed Larus.

"Get your rest too my son," Father Thomas said to Hunter. Standing up, he crossed over to the door. Then with a final glance back to Hunter, he left the room, closing the door behind him.

Patting Hunter on the forearm, Larus said, "Try to get some sleep."

"I doubt if I can," he replied. As Larus stood up from the bed and went over to sit in a nearby chair, Hunter again looked at his blood-stained fingers. "First thing though," he said as he moved to sit up on the edge of the bed, "is to wash this off." A shudder went through him at the thought of Father Thomas' flesh still beneath his fingernails. Getting up, he was soon at the wash basin using a less than clean towel to scrub it off.

Larus watched him as he stood cleaning himself by the basin. "Are you sure you are feeling okay?" he asked.

Hunter paused in his work and glanced back toward him. "I feel fine," he said matter-of-factly. "I still can't believe I did what you claim. If not for the scratches and..." pausing, he held up his partially clean hand, "I'd call you both liars." Returning his hand to the basin, he resumed scrubbing.

Once his hand was thoroughly clean, in some places painfully so, he returned to the bed. Sitting down on the edge, he glanced over to Larus. "I don't feel like going back to sleep."

"You should try," advised Larus.

Hunter sighed and then laid back on the bed. "Aren't you tired?" he asked.

"A little," he said. "But don't you worry about me." Leaning forward, he blew out the candle and the room was plunged into darkness.

After a few minutes, their eyes adjusted sufficiently so that Hunter could see Larus' gray, shadowy form still sitting at the table. "Larus?" he asked softly.

"Yes?" came the reply.

"Thank you for stopping me from hurting Father Thomas more than I did," he said.

"You're welcome," Larus replied. "Now, get some sleep."

Sleep did not come easy to Hunter as he lay there. Visions of his attack on Father Thomas as the other two had related replayed over and over in his mind. When he finally managed to fall asleep, the sun was just beginning to rise.

Two hours after sunup came a knock on the door. Larus stepped softly as he quietly made his way over to let in Father Thomas. "He's still sleeping," he whispered to the priest. "I thought he could use the extra rest."

Father Thomas nodded. Then after a quick look to see Hunter lying still and quiet upon the bed, he said, "I will go and have our morning meal brought to us here."

While Larus was waiting for Father Thomas to return, he took out the crystalline arachnid and set it on the table before him. It was a curious thing, this item Hunter had found. It was harder than the average crystal should be and had been crafted by a master artist. From the tip of one of its double joined legs to the tip of another, it was seamless.

He hoped that they were correct in their determination that it was a sign from the Goddess, directing them toward the temple of the Or'tux. But was that all it was? He couldn't help but feel that there was more to this small crystal figurine than being a mere directional indicator.

Just then, he heard footsteps of more than one person out in the hallway approaching. When they came to a stop outside the door, he quickly placed the crystalline arachnid within his shirt to hide it from view. A moment later, the door opened and Father Thomas entered followed by two servants bearing food laden trays and a pitcher of ale.

"Thank you my sons," he said quietly to the two boys.

"You're welcomed Father," the older of the two replied. "Is there anything else we can do for you?" He kept his voice low in difference to the sleeping man still lying in bed.

"No," Father Thomas assured him. Producing two silvers, he gave each of the boys one as he escorted them back to the door. With a quick blessing of good health, he sent them back to the kitchen.

"Still asleep is he?" Closing the door, Father Thomas turned back to where Larus was already tearing off a bit of bread and beginning to eat.

Larus nodded. Biting off a corner of the bread he held, his attention was suddenly drawn to the bed as Hunter began stirring. Motioning for Father Thomas to stay back just in case Hunter proved violent again, he moved closer to the bed. "Hunter?" he asked.

"Mmmm?" murmured Hunter sleepily. Cracking open an eye, he saw them standing there staring at him. Coming fully awake, he suddenly sat up in bed. His sudden reaction caused Father Thomas to take a step back. "Is everything okay?" he asked, worried.

Nodding, Larus gave him a grin. "It looks that way," he said, relieved. There was no trace of the madness Hunter had exhibited upon awaking the previous two times. Turning to Father Thomas, he saw the relieved look he felt mirrored in the priest's eyes. "He's fine."

"Thank goodness," Father Thomas said.

Returning his attention to Hunter, Larus gestured toward the food and said, "Breakfast's ready."

Hunter audibly sniffed the air and smiled. "Smells good," he said satisfactorily. Coming from off the bed, he made his way to the table where he loaded his plate. "So," he began once the plate was filled to his satisfaction, "how far is it to... uh... Sharstan was it?"

"Two days," replied Father Thomas. "If we don't tarry and the weather remains good."

Hunter glanced out the window and could see the crystal blue sky peeking in through the mass of limbs and leaves enshrouding the tree just outside their window. A soft breeze rustled its way through their loosely packed mass. "I don't think that is going to be a problem."

Father Thomas shook his head. "No, the Goddess will see to it that we have clear weather," he said matter-of-factly.

Larus grinned at that. While it was true Qyaendri did have some ability in affecting the weather of a world, they would rarely do such. Changing weather patterns was no small thing. It was a major event which not even the greatest of the Qyaendri would dare. It could wreak devastation on a mammoth scale, turn farmland into desert, and in the most extreme instances set into motion events which could kill off every living thing upon the surface of the world. So no, despite Father Thomas' absolute belief that fair weather would be theirs, there would be no supernatural interference to make it so.

After making short work of the remainder of the food, they were soon down to the stables and had their mounts ready for travel. From the inn's courtyard, Father Tomas led them to the northern edge of town where a road of sorts began making its way northward through the tree lined hills.

Not much wider than what one wagon could easily traverse, the road at least did show signs where the locals had attempted to grade it to prevent the ruts created by the wagons from becoming too bad.

The first couple miles out of Milltown were fairly pleasant. Trees and bushes had been kept back, a good sturdy bridge spanned a creek, and the road had had a recent layer of small rocks spread across its surface to aid in the prevention of ruts. Along the way they came across several outlying farmsteads, but once the last had fallen away, the road quickly worsened.

No longer were the trees cut back. Their long, outreaching branches would at times stretch far out over the road. The road began showing deep ruts, and at the streams and creeks, there were no bridges to ease their crossing.

"We're really out in the boonies aren't we?" asked Hunter after they had forded the fifth stream since leaving Milltown. Traveling through rugged country and not having seen another living soul for hours lent a desolate feel to this part of Casdra.

"You could say that," replied Larus. Though he didn't understand what a 'boony' was, Hunter's meaning was clear.

It took a little over two days, but near noon of the third, they arrived in Sharstan.

Chapter 19

A small ramshackle collection of huts or a shanty town right out of the Depression was what came to mind when Hunter saw Sharstan for the first time. A score of buildings in all, none very large and all in desperate need of repair, sat on the southern shore of a fair sized lake. North of the lake rose a snow capped mountain range that stretched east to west. Somewhere within those peaks lay the temple of the Or'tux.

"Not much to look at," commented Hunter as they rode the last distance to the outskirts of Sharstan. The people were not much better than the town in which they lived. Dirty, disheveled, and at least from Hunter's point of view smelling right foul, they were a nasty lot.

"Perhaps not," agreed Father Thomas, "but they are good people."

"We'll see," added Larus. Like Hunter, he wasn't much impressed by the locals.

As they drew close to the first building, the locals began noticing their approach. Most simply went about their business. Two individuals leaning against one of the nearby buildings came to greet them.

One was a tall, thin man with several missing teeth, whose clothes hung loosely about his lanky frame. Despite the fact of being a man in his mid twenties, he looked like a kid forced to wear his older brother's hand-me-downs.

The other was just as lanky but whose clothes were a better fit. Both men were dirty and as they drew closer, the three newcomers were soon enveloped in an aura of pungent odor.

"Father," greeted the man whose clothes fit best. Ignoring the other two, he and his friend came to stand beside Father Thomas's horse. "Welcome to Sharstan."

"Thank you my sons," Father Thomas replied.

Next to him, Hunter was wrinkling his nose in an attempt not to inhale the stomach turning odor, all the while trying not to show it.

"I'm Tom," the man said, "sort of the mayor of Sharstan you might say." Gesturing to the other, he added, "This is Yoll."

"Good to meet you Tom, Yoll," nodded Father Thomas. Then indicating Larus and Hunter, he introduced them as well.

"What brings you this far north, Father?" asked Tom. "It isn't often we see one of the Lady's own up here."

"We are on a quest of sorts," explained Father Thomas.

Yoll's eyes widened. Then in an awed voice he asked, "For the Lady?"

Father Thomas grinned at his reaction. "Yes, Yoll," he affirmed.

"We were told someone in this area could help us," interjected Larus. "A trapper by the name of Bellion Shank."

"Shank?" exclaimed Tom in disbelief. "That layabout?" The look on his face said his opinion of Bellion Shank was rather low.

"So we were told," replied Father Thomas.

"Do you know where we might find him?" asked Larus.

"Sure," replied Tom. "He's where he always is at this time of day."

"And where would that be?" Larus asked.

Turning slightly, Tom pointed toward the middle of Sharstan, to one of the smallest, dilapidated buildings. One side had a gaping hole that was inefficiently covered by what looked to be the lower half of a broken rowboat. "He'll be in there."

"Thank you," said Father Thomas. Then as he nudged his horse into motion he added, "May the Lady bless you."

"It's good to have you in Sharstan Father," Tom said as the three riders began moving away.

"What a dump," commented Hunter in disgust. How people could live like this was beyond his ability to comprehend.

"I think that if it should prove necessary to spend the night here," began Larus, "we should camp near the lake." He pointed off toward the shore some distance away from the edge of town.

"I agree," said Hunter. The mere thought of remaining within such a place for any length of time made his stomach churn.

The building wherein they were told they could find Bellion Shank was little more than a single room domicile. Tendrils of smoke escaped through cracks in the roof, evidence that someone was within. An errant breeze blew the smoke toward Hunter, and its acrid stench threatened to empty the contents of his stomach.

"Man, what is that?" he asked. No longer able to hide his dislike for the smell of the place, he produced a cloth and pressed it to his nose and mouth.

Father Thomas shook his head. "I do not know," he replied, then pulled the collar of his robe higher to cover his mouth too. Before they reached the hole in the wall which must be the domicile's entryway, a head poked out and looked in their direction.

The head belonged to a man. Unruly and unkempt dark hair framed a face wild with facial hair and dark, bushy eyebrows. His initial expression was one of annoyance until his gaze fell upon Father Thomas. Then it turned into one of downright irritation. Without saying a word, he ducked back inside.

"Hello," Father Thomas said in friendly greeting as he stared at the recently vacated opening. No reply was forthcoming. He glanced to Larus who only shook his head.

"Hello," replied Father Thomas a bit louder than before. He paused for an answer and when it didn't come added, "We are looking for Bellion Shank."

"Go away," came a gruff voice from within.

"We are on business of the Lady," stated Larus.

"I don't care if you are the Lady herself!" the voice exclaimed.

Father Thomas gasped at such blasphemy. He was about to respond when Larus stopped him. "Don't," Larus said. "He's trying to bait you." Swinging a leg over, Larus dismounted. "Stay here," he said to the other two. Then he turned and walked toward where the section of boat leaned against the hole in the wall.

"We need to talk with you," Larus said. Pausing next to the section of boat, he peered through the hole and into the hut.

Inside was a mass of shadows enshrouded by a thick layer of smoke. What light managed to make its way through the cracks in the walls and ceiling did little to diffuse the smoke. One of the shadows moved, a rather large shadow. In the hand of the shadow was a glint of metal indicating a bared blade.

"Go away," the voice said again. "Leave me alone."

"We have need of information that we believe you possess," explained Larus. "Allow us to talk with you and you'll never see us again."

"Hah!" the voice shouted. "I know your tricks. Now leave me be!"

Undaunted, Larus stepped forward toward the opening. Within, he heard a growl coming from the man. Knowing full well that he would be attacked, he ducked under the boat and entered.

"*Get Out*!" screamed the man as the shadow burst into motion.

Larus saw the glint of metal coming for him and quickly dodged to the side. As the blade passed within mere inches of his side, he struck out at the arm holding it.

"Ahhhh!" cried the man as Larus' fist connected just up from the man's wrist. The force of the blow stunned the muscles, forcing the hand to release its grip on the knife. Another blow to the man's midsection knocked him backward, deeper into the darkness. Larus quickly followed and heard more than saw the man crashing into, and then through, a wooden table.

He didn't give the man a chance to launch another attack. Pouncing, Larus struck him with a one-two punch that easily subdued his attacker. A quick check to make sure he didn't kill the man, he was relieved to find him only unconscious. Coming to his feet, Larus returned to the hole in the wall and knocked the boat aside to the ground.

"What happened?" asked a worried Father Thomas. "Is he okay?"

Larus nodded. "He won't be causing any further trouble," he replied. Then he noticed where Tom and Yoll stood with a dozen others, watching. He dismissed them since they only seemed curious about what was going on.

He helped Father Thomas dismount and told Hunter to remain with the horses. When Hunter started to object, he discreetly nodded over to the crowd watching them. "We don't want to find our horses gone when we come back out."

Hunter glanced over to the onlookers and nodded. "I understand," he said.

"If any trouble should develop, holler," Larus told him.

Giving him a grin, Hunter replied, "You don't have to worry about that."

Larus nodded and then with Father Thomas following close behind, reentered through the hole in the wall.

With the boat no longer before the gaping hole, the interior was much better lit and the air was beginning to clear. The large man whom they believed to be Bellion Shank still lay unconscious on the floor.

Father Thomas moved over to a cloth hanging before a shuttered window and pushed it aside. Flinging open the shutter, he felt a breeze pass through which greatly aided in dispelling the noxious cloud of bitter smoke.

"Look here," said Larus, drawing the priest's attention to a smoldering copper brazier. It proved to be the source of the vile smelling smoke. "What should we do with it?" he asked.

Wrinkling his noise Father Thomas said, "Put it out."

"As you wish." Collecting a large globule of saliva, he spat upon the smoldering ember, extinguishing it. Once it quit producing the acrid smoke, the breeze coming through the window was better able to clear the remainder still in the air.

They left the man on the floor and took seats in the only two chairs within the hut. After only a few minutes of waiting, the man began to stir. First a groan as he lifted his hand to his jaw, then a startled gasp when he realized they were there.

Larus saw the man's eyes narrow and said, "We don't want trouble. But we do need to speak with you."

The man ignored him as his eyes went first to the opened window, then noticed the absence of the boat at the hole in the wall. His head swiveled quickly toward the brazier and a cry escaped him when he saw smoke was no longer rising from it.

"Damn you!" he cursed as he lurched to his feet. "You had no right to do that!" Moving toward the brazier, he was abruptly stopped when Larus stepped in front of him. "Out of my way!" he roared. Reaching to force him aside, the man instead was dealt a blow by Larus which knocked him backward to the floor.

"Not until you answer our questions," stated Larus.

Once again the man rose to his feet and tried to reach the brazier. And once again, he was thrust backward. This time, Larus' blow took him in the jaw and lifted him off his feet.

As the man landed on the floor with an 'oomph', Father Thomas gave Larus a look and asked, "Is all this really necessary?"

"It is if you want your information," he replied. Turning his attention from Father Thomas back to the man, he said, "I can do this all day." The man glared at him. "The sooner you talk to us, the sooner we are out of here." He paused a moment then asked, "You're Shank aren't you?"

The man may not have been the smartest person in the world, but he realized that he wasn't going to be able to budge Larus by force. Giving in to the inevitable, he nodded. "What do you want to know?" he asked.

"Father," Larus said, indicating for him to do the talking.

"We are looking for the temple of the Or'tux," he explained. "Have you ever heard of it?"

From the blank expression on his face, it was clear that he hadn't. Shaking his head, he said, "No."

"It would be located somewhere in the mountains, far to the north," he explained. When that didn't elicit a response, he added, "It has been rumored the place is cursed."

His expression changed subtly at that for a fraction of a second before returning back to normal. It happened in the blink of an eye, but not so fast that Larus failed to notice. Shaking his head, he said, "Sorry. I haven't heard of any place like that."

"It would be high in the mountains," continued Father Thomas. "A temple carved from rock encircled by a deep abyss."

"No," said Shank. "Haven't seen anything like that."

"Are you sure?" asked Larus.

Turning his gaze toward him, Shank reiterated, "Yes."

Larus knew he lied. He did know something.

"Would you know of anyone here in Sharstan who might know?" asked Father Thomas hopefully.

Shrugging, Shank said, "Maybe *Mayor* Tom could help you." The way he said mayor clearly indicated how little he felt about Tom.

"We should go," Larus announced. When Father Thomas glanced questioningly at him, he gestured toward the hole in the wall with a nod.

"Sorry for bothering you," Father Thomas said.

"You and your kind are always coming around and bothering me," he said vehemently. "Why don't you all just leave me alone!"

Larus had Father Thomas leave first while he followed, backing away from Shank, never taking his eyes from the man. Once he had moved out from between Shank and the brazier, Shank leaped forward and hurried toward it. As Larus was leaving, he heard flint striking stone as Shank worked to relight the brazier.

"Well?" asked Hunter as Larus emerged from the hut.

Not immediately answering the question, he crossed over to the horses. "He's lying," he whispered to the other two.

"Are you sure?" asked Father Thomas.

"Yes," Larus replied. "When you mentioned that the place was cursed, he reacted."

"But why would he lie?" Father Thomas wondered.

Larus turned his gaze to Father Thomas. "There are many reasons men will lie," he explained. "Some do it simply because it is in their nature."

"Father Biern directed us to this man," he said. "There must be a reason."

"He knows where this place is," Larus said. About to swing up into the saddle, he noticed Mayor Tom and the others still standing some distance away, watching. "But I intend to find out what he knows. Stay here." Leaving the other two by the horses, he walked over to the crowd.

Mayor Tom gave him a halfhearted grin as he approached. "Was Shank any help?" he asked.

"No," replied Larus.

"Didn't think he would be," Tom said. "All he wants to do is stay in there all day and burn his weed."

Another of the bystanders, a man of middling years with the looks of a woodsman, asked, "What did you want with him anyway?"

"We're looking for a place high in the mountains," he explained. "A colleague of my friend indicated that Bellion Shank might be able to help us find it."

"Why would he think that?" questioned another.

"I don't know," Larus admitted. Glancing around at those standing nearby, he said "Maybe one of you has heard of some place rumored to be cursed?" Many maintained a blank look, but two of them reacted as had Shank, a momentary flicker of recognition which quickly vanished.

"Well," Larus said, "if any of you remember anything, we'll be camped over by the river." He started turning to head back to where Father Thomas and Hunter waited when he paused. "We would make it worth your while." Leaving them to think about it, he made his way back to the other two.

By this time, the section of the broken boat had been returned to its place blocking the hole in Shank's wall, and wisps of smoke could once more be seen emerging through the structure's cracks.

"Shank's not the only one who knows something," Larus quietly told Father Thomas.

"But why will they not tell us?" questioned the priest.

"Who knows?" replied Larus. Taking hold of the saddle horn, he swung up into the saddle. "Let's make camp and see what we can figure out."

"So we're spending the night?" questioned Hunter after Larus explained the situation.

"Not in Sharstan we're not," he assured him. "We'll be better off further down the lakeshore." ...and away from the smell.

In fact, once they had left the last ramshackle buildings behind, the air freshened up dramatically. They continued along the shoreline until coming to a small clearing up from the beach where the trees would shield them from the wind throughout the night, as well as blocking any view of Sharstan. The clearing also afforded them a perfect view of the lake and the mountain range to the north.

Father Thomas was most pleased with their campsite. "Very nice," he said. Dismounting, he stood and gazed over the blue waters to the snowcapped peaks rising to the sky.

Larus came up behind him and laid a hand on his shoulder. "Don't get too comfortable," he told him. "I hope for us to be out of here before long."

"I understand," replied Father Thomas.

"How long do you suppose we'll be here?" Hunter asked.

Shrugging, Larus turned toward him. He could see a hint of something behind his eyes, as well as a furrowing of his brow. "Not long, I assure you," he replied.

Hunter nodded and then began gathering wood for the fire.

Larus watched their comrade for several moments as he passed within the trees and began picking up fallen twigs and branches.

"He has not shown any sign of the madness since leaving Milltown," Father Thomas announced as he came up behind Larus.

"I know," replied Larus. "Let's hope it doesn't return."

Ever since Hunter's initial attack on Father Thomas at the inn, they had exercised great caution every morning when Hunter awoke. But each time, he awoke normal without any vestiges of the madness which had driven him to attack.

"I'm going to return to Sharstan and see if I can learn anything further," Larus told the priest. "Those people know something and I intend to find out what."

"Please do not do anything rash," cautioned Father Thomas.

Larus turned toward him with a reassuring grin. "Be at ease Father," Larus said, "I'm not going to hurt anyone." *But that doesn't mean I may not twist a few arms if such means become necessary,* he added silently to himself.

Father Thomas merely nodded.

"Keep an eye on Hunter and don't let him wander away," Larus said then turned toward Hunter. Raising his voice, he hollered, "Hunter, I'm returning to Sharstan to see what else I can learn."

Hunter paused in the middle of reaching down for a branch. "By yourself?" he asked.

"Yes," Larus said. "I won't be too long."

"Okay," he replied. "We'll have the camp ready when you return."

Larus gave him a grin and a thumb's up. Noticing Father Thomas' quizzical look, he did the thumb's up again and said, "It's a sign of agreement or affirmative response from his world."

"Oh," Father Thomas said.

As Larus started turning, he saw Father Thomas mimicking the thumb's up. Grinning to himself, he headed for the beach and began making his way back to Sharstan.

Questions passed quickly through his mind as he walked along the shoreline. What did Bellion Shank know? Why won't he cooperate? And perhaps most puzzling, why would Father Biern direct them to a man who wasn't going to help them? Questions and questions! All the while time was running out. He didn't know how much was left to complete whatever it was Hunter was supposed to do. Could it already be too late? He didn't think so. If it was, he was certain the sense of urgency propelling him along would be gone. But there was no time to dilly-dally with Bellion Shank. He had to know where the temple was!

The first outlying building of Sharstan was appearing out of the trees ahead when the sound of someone moving through the forest drew him out of his reverie. Slowing but not stopping, he turned his gaze toward the source of the noise. To his surprise he saw that it was Mayor Tom. Coming to a stop, he was about to greet the man when Tom put finger to lips in a gesture indicting him to remain silent. Then the Mayor indicated with a nod of the head for Larus to return back down the beach.

Curious, Larus turned around and complied. While he worked his way along the shore line, Mayor Tom kept pace with him all the while remaining within the trees. Larus glanced at Tom several times before the mayor finally altered his course and left the confines of the forest. Just before emerging from the trees, he glanced back down the beach toward Sharstan. Seeing that the outlying buildings were no longer visible due to the forest, he joined Larus on the beach.

"Good day to you Mayor," greeted Larus.

"Let us continue further, shall we?" he asked. After another glance over his shoulder toward Sharstan, Mayor Tom set out at a quick pace.

"What's going on?" asked Larus.

"I don't want anyone to know that I've spoken with you," the Mayor said.

"Oh?" Larus questioned. "Why?"

"Let's just say it would cause certain complications," he replied. "My life wouldn't be worth spit if Shank found out."

Larus nodded. That would explain why no one had been willing to answer his questions earlier. Lowering his voice, Larus asked, "Has this something to do with what my friends and I are here to discover?"

"Maybe," Mayor Tom said. About every fifth step he would glance back over his shoulder to see if they were being observed.

After the sixth time, Larus reached out and gripped Mayor Tom's arm bringing him to a stop. "Tell me," he said urgently.

"Bellion Shank used to be one of Casdralla's priests," he said. "I don't know what his real name is, but it isn't Bellion Shank."

"Is that how Father Biern knows him?" asked Larus.

Mayor Tom shrugged. "Not knowing this Father Biern, I couldn't say," he replied. "I do know that Bellion Shank has never mentioned him before, nor any other priest for that matter. I learned of Shank's past from another, many years ago."

"What connection is there then?" Larus knew Mayor Tom was trying to get at something, something which would make his life problematical if those in Sharstan were to learn of it.

"I'm getting to that," replied Mayor Tom. "It has to do with that weed he burns."

"The weed?" asked Larus.

Mayor Tom nodded. Turning his gaze to the mountain range in the distance, he said quietly, "He gets it from somewhere up there, in a location which he holds as a closely guarded secret. To even ask him about it could result in immediate attack. I think the constant breathing of the weed's smoke has addled his mind."

"He gets it in the mountains?"

Mayor Tom nodded. Lowering his voice still further, he added, "In a place where the spirits of the dead walk." He met Larus' gaze. "Or so I've heard."

Definitely seeing the possible connection now, Larus asked, "Do you know where it is?"

Shaking his head, Mayor Tom said, "Like I said, Shank keeps the location to himself. He disappears every once in a while, presumably to replenish his stock of weed." He grew silent for a moment before saying, "He hasn't made a trip up to the mountains for over a month. His stock should be running very low by now."

Larus began to see where this was going. "How much does he have left?"

"No idea I'm sorry to say," he said. "And it wouldn't be a good idea to ask him."

Remembering their encounter with the man, Larus could see where that would be a bad idea. A plan began to formulate in his mind. "You wouldn't happen to know where in his place he keeps his stash do you?"

"No," Mayor Tom said, shaking his head negatively. "I try not to have any dealings with Bellion Shank. And please, don't mention that I've spoken with you."

"Not to worry," Larus assured him, "your secret is safe with me."

Glancing back up the shoreline, he said, "I better be getting back."

"Thank you for your help," Larus said gratefully.

"I've done many things in my life of which I am not very proud," he replied. "If you are truly on the Lady's business, then perhaps my aiding you will count for something when the time comes that I stand before Her."

"I'm sure it will," assured Larus. "I'll have the good Father pray for you and give you her blessing."

Relief washed over him. "Thank you," he said. Then with that, he glanced once more toward Sharstan before hurrying into the treeline.

By the time Mayor Tom disappeared from sight, Larus was already running back toward the clearing where he had left the others.

"Do you think that would work?" asked Father Thomas.

Larus had filled them both in on what Mayor Tom had said. Father Thomas was most upset when he learned that Bellion Shank had once been a priest of Casdralla. When asked, he replied that Shank didn't look familiar.

"It should," affirmed Larus. His plan was to wait until dark and then sneak into Shank's place and remove the remainder of his stash of weed, thereby forcing Shank to return to where he harvests it to get more. It would then be a simple matter to follow him.

"What if you can't find his supply?" Father Thomas asked.

"Then I'll have to question Shank directly," he replied.

"But from what Mayor Tom said, it is unlikely he will cooperate," argued Father Thomas.

"I realize that," he stated. "But let's worry about that when it happens." He gazed to Father Thomas and the priest understood that should Larus not find Shank's stash, then the man would have to be forced to talk, one way or another. The people of Casdra depended on it!

Larus suggested for them to get what sleep they could until it was time. For should he succeed in removing the weed, then they must be ready to follow Shank at a moment's notice. While the other two lay down to rest, Larus kept watch as the sun dropped to the horizon.

Several times throughout the afternoon, curious locals came up the beach to see what was going on with them. Larus would allow them to come to within a certain distance, just close enough to see for themselves that there was nothing to see, before shooing them away. Before too long, the locals stopped coming around.

He waited until darkness had covered the land for many hours before waking the others. Coming to where Father Thomas and Hunter lay, he woke them. "It's time."

Chapter 20

Sharstan was dark and quiet. Only two windows glowed with light from within indicating not everyone had turned in for the night. Fortunately, neither of them were Shank's. Larus had left Hunter and Father Thomas some distance back in the forest while he went on alone. Now standing at the fringe of the trees encircling Sharstan, he waited and watched.

A lone individual made his way from one of the darkened buildings to one of those with light. Larus watched from the shadows as the man, who was obviously inebriated, staggered his way to the door. It took him some time before managing to open the door and enter.

Once the door was closed, Larus again scanned the darkened streets of Sharstan and found them deserted. Moving out, he slowly made his way to Shank's hut. Even in the darkness, his place was unmistakable as it was the only one with part of a boat leaning against it.

Larus moved silently through the dark, simply another shadow among shadows. He made his way to the boat covered hole and came to a stop. There he stood motionless as he listened to the night; the far away hoot of an owl as it searched for prey, a wisp of conversation from a nearby building, and coming through the hole by which he stood, the clearly identifiable sound of snoring.

With a quick glance around to make sure Sharstan remained still and quiet, he moved aside the boat just far enough so he could enter. In the darkness of the hut, Larus could see the glow of the smoldering ember of the weed as it burned in the brazier. The stench filling the hut was just as intense as it had been during their earlier visit. Stepping carefully, Larus slowly made his way inside.

First a step…then he paused to make sure Shank still slept. When a snore came, he moved a little bit further only to pause once more to await another. Step by step he made his way over to the burning brazier. If the weed were to be anywhere, it would most likely be kept readily accessible to refill the brazier.

Even Larus' vision had a hard time dissimilating the shadows within the hut. When the red ember of the smoldering weed was next to him, he came to a stop. Then moving his hands slowly and cautiously, he began feeling around for a container in which Shank might keep the weed.

First item he found was a sheathed knife, next was a cloth lying rumpled beneath it. He spent several minutes working his way across the small tabletop until he was sure what he sought was not there.

Next he knelt down and moved his search to beneath the table where he found a large cloth bag. Pressing his hand gently upon the top of the bag, he heard the faint crackle associated with dried leaves. Nodding to himself, he lifted the bag from off the floor and opened it.

The odor coming from within said that he had found Shank's stash. Reaching his hand inside, he grabbed a handful and pulled them forth. In the dark he couldn't tell what they looked like, but could tell that they were all but dried out. Transferring the weeds to his other hand, he reached in and pulled out another small amount which was the last of it.

From the bed where Shank slept, the snores continued to come as Larus replaced the now empty cloth bag back where he had found it. Once it was in place, he returned to his feet and turned for the door. Using the same care as he had upon entering, he crossed the room and passed through the hole. Behind him, the snores continued to come.

Once the boat was back in place, he paused to glance around the darkness to see if anyone was about. Not finding anyone, he quickly made his way back to where the other two waited with the horses.

"Did you do it?" asked Hunter when he rejoined them.

Larus nodded and held up the leaves clutched in his hand. "Shank will have to go get more if he wants to keep breathing the smoke," he replied. "Right now he's still sleeping. I don't know what he'll do upon awakening."

"What do you mean?" questioned Hunter.

"If the weed's addled his mind then he may not realize he had more before going to sleep," he explained. "If not, then he may come looking for whoever took them."

"You mean us?" Hunter didn't like the sound of that.

"Who else?" Larus put the weeds in his saddlebag before saying, "We arrived just before his weeds came up missing. And if the place we were questioning him about is truly where he gets them, then he'll doubly suspect us of taking them."

To Father Thomas Larus said, "Let's find a place where we can hole up until he wakes. I'm sure we'll know when he does, then watch what happens."

Father Thomas agreed with his plan and they moved into the forest near the edge of town, not far from Shank's hut. They moved the horses even further into the trees and secured their reins to the limbs of a fallen trunk. Hunter and Father Thomas remained with the horses again while Larus returned to the edge of the forest and settled down to watch. Still a couple hours left before dawn, he didn't expect anything to happen until the sun rose. And he was right.

A roar snapped him out of a light doze. Gazing through the trees toward Shank's hut, Larus saw the bull of a man emerge holding the empty cloth bag in one hand, and a long knife in the other.

Locals scattered as he began accosting them, accusing them of taking his weed. One wasn't able to flee quickly enough and received a nasty cut along his forearm. Finally, Shank's attention was directed down the shoreline toward where they had set up camp. Other locals joined the chorus of accusations leveled toward Larus and the others. Larus was sure they were simply accusing him and the other two just to redirect Shank's wrath. Little did they know that they were right on the money.

As Shank stormed off toward their now deserted campsite in the clearing, the locals gathered together and discussed what could have happened. Several snippets of the conversation drifted to where Larus hid. Half seemed to believe he and the others had taken it while the other half thought Shank had finally lost his mind completely. Curiously, Mayor Tom and his buddy Yoll were not to be seen.

The group of locals continued talking about Shank's behavior until he reappeared, returning from finding the campsite deserted. The look on his face was one of stark rage. Two seconds after he was spotted returning to Sharstan, the locals scattered. In no time at all, the only thing moving within Sharstan was Shank.

If anger had a name, truly this day it would be called, Bellion Shank. He absolutely oozed it from every pore. In his rage, he struck the side of a building in passing, leaving a fair sized hole. Larus could hardly credit that this man had once been a priest of Casdralla. Surely Mayor Tom's informant had to have been wrong.

Shank paused near the hole in his wall and scanned the town. If looks could destroy, there would not have been two stones left atop each other. Then knocking aside the section of boat, he stalked into his hut.

So far so good, Larus thought to himself.

He didn't have long to wait before Bellion Shank reemerged from his hut. This time, he carried not only the cloth bag, but a pack filled to bursting. He left behind his hut and turned toward the lake. Along the shoreline were several old docks, all but two having lapsed into such a state of disrepair that most of the planks and pilings were either broken or gone. Of the two remaining docks, one had three boats moored to it while the other held but two. Shank headed to the one with two.

When Shank moved out of sight behind his hut, Larus was forced to emerge from the trees to keep him in sight. Moving quickly, he reached the side of the hut and peered around it. Shank had already reached the dock and tossed the cloth sack into the bottom of the boat. He then climbed in and sat on the bench.

Once seated, he opened his pack and removed the brazier, placing it atop the other bench. To Larus' surprise, he could still see smoke rising from the last smoldering vestige of the weed. Why his pack hadn't caught fire was a mystery.

After setting the brazier in place, Shank removed the guy rope from the piling and pushed the boat away from the dock. Taking an oar in either hand, he began rowing directly away from shore. Larus only watched him for a few moments before turning to head back to the others.

"You're going to follow him, right?"

Larus paused and turned to find Mayor Tom standing in a nearby doorway. Larus nodded, "That's right."

"Do us a favor and see to it that he doesn't return," Mayor Tom said.

"I'm not a murderer," argued Larus.

"I doubt if it would come to that," Mayor Tom replied. "Once he sees you it will be more like self defense."

"If that's the case..." Larus said with a shrug, leaving the sentence unfinished.

"Good luck," Mayor Tom said as Larus hurried away toward the forest.

When he reached Father Thomas and Hunter, he had them in the saddle quickly. "He's heading northeast across the water," he explained. "There's no time to lose."

"Then let us hurry," Father Thomas said.

With Larus in the lead, they broke into a gallop once they emerged from the treeline. Racing to the shore, they began working their way around the lake. When Hunter saw the lead Shank already had on them, he thought how fortunate it was that the outboard motor hadn't yet been invented on this world. The man was rowing furiously across the lake.

Moving quickly, they soon left Sharstan behind and entered the forested hills on the western side of the lake. The going was difficult seeing as how there was no road or trail for them to follow. About the only thing in their favor was the fact that Shank couldn't keep up such a fast pace. By gauging his route across the lake, he would make landfall on the far side. Too far for one man to sustain such a furious speed.

Over the course of the next couple of hours, the shore gradually drew further away from the course Shank was setting until finally, he was so far out as to be almost invisible. Despite the fact that they eventually lost sight of him, they had a pretty good notion as to where he was heading. So keeping a good pace, they continued to follow the shoreline, all the while casting glances out over the water for glimpses of their quarry. It wasn't until after reaching where the shoreline began curving more to the east did they at last see him again.

The afternoon sun was beginning to cast long shadows when during a short break to rest the horses, Larus looked out over the water and saw Shank. Standing on the shore atop a boulder, he turned back to the others and said, "He's stopped."

"Stopped?" asked Father Thomas.

Larus nodded. "Looks like it."

Moving alongside the boulder, he accepted a helping hand from Larus and was soon up on top standing next to him. Larus directed his gaze over the water a little south of east. There he saw a black dot and could barely make out Shank's silhouette against the backdrop of the water.

"What is he doing?" Father Thomas asked.

"I'm not sure," replied Larus. "Looks like he's holding the brazier."

"Could be the weed no longer burns," suggested the priest.

"Perhaps," he agreed. "Either way, with him stopped as he is, we can afford to rest for a short time. He's still an hour or so away from the mouth of that river, which I think he may be trying for."

About a mile or so further east along the shoreline, a river entered the lake. From where they stood on the boulder, the mouth of the river looked to be over a hundred feet across.

"I do not think we should tarry too long here," argued Father Thomas. "Would it not be better to reach the river first and find a ford to the other side?"

"That would be a good idea," agreed Larus, "if we were sure he was going to land on the other side. For all we know, he could land on this one." Then glancing back to where Hunter sat leaning against the bole of a tree, he said, "Besides, we didn't get much rest last night. A short break will do us good."

At the mention of rest, the fatigue Father Thomas felt made itself known as an unexpected yawn escaped him. He gave Larus a grin, "Perhaps you are right."

"I'll keep an eye on him while you two rest," Larus said. "If he starts moving again, I'll be sure and wake you."

"Very well," agreed Father Thomas. Then with a helping hand from Larus, he climbed down from the boulder and walked over to a tree near Hunter where he settled down to rest. He said a short prayer for all of them, and another for Hunter whose eyes were already half closed. With yet another yawn escaping him, he leaned his head back against the tree and closed his eyes.

As his two companions slept, Larus remained atop the boulder, keeping watch on Shank.

"I made it! I'm not too late!"

He was in the city, a city with towering walls besieged by darkness. The same darkness which had haunted his steps for so long.

In the heart of the city glowed a light which gave comfort and courage. He knew that the darkness encircling the walls wanted nothing more than to extinguish that light for good. How he knew this he didn't know, he just did.

Along the streets were countless frightened people, some huddled in groups while others cowered alone against the stone walls of neighboring buildings. Then suddenly from out of the confusion appeared a man. Dressed in armor as he was, Hunter took him to be a guard. The coat of arms emblazoned upon his chest was that of five stars forming a semi-circle. Light reflecting off of them made them dazzle.

"Come on!" the guard shouted. "There isn't time." Without waiting for a reply, he turned and hurried away. Hunter followed.

It soon became clear their destination was a doorway leading to one of the defensive wall's guard towers. As the guard reached the door, he paused and turned back toward Hunter. "Hurry!" he shouted, then disappeared within.

Hunter ran after, racing through the opened doorway. Inside, he came to a stop when he found wounded fighters lying in rows of pallets upon the floor. Red-tinged bandages binding extremities, screams and cries from where surgeons worked to save lives, fear began to grow inside him. Looking to the spiral steps leading up to the ramparts above, he saw the back of the guard disappear around the first curve.

His fear grew as he raced for the steps, cries of the wounded followed him as he took the steps two at a time. Coming from further up the stairwell, he heard the guard say, "Hurry!"

Wham!

A shockwave ran through the stone and knocked him backward. Bracing his hand against the side of the stairwell, he regained his balance. Moving once again, he continued for the top.

Wham!

Again he was thrown off balance as something struck the outer wall. And again he righted himself and continued upward.

Wham! Crack!

Shards of masonry pelted him as the wall cracked from the blow, dust filled the stairwell. Undaunted, he rounded another turn in the stairwell and continued.

Wham! Crack!

A giant stone struck the tower's wall not three feet above his head, completely shearing it off. Hunter was thrown to the stone steps as stones from the destroyed tower rained down upon him. One struck his head and another crushed his ankle. When the dust cleared enough so he could see, he saw where the tower now ended in a ring of jagged masonry five feet further up.

"Give me your hand!"

The guard whom he had followed now crouched on the rampart above. Blood flowed from the guard's temple and his left arm hung limp. Reaching down his right hand, he shouted again, "Give me your hand!"

Despite the pain throbbing in his head and his crushed ankle, Hunter raised himself up just enough to reach the offered hand. A cry of pain escaped him as the guard hauled him atop the wall.

"Come on!" the guard shouted as he helped Hunter to outer edge overlooking the darkness besieging them.

Hunter's heart froze when his eyes gazed upon the miasmic, pulsating darkness below. There was no form to it, it just was. Terror beyond imagining swelled within him at the sight.

"Do you have it?"

Wham!

From out of the darkness came a dark mass which struck the wall not far from where they stood.

Mind numb with fear, Hunter didn't at first realize the guard was speaking.

"Do you have it?" the guard shouted.

From somewhere deep within him, he found the courage to voice, "What?"

"The ring!" the guard said. "Do you have the ring?"

"Ring?" he asked confused. Holding up his hands, he gazed at ten fingers, all unadorned by any form of jewelry. "No."

For a moment, the world grew still as a brief breeze seemed to come and ruffle the guard's hair ever so slightly. "Then all is lost."

Wham! Crack!

A massive concussion wave knocked Hunter backward, a scream of pain tore through him as he stepped upon his ruined ankle in an attempt to remain standing. Before him, the guard stood amidst a cloud of rising dust. Then...

Wham! Crack!

...the guard and the section of wall beneath him disappeared in a thunderous impact by another of the dark projectiles. A roaring filled the air and Hunter realized this entire section of the wall was collapsing beneath them. Falling to the stone rampart, he began scooting backward but the stones upon which he lay gave way.

Panic filled him as he fell, pain of mammoth proportions coursed through his body as falling stones crushed him. When he finally came to rest, he was pinned underneath a pile of crushing rubble. He could feel himself growing weak and knew his life would soon be over.

But then he saw the darkness, the evil, malevolent darkness which had stalked him for so long, surge through the gap in the wall. With life fading away, he listened to the screams of terror coming from all around as the darkness destroyed every living thing within the city. He saw the shining light at the heart of the city grow dim as the darkness rushed forward and attacked. Then before death finally took him, he saw the light go out.

A feral scream broke the quiet, drawing Larus' attention away from Shank and back to where Hunter and Father Thomas lay. Father Thomas was backing quickly away from Hunter who stood with his back to the priest. The madness had returned! Leaping from the boulder, he raced toward Hunter.

Drawn toward Larus' movement, Hunter turned eyes full of madness toward him. Curling his hands into claws, he growled deep within his throat and sprang forward.

Larus kicked out with his foot and caught Hunter in the side of the chest, forcing him off balance. Then before Hunter could right himself and resume the attack, Larus lashed out with his fist.

Air was quickly expelled as his fist landed a hard blow to Hunter's chest. Knocked backward, Hunter came to a sudden stop when his back smashed into a tree.

"Don't hurt him!" warned Father Thomas.

Larus ignored the priest, his attention being fully fixed on the man before him. He stood there, poised to deal Hunter another blow as he watched reason slowly return to the eyes of his friend. Then, just as his guard began to relax, the madness returned. Without uttering a sound, Hunter leaped forward only to crash to the ground when Larus' fist impacted with the side of his head.

Larus remained ready to continue the fight, but quickly realized Hunter was out cold. "It's okay Father," he said to Father Thomas.

"Oh my son," Father Thomas said as he came and knelt by Hunter's side. "What is going on inside your mind?" Soft, barely heard words issued from the priest as he began to pray.

While the priest prayed, Larus went to the horses and retrieved a length of rope with which to tie Hunter's legs and arms.

"Is that really necessary?" Father Thomas asked once he was done with his prayer.

"I'm afraid so," replied Larus. "We can't afford to take the risk of him regaining consciousness while still under the affect of the madness." After tying Hunter's hands together, he began working on his feet. "Once we're sure the madness has passed, we'll untie him."

Father Thomas didn't like the idea of treating Hunter so, but understood the necessity.

Now with his hands and feet securely tied, Larus picked up their unconscious friend and propped him up against a nearby tree. "Keep an eye on him," Larus said to Father Thomas. "I'm going to check on Shank."

Leaving the priest to minister to Hunter, Larus returned to his lookout atop the boulder. Gazing out over the water, he saw that Shank had once again resumed rowing toward shore. He hadn't made it very far from his earlier position and Larus figured he still had an hour or more before making landfall.

Hopping down from the boulder, he said, "Time to go. Shank's moving."

"What about Hunter?" Father Thomas asked.

Larus came over and picked him up. "Only one thing to do," he said. Carrying Hunter over to the horses, he laid him across the back of his horse and proceeded to tie his hands and feet together with a rope passed beneath the horse's belly. When Hunter was secure, he turned toward Father Thomas. "We'll untie him when he regains his mind."

Father Thomas nodded. "Let us pray that he does," he said as he mounted.

Larus led Hunter's horse while Father Thomas brought up the rear. By the time the mouth of the river came into view, Hunter still hadn't regained consciousness.

Chapter 21

Hidden within the trees, Larus watched as Shank rowed closer to shore. It was soon clear he meant to make landfall east of the river's mouth. Silently they watched as he reached the shore. There, he pulled his boat out of the water and dragged it across the shore to the trees where he secured it.

Shank paused only a moment as he glanced around, almost as if he sensed being secretly observed. Then he removed his pack from out of the boat and slung it over his shoulder. Peeking out from under the flap was the cloth bag he used to hold his weed. Next, he took the brazier from off the bench and brought it close to his face.

From his position, Larus could see the brazier no longer emitted the noxious fume of burning weed.

A barely heard stream of expletives issued forth from Shank as he turned and began following the river up into the mountains. Larus waited only long enough for Shank to disappear into the trees before returning for the others. Father Thomas waited half a mile back with the unconscious Hunter. When he rejoined them, he discovered Hunter had regained consciousness.

"I tell you I'm fine," Hunter was saying to Father Thomas in a reassuring tone as Larus appeared. Still bound hand and foot, he was propped against the bole of a tree glaring at the priest.

Father Thomas for his part stood back and said nothing.

"He's telling you that he is okay," Larus told the priest as he emerged from the trees.

Turning at his voice, Father Thomas nodded. "I thought as much," he responded. "But I thought it wise to wait until your return."

"Understandable," agreed Larus.

"It happened again didn't it?" asked Hunter. There was a haunted look in his eyes.

"If you mean you trying to attack us," clarified Larus, "yes it did." Coming to Hunter's side, he grabbed his head and looked deep into his eyes. They appeared clear and rational.

"Well, I'm over it now," stated Hunter. "Untie me, okay?"

Larus nodded and started removing his bonds. "Shank has landed and is heading upriver," he announced.

When he was free of the rope binding him, Hunter rubbed his wrists and said, "Thanks."

Shrugging, Larus replied, "Stop trying to attack us and this won't be necessary."

"I don't even know I'm doing it," he explained. "I can't even remember that I did."

"I know," Larus assured him. "I just wish we knew how to stop it."

"Don't let me go to sleep," joked Hunter with a grin.

"Maybe we'll try that," Larus said in return. "Now, let's mount up and find a place to ford the river before we lose Shank."

"You know," Father Thomas said as they got underway, "I took a look at those weeds you removed from his hut while you were gone."

"Oh?" asked Larus.

"I think they may be from a plant known as theshil," he said. "If so, it is very rare. I do not know much about it, but I do know that a powder made from its leaves is used during certain rites at the Temple." A moment went by before he added, "Rites for the dead."

"Wonderful," replied Hunter when Larus gave him the translation. "I hope he's not going to say rites to bring back the dead or anything like that."

When Larus translated Hunter's comments, Father Thomas shook his head. "Nothing like that, no," he explained. "The Temple is very much against all things to do with necromancy. It is traditionally burnt during funerals, if the family could afford it that is, it is very expensive."

"So it does have something to do with the dead," Hunter mumbled to himself. Visions of zombie movies started flashing through his mind. Will there be someone saying, *'They're coming to get you Hunter?'* Hunter chuckled at his active imagination and shook his head.

Once they were mounted, Larus retraced his steps back through the trees. "There's the river," he announced quietly when it came into view.

Up ahead, the water flowed from out of the mountains and into the lake. Trees were thick on either bank with no discernible trail to be found. "Can we cross here?" asked Father Thomas.

Larus rode to the water's edge and gauged their chance. "Maybe," he said. "Let me see." Nudging his horse forward, he began entering the current.

"Wouldn't it be better to try a little further upriver?" questioned Hunter. "You would think it would be shallower the further up you go."

"True," replied Larus. "However, we would run the risk of losing Shank if he should leave the river's edge."

Hunter could see the logic and remained silent while Larus worked to ford the river.

Larus kept his horse at a slow pace while he scanned the riverbed as best he could for a viable route. Weaving in a zigzag pattern, he eventually reached the middle of the river. By this time the lower half of his horse was completely submerged and the current made it difficult for it to keep its balance.

"Easy boy," Larus said soothingly as he nudged his horse into motion once again. This was the trickiest part, crossing the center where the water flowed deepest. If he could make it several more feet, he would be home free. Step by step, the horse worked its way through the strong current.

Once it had moved far enough so that its belly was no longer under water, Larus turned back to the other two. "I think you can make it," he said. "Just follow the way I went and take it slow and easy."

"Right," agreed Father Thomas. Then to Hunter he gestured to the river and said, "After you."

Hunter didn't need Larus to translate, he knew Father Thomas wished him to go first. Nodding to the priest, he said, "Okay," and headed for the water. His horse balked only a short moment before entering, but then settled down and began to cross. He tried to keep as much to the route he remembered Larus taking, and eventually made it to the other side. After he was out of the dangerous part of the river, Father Thomas started across.

When he was sure Hunter would no longer be in danger, Larus rode further into the trees where Shank had disappeared. He could clearly see part of an impression of a foot in the edge of a mud puddle. Scanning the ground further in, he found another.

"Any sign of him?" asked Hunter when he came to join him.

Larus nodded. "A couple tracks," he said. The forest before him was wild and thick. He hoped further signs of Shank's passing would continue to be forthcoming.

Father Thomas was soon across the river and they set out after Shank. "Keep your eyes open." said Larus. "Until we know exactly where Shank is, it might be best to remain quiet. We wouldn't want to alert him that he's being followed." The other two nodded their agreement and kept silent.

As they left the lake shore and headed into the untamed forest, Larus rode point. He kept a slow pace as he scanned the ground for footprints and other signs of Shank's passing. It was clear by the total disregard Shank had for leaving a trail that he did not suspect they were following.

Shank's trail continued to stay within sight of the river and was easy to follow. Larus kept the pace slow but steady so as not to catch him too quickly. As long as the trail was clearly visible before them, caution would mandate their actions. Though once the shadows grew long with the drawing close of the day, Larus grew worried about the possibility of losing their quarry once night had fallen. With any luck, Shank would stop and make camp. But the trail continued on even when the sun dipped below the horizon and the first star made its appearance in the heavens above.

By this time, the river had climbed its way up through the foothills bordering the lake and passed into the mountains. Peaks of moderate size rose about them while others further away towered even higher into the sky. In the last vestiges of light, they saw where the river emerged from a high walled gorge. Larus grinned as he turned back to the others. Pointing to the gorge, he said, "We'll not lose him now." Quickening their pace, he hurried toward the gorge. The trees began to thin as they reached the mouth of the gorge and the view of the slopes rising away from the river grew clearer.

"Larus!" Hunter whispered urgently.

When he turned around to see what Hunter wanted, he saw him looking at the slope some distance above them. Moving his gaze upward, he saw a lone figure some hundred feet above. From the direction Shank was heading, it appeared he was not making for the gorge. Rather, he was heading for a 'v' formed between the eastern wall of the gorge and the slope of another rising mountainside.

"How did he get up there?" Larus asked. In the dim light of dusk, he looked back down the slope Shank was upon, in the direction from which they had just come. He saw where the slope between the river and the trail upon which Shank strode grew less steep and may afford them a way to follow. "This way," he said. Moving quickly, he led them back to try and reach the trail Shank was following. To his surprise, they came across a somewhat level path leading up the side of the mountain. In the faint light still illuminating the world, a footprint was barely visible. With a grin, Larus turned onto it and moved to follow.

The light faded rapidly and soon, all they had left with which to see was that coming from the stars. They knew Shank was ahead, but not how far. Larus kept them to a pace slightly faster than a man could walk in an attempt to close the distance.

As they made their way along the path, Larus began to realize that what they were on may be the remains of an ancient road. Though it followed the twists and turns of the mountainside as it rose, the path retained a somewhat uniform width as it climbed toward the 'v'. Its surface was smoother than what one would expect of a naturally occurring path.

Through the deepening dark, they followed after Bellion Shank. When they reached the 'v', all that was visible were the silhouettes of the mountains against the backdrop of stars. Larus had them pause a moment as he listened for signs indicating the presence of Shank. After a minute of fruitless searching, he nudged his horse into motion and passed through the 'v'.

For some time after that, they were in almost absolute darkness as they followed the path. At least, Larus hoped they were following the path. All they could be sure of was that they were making their way through a depression between one mountainside on their right, and a steeply sloping hill on their left.

"Think this old road could lead us to the temple?" Hunter asked quietly.

Unseen in the dark, Larus nodded. "I was thinking the same thing," he replied.

They followed the depression as it wound its way through the mountains for over an hour before the moon finally made its appearance. With its added light, Larus was able to determine that they were still upon the ancient road which had taken them initially through the 'v'.

"Larus," said Father Thomas, "it might be wise for us to wait until morning before continuing. The sky is clear and any tracks will still be there when the sun rises."

His first inclination was to argue the point and insist upon continuing. The pressing need for urgency still was very much a presence within him. But then logic took over and he realized that none of them had had much sleep in over twenty four hours. Also that Father Thomas was right, Shank's tracks would still be there in the morning.

"What if he moves off this road?" questioned Father Thomas. "In our hurry, we would miss that."

Larus brought his horse to a stop. "Very well," he said. "We'll make camp right here." After dismounting, he added, "But no fire."

"Man," argued Hunter, "It's going to be freezing by morning." Already, the wind whipping along the depression had grown quite cool.

"Then I would suggest you pull your blanket close about you," replied Larus. "No fire!"

"Okay," agreed a less than happy Hunter.

Leaving the horses saddled, they tied their reins to a nearby tree then settled in to get as comfortable as possible. Hunter took Larus' advice and pulled his blanket tightly around him, though it didn't seem to be all that affective in warding off the cold. Tired as he was though, he fell asleep right away. In fact, he slept the sleep of the dead until a hand gave his shoulder a little shake and an intruding voice said, "Hunter."

When he didn't at first respond, the hand shook a little harder. "Wake up Hunter," the voice said. "It's morning."

Cracking open an eye, he saw Larus crouched next to him with Father Thomas standing several feet back wearing an anxious look. Though the world was already growing light, he did not want to get up so tired was he.

"We're wasting daylight," admonished Larus. "Get up."

As Hunter groaned at having to get up when his body cried out for more sleep, he heard Larus say to Father Thomas, "He's alright."

"Of course I'm alright," Hunter said. Sitting up, he gave out with a loud yawn and wiped his eyes. "Man, didn't we just go to sleep?"

Larus gave him an amused grin. "Actually, it's been six hours since we stopped," he replied.

"Six hours? Feels more like six minutes." After getting to his feet, he was handed several strips of dried beef from Father Thomas. "Thanks," he said as he took them and ripped a portion off with his teeth.

"Get mounted and let's get going," Larus said. "Found one of Shank's footprints further up the road, so we didn't lose him in the dark."

"Wait a second," Hunter told him. "I gotta go." Moving off a ways to behind one of the larger trees in the area, he went about his morning business. While standing there his eyes roved across the ground, not really looking at anything until he noticed something protruding from the ground several feet away. It protruded four inches out of the ground, was round, and about the size of his hand.

"Hey!" he hollered to the others as he quickly brought his business to a close. Crossing over to the protrusion, he reached down, grasped, and pulled.

"What is it?" Larus asked, interest piqued.

It took some effort, but when the ground finally gave way and what he had hold of broke free, he discovered it had been the bottom end of an urn. "Doesn't this look like..." he began then trailed off as he glanced toward the other two.

"Yes it does," agreed Larus. "The patterns are the same as those found on the smashed shards of the urns near where we found you."

The urn was more or less intact with only a small part of the lip missing. Other cracks could be seen marring its surface, but over all, it was whole.

"We are close," said Father Thomas.

Hunter didn't understand what he said, but nodded for the tone he used spoke volumes. Raising the urn over his head, he proceeded to smash it on the ground. When it hit, it shattered and revealed that it had been packed with dirt.

"What did you do that for?" Larus asked, perturbed.

"Didn't you say the crystal spider I found might have been secreted within one of the urns in the Grotto?" Hunter said.

"That was one theory, yes," he agreed.

"Okay then," Hunter stated. "Then maybe there is something in this one too." Crouching down over the shards, he grabbed a small stick from off the ground and began poking through the chunks of dirt. After breaking all the clods of dirt into much smaller pieces, he finally had to admit there was nothing to be found.

"Oh well," he said. Standing up, he turned and found Larus staring at him. "You never know."

Once he was mounted, they left the site of the smashed urn and resumed their pursuit of Bellion Shank. The ancient road along which Shank's tracks followed extended in a fairly straight manner for half a mile before reaching a point where the hill to their left abruptly fell away to reveal the gorge with the river far below. Gauging from the depth of the gorge, they must be well over five hundred feet from the bottom.

At that point, the ancient road curved to follow the lip of the gorge. For the most part, it remained ten to twenty feet from the edge. Though at times, years of erosion had brought the distance down to less than a foot. And still, Shank's footprints continued on.

"I don't think he stopped during the night," commented Larus. Now two hours after heading out this morning, they hadn't come across any sign of Shank making camp.

"His need for the weed must be strong," suggested Father Thomas.

"Perhaps," agreed Larus.

"Is this weed a narcotic of some kind?" asked Hunter.

After receiving the translation, Father Thomas shook his head. "Not that I ever heard," he replied.

"There must be some reason that he needs it," Hunter continued. "From the way he acts, I'd say he was hooked."

Father Thomas shrugged. "It could be," he agreed. "I have never heard of anyone inhaling the smoke of the theshil leaf for any length of time. I suppose doing such could create a need for the continued inhalation."

"One thing is for sure," Hunter said. "We'll know when Shank has reached wherever he gets the weed." When Larus glanced over to him, he added, "'Cause we'll be able to smell it."

Larus nodded. "Good point," he agreed.

The ancient road continued making its way along the lip of the gorge throughout the morning hours. At times the eroding of the gorge's rim would encroach very close, only to back away again further on. In one place the eroding had advanced to such an extent that over half the ancient road had fallen into the gorge. Fortunately, the mountainside to their left had a gentle upward slope and they were able to bypass it easily.

As the road climbed higher, so too did the way grow narrower. The mountainside to their left continued growing closer and steeper until the right side of the road abutted a now steeply inclined slope. And with the effects of erosion to their left, the way at times grew very narrow indeed.

It was sometime after noon when Larus brought them to a sudden halt. "I think we found Shank," he announced.

"Where?" questioned Father Thomas.

Pointing to a point some hundred feet ahead where the road curved around an outcropping of rock, he indicated a dark form lying unmoving upon the ground.

"Is he dead?" asked Father Thomas.

"Could be he's sleeping," suggested Hunter.

"That was my thought too," Larus agreed. "If he's dead, there is nothing we can do for him. If he's asleep, we don't want to let him know we are here."

Looking at the still form, Father Thomas couldn't help but think the man may be injured. "He may be hurt," he said. "We should go and find out."

Larus gazed at the form lying on the road and shook his head. "I don't think he's just hurt," he explained. "A hurt man would hardly be lying motionless." Then he turned his attention to the sun overhead. "Still have quite a bit of time before dark," he said. "Let's move back down the road as far as we can and still keep him in sight. If after two hours he hasn't moved, we will go see if he's dead."

Father Thomas being the priest that he was, wanted to immediately go and see if Shank needed help. But their mission for the Lady took precedence over everything else. And staring at the still form, he had to admit the logic in what Larus had said. So they moved back down the ancient road until Shank's form was an all but indistinct dark blob. Then, they waited.

During the next two hours, horses were fed and watered. After which, food was passed around while Hunter and Father Thomas relaxed against the hillside. Larus on the other hand, kept constant vigil as his gaze never once left the immobile form of Shank. When finally the two hours were up and Shank still had not moved, the consensus was that he was dead.

"Let's go," Larus said as he swung up into the saddle. Once the other two were mounted, they rode quickly along the ancient road until reaching Shank.

From where he trailed behind Father Thomas, Hunter hollered, "Is he dead?"

Looking down on the face of the weed burning, once priest of Casdralla, Larus knew the answer immediately. "Yes," he replied. "He's dead."

The brazier with which Shank burnt his weed was clutched tightly to his chest, his arms wrapped around it almost protectively. His lifeless eyes were open, mouth slightly agape as if he was speaking at the moment of death.

"Wonder what happened?" asked Hunter. A shiver went through him when he came and looked upon the dead man. Something about Shank's expression unnerved him.

Larus glanced back to Hunter and said, "Good question. It doesn't look as if he was attacked by an animal, and I doubt if he died from the elements. It just wasn't that cold last night."

"Then what killed him?" asked Hunter once again.

Larus kept quiet as he continued to inspect the dead man. "I suppose it's possible he could have had a heart attack or something," he finally said. "But that seems unlikely." Standing, up, he turned to Father Thomas. "What do you think?"

"I have ministered many people in their last hours," he said softly. "But never have I seen anyone pass from this world with an expression on their face matching his. The way the skin around his mouth and eyes is set makes it appear that he died rather unpleasantly." Bending over Shank, he moved his hand closer to the dead man and pointed to the eyes. "See how the lids are raised above the pupil showing some of the white?" When Larus affirmed the observation, he added, "That would seem to indicate he was surprised, or frightened just prior to dying. I could be wrong though."

When Larus communicated Father Thomas' observation to him, he asked, "But wouldn't the eyelids have relaxed in death?"

"One would think so," replied the priest.

"Now what?" asked Hunter. "If he did know the location of the Or'tux temple, he can't tell us now."

Gazing to the surface of the ancient road, Larus saw Shank's tracks leading to the point where they found him, then stopped. "All we can do is continue along the way he was heading and hope for the best."

"But first," interjected Father Thomas, "we need to give this man a proper burial." He looked to Larus expecting an argument about wasting time and was surprised to find him nodding.

"There was a widening of the road some ways back that would work," he said.

They wrapped Shank tightly in his cloak and when Larus lifted him from the ground, the brazier came loose of Shank's grip and clattered to the ground. "Bring it," Larus said to Hunter.

Hunter nodded and picked it up.

It took a few minutes to return to the widening of the road. There they found the ground to be almost solid rock with just a light coating of dirt. "We shall have to build a cairn," said Father Thomas.

It took almost an hour before sufficient rocks could be gathered to completely cover Shank. Father Thomas said a brief prayer, beseeching Casdralla to have mercy on Shank and to aid him in his journey to the afterlife.

Throughout the gathering of the cairn, Hunter couldn't shake the cold feeling that had settled over him. He hadn't forgotten what others had said about this place, that it was cursed. He wondered if Bellion Shank had been struck down by whatever cursed this place. If so, was the same fate to be theirs? Shivering, and not completely due to the kiss of the wind, he was quite thankful when Father Thomas concluded the ceremony and they got underway. But strangely enough, leaving Shank's cairn and heading further along the ancient road did little to quell his unease. If anything, it only grew worse.

Chapter 22

Not long after leaving Shank's cairn, they came to where a thin column stone rose against the side of the cliff to their right. Across the ancient road from the column were the remains of another, a jagged base rising no more than two inches from the base of the roadway.

Larus brought them to a halt just before reaching the columns. "From the time of the Or'tux would you think?" he asked Father Thomas.

"Most likely," Father Thomas replied with a nod. Moving closer to the intact one on the right, he gave it a brief examination which revealed little. The column bore no markings or designs, just a smooth, weatherworn surface.

"Should be close then," observed Hunter.

Larus shrugged, "Perhaps. Keep your eyes open." Moving forward, he passed through the space between the column and its broken counterpart.

Hunter gazed at the column as he passed, his unease growing. "We should hurry," he urged after reaching the other side. Glancing to where the sun sat not far above the peaks to the west he said, "I wouldn't want to be caught on this trail after nightfall."

Nodding, Larus increased their speed until they were moving at fast canter.

After the columns disappeared behind them, they came across another, this time standing a lonely vigil beside the road. Whether or not there had been another standing on the left side would forever remain a mystery. Erosion had pushed the lip of the gorge back, removing a good third of the ancient road. As they passed, they saw this column was an exact duplicate of the previous pair.

Twice more they encountered the columns, the only completely intact pair being the last. After which, the columns no longer made an appearance though the road continued on its rise from the river below. Glancing over the side, Hunter saw how far it was to the bottom. Shivering, he kept his horse as far from the lip as he was able.

In his mind he could still see Shank's lifeless face. His imagination came up with all sorts of explanations for the man's untimely death, none of which did anything to quell his unease. In the back of his mind was the knowledge people considered this place cursed.

So spooked did he become that even the wind rustling the scant vegetation bordering the road created an eerie cacophony that increased his anxiety. And as the shadows lengthened, his nervousness rose. At one point, when a loose branch fell from high above and landed on the road not two feet away, he actually cried out.

"Relax," Larus told him. "There's nothing to worry about."

Hunter flashed him an uneasy grin and nodded. "Yeah," he said. "Okay." But still, the uneasiness was a constant companion. *Cursed. Cursed.* The word kept returning despite his efforts to banish it. First would come Shank's lifeless face. Then...*Cursed!*

A glance to the western peaks revealed the sun was beginning to disappear from sight. The realization they were not going to get off this cliff before it grew dark sent a shiver of fear coursing through him.

Hunter wasn't the only one feeling ill at ease. Father Thomas too had felt a growing sense of foreboding develop over the last couple hours. Prayer did little to dispel it, bringing only a momentary comfort which was soon gone.

Ahead, the ancient road continued onward, disappearing around a bend as it followed the natural contours of the cliff. Larus, sensing the unease his two fellows were feeling, picked up the speed even further. It's difficult to ruminate on unknown fears when you are galloping along a narrow road adjacent to a deadly drop. Your whole attention must be focused on the task at hand or you risk a misstep.

Moving along now at almost a gallop, he rounded the bend and saw the road continue for another two hundred feet before disappearing from sight once more. A quick glance back showed Father Thomas and Hunter leaned over the necks of their horses bearing looks of intense concentration. Smiling to himself, he returned his gaze to the fore.

As he reached the next bend, the last rays of sunlight faded as the sun sank behind the western peaks. He rounded the bend at a gallop then quickly came to a stop. For on the other side of the bend the road came to an abrupt stop not fifty feet away.

They had found the temple of the Or'tux.

A small plateau of sorts, ringed by the tall, sheer walls of the mountainside, extended away from the edge of the gorge. Not far from where Larus had stopped, a twenty foot wide chasm completely divided the plateau in two. On the other side was what had to be the entrance to the Or'tux temple.

The mountainside which made up the face of the temple had been formed in such a way that the eyes had a hard time making out what they were seeing. Strange angles and protrusions gave it a surreal feel. A single arched opening tall enough for a giant, which could comfortably see two wagons pass through side by side, was the only access. The temple face was completely devoid of windows or other openings one would expect to find. The only way in was through the arched opening.

Larus quickly took in the temple as Father Thomas and Hunter caught up with him. "We made it," breathed Hunter when he reached Larus' side.

"Not yet," said Larus as he glanced sidelong toward him. "There's no way across." Indeed, where the road met the chasm sat the remains of a bridge that once would have connected with the other side. Two posts and the jagged edge of a stone walkway that jutted out half a foot was all that was left. A similar remnant was to be found on the opposite side with a gap far too wide to jump in between. At some time in the past, the middle section had collapsed.

Moving to the edge, they looked down to find the chasm disappearing into darkness below. During the infrequent moments in which the wind calmed, they could hear the sound of water crashing on rocks far below.

"Care to jump across?" Hunter quipped.

Larus gauged the distance for a moment then said, "Might make it."

"You're kidding!" exclaimed Hunter.

"No," replied Larus in all sincerity. "But the point is moot. You and Father Thomas could never make the distance and I'm not about to leave you two out here alone."

"So what do we do?" Hunter asked. His gaze kept returning to the façade of the temple and the dark maw of the entrance. Whenever his gaze passed over the dark opening, a shiver ran through him.

"Shank was heading in this direction," stated Larus. "And the fact that we didn't pass any patches of his weeds, would seem to suggest the temple was his destination. Somehow, he was going to get across." Glancing to Larus and then to Father Thomas, he added, "The light won't be completely gone for an hour. Let's use that time and search for another way over. Shank could have a rope bridge or something similar hidden around here."

As he and Father Thomas started moving about the plateau, Hunter stood staring at the opening. Something…

"Hunter!" Larus hollered, drawing his attention away from the opening. "We don't have time to just stand around."

"Right," he replied. Then with another quick glance to the temple's entrance, joined in the search.

From one side of the plateau, which fortunately wasn't all that big, to the other, they sought the means with which Shank planned on reaching the far side of the chasm. From what Mayor Tom said, Shank had been on trips to gather his weed many times. Therefore, it stood to reason that there must be some way to reach the far side. For there certainly hadn't been any other way to go from the ancient road other than scaling the cliff to the heights above, or dropping down into the gorge.

However, to their dismay they failed to find any indication of how Shank had performed such a feat. By the time they had searched the entire plateau, it was twilight. "We'll have to resume our search in the morning," announced Larus.

When Hunter saw Larus begin removing packs from his horse, he said, "We shouldn't stay here." A trace of fear was in his voice as his eyes returned once more to the now barely seen arched opening.

Larus lifted an eyebrow questioningly, glanced briefly toward the temple, then turned his gaze toward Father Thomas. "What do you think?" he asked.

"There may be some wisdom in not remaining so close to a place where evil rituals were performed," he said. "I too feel ill at ease in the shadow of this place."

Glancing between his two comrades, Larus nodded. "Alright then. Gather what wood we can and we'll head back down around the bend. The lee there should provide some shelter from the worst of the wind."

"Good," Hunter quickly agreed, turning his back to the temple. Bending over, he picked up a fallen branch and then moved to gather another.

Larus replaced his packs behind his saddle then gathered wood too. There wasn't much, the plateau being mainly barren stone. What there was had fallen from trees growing along the heights above.

Once every piece larger than a twig had been gathered, they carried their scavenged bounty back down the road and around the bend. When the temple could no longer be seen, they made camp and soon had the beginnings of a fire going.

Hunter's uneasiness subsided in the glow and warmth of the fire. The normalcy of the crackling and snapping as the wood was consumed did much to alleviate his feelings of dread.

"Any ideas on how we're going to reach the other side of the chasm?" Hunter asked.

"Not right now," admitted Larus. "In the morning we'll discover a way."

"Then what?" When Larus glanced toward him, he said, "We still don't know what we're here for."

Larus translated for Father Thomas who replied, "The spider you found in the Grotto is important somehow. Once we have reached the temple, then we will need to search for why it is important. You were not given it for nothing."

"How can you be so certain?" argued Hunter. "Maybe I just picked it up in passing? After all, I have no recollection of what transpired within the Grotto. Not until you two found me that is."

Father Thomas was quiet for a few moments before replying. "You are our Lady's champion, her chosen one as it were," he began. "You would not have been brought here to our world and allowed to stumble along blindly. That is why you were given into my care, and why Larus travels with us too. He and I are here to interpret the signs, guide you along the way. And we both agree that the fact you were found in possession of the spider means we need to find a way inside this temple." He glanced to Larus who was translating and received a nod in agreement.

"Alright," Hunter said. "We need to get into the temple. But why?"

Grinning, Larus shrugged. "Haven't a clue. My guess would be that we'll learn once we get in there. Such is the way with these things." He knew Hunter wasn't satisfied with his and Father Thomas' explanation. But there wasn't anything else for them to go on. How could be possibly explain to him that this was exactly how mortals were directed by Qyaendri in doing their god's work. Signs, portents, uncommon happenstances, and other incongruous means were the methods by which they guided those working on behalf of their god. Those such as Hunter, and by association, himself and Father Thomas.

"You should try and sleep," Larus told Hunter. "Tomorrow may be a long day."

"Very well," agreed Hunter. Though how he was going to fall asleep exposed to the chilling wind as he was he didn't know. He moved over to where the road met the cliff face and wrapped his blanket tight around him. Still close enough to feel the warmth of the fire, he laid down and tried to get comfortable.

The part of his body closest to the fire remained comfortable while the other half froze. It seemed as if the protection Larus had expected did little to shield them. The wind continuously cut right through the blanket, sapping the warmth from him. And if that wasn't bad enough, the surface of the road he lay upon sucked what little warmth the wind left him. Miserable, he tossed and turned for quite a while before finally managing to doze off.

"Larus isn't getting it is he?" asked Ftheril.

He and another low ranking Qyaendri were in attendance on the ancient road where the three mortals sought the comfort of fire and blankets.

"No," agreed Aell. Like Ftheril, he too was one of the Qyaendri beneath Daeson who worked closely with mortals. "Are we going to implant another dream?"

Ftheril shook his head. "No," he replied. "We don't dare." Mortals tended to react negatively when their dreams were altered. One alteration here or there wouldn't affect them very much. But ever since his arrival at the High Temple, Hunter had been bombarded with visions almost nightly and his mind wasn't taking it very well.

Each mortal reacted differently to a Qyaendri's incursion into their subconscious, though always negatively. After the first couple incursions, Hunter had grown violent until they backed off and gave his mind a chance to stabilize. Ftheril was the one charged with implanting the visions, and he knew that Hunter's mind was close to the breaking point. He had to allow him time to repair the imbalance caused by the incursions. In the past, there had been Qyaendri who pushed too hard and caused a total collapse in the subject's mind, some to the point where sanity never returned.

Ftheril wasn't going to allow that to happen. There was still one vision that must be implanted, and Hunter's mind had to have a couple more days to heal before the attempt was made. If only Larus would have caught on by now, the last couple of visions would not have been necessary.

"What do you plan to do?" Aell asked.

There were other ways to influence mortals. Turning his eyes to the horses, a plan began to form.

"Can't sleep?" Larus asked. Father Thomas was sitting up and looking in his general direction.

"No," he said, shaking his head. A glance over to Hunter revealed he was still sleeping by the fire. Coming to his feet quietly, he wrapped his blanket tightly about him and walked over to where Larus stood gazing out over the moonlit landscape of the gorge.

They stood quietly together for several minutes, the only sound disturbing the stillness was the crackle and pop of their fire. Breaking the silence, Father Thomas said, "We have not done the Ritual of Dedication as yet."

"What?" asked Larus.

"When we first met, you mentioned wishing to dedicate yourself to Casdralla," explained Father Thomas. "Do you still wish to so dedicate yourself?"

Larus turned his gaze from the darkness and glanced toward the priest. "It might be best to wait until this is all over," he replied. In truth, he didn't believe it would be all that necessary any longer, especially after the revelations unearthed in the High Temple.

"I understand," Father Thomas said. "Often during moments of hardship, a man wishes to become closer with something greater than himself. Then once those times are past, feels the need less."

"It's not like that," Larus assured him. "Nothing is more important to me than the Lady." When Father Thomas remained silent, he glanced over toward him and saw a knowing look in his eyes. Just what the priest was 'knowing' wasn't clear, though he had a pretty good idea. If Father Thomas suspected he was a Qyaendri in human guise, he failed to voice the question, much to Larus' relief.

Then from the part of the ancient road where the horses were positioned, they heard one of the horses snort, then another.

"I better go check on them," Larus said. "Might be one of the local predators looking for a meal. Stay here and keep an eye on Hunter."

Father Thomas nodded before returning to the fireside.

The horses were huddled together not far up the trail just within the outer fringe of the campfire's glow. Larus could see all three were gazing down the trail in the direction of the Or'tux temple. Whatever was spooking them was coming from up there. "What is it boy?" he asked, coming up alongside his mount.

Laying a hand on his horse's neck, he could feel the beast trembling. "It's okay," he said soothingly. Patting him on the neck twice, he moved away from the horse and headed up the trail.

He went several yards into the dark before coming to a stop. Search as he may, he couldn't see the source of what was upsetting the horses. Then from behind, came the sound of terrified neighing. Pivoting fast, he saw one of the horses rearing on its hind legs. Eyes rolling white in terror, the horse let out another screech of terror, the other two reared up as well.

As one, the three horses turned and bolted toward the camp. "Watch out!" Larus shouted an instant before they tore through the camp.

Father Thomas barely jumped out of the way and tripped over Hunter. Stumbling, he heard Hunter shout what had to have been an obscenity as he regained his balance. "What is it?" he shouted to Larus.

"I don't know," Larus shouted back. Remaining where he was, he kept his back to the campfire and stared into the darkness. "I'll check it out. You and Hunter get the horses." A brief glance behind showed the horses had already passed beyond the campfire's light. "You better hurry before their terror makes them run off the side of the cliff."

"Right," Father Thomas agreed.

"Hunter," Larus shouted. "Go with the Father and get the horses."

"What happened?" Hunter asked, now fully awake.

"Something spooked them," Larus replied. Turning back to the darkness, he held his sword at the ready then proceeded to walk up the trail.

"Hunter!" shouted Father Thomas. Hurrying after the horses, he glanced back to see Hunter still standing by the fire staring up the trail to where Larus had disappeared into the night.

"Coming!" Hunter hollered as he turned and followed.

Father Thomas found the first horse not far down the ancient road. The beast was trembling but at least was remaining motionless. From further down, he heard another neighing. Sending a prayer up to the goddess, he left the horse where it was and hurried after the other two.

Surprisingly, Hunter caught up with him fairly quickly. Unable to communicate, they ran quietly after the horses.

"Ahhhh!" exclaimed Hunter as his foot snagged an exposed root and tripped, hitting the ground hard.

Coming to a stop at Hunter's cry, he glanced back and asked, "Are you alright my son?"

"I tripped on a root," replied Hunter though he knew Father Thomas wouldn't be able to understand him. That was when he realized he was but a foot from the edge of the cliff. Breathing a sigh of relief, he started climbing to his feet when the ground gave way beneath him. Screaming, he flailed about in an attempt to stop his fall when his hand brushed against something firm. Out of sheer reflex, he grasped at it.

His fall was abruptly stopped when the root he grasped grew taut. Eyes closed, knuckles white from the force of his grip, he dangled against the side of the cliff.

"Hunter!" Father Thomas shouted.

From somewhere just above him, he heard Father Thomas call his name. Opening his eyes, he glanced up and saw Father Thomas' silhouette against the backdrop of stars. "Here," he said.

"Are you okay?" asked the priest.

Hunter didn't know what the priest was saying, but at least he was comforted by the knowledge help was just a few feet away.

"Can you reach my hand?" Father Thomas asked. Lying supine upon the ground, he reached his hand downward.

Hunter could tell by the way Father Thomas was positioned that he was trying to reach him. For a moment, panic held reign and he was unable to let go of the root, both hands clinched tightly in terror.

"You can do it my son," came the soothing voice of Father Thomas.

Another moment of indecision, then his right hand let go of the root and reached upward. In the darkness, he couldn't tell where Father Thomas' hand was and started waving his back and forth in an attempt to find it. When at last their fingertips brushed against each other he was filled with a great sense of relief.

Father Thomas stretched further to take Hunter's hand. Just as their hands began coming together, he felt the root to which Hunter grasped, shift beneath him.

A primal scream of terror filled the gorge as the root broke free. Hunter was still screaming when realization sank in that the root had grown taut once more, stopping his fall several feet further down the cliff face.

"Hunter?" Father Thomas asked fearfully. A moment went by and there was only silence. "Hunter?" he asked again.

"Still here," he replied, terror very much present in his voice. Both hands were again clinched tightly around the root and his eyes were shut. "I'll never reach you now. Go get Larus."

"Larus, right!" he hollered.

The sound of Father Thomas leaving the edge of the cliff and rushing back toward their camp gradually faded away until Hunter was alone, hanging in silence. He could feel the side of the cliff and for a fleeting moment thought about trying to find a handhold. But he was much too scared to make the attempt as visions of the root completely breaking free and plummet to his death continued coursing through his mind.

When the sound of returning footsteps began to be heard, he opened his eyes and saw a light coming toward him from down the road. Larus held a torch as he ran alongside Father Thomas. For some reason, the feeling that he had done this before came over him. Glancing to the darkness above the lip of the gorge, he watched as the light rapidly came toward him.

"Hunter!" Larus shouted. Scanning the edge of the cliff as he approached, he finally saw where the tautly stretched root emerged from the middle of the ancient road and went over the side. Coming to the edge, he held out his torch and looked over. Below he saw Hunter dangling above a sheer drop that disappeared into darkness.

"Kind of in a pickle aren't you?" he asked with a grin.

"Do something!" shouted Hunter.

Handing his torch to Father Thomas, Larus bent down and took hold of the root. "I'm going to pull you up," he announced. "Ready?"

"What a dumb question," retorted Hunter. "Of course I'm ready!"

"Okay," Larus told him as he positioned himself for best leverage. "Here we go." Ever so gently he began pulling up the root, making sure to keep a steady tension on the root to minimize the possibility of breakage.

Father Thomas stood next to him where he gazed over the side and kept track of Hunter's progress. "Halfway," he said after a minute. Then when Hunter was only a foot from the top, he knelt down and extended his free hand down. "Take my hand," he said.

Looking up at the sound of his voice, Hunter saw the extended hand and reached up to take it.

As soon as he had a firm grip on Hunter's hand, Father Thomas added his strength to the endeavor. With a final heave, the upper half of Hunter's torso crested the lip. Larus quickly grabbed his jacket with one hand and hauled him the rest of the way over the edge.

"Thanks!" exclaimed Hunter as he turned and lay on his back. Arms sore and trembling from having gripped the root for so long and so tightly, he just laid there.

"Are you okay?" Larus asked. When Hunter nodded, he said, "You stay here with Father Thomas while I round up the horses."

"No problem," Hunter replied.

Father Thomas held the torch out to Larus who shook his head. "You keep it," he told the priest. "I'll be back soon."

As Larus moved off down the ancient road in search of the remaining two horses, Father Thomas wedged the torch in between two stones. "Praise the Lady you are safe," he said to Hunter despite knowing his words would not be understood. Hunter glanced at him and nodded then laid back and closed his eyes, which for some reason caused Father Thomas to smile.

It took more than a few minutes for Hunter's pulse rate to quiet down. First he closed his eyes and thought about how close the end had come. Then he realized focusing on his near death experience wasn't helping much in relaxing him, so he tried to quiet his mind and think about nothing.

So well did he succeed in thinking about nothing, that he was surprised to be startled awake by the snorting of a horse. Larus had returned with the two frightened steeds.

"They were down quite a ways," he told them. "Fortunately neither one had gone over the edge in their panic."

"I am sure the Lady kept them safe," stated Father Thomas. "She watches out for her people."

"Are the horses her people?" Hunter asked when Larus gave him the translation.

"I think the Father was talking about us," explained Larus. "That She made sure we would not be stranded high in these mountains without transport."

"Oh," replied Hunter. Nerves once again under control, he came to his feet and took charge of one of the horses as they began returning up the ancient road to their camp. He didn't take more than a couple steps before catching a momentary twinkling out of the corner of his eye. Stopping, he turned toward the cliff face rising alongside the road but the twinkling was gone.

Larus took note of him standing in the middle of the road, staring at the cliff face. "What is it?" he asked.

Hunter shrugged. "Nothing I guess," he said. Then as he turned to proceed up the road again, the twinkling reappeared. "There!" he exclaimed.

"There what?" asked Larus.

"Something...," Hunter began, then stopped. "Bring the torch closer." As Larus brought the burning brand closer to where Hunter stood by the cliff face, the torch's light began to be noticeably refracted by a portion of the cliff face.

"It looks like quartz of some kind," commented Larus. "Quite common in these types of mountains." Beside him, Hunter had grown quiet. Glancing to his comrade, he found his expression to be unreadable.

"Give me the torch," Hunter said quietly.

"What?" asked Larus, not sure if he had heard him correctly.

Turning to Larus, Hunter held out his hand and said with more authority, "Give me the torch."

Larus gazed at his comrade a moment then relayed Hunter's request to Father Thomas who handed him the torch. Then they both watched as he brought the burning end closer to the vein of quartz. When he moved the burning head of the torch into a cavity behind the quartz, they were bedazzled by the explosion of colored light refracting outward. The light lasted only for a moment before Hunter withdrew the torch and began running it along the rock face.

"What is he doing?" whispered Father Thomas.

Shrugging and never taking his eyes from where the torch moved along the rock wall, Larus replied, "I don't know."

Hunter was concentrating intently upon the torch as he moved it along. A sweat had broken out on his brow despite the cold wind coursing through the gorge. Deep in the recesses of his mind, a memory was being triggered, one that he could barely, consciously remember. Fear accompanied the memory though there was no rational explanation as to why.

When he had seen the second twinkling of the quartz refracting the torch's light, the memory had begun to emerge. Not in its entirety to be sure, just bits and pieces. The sparkling quartz, a light moving along the side of the rock wall, and permeating it all was an underlying current of fear.

He could hear the other two speaking, but it was no more than background noise. The torch was following a path, a path taken by...something. Whether that something was good or bad he didn't know, only that he had to follow. For *it* was coming! Time was all but gone!

"Hunter," Larus said as he laid a hand on his shoulder.

The contact intensified the fear and Hunter struck out with the torch causing Larus to stumble backward to avoid being burned. "Don't touch me!" Hunter screamed with a touch of hysteria in his voice.

Larus glanced worriedly to Father Thomas and could see the same question mirrored in the priest's eyes. *Had the madness returned?*

Returning the torch to the wall, he continued following an unseen path across its surface. Then, the torch reached a hard to see recess a little larger than what would allow a single man to pass.

"This is it!" Hunter breathed.

"This is what?" asked Larus.

"The way," he said. "The way to avoid the darkness."

Larus glanced again to Father Thomas. Silently, he mouthed *'Darkness?'* Father Thomas shrugged indicating he didn't understand either.

Hunter made to step within the recess and Larus took him by the shoulder again. This time however, the torch did not strike out at him. Instead, Hunter looked back over his shoulder with eyes that weren't really seeing the here and now.

"Just a minute," Larus said then pulled Hunter ever so gently away from the recess. "You better let me check it out first." When no argument was forthcoming, he took the burning torch from Hunter's grip and stepped to the opening in the side of the cliff.

He took a moment to inspect the opening in better detail. It was a marvel of construction now that he knew it was there. Masterfully crafted to blend into the side of the cliff, unless you knew what to look for, you would never know it was there.

The recess itself was barely three feet wide and as he stepped within, could see that it extended to the right for close to ten feet in a course paralleling the road. Then, it turned abruptly and disappeared further into the side of the cliff.

Larus glanced back toward where Father Thomas now stood next to Hunter. "It seems to go on for some distance," he explained.

"Should we follow it do you think?" asked Father Thomas.

"Not in the dark," he replied. "Who knows what dangers may be waiting for the unwary?"

His words caused Hunter to grow agitated. Hands shifting nervously and his head darting about looking for who knew what, he said, "We can't afford to wait any longer." With rising distress, he looked back down the road before adding, "It will be here soon."

"What?" Larus asked. Leaving the recess, he moved to stand before Hunter. "What will be here soon?"

"I..." he began then a confused look came over his face. "I don't know," he said.

The eyes turned toward Larus had the look of returned sanity. The faraway glaze that had been there before was gone. "Is it the darkness?" he asked.

Hunter nodded, but then looked confused. "Yes...I think so," he replied.

Darkness was all around them, and would be until the sun rose in a couple hours. "The sun will rise soon," he explained. "It would be better to wait until then before moving through such a close and tight space."

Hunter gazed at him for a moment before nodding. "If you think that is best," he said.

Father Thomas laid a hand on Hunter's arm and said, "We should return to camp and get what rest we can until then."

Turning his eyes to Father Thomas, Hunter nodded.

"At first light," Larus said as they began making their way back up the road, "we'll see where that goes."

"Do you think it could be the way to the Or'tux temple?" asked Father Thomas.

Larus was quiet for a moment, then shrugged. Lowering his voice, he said, "I don't know. But one thing is for certain, the way Hunter found it and how he acted suggests we need to investigate further."

Father Thomas nodded. As they completed their return to camp, he couldn't help but think of the crystalline arachnid and how Hunter had been led to it. Could this have been something similar?

Chapter 23

The morning dawned sunny. Off to the north could be seen a possible storm front building, nothing major just a more congested congregation of darker clouds. The wind was cold and the intermittent gusts bit like icy fangs. With the peaks rising tall to the east, it would be some time before any direct sunlight would reach the ancient road and those shivering upon it.

Father Thomas stood silent vigil as the world burgeoned into day. Larus and Hunter lay next to the fire which wasn't much more than coals. He was tempted to put more wood on the fire, but didn't want to waste their meager supply. They may need it before they headed back.

With the world brightening, his curiosity got the better of him and he walked around the bend in the road and gazed over to where the temple sat on the far side of the crevice. Even in the light of day it held an ominous feel. There was nothing to which he could attribute the unease it produced, just the sight of the place gave him the creepy-crawlies.

A noise back at the camp drew his attention and he returned to find Larus on his feet looking for him. "Over here," he said as he rounded the outcropping. "I was looking at the temple."

Larus was relieved to see the priest. "We shouldn't become separated," he warned. "Not here." A shiver went through him and whether it was the bite of the wind or something else, he couldn't be sure.

A smile came to the priest. "I only stepped around the bend," he explained.

"Still...," Larus said, leaving the rest of the thought unspoken.

Their voices penetrated Hunter's sleep and he too was soon awake.

"How are you this morning my son?" Father Thomas asked him. Gazing into his eyes, he sought any trace of madness. With relief he found none.

"Fine," replied Hunter. "A bit tired but otherwise, I feel pretty good." Then he saw the way in which he was being scrutinized by not only Father Thomas but Larus as well. "Why?"

"Do you remember anything about last night?" Larus asked.

Hunter's gaze went from one to the other before answering. "If you are referring to chasing the horses down the road and almost falling off the cliff," he began, "then yes, I do."

Father Thomas stepped closer to Hunter and asked, "And after that?"

"After?" asked Hunter. Turning his mind on the event of the night before, he vaguely remembered being pulled from his precarious position above the gorge and laying down. After that, things grew a bit fuzzy.

"I laid down," he said as he watched the other two's expressions. "And…then we came back here."

Father Thomas nodded. "I thought so," he said.

"Thought so about what?" he asked.

After first casting a glance to Larus, Father Thomas related the finding of the recess that led back into the side of the cliff face.

When Father Thomas finished, Larus could see Hunter worked to remember what the priest had recounted. "You also mentioned something about a darkness."

As soon as he said 'darkness', the skin around Hunter's eyes tightened. "Darkness…," he began as he tried to recall the events more clearly.

"You said it would be here soon," Father Thomas said. When Larus translated the words, Hunter grew even more confused.

Looking to Larus, he shook his head. "I don't recall anything about a darkness, other than it was night," he said. "I do seem to recall a rainbow." He nervously chuckled at that. "You probably think I'm daft. A rainbow in the dead of night."

Larus shook his head. "No," he assured him. "Actually there was one." He then went on to explain how the torch passing behind the vein of quartz had produced a momentary rainbow-like refraction.

Hunter grew quiet as he sought an unattainable memory. "Why can't I remember any of this?" he asked.

"It's just like what happened in the Caves," explained Larus.

A look of growing horror came over him as he asked, "You mean something had hold of me? Controlling my actions?"

"So it would seem," answered Larus.

He looked to Father Thomas. "Was it this goddess of yours?" he asked.

When Larus translated the question for the priest, Father Thomas' first inclination was to answer a resounding 'yes'. He had opened his mouth to speak then abruptly stopped. How could he be so sure? Casdralla was not the only force on this world. Not to mention they were in close proximity to the site where another god had held sway. How could he be certain that it was Casdralla or one of her minions that had taken hold of Hunter? In the back of his mind, he recalled how this place was rumored to be cursed. Could what happened to Hunter have been a manifestation of that?

"Father?" asked Larus.

"What?" he exclaimed, then realized the other two had been waiting for an answer. "Oh, sorry. To answer your question Hunter, I do not know." He saw the worry in his eyes as Larus relayed his answer. "I would like to believe that it was, but I am afraid there is no way for us to know for sure."

"Great," moaned Hunter.

Larus came and patted him on the back. "Don't worry," he said. "There was no feeling of malignant forces at work, and you were fairly lucid throughout the whole event. I doubt if you have anything to worry about."

Yeah, right! he thought to himself. Visions of head spinning and pea soup flying flashed through his mind which he immediately tried to banish. *Man, I've watched way too much television.*

"Relax," Larus told him. "On the bright side, Father Thomas and I believe what you found may be a way into the Temple."

Hunter looked doubtful.

"It's close enough to the entrance and is hidden very well," he explained. "Add that to the fact Shank had to have a way across the crevice currently barring access to the temple, then it makes sense. Also, Shank didn't have any means with him for crossing to the other side." Patting him on the back again, Larus grinned. "Let's go see if we're right."

A glance to Father Thomas showed him to be in agreement. "Alright," agreed Hunter with only marginal enthusiasm. Worry about what may await down the narrow passes on the other side of the recess gnawed at him as they made their way down to the opening

Larus had them remove all the equipment from the horses and stack it just within the recess "We can't take the horses with us," he explained as he removed his saddle and carried it through to the inner passage. "Too narrow." Setting it down, he returned for his bedroll and packs. "There's nothing out here but a few roots to tie their reins to and if something should spook them again like last night..."

"Maybe one of us could stay here with them?" suggested Hunter.

"No," asserted Larus. "I would rather lose the horses than have us separated?" Bending over to grab his packs, he then straightened up and gazed to Larus. A grin came to him as he said, "Besides, I thought you didn't like horses."

"That was before," replied Hunter. "Now that I can ride it's different."

Tossing his packs in with his saddle, Larus chuckled.

Once their equipment was stashed far enough down the passage behind the recess so as to be unseen from the ancient road, Larus tied the horses' reins to the root Hunter had hung on for dear life the previous evening. "This should keep them here unless something spooks them," he said after securing the last one.

"Unless we don't return," added Hunter.

Larus glanced to him and shook his head. "No thinking like that now," he advised.

Father Thomas had a pack slung over his shoulder containing their food, blankets, and several sticks they could use for torches should the need develop. "Ready?" he asked.

"Yes," replied Larus. "Let's see if our guess is correct." Turning toward the recess he said, "I'll lead, Hunter you follow close," and then changing to Father Thomas' language, he added, "Father, you bring up the rear."

"As you wish," he said.

The three horses tied to an exposed root in the middle of the road painted a strange picture. Larus cast a final look their way before passing through into the hidden passage behind the recess. With a wish that they will be there upon their return, he entered the passage.

It was narrow, their shoulders constantly rubbed against one side or the other. The rock itself looked natural, as if the passage was created through forces of nature and not through the ingenuity of man.

Moving at first to parallel the ancient road, it quickly turned left and moved deeper into the mountain. Larus thought for sure the ceiling of the passage would close and form a tunnel. But instead, there was a constant opening through which the sun's light was able to pass.

Once past that first turn, the passage began to slant downward at a gentle angle as it began curving first one way then the other. Past the third curve, the sound of cascading water began to be heard. At this point, the passage started slanting downward at a greater angle.

The reverberation of cascading water grew louder the further they went. It didn't take long before mist began to be felt in the air. "Be careful," warned Larus. "The ground is beginning to get slick."

Indeed, patches of algae and moss could be seen here and there along the ground of the passage as well as the walls. With the limited sunlight reaching them through the crevice above, it was difficult to discern the slick patches clearly.

Hunter slipped twice, each time saved by Father Thomas from landing on the ground, before the passage widened and the roar of water grew louder. At this point the mist which had been barely noticeable before, intensified.

"Sounds like a waterfall," commented Father Thomas.

Larus paused as he glanced back and nodded. The day before when they had stood before the crevice barring the way to Or'tux temple, the sound of water could be heard deep within its shadowed depths. What lay ahead could be the source of that sound.

Resuming their progress, they quickly reached a widening of the passage that quickly grew into a mist shrouded cavern. Light filtering in from up above made the water particles sparkle iridescently.

The cavern wasn't very large, barely sixty feet from one side to the next. It held a roughly, uniform shape from where it began high above them until it disappeared into darkness below. The dominant feature of the cavern was the waterfall.

Not a great cascade of water by any means, still the sound of it crashing on the rocks below reverberated through them as they drew closer. Pouring into the cavern from the upper reaches, it cascaded down the right side of the cavern, past the cavern floor, and crashing into rocks somewhere below.

"Impressive," Father Thomas said in appreciation of nature's display.

"Indeed," agreed Larus.

Once they reached the edge of the cavern they discovered where the passage came to an end. It went straight to the waterfall then fell away.

"This can't be the end," Larus said loudly to himself. The signs all said this was the way to go. Or could he be misinterpreting them? A moment's reflection failed to unveil a misstep in his thinking. "Where would Shank go from here?"

"Providing of course that this had been his intended route," stated Father Thomas.

The walls of the cavern rose sheer on all sides, the passage in which they stood ended at a jagged drop-off several feet from the falling water. It didn't seem as if there was another way to go. While Larus considered the situation, Hunter moved closer toward the waterfall. From where the passage came to an end, the falling water was almost close enough to touch.

Leaning against the cavern wall for support, he stretched out his hand to feel the power of the falling water, and was impressed. Hard, but not so hard as to sting.

"Be careful!" Larus shouted over the roar of the falls.

Hunter glanced back and nodded to him reassuringly. Taking a step back, he continued to marvel at the falling water. Never had he ever been so close to one. Oh sure, there had been many trips he had taken during which they saw waterfalls. But never this close. He thought to himself how cool it would be to stand behind it, watching it fall mere inches before him. Such a thing was something he had always wanted to do.

So with that thought in mind, he moved so he could see behind the waterfall and discovered a narrow shelf running along behind it. Wet, slick, and with barely enough room to stand, he knew his dream of standing behind a waterfall would continue to elude him. He wasn't about to take the risk of slipping off and falling.

A glance over to the other two showed them to be in conversation, paying him little heed. It irritated him that he and Father Thomas couldn't communicate. Even though he knew that Larus would inform him of anything important, he would still love to know what was being said. He was sure Larus didn't relay everything that was being said.

Returning his gaze to the falling water, he backed up out of the spray area and found a relative dry spot in which to wait. He felt peaceful right now, more peaceful than he had felt since coming to this crazy world.

Why anyone thought he would be suitable as a Chosen One was beyond reason. His life could be summed up in just one word, mediocre. There were no great feats of anything in his past. In school he had a 2.4 average, his job was mind numbing with little future. He didn't even have anyone in his life. Not for the first time he wondered about the wisdom of his being chosen for this. If this job required a person with no special skills, mental acuity, or wisdom, then yes, he would be the prime candidate. Shaking his head, he chuckled sadly.

Hunter alternated between watching Larus and Father Thomas, and the waterfall. Of the two scenes before him, the waterfall held his interest more. He wondered how long the water had been falling through this cavern. If the information Father Thomas had on the Or'tux was accurate, then this cavern would have had to have been in existence for a long time. Which meant that it may have started out much smaller, with the waterfall having eroded much of it away over the years. Or maybe the waterfall hadn't even been in existence when the Or'tux inhabited the temple. Could the waterfall have eroded through and removed the passage, perhaps a stream that had eaten its way through the bedrock above?

Excited at the idea, he sat up. How long would it take for water to erode that much rock away? Of course any earthquakes or other seismic activities would have accelerated the process. His eyes flicked back to the narrow shelf running along behind the waterfall. Could that be all that was left of the passage? If so, would Shank have used it?

Climbing to his feet, he started toward the edge of the waterfall again then stopped. A glance over to the other two showed them to still be in conversation. He almost spoke up about his idea but thought better of it. They might think him foolish. So moving to where the passage ended near the waterfall, he began looking for evidence indicating that Shank may have intended to go this way.

It took him all of five seconds to find an eye ring pounded into the side of the wall. With only a modicum of rust marring its surface, the eye ring looked relatively new compared to the rock wall it was driven into. And Shank had carried a rope! Tie that to the ring and you would have a way to anchor yourself as you worked your way across the narrow shelf behind the waterfall.

"Hey!" he hollered. Glancing to the other two, he waved for them to join him. When they came, he pointed out the eye ring and then the narrow shelf running behind the waterfall. "I think Shank went that way." He then explained his thoughts on how the waterfall may have eroded away the passage.

Larus was quick to agree. "Good thinking," he praised. Taking the rope from his pack, he tied one end through the eye ring. The other he tied about his waist. "I'll go first and make sure there is a passage on the other side. If so, I'll hold the rope secure while you two come across."

"Okay," said Father Thomas. "Be careful my son."

"Don't plan on being anything else," Larus replied with a grin. "Wait for my signal then come across one at a time." With that, he moved to the edge of the drop-off and placed a foot upon the shelf.

Immediately, the water from the fall began pelting him. Droplets of icy water quickly had his clothes drenched as he worked his way along the shelf. The water coating it made for treacherous footing, but he took each step carefully. With his body firmly pressed against the cavern wall, he found what handholds he could as he scooted his left foot forward. Once it was firmly in position, he would slide his right.

Barely two feet separated the falls from the wall and when he reached the main body of falling water, felt it begin to intermittently strike his pack with force. As long as he kept a firm stance on the shelf, the force of the water wouldn't knock him off. From this point on, handholds became much more important, especially during the times he was sliding his feet.

A handhold here, sliding his foot there, inch by inch he made his way along the back side of the waterfall until he reached the far side. Through the mist, he could see where the shelf began to widen as it continued on toward a dark opening. It was the passage!

Once past the falling water, he quickened his pace until he stood upon the rock floor of the passage. A quick examination of the walls revealed another eye ring similar to the one on the other side. Untying the rope from around his waist, he securely threaded it through the eye ring then pulled it tight until the rope was stretched taut across the back of the falls. Then he tied it off.

"Okay!" he hollered to those waiting on the far side of the falls.

So thick was the spray coming up from where the water impacted below that the far side was totally obscured. He waved his arms and shouted again, this time as loud as he could. If they heard him, their reply was lost in the waterfall's roar. Did they hear him? He had no way of knowing. If they did, someone should be starting across now. Hoping that they had, he returned to the rope stretching between the two eye rings and waited.

As he waited, he could see the rope moving, but whether from the water from the falls striking it or one of the other two crossing, he didn't know. Fortunately, he only had a minute to wait before Hunter appeared making his way across. Once Hunter was close enough, Larus reached out and helped him across the last few feet. Hunter was soaked.

"Any trouble?" he asked.

Hunter shook his head. "No," he replied as he moved an errant strand of sopping wet hair from out of his face. "Slipped once but with the rope was able to right myself and continue on." He grinned as he added, "I'm not ashamed to admit the crossing terrified me."

Larus patted him on the back and was about to comment when Father Thomas appeared along the shelf. He had one knee on the shelf and the other leg dangled precariously below. Trying to stand, he was knocked back down by the force of the falls.

"Father!" Larus cried. "I'm coming!" Leaving Hunter's side, he rushed to the rope and started to make his way out to Father Thomas. "Just stay where you are!" He saw Father Thomas glance toward him and nod.

Scooting along the shelf, Larus reached the priest's side. Then with one hand maintaining a grip on the rope, he used his other to grab the straps of Father Thomas' pack and lifted. With the added stability Larus gave him, Father Thomas was able to bring both feet back to the shelf and stand on wobbly knees.

"Can you make it?" Larus asked.

Father Thomas shook his head. He made a reply but it was lost in the roar of the falls.

"Then we'll do it together," Larus shouted. Keeping a grip on Father Thomas, he helped the priest work his way to the far side until both were finally standing upon the dry, rocky floor of the passage. Father Thomas quickly sank to the ground.

"It might be a good idea to rest for a few minutes before continuing," Larus suggested.

"I agree," replied Hunter. His legs were a bit on the wobbly side too though he wasn't about to admit it.

Larus went to where the passage continued and gazed into the opening. Not far from where it resumed after the waterfall, light faded completely as the ceiling finally came together to form a tunnel. Returning to the other two, he commented, "We'll need light to continue."

"Are the sticks wet?" asked Hunter.

After opening his pack and checking on the sticks of wood they planned to make into makeshift torches, Larus nodded. "A bit wet," he explained. "But not so bad as to make them unusable." Within his pack was some cloth which he removed and wrapped around the end of one of the sticks. A bit damp, but with a little effort could be coaxed to burn.

By this time, Father Thomas' breathing had calmed and the shaking in his legs had diminished. When Larus glanced his way he said, "I will be fine. Took a misstep going under the falls and thought my time had come. The rope saved my life."

"Glad not to have lost you Father," Larus replied. "Do you think you will be able to continue now?"

"Yes," Father Thomas answered. Holding out his hand he said, "If you would be so kind as to lend me your hand?"

Larus gave him a grin. Coming over, he took the hand and helped him to his feet. Indicating where the passage continued he said, "Looks like it continues to descend."

"Do you still think this goes to the temple?" Father Thomas asked.

"Maybe," replied Larus.

"I've been thinking," interjected Hunter. "The weeds Shank harvested may grow in an underground cavern." As Larus turned toward him, he rose to his feet. "We may be taking a long way to nowhere."

"Always a possibility," he said. Turning to Father Thomas he asked, "What do you think? Are we going the right way?"

About to answer, Father Thomas stopped and then closed his eyes. After a moment's prayer he opened them and shrugged. "I do not know."

"Well," Larus said, "there's only one way to find out." Kneeling down, he removed his flint from his pouch and proceeded to strike sparks. As they landed upon the cloth tied to the stick of wood, he gently blew glowing sparks until they caught. Now with the torch burning, he came to his feet and said,

"Let's go." Leading the way, he entered the passage. Father Thomas and Hunter followed close behind.

Moving down the passage, the light from above rapidly faded until they were completely shrouded by darkness, with the only source of light being that of the torch. Not far after the light faded, the passage narrowed until it was again the width it was when they had first left the ancient road.

They traveled through the narrow confines for only a short span before they again heard the sound of water ahead. A minute later, the passage came to an abrupt end at a dark chasm.

Wider than what the torch's light could illuminate, the chasm opened up before them. Above, the wall rose several feet before curving to move almost horizontally away from them. Where the passage ended was a drop off that sloped at a steep angle down and away into darkness. It was out of that darkness before them that the sound of fast moving water emerged.

Larus held the torch out as far as he could and scanned the rocky slope below them.

"Do you see anything?" Father Thomas asked. Larus shook his head.

Hunter searched the area too, then the thought occurred to him to look for eye rings similar to what they had found by the falls. A minute's search revealed there were none.

Then, Larus suddenly pointed to a point some distance down the rocky slope. "Look," he said.

Directing his gaze to where Larus indicated, Hunter found what looked like steps carved into the rocky surface. "Steps?" he asked.

Larus nodded. "If you look at the slope from there to here," he said, "you can see others." Indeed, the first step was just below where they stood. It was an ingenuous design in that it blended almost perfectly with the rocky surface. So well did it blend in that you wouldn't see it if you didn't know what to look for.

But now that they knew, it was easy to see the series of steps carved in a non-linear pattern down the steep slope. Each step was of different size, shape, and position. Yet when they began making their way down from where the passage ended, found each to be immobile and sturdy. They were a marvel of craftsmanship, not what one would expect from a blood thirsty people such as the Or'tux were said to be.

Larus of course went first with Hunter next and Father Thomas bringing up the rear. The steps held no discernable pattern or path other than taking them further down toward the sound of rushing water. Forty steps later, they came to the source of the sound. It was a small underground waterway, carved naturally from the bedrock.

Its depth was unknown as their sight could not pierce its churning mass. Peppered with rocks jutting from the water as it were, the water was in a state of constant turbulence.

The last step came to within a foot of the waterway's edge. This step being large enough for all three to comfortably stand upon it at one time, they paused to consider where to go from there.

"I'd say we follow the water," suggested Larus. Downstream to their left, the surface of the ground abutting the waterway was fairly level and smooth, while upstream looked to be much more rugged. The others indicated their agreement.

Hunter gazed upon the water with trepidation. "I hope we aren't going to have to wade across," he said.

Larus gave him a grin. "Let's worry about that when we have to shall we?" he asked. Moving off the last step, he began walking along the side of the underground waterway. For the most part it ran fairly straight with only gradual twists and turns. All the while, the semi-level path running alongside continued to match its course.

After about ten minutes of walking, faint light began to be noticed ahead along the river's path. Also, the sound of water seemed to increase.

The light was a welcomed sight to Hunter. He hadn't much cared for trudging around underground as they had been. But as they drew closer, the light didn't grow much brighter as he had hoped. When they finally reached where the waterway emerged from underground, they realized why.

The waterway had emerged from the side of a deep, narrow crevice where it cascaded down into unknown depths below. Above, the crevice extended at least fifty feet, maybe more before reaching open air.

"This is it!" Larus exclaimed excitedly. Pointing just below where they stood, he indicated a series of ten steps that led down to a narrow landing. From the landing, a four-foot wide drawbridge extended across the crevice to an opening on the far side. "It's the way inside the temple!"

Chapter 24

The drawbridge was hinged on the far side and the remnants where chains had once connected to it showed how it could have been raised. Made of stout beams of wood, it had survived the years in surprisingly good shape.

An arched opening loomed on the far side. The stone bordering the dark, ominous opening had been worked and shaped to form columns, columns very similar to those encountered along the ancient road.

Father Thomas gazed at the darkness within the arched way and felt his skin crawl. Never before had he felt so strong a sense of wrongness as he did now.

"Are you okay?" Larus asked.

Barely able to turn his gaze from the opening, he saw Larus looking at him with concern. "There is something...," he began, then stopped.

"What?" asked Larus. Moving his gaze toward the arched opening across the chasm, he tried to determine what had Father Thomas spooked.

"I...I do not know," Father Thomas stated. "A wrongness."

"Wrongness?" Larus returned his gaze to the priest.

Father Thomas nodded. "I cannot explain it better than that," he replied. "The thought of going in there..." Suddenly, a nervous shiver ran through him.

"But that is where we have been led," Larus said. "We must."

In a barely heard whisper, Father Thomas said, "I know." Then taking a deep breath, he offered a prayer up for courage, then nodded.

Father Thomas' reaction caused Larus grave concern. A priest often was more in tune with forces that other mortals were not. Placing a hand on his sword, he laid the other on Father Thomas' shoulder. "Are you going to be able to enter?" he asked.

"Yes," Father Thomas assured him though his tone said he wished to do anything else but that.

"Okay then," he said. "Tell me immediately if whatever you sense becomes worse."

"Rest assured I shall," Father Thomas said.

Larus didn't translate that particular conversation for Hunter, but Hunter knew something was up. The tone of voice and facial expressions spoke volumes. He glanced questioningly to Larus who said, "It's a rival god's temple. He's having a hard time with entering."

"Oh," he replied.

Larus glanced to Father Thomas again and hoped he was right about what was bothering him. Some priests do react adversely when in the presence of another deity. For their sakes, Larus fervently hoped that was the case now.

Stepping toward the drawbridge, he placed a foot upon it to test its strength. When it easily supported his weight, he started across. Upon reaching the other side, he glanced back and saw Father Thomas motionless on the far side making no move to cross.

Apprehension bordering on fear was plainly visible on the priest's face. "It's okay to cross," he hollered over the crash of the water below.

Father Thomas licked his lips and took a step onto the drawbridge then paused. First a glance to Larus, then one to the darkness extending to unknown depths below the drawbridge. Finally, he took another step and rushed across. Behind him followed Hunter.

Larus extended his hand to help him across the last few feet which Father Thomas gladly took. "Thank you," he said in a raspy whisper. His grip on Larus' arm was surprisingly strong.

"You're welcome," replied Larus as he saw Father Thomas perspiring. "Are you sure you are okay?" he asked.

Father Thomas gave a halfhearted grin. "As well as I can be," he assured him. In his mind he silently said a prayer to Casdralla, trusting in her to see him through.

Larus again looked him in the eyes, searching.

"I am fine," asserted Father Thomas.

From the way perspiration still beaded the priest's forehead and the fact that he was a bit paler than normal, Larus knew he was anything but fine. Not pressing the point any further, he turned to face the arched opening.

Before him, a passage extended into darkness, past the reach of the torch's light. The floor of the passage was smooth as were the walls and ceiling. Easily wide enough for two men to walk side by side, the ceiling was high enough to allow all but the tallest of men to walk erect without fear of scraping.

"I don't suppose any of us have figured out why we are here?" Hunter asked.

Larus turned back toward him. "No," he said, shaking his head. Then he pulled forth the crystalline arachnid and held it before him. "But I'm sure this will aid us in some manner." Slipping it back within his shirt, he turned and started into the passage. To Hunter he said, "No matter what happens, stay close to Father Thomas."

"Wh...what do you think is going to happen?" quavered Hunter's voice.

"I don't know," he said without looking back. "Just stay near him. He may need your help." A glance over his shoulder showed Father Thomas doing slightly better. The perspiration had diminished though in the torch's light, he still looked a bit pale. Returning his attention back to the passage before them, he kept alert for any sign of danger. Father Thomas' nervousness was beginning to get to him.

Not far past the arched entryway, the passage opened onto a bare, rectangular room. Not much more than thirty feet by forty, it may have once been a guard room. There were two other exits leading from the room. One was a passage directly across from where they entered. The other was the beginning of an ascending stairway in the wall to their right.

Larus came into the room and paused to consider which way to go.

Hunter walked around over to the passage extending from the room and peered into the darkness beyond. A noise caused him to turn and find Larus approaching.

"So," began Larus. "Which way?"

Surprised to say the least that Larus would ask him, he asked, "How would I know?"

Larus pulled forth the crystalline arachnid. "This led us here," he explained. "And you were the one found with it."

Hunter stared at the arachnid but didn't take it. Something about it bothered him though he couldn't say what. Then he turned his eyes back to Larus.

He could see Hunter was reticent about taking the crystalline arachnid. He could also tell Hunter wasn't about to be any help in deciding which way to go. Sighing, he slipped the arachnid back within his shirt and turned toward Father Thomas. The priest stood over by the flight of steps, looking up into its dark recesses. Crossing the room he was soon by his side.

Father Thomas heard his approach and turned from the steps.

"Any feelings on which way to go?" Larus asked. When Father Thomas shook his head negatively, Larus asked, "Which way don't you want to go?"

Hesitating only slightly before pointing toward the steps, he said, "That way feels wrong."

"Wrong?" questioned Larus. "In what way?"

"It just does," replied Father Thomas. "More so than the rest of it." Turning his eyes back toward the steps leading up into darkness, he shuddered.

"Hmmmm," murmured Larus. Stepping closer to the steps, he gazed up into the darkness but failed to feel whatever apprehension plagued the priest. *Must have something to do with rival gods,* he theorized.

Nestled within his shirt he could feel the cold body of the arachnid. Its importance had yet to be determined, but he was positive it was more than just something to lead them to this place. From what Father Biern had said back at the High Temple, the spider was the symbol of the Or'tux god. Was it mere chance that the crystalline arachnid found its way into the Caves, ultimately to be found by Hunter? Larus thought that very unlikely.

Moving the torch into the stairwell opening, he raised it as high as he could to illuminate as much of the upper reaches as possible. The steps rose steeply for several feet before curving and disappearing to the right.

The touch of a hand on his arm startled him and he almost dropped the torch. Glancing back, he saw the hand belonged to Father Thomas.

"We should move on," advised the priest.

Larus nodded and stepped back from the stairwell.

"Over here!" exclaimed Hunter excitedly. Still standing by the mouth of the other passage, he waved for them to join him. When Larus and Father Thomas moved across the room, he pointed toward the floor. "I think Shank went this way," he stated.

In the light of the torch was the barely perceptible impression of a boot in the dust covering the floor. Larus was no expert in such things, but it did look as if the boot print had been there for some time.

"It isn't mine," Hunter assured the others. Putting his boot next to the print, he showed them that the other was an inch longer.

"Alright," said Larus. "We'll follow Shank a little bit longer." Next to him he heard Father Thomas breathe a sigh of relief. Stepping into the passage, he held aloft the torch and said, "Come on."

The passage led straight for over a hundred feet. Occasionally there would be other passages joining theirs, but after searching for boot imprints in the dust, found Shank had bypassed them all. Continuing on, they followed the indistinct prints until the passage opened onto another room, smaller than the previous one.

As the light of their torch began illuminating the room, they discovered this room was not left bare as had the previous one. An oval room, it was dominated by a stone table situated in the middle.

Intricately carved in what looked to be arcane symbols, its exact nature was hard to determine, for their eyes had difficultly remaining focused upon it. The more one stared, the worse their vision became. Looking away brought a person's vision back to normal almost instantly, though if one looked at the table again, their vision would quickly falter.

"What is causing that?" Hunter asked after several failed attempts to get a satisfactory look. Rubbing his eyes, he gave up looking at it for his head had begun to ache.

"I don't know," replied Larus. "Must have something to do with the Or'tux god I would think." He too was having difficulties with seeing the table. Turning to Father Thomas, he saw the priest had broken out in a sweat again and was even paler. "Father?" he asked.

"I…I," he began then closed his eyes and took a calming breath before turning his attention to Larus. "It is like nothing I have ever encountered before." Moving his head, he directed his gaze away from the center of the room, and the table. "I have never even heard of anything affecting a person so."

"Shank went through here," Hunter said. Not far from where they stood, another boot print was clearly visible further into the room. "It looks like he went over there."

Larus followed the prints as they went around the table to the right and saw where they entered an opening beyond which was the beginning of steps disappearing down into darkness. Aside from the steps, the only other way from the room other than the way they had come was an arched entrance to another passage on their right.

Hunter turned back to Larus and asked, "Should we continue to follow?"

Before Larus could reply, Father Thomas said in a raspy voice, "Yes."

Both turned toward the priest. "Are you sure?" Larus asked.

Father Thomas nodded. "Take another look at the wall on either side of the opening leading to the steps," he said.

Larus turned and was quick to see what Father Thomas was talking about. For mounted on the wall at eye level on either side were stone carvings, carvings which were an exact match for the crystalline arachnid resting within Larus' shirt. "I think you may be right," he agreed. They were made of the same material as were the walls and at first hadn't been noticed. Their eight legged bodies looked as if they had been frozen in motion, head down. The other passage leading from the room didn't have them.

Keeping to the edge of the room in order to maintain as much distance between himself and the table, Larus led the others to the top of the steps. Once there, they found the stone spiders to be torch sconces. There was an opening within the thorax of each where a torch could be inserted.

"Stay close," Larus advised the other two as he stepped onto the first step. The torch's light revealed steps winding around in a tight circle, disappearing into the unknown. "And watch your step," he said as he began the descent. For three complete revolutions did they follow the winding steps before emerging at another room that was larger by far than the one above.

"Oh my," breathed Hunter when he saw the gigantic spider statue taking up the entire wall to their left. It had to be ten foot high with each of its eight legs being at least twenty feet in length. Its jewel faceted eyes seemed to peer at them, almost as if questioning their right to be there.

Sitting before the spider could only be the Or'tux altar. Massive in its own right, the altar was a ten foot wide block of black obsidian, oval in shape, and concave. Dark stains marred the surface, evidence of the ritual sacrifices the Or'tux performed for their god.

Over a dozen niches dotted the other three walls of the room. Each stood in empty prominence, all but a couple bore red stains similar to those upon the altar. There were five pedestals within the room as well, what once stood upon them was now lost to time.

"The altar of the Or'tux," Father Thomas said.

A glance to the priest revealed that the pallor of his face had vanished only to be replaced with a grim expression of determination. When Larus turned to enter, Father Thomas stopped him by laying a hand upon his arm. "No," he said. "I shall lead here."

Larus paused a moment then gave the priest a nod. "As you wish Father," he said. Taking a step back, he allowed Father Thomas to precede them into the room.

"Bad things happened here," Father Thomas said. Moving toward the altar, he silently sent a stream of prayers up to his goddess. The sight of the giant spider and the altar before it had at first sent fear coursing through him, practically rendering him immobile. Being before such objects of evil worship had threatened to overthrow him.

But then, his hand brushed the sliver of wood he had carried with him since just before the Qyaendri appeared to him in the ruins of his temple in Billin. It gave him comfort, banishing the fear. Then from somewhere deep within his soul, the strength of faith flared anew bringing with it a renewed sense of purpose, of hope. No longer would Father Thomas quail at the fear this place sought to instill in him. Was he not an anointed priest of Casdralla? Was he to bow to the forces of another?

His faith clothed him like an armored shell as he strode across the room toward the spider and the altar before it. Negative energy railed at him from the altar, perhaps sensing he served another. A glance behind him revealed that neither Hunter nor Larus appeared to be affected by what he felt. "Do you feel that?" he asked.

"Feel what?" asked Larus.

"A malevolence," he replied. "Traces of hatred, of rage, of evil."

Larus shook his head, as did Hunter when Larus translated Father Thomas' words for him.

"It does not want us here," Father Thomas added as he turned back toward the altar.

The altar itself was relatively simple as altars go. The concave center just large enough to allow an average sized human to lie within. Dotting the bottom of the concave surface were several openings barely an inch in diameter. What they were was soon revealed when Father Thomas led them around the altar to the other side. There they found an outflow where the Or'tux high priest could collect the blood of those sacrificed.

Now that they were close to the giant spider which they believed to be the representation of the Or'tux god, they could see that each of the six eyes was composed of a dozen gems set close together. Curious, Hunter reached out to touch them.

"I would not do that," warned Father Thomas.

Hand poised a mere inch from the nearest eye, Hunter glanced back toward the priest. He could see the implied warning in the priest's eyes of untold danger.

"This place is better left undisturbed," stated Father Thomas. Beside him, Larus nodded agreement.

Bringing his hand back, Hunter acquiesced to their judgment. He then turned his attention to the spider as a whole and noticed how on either side of the massive body, the legs arched in such a way that a man could walk beneath. Each set of four legs formed their own walkway running alongside the spider. Intrigued, he went to the legs on the spider's right to inspect their construction further. That was when he saw the doorway situated at the far end of the walkway formed by the legs.

"Hey!" he hollered to the others as he moved beneath the arched legs. "There's a door here." Pausing beneath the second leg, he glanced back to the others and waved for them to join him.

"Wait!" cautioned Father Thomas as he rushed forward.

Ignoring Father Thomas, Hunter turned back toward the doorway. Excited by the prospects of what could lay beyond the doorway, he started forward. Now that he was within the walkway formed by the legs of the spider statue, he could clearly make out what was left of the door that had once stood within the doorway. Now little more than a shattered remains of its former self, the door sat askew, still connected by a single hinge to the door jamb two feet from the floor. As the other two hurried to join him, the light from the torch Larus carried was reflected by a piece of crystal still adhering to the door.

"Hunter," Father Thomas said as he entered the walkway behind him, "stop!"

Though the word was foreign, his meaning was not. Hunter came to a stop and waited for the priest to join him. Pointing to the cracked shard of crystal on the door, he asked, "Is that what I think it is?"

Taking a step past Hunter, Father Thomas paused as he gazed toward the shard of crystal glittering in the torch's light. "Larus," Father Thomas said, turning toward him, "let me see the spider."

Removing the spider from his shirt, Larus handed it to the priest.

Holding it before him, Father Thomas crossed the remaining distance to the door. Looking from the shard on the door to the crystalline arachnid, then back again, he nodded. "There used to be another of these spiders mounted upon this door." Then with a wave, he indicated for the other two to join him.

"It must have been shattered when the Or'tux were overthrown," theorized Father Thomas. "Most likely some of the priests may have been hiding within that room and our people broke down the door to get to them, resulting in the shattering of the spider."

"What is back there do you think?" asked Hunter.

Father Thomas shrugged. "I do not know," he replied. "Only one way to find out." Keeping the crystalline arachnid in hand, he stepped through the doorway and into a short hallway that curved sharply to the left after three feet. The other two followed close as he walked to, and then around, the corner.

There they discovered the hallway continued for only a few more feet before ending at a small room barely ten feet by fifteen. It was rather plain, whatever furnishings it may have once held were gone. Markings found on the floor gave the indication this had been someone's living quarters. One set was shaped similar to a bed, while another could have been made by a chest of drawers. Two others could have been other furnishings like small tables or stands. The walls themselves were plainly formed, merely cut stone set one atop the other. No wall sconces, niches, or anything else to break the mundaneness of the room.

"Could this have been the high priest's room?" asked Larus.

"Most likely," agreed Father Thomas, "especially given its close proximity to the altar and statue in the other."

Hunter was disappointed. Where was the treasure? Weren't old temples of evil gods supposed to hold treasure for the bold adventurers to find? Apparently years spent watching television and reading books had been misleading. He wondered what Indiana Jones would do in a situation like this.

Larus saw the look of disappointment Hunter wore. "Everything of value they found was taken back to the Caves," he explained. "I seriously doubt if we'll find anything."

Turning to Larus, he asked, "Then why did we come? If they took everything, then there is no reason to be here."

In the face of that logic, Larus had no immediate response.

Hunter looked around the room for a moment before abruptly coming to a stop. "The other side!" he exclaimed.

"The other side of what?" questioned Larus.

Turning about, Hunter hollered as he made to leave the small room, "The other side of the spider! If by passing beneath one set of the spider's legs you reached this room, then doesn't it seem logical another room could be reached by doing the same thing on the other side?"

As Larus followed Hunter from the room, he quickly translated Hunter's theory for Father Thomas.

Hunter had already passed through the doorway and was making his way beneath the arching legs of the spider when Father Thomas reached the doorway and hollered for him to stop. Emerging from beneath the legs, Hunter came to a stop before the spider.

"We must exercise the greatest amount of caution here," the priest warned him. Drawing abreast of him, Father Thomas added quietly, "We are not alone here." Larus translated.

Startled by the priest's words, Hunter looked around the large altar room for others. "I don't see anyone," he said.

"Neither do I," agreed the priest. "But nevertheless, there is something here which should not be awakened." Pausing only a moment, he then added, "I feel it."

"What is it that you feel?" questioned Larus.

"Just…a presence," he replied. "I do not think it realizes we are here."

"How do you know this?" Larus was beginning to look worried.

Giving the one-time Qyaendri a halfhearted grin, he said, "I just do." Then he crossed in front of the spider to the walkway formed by the spider's other four legs. And sure enough, there at the end was another door exactly like the one they found on the other side. Only this time the door had survived intact. All that was left of the crystal spider that had once adorned it was a vague impression left behind. The door stood ajar.

Indicating the vacant spot where a crystal spider had sat, Hunter asked, "Was that where our spider came from?"

Father Thomas brought their spider up and placed it against the door. It was a perfect match. Glancing back to Hunter he said, "Looks like it. But it could also be that there are dozens of these throughout the temple, all made exactly the same." After handing the spider back to Larus, Father Thomas laid his hand against the door and pushed.

At the opening of the door, a most unpleasant odor came wafting out to envelope them. "Gah!" exclaimed Hunter as the smell assaulted his olfactory senses. Then through hands covering his nose and mouth he muffled, "What is that?"

With the collar of his robe pressed tightly over his face, Father Thomas turned back and shook his head silently. His reply was lost enroute through the thick material.

"I think we have found the source of Shank's weed," announced Larus. Though his nose was wrinkling from the stench, he refrained from covering it as the others had. "This smell is much more intense than what we experienced in his tent, but it is definitely the same."

"You are correct," acknowledged Father Thomas. Removing his robe's collar from in front of his face, he took a hesitant breath which resulted in giving him a nauseated expression and a slight green pallor.

Hunter on the other hand wasn't ready to face the full brunt of the odor and kept his hands firmly in place. "We're not going in there are we?" he asked.

Larus moved to stand next to Father Thomas and pushed the door open the remainder of the way. As the door continued to open and the light filled the room, he knew they would. For the light revealed a tomb sitting prominently in the center of the small circular room. And sitting atop the tomb with its eyes staring toward the doorway in which they stood, was another crystalline arachnid.

The tomb sat upon a rectangular block of stone. The block of stone was in turn surrounded by wavy fronds growing from out of a pool of dark liquid. Circular and filling the entire room but for a small foot and half path along the walls, the pool of dark liquid seemed to draw the torch's light toward itself.

But perhaps the most ominous facet of the room was the fact that the fronds were moving as if blowing from a wind, a wind that was nonexistent. Ripples of waves would slowly make their way across the small field of fronds, each having their start in disparate locations.

"Creepy," mumbled Hunter.

"You could say that," agreed Larus. Turning to Father Thomas, he saw the priest staring intently at the waving fronds. "Is it safe to enter?"

"I would think so," he replied. "Shank had to have entered to harvest his weed. And the fact that he survived would indicate we will too." He glanced to Larus and saw him move to step into the room. "Still, I would advise against disturbing anything."

Larus nodded and stepped onto the narrow path circumventing the room. On the far side sat another exit, a darkened arched opening which he began moving around the dark pool toward. As he reached the halfway point, he glanced over to the arachnid sitting atop the tomb and could see where its back half had been shattered. Most of its thorax and four legs were missing.

From behind him he heard Hunter ask, "Why didn't those who destroyed the Or'tux also destroy the tombs?"

"Respect for the dead I would imagine," replied Larus. "Even the dead of the enemy demand a certain amount of respect and honor." He paused a moment before adding, "For the most part."

Nodding, Hunter gazed toward the tomb, wondering who it might be that was within. A noble? Priest? Could there be a curse in place for those who disturbed these men's rest as there was rumored to be in ancient Egypt? A shiver ran through him at the thought of some mummy coming after them. If only they had a cat. Hurrying to catch up with Larus, he did so just as Larus reached the arched opening.

It was the beginning of a short passage which ended at another room, larger than the first. There they found two of the tombs encircled by the dark liquid and wavy fronds. Each of the tombs also bore the remnants of a crystalline arachnid. On one there was but three stubs of legs, whereas the other was missing the head.

The tombs within their circular areas of fronds sat side by side with a walkway running between them. Along the outer fringe of the room ran a stone walkway as encountered previously. Another dark opening loomed on the far side of the central walkway.

"Wouldn't destroying those spiders atop the tombs be considered a desecration of the dead?" wondered Hunter.

Larus nodded. "I would think so," he agreed.

"Then why would they do it?" Hunter asked. "If as you say they felt respect for the dead?"

"Anger maybe?" he replied. "Retaliation for the destruction of the original High Temple? People do things when under the onus of strong emotions that they would not otherwise."

Father Thomas, after receiving the translation said, "Who is to say this was done by those who destroyed the Or'tux people? For all we know, Bellion Shank could have done it, or perhaps another with a grudge against them."

Hunter could see the logic in the priest's argument.

After a brief visual inspection of the room, Larus started across the walkway running between the two tombs. With fronds waving on either side of him, he had to take extra care in ensuring the fronds did not touch him since the walkway was barely two feet wide. For some reason, the thought of being touched by them made his skin crawl.

He still didn't know what they were doing there, but it felt right that they were. Even Father Thomas agreed that this was where the crystalline arachnid had led. Larus had been slightly on edge ever since Father Thomas announced they were not alone. Saying there was a 'presence' was a bit vague, but centuries of dealings with humans had given him a respect for their innate senses, especially those called to the priesthood. There was little doubt that in his original Qyaendri state, he too would be aware of this presence.

Once at the arched opening, the torch's light revealed a junction ahead where another passage crossed theirs. Moving forward, he came to stand at the junction. The passages moving to the right and left both opened up onto other rooms not far from where he stood. Within he could barely make out the outline of tombs similar to the ones already encountered. The passage which continued straight ahead passed out of the torch's range.

Turning back to Hunter he asked, "Straight ahead?"

"As good as any," shrugged Hunter.

Looking to Father Thomas, he asked the same question.

After a moment's contemplation, he nodded. "We can always come back to these," he said.

"That presence you feel wouldn't by chance be down there would it?" he asked, indicating the passage ahead.

"Possible I suppose," replied Father Thomas. "I feel it as an echo in the background. It is neither close nor far away, simply there, all around us." He shook his head. "I am afraid it is a bit hard to explain."

"Well," began Larus, "just make sure you holler if you feel it change in any way."

"I shall," agreed the priest. "So far, it has remained constant."

"Good," grunted Larus. Then turning back to the passage stretching out before them, he raised the torch and moved into it.

This passage continued straight for twenty feet before coming to another cross passage. Just as at the previous one, they could see rooms with tombs down to their right and left. Ahead, the passage continued on into darkness.

Larus gave the two rooms a cursory glance before continuing to follow what he had begun to think of as the 'main' passage. Once past the junction, it continued on for a good fifty feet before reaching a point where the torch's light began illuminating another room.

As they drew closer, they saw how this room was larger than any of the other tomb-bearing rooms. Upon reaching the end of the passage, Larus brought them to a halt as the light from the torch revealed four tombs lined up in a row before them, each with their own circle of dark liquid and waving fronds. Only this time, the fronds were more than twice the size of any they had yet encountered.

Rising tall from the pool of dark liquid, the fronds stood almost three feet high and each was the width of a man's hand at its widest. Unlike the other tomb rooms they had passed through, this one did not have stone walkways allowing passage between the tombs, nor were there walkways around the outer fringe of the room. The stone separating one dark pool from its neighbor had a width of less than three inches.

But the four tombs and large fronds was not the most striking aspect of this room. Instead, it was the single tomb lying upon a raised stone platform beyond the four tombs, and the wall above it.

Intricately carved and adorned with gems, the tomb was a dazzling sight in the light of the torch. Atop the tomb sat a crystalline arachnid, larger than any yet seen. From where they stood it didn't appear as if it had suffered any damage as had the others.

Five other of the smaller crystalline arachnids stood sentinel in an arch upon the wall above the gem encrusted tomb. Inscriptions within the confines of the arachnid formed arch appeared to be some sort of religious symbol, though composed primarily of small circles and squiggly lines, as a whole there seemed to be some sort of a pattern to the design. Also, their eyes had a hard time focusing on it just like the stone table they had encountered earlier.

Hunter's breathing began growing labored as he stood just within the room. Gazing across to the five crystalline arachnids that glistened in an arch upon the far wall, he felt fear that had been locked deep within surge forth.

Buried memories accompanied the fear, making their presence known as they fought for supremacy with his conscious mind. His mind fought back, sweat beaded and streamed down his face, but the memories were not to be denied.

Light dying. Darkness welling. Hope lost.

Do you have it?

A question out of the dark recesses. A kernel of hope.

Do you have it?

A besieged city, a guard.

No longer within the bowels of the Or'tux temple, he once again stood upon the wall. Looking out over the darkness seeking to enter, fear nearly stole his reason.

"Do you have it?" shouted the guard.

The voice broke the spell fear had over him and was able to turn away from the darkness. There before him stood a guard dressed in plain armor bearing the emblem of a five star arc emblazoned across his chest.

Screams of terror broke the night as he locked gazes with the guard. From somewhere nearby, a loud crashing noise came as a projectile hurled out of the darkness struck the outer side of the wall.

"Do you have it?" demanded the guard.

Hunter was about to answer when a crack formed beneath the guard's feet. He gazed in horror as black, acidic ooze emerged from the crack and began enveloping the guard's feet. As the ooze worked its way up the guard's torso, a scream tore from the man's throat, "Do...you...have...it?"

Around him the wall was shattering. More globules of ooze surged through the cracks, devouring everything it touched. Everywhere there were screams. The last thing he saw before the black ooze completely swallowed the guard was the five stars emblazoned upon his breast.

Whack!

"Hunter!" shouted Larus. When he failed to respond, Larus struck him across the face again.

"I don't have it!" Hunter wailed just before his eyes rolled up in his head and collapsed.

Chapter 25

Voices speaking in an unintelligible language was the first thing Hunter knew. As consciousness returned, he discovered his hands and ankles were bound. The voices grew clearer and soon realized Larus and Father Thomas were speaking quietly to one another not far from where he lay on a cold stone floor.

Opening his eyes, he could see the flickering torchlight from where it sat wedged in a cracked section of wall near Larus' head. He wasn't sure where they were until the wavy fronds growing from the black pools caught his attention. Then it came back to him. They were still within the Or'tux temple.

He must have moved or given some other sign that he had awoken for the other two ceased talking and turned toward him. "Hunter?" asked Father Thomas.

"Yeah," he replied through a mouth as dry as cotton. "What happened?"

Getting up, they walked over to him. Larus looked upon him with concern in his eyes. "You had another episode," he explained.

Moving his bound wrists, Hunter asked, "Is that why my wrists are tied?"

Larus nodded. "We were afraid you might accidentally hurt yourself," he explained. Kneeling down at his side, he looked into Hunter's eyes, searching.

Hunter put up with the examination for only a short time before asking, "Can you untie me now?"

"Of course," replied Larus.

Soon, Hunter's hands and feet were free. Sitting up, he rubbed them as he looked at the other two. Both showed nothing but concern for him. "So...what happened exactly?" he asked.

"We've been discussing that since it happened," explained Larus. "As near as we can figure, shortly after you walked into the room, you froze. Then tried to walk into that." Pointing, he directed Hunter's attention to the nearest group of fronds growing out of a dark pool.

A shiver went through him at the thought of contact with those waving fronds.

"We stopped you and tried to bring you around," continued Larus. "Just before you passed out you shouted, 'I don't have it'.

"I don't have it?" queried Hunter. "Why would I say that?"

"You don't remember?" asked Larus.

"I…," he began then stopped. There was something. "I don't have it," he mumbled to himself in an attempt to make the words spark a recollection. "I don't have it." Turning his attention back to Larus he asked, "Is that all I said?"

Larus nodded. Pointing to a spot not two feet away he said, "You were standing there immobile for over a minute before making the attempt to enter the fronds. Father Thomas believes it has to do with why we are here."

"That would make sense wouldn't it?" stated Hunter. "I don't have it," he mumbled again. Gazing to the spot where he stood immobile, he tried to recall what happened. But the last thing he remembered was entering the room and the four tombs standing in line before him. "I don't have it," he said again, and a vague memory came to the fore of another person.

Larus and Father Thomas remained silent as Hunter worked it out. Standing up, he crossed over to the place where he had stood immobile. Immediately, Larus came to his side. "I don't think there is anything to worry about now," Hunter assured him.

Giving him a half grin and a shrug, Larus remained where he was.

"So," Hunter said turning toward the room's entrance, "we came in there and I walked to here and then stopped." Seeing Larus nod, he turned with his back to the entrance and looked toward the tombs.

"I would have looked out upon those four tombs," he said as he gazed upon each one in turn. "And then I would have…" Growing quiet, he felt something, a tremor of nervousness when he gazed over the four tombs toward the wall on the far side. The sparkle of the five crystalline arachnids caused the nervousness to grow.

"Hunter?" Larus said quietly.

"I'm okay," he replied as he glanced toward him. Giving Larus a grin of reassurance, he turned his gaze back toward the wall.

Larus watched him carefully as he stared in silence. When a bead of sweat formed on Hunter's brow, he gestured for Father Thomas to come closer. As Father Thomas took position on the other side of Hunter, Larus asked, "What do you see."

A shake of the head was the only answer forthcoming.

"Is it the…darkness?" asked Larus. A sudden intake of breath from Hunter said Larus knew he may be on to something.

"Whatever we do," Father Thomas said to Larus, "we cannot allow him to lose consciousness if we wish him to remember. We have to know what is going on in there if we are to help him."

Larus nodded. Returning his attention to Hunter, he saw that Hunter's breathing had quickened and sweat had begun to form in earnest. "Hunter?" Larus asked.

Hunter's eyes flicked to him and a trace of intelligence could still be seen. Reaching out, Larus laid a comforting hand on Hunter's shoulder and could feel him trembling. As Hunter's gaze began to turn from him back toward the wall, he said in a commanding voice, "Hunter, keep your eyes on me!" With relief, he saw Hunter swivel his eyes back toward him.

"Keep focused on me," Larus demanded.

Ever so slightly, Hunter nodded. Somewhere behind those eyes, he knew that Hunter was at least partially elsewhere.

"Now," Larus said, eyes locked with those of Hunter, "what are you supposed to have?" This was the moment he and Father Thomas was dreading. Could he answer? Or would the question push him over the edge.

Larus' eyes were as an anchor in a sea of turbulence. Without them he knew he would be lost. Hunter was again on the wall, yet at the same time stood before Larus in the temple of the Or'tux. His mind railed against the disparity, but Hunter somehow kept focused on Larus' eyes and retained his sanity.

"Do you have it?" the guard demanded.

"What is it you are supposed to have?" Larus' question but a breath behind that of the guard's. Mind alternating between reality and dream, his vision wavered and felt his state of consciousness growing precarious.

Darkness swelled upon the wall, quickly enveloping the guard. The stars emblazoned on the front of his armor seemed to blossom into life and began to glow as the darkness took him.

"Hunter," came a voice, "stay with us." Then the vision atop the wall faded slightly as Larus' face once again came into focus.

On the verge of collapse, mind barely able to differentiate reality from dream, a flash of light in the real world drew his attention from Larus' eyes. On the wall far behind Larus, the five arachnids sparkled in the torch's light. For a brief moment, the five stars from the guard's uniform were superimposed upon the arachnids. They aligned perfectly. And he knew.

"Hunter!" Larus cried as he saw Hunter's eyes begin to roll backward. To Father Thomas he said, "We're losing him! Now!"

Taking the opened water bottle held in his hand, Father Thomas sprayed Hunter's face while Larus cried his name again. "Hunter!"

Like a rag doll, Hunter collapsed to the floor. Immediately, Father Thomas was there with the water bottle and emptied the rest of its contents onto Hunter's face in an attempt to revive him. As the water hit his face, Larus slapped him hard. "Wake up!" he hollered. Shaking him, he didn't stop until Hunter began to sputter from the water that had entered his mouth.

Coughing, Hunter's eyes flew open. Larus ceased shaking him and took his head between his hands to lock gazes with him. "Hunter?" he asked quietly as he sought for signs of reason.

One of Hunter's hands came out of nowhere and thrust Larus away. Caught unawares by the blow, Larus was knocked off balance and pushed to the side. Hunter immediately turned to the side and continued coughing while holding up a hand to forestall any forthcoming 'aid' from Larus. He could see the concern they had for him and between coughs allayed their fears by indicating he was okay.

"Do you remember?" asked Larus when it looked like the coughing fit had passed. "Do you know what you are supposed to have?"

"Yes," he replied. Sitting up, he turned haunted eyes toward Larus and Father Thomas. Memories came to him. The most detailed were the ones associated with the wall and its subsequent fall to the besieging darkness.

"Sounds like the wall of his dream may be that of Xith," commented Father Thomas at one point. "Perhaps the darkness is symbolic of the Ullentites." He glanced to Larus. "If I am correct, then Xith will fall." A pause then... "And so too will Casdra. I pray that I am wrong."

"Unless we get what we came here for," stated Larus. Turning to Hunter he asked, "Do you remember?"

Shakily, Hunter nodded. Then he began speaking of the dreams.

Throughout Hunter's narrative, Larus repeatedly berated himself for being a fool. Hunter's bouts of madness had not been the result of being taken from his world and transplanted to this one as he and Father Thomas had originally theorized. No! They had been the result of dreams implanted by Qyaendri and he hadn't the wisdom to recognize them for what they were. Idiot! *'Remember the ways of the Qyaendri'* Ftheril had told him during their encounter back in the Caves. At the time he had taken Ftheril's words as advice rather than a hint of what was to come. Fool!

"...keeps coming back to me on that wall, and the guard," concluded Hunter. "What can it mean?"

Putting aside his self-deprecating thoughts, Larus said, "These visions were given to you for a purpose. I believe if we correlated the times of the dreams with the times of madness, we would see them match perfectly." Nodding over to the priest, he added, "I also think Father Thomas was correct in that the wall in your dream is that of the city of Xith."

"And the darkness being the Ullentites?" queried Hunter.

Larus nodded. "Yes," he replied.

Hunter was quiet a second then, "But why did my earlier dreams always begin back on my world then end up on this one?"

"You have to understand that dreams implanted by the gods are not like movies playing out before you," explained Larus. "Rather, they are thoughts that are placed within your subconscious which in turn have to be assimilated by your mind. That assimilation invariably manifests as dreams, dreams which use images you as the recipient can understand."

"I guess that makes sense," Hunter said. "But why couldn't I remember them until now?"

"Most times these dreams are implanted in anticipation of a specific event coming to pass," Larus told him. "Once past the initial assimilation, they lie dormant until triggered by something. In your case...," pausing, he pointed toward the five crystalline arachnids on the far wall, "it was the sight of those."

"So that would mean they have special significance?" asked Hunter.

"In one way or another, yes," replied Larus. Indicating the crystalline arachnid they possessed, he added, "Between this and those over there on the wall, I believe we will find that which we were brought here to find."

"The ring?" offered Hunter.

Larus nodded. "The guard on the wall asked if you had it. From what you said his armor had five stars which were arrayed just as those five spiders are over there. There has to be a connection."

"But what?" Hunter looked over the waving fronds to the five crystalline arachnids glittering in the torch light.

"We won't know that until we get over there," Larus stated.

Between where the three of them now sat and the wall with the five crystalline arachnids sat a waving field of fronds. Unlike the previous room where there was a walkway passing between adjacent stands of fronds, this one had little more than a narrow ledge separating each from their neighbors. With the way the fronds were swaying to and fro as if to a nonexistent breeze, there would be no way to traverse those ledges without coming into contact with the fronds. And that was something none of them wished to do.

"How do you propose we reach the far side?" asked Father Thomas.

"There's nothing that says all three of us must cross," observed Larus. Tucking their crystalline arachnid within his jacket, he stood. "I'll cross and get the ring." Turning to the other two, he said to Father Thomas, "If it should prove necessary for all of us to cross, we'll worry about that when the time comes."

"Good luck," offered Father Thomas.

"Thank you," replied Larus. "Oh, and if Hunter starts acting weird again, take him from the room."

"I will," Father Thomas assured him.

"I'll be back," Larus said to Hunter and was surprised when Hunter started laughing. Why anyone would think this was funny was beyond him.

Turning toward the waving fronds, Larus gauged the distance from the pool's edge to the tomb sitting in its center. Then with a running start, he raced for the edge and leaped. His two companions held their breath as he arced over the dark pool and its fronds, finally slamming into the top of the crypt and knocking off the tomb's crystalline arachnid into the fronds.

Grabbing onto the ornate surface adorning the top of the tomb, he sought handholds as his momentum continued carrying him forward. Just before reaching the edge and plunging over the side into the waiting fronds, his fingers found a projection and clenched onto it tightly. He came to a stop with head jutting several inches past the edge of the tomb. Inches away were the tops of the fronds.

Very nimbly and carefully, he pulled himself from the edge and brought himself upright onto the tomb. He waved back to the others, informing them he had safely made it this far. Then he readied for the second jump, this time without the benefit of a running start. At least he could leap with everything he had without fear of overshooting.

Moving as far back as the top of the tomb allowed, he took a breath, let it out, then ran. Three steps were all the space afforded him before he leapt with every ounce of strength. Sailing over the fronds, he cleared their edge by a good seven feet.

"I made it!" he hollered back to the others. Seeing their answering waves, he turned back to the tomb and the five crystalline arachnids arching across the wall above it. His eyes went first to the tomb. He had a good idea that the ring would be within the tomb, residing upon the finger of whoever was entombed.

Crossing over to stand next to it, he could better see its construction. The tomb itself was squarish in size and larger than the others they had encountered thus far. Though ornately carved, the top was just a lid that once removed, should reveal the occupant lying within. Now the trick was in removing the lid. With only the use of his own strength, Larus was fairly sure he would be able to lift it. Giving it a careful examination, he quickly found handholds which would afford him decent leverage. Moving into position, he gripped the lid and lifted.

From the other side of the room, Father Thomas and Hunter stood silent vigil as they watched Larus first move to, and then around, the tomb. When he finally came to a stop and gripped the lid of the tomb making ready to lift, Hunter found himself holding his breath in anticipation.

"He may not be able to lift it alone," he said.

Standing next to him, Father Thomas may not have understood his words, but he did pick up on the concern in his voice. Nodding, Father Thomas replied, "We may yet have to cross over and help." A prospect he did not relish.

Eyes fixed upon Larus' efforts to lift the lid, Hunter nodded uncomprehendingly. On the far side of the room, Larus continued straining to lift the tomb's lid. "Come on," breathed Hunter when Larus paused in his attempt for a brief moment then resumed. Even from this far he could see the sheer effort Larus was putting into lifting the lid, though with little success. When after the third attempt Larus stepped back and didn't return, Hunter knew he was having problems.

It can't be that heavy, Larus thought. Even though not fully restored to full Qyaendri abilities, he knew that his strength was that of at least two, maybe three men. He should have been able to at least budge the top of the tomb. But it hadn't even moved a hair's width! Something must be keeping it closed. A lock maybe?

He did have some knowledge of the inner workings of locks. Once he had been sent to the aid of a man who had begun to stray down dark paths. In the course of helping the man back to the ways of Casdralla, he had seen the picking of locks many times. He even watched as locks had been completely dismantled and studied by the man. If there was a lock of sorts preventing him from opening the tomb, then there must be a way to release it. Giving the tomb a once over, he wondered what guise it would take.

First he searched the outside of the tomb in its entirety for a keyhole as that would be the simplest, but failed to find any. Then he tried looking for a release, some node on the tomb that may yield results when manipulated. Again his efforts were met with failure.

"Irritating," he quietly mumbled.

Next he turned his attention to the large crystalline arachnid atop the lid. All attempts at moving legs, body, or any combination of such proved futile. He even took out the crystalline arachnid they had carried since the High Temple and tried placing it in various positions on the lid thinking it may have been a key. When that proved useless, he set it piggy-back atop the larger one affixed to the tomb. Again, nothing.

"Why won't you open!" he shouted at it. A glance around this side of the room revealed nothing that could be used as a crowbar to pry the lid off. If he had a hammer he'd try smashing his way through. Oh how he wished he would have thought of bringing one. But who would have thought it would be needed?

Frustrated, he felt like smashing the lid with his fist, but knew all such an action would accomplish was injury to himself. Taking a step back, his gaze roved over the lid as he tried to calm himself and consider the problem logically.

His gaze continued returning to the five crystalline arachnids forming an arch on the wall above the tomb, trying ineffectually to focus on the area of squiggles and circles within. Try as he might, the more he focused on the area, the worse the distortion and feeling of discomfort became.

In his mind's eye, he pictured the guard Hunter had described from his dream, how upon his uniform were five stars matching the formation of the crystalline arachnids. Was it merely a guide, a direction to lead them to this specific tomb? Or was it more?

Each of the five crystalline arachnids was positioned so their heads were pointed toward the area within the arch comprised of squiggles and circles. In fact, if you drew a line through the center of each and continued it through the area of squiggles and circles, the five lines would intersect at the same point. Intrigued by the revelation, he tried to focus on the spot of intersection with little success. He at least could tell that one of the circles did lie there.

Turning his gaze back to the crystalline arachnid he had sat atop the larger one of the tomb, the thought that it may be a key once again crossed his mind. *Could it be?* Hoping that would be the case, he climbed atop the tomb and grabbed Hunter's arachnid.

The squiggle area was now at eye level. Looking upon it that close gave him a feeling of nausea whenever it came into sight. *I hope this works*, he thought to himself as he raised the crystalline arachnid to the area of squiggles and circles.

"What is he doing?" Father Thomas wondered. From where they stood on the far side of the field of fronds, they watched as he climbed atop the tomb.

Beside him, Hunter nodded. Larus' actions were inexplicable and Hunter hoped he knew what he was doing. A moment after Larus stood erect upon the tomb, a feeling of foreboding came over Hunter as a cold chill coursed its way down his spine. On the back of his neck, he could feel all the tiny hairs standing on end. That's when he noticed the fronds which had been in constant motion since their first entering the tomb area were still. Looking from one side of the field of fronds to the other, he saw each stalk standing perfectly erect. The sight deepened his feeling of unease.

"Fa...," he began when a flash of light flared from the far side of the room.

His gorge was rising as he moved the crystalline arachnid toward the area where the five imaginary lines extending from the arachnids intersected. As he moved it up toward the center, the arachnid in his hand began interposing itself between him and the area of squiggles and circles. The nausea started diminishing.

Afraid that placing it in the wrong position may have disastrous repercussions, he moved it ever slower as it drew closer to the wall. Then when it was less than two inches away, the crystalline arachnid in his hand suddenly turned clear. The body that once was translucent was now completely transparent. The sudden change startled him and almost caused him to drop it. But keeping his grip firm, he prevented it from smashing onto the floor.

"Oh," he breathed as he looked through the thorax of the crystalline arachnid and upon the pattern of squiggles and circles. It was now clear and easy to look upon, all vestiges of his earlier nausea having vanished. So long as he looked upon it through the arachnid in his hand, there was no ill affects.

A grin came to him when he saw eight small circles in two slightly broken lines running perpendicular to the floor. Moving the arachnid closer, he saw that its eight legs would match perfectly the pattern of the eight small circles. *Triumph!*

With their goal in sight, he brought the arachnid forward until the eight legs rested upon the eight circles. When nothing happened, he pushed upon the back of the arachnid and felt it sink into the wall. A second later, the five arachnids arching upon the wall flared in a blinding flash.

Chapter 26

Momentarily blinded by the flash, Larus was knocked off balance and fell from the tomb as the lid upon which he stood began to move. Blinded, he heard the sound of stone grinding on stone. By the time the grinding noise ceased, his vision had sufficiently returned for him to see that it wasn't just the lid which had moved, but the entire tomb.

"Larus!" Father Thomas shouted from the far side of the room. "Are you alright?"

Regaining his feet, Larus turned toward the voice and waved. "Yes," he replied. "Startled me is all." Shaking his head in an attempt to further clear his vision, he saw where the sliding of the tomb had revealed an opening wherein steps descended down into darkness. "There's an opening here!" he shouted to the others.

Moving toward it, his excitement grew. Stepping onto the first step, he gazed into the darkness then over to the others. "Be right back!" he hollered then began making his way down the steps. He heard one of the others shout something but so intent was he on the steps that he paid little attention.

The descending down the steps soon had him completely enveloped in darkness. Knowing the others would be unable to see him, he allowed the glow which had appeared back at the Ullentite camp to shine forth. Though not bright by any measure, it was sufficient for him to make out his surroundings.

On either side, figures were etched into the walls. The glow emanating outward from his skin gave them a haunting feel as he continued down the steps. Seventeen in all, they finally came to an end at a small room where a single skeleton was laid upon an open bier. Dressed in robes having long since succumbed to time, Larus could tell they once had been made of the finest materials. The man, for that is what Larus took the skeletal remains to have once been, laid with arms crossed across his chest.

Pausing but a moment on the bottom step, Larus gazed to the man with its vacant eye sockets staring up toward the ceiling. The sight of the skeletal face gave him pause as an uncontrollable shiver took him for the briefest of moments. When the shiver passed, he stepped into the room.

Crossing over to stand next to the bier, his gaze sought the hands of the dead man. Flesh long since turned to leather bound tightly upon the bones. They lay upon his chest in a relaxed state. His heart quickened when he saw a ring adorning the forefinger of the right hand. A quick visual check revealed the other nine fingers were bare of adornment.

With eyes now locked onto the ring, he said in a quiet whisper, "That has to be it." The details of the ring were unclear in the miniscule luminosity of the glow emanating from him. What was apparent was the shape of the ring's stone, oval.

Reaching out, he gripped the ring and slid it easily from the dead man's hand.

The motionless fronds were even more unnerving than when they had been waving as if to an unfelt wind. Hunter and Father Thomas waited anxiously, their eyes locked to the opening in the floor through which Larus had disappeared. Above the opening, the arch of five arachnids glowed with a dim, white light. The sixth, the one Larus had placed in the middle that had initiated the opening of the secret way, glowed much more darkly, pulsating in a slow, barely perceptible rhythm.

Standing next to Hunter, Father Thomas fidgeted with his hands, wringing them over and over while mouthing silent prayers. Ever since the flash of light, Father Thomas had grown nervous, which of course did little to ease Hunter's own feelings of impending doom.

"I hope the ring is in there and we can get out of here," he said to the priest. Glancing over to his companion, Hunter saw him make no attempt to reply. A closer looked showed Father Thomas' eyes closed as he continued mouthing silent prayers.

"Father?" he asked. Again, no response. Turning his eyes back to the opening in the floor, his fear grew.

"Got it," Larus said as the ring came free of the skeletal hand.

Turning for the steps, he suddenly came to a stop. Something had changed. Glancing around the room, he tried to determine what had produced such a feeling. Then he understood. The glow emanating from him had dimmed.

From deep within, a sense of urgency surged forth and he rushed for the steps. As his foot settled upon the bottommost step, a lance of cold struck him square in the back. Pain flared as the lance exited out his chest. Then it was gone.

"Ah!" he cried as the unexpected pain caused him to stumble, forcing him to brace a hand against the side of the stairwell to keep from falling.

Then a barely heard noise drew his attention back to the bier. His eyes widened as he saw the robes begin settling in upon themselves. Almost as if the bones were no longer there or had disintegrated into dust.

The shock of seeing the robes settling down onto the bier was broken as from above, the sound of stone grating across stone was heard. A glance up to the opening showed him the horrifying truth. The tomb was sliding back across the opening to its original position. If it closed, he would be forevermore trapped down there. Pushing off from the wall, he raced up the steps.

A shattering noise brought him from his prayers just as Hunter shouted, "Father!" Hunter's hand gripped his arm as they both looked across to the wall above the opening in the floor. The five arachnids which had glowed since the tomb had slid across were dark. The sixth which had been fundamental in opening the secret way, lay shattered on the floor below. Then the grinding noise came as the tomb began sliding back in place.

"Larus!" Hunter shouted. "We must help him." Meaning to run and leap across the field of fronds just as Larus had, he was stopped by Father Thomas snagging his sleeve.

"No!" he said as he brought Hunter to a stop. There was no way either of them could reach the tomb before it closed. It was more than halfway shut now.

"Let go!" Hunter yelled and pulled his sleeve from the grip holding him back. "We have to help him!" Turning back to attempt the leap across to the tomb amidst the fronds, he heard a yell from the other side. A fraction of a second later, Larus flew out from the rapidly closing opening and landed on the cold stone floor several feet away. For a brief moment Hunter thought he detected something around Larus, a glow maybe, but then it was gone. As Larus stood up, the grinding ceased. The way was again sealed.

"Yeah!" Hunter yelled in jubilation. But it was short lived as movement caught his eye. The fronds were in a frenzy. No longer standing motionless, they now waved back and forth as if in gale force winds hitting them from all directions at once.

Beside him, Father Thomas yelled something to Larus then grabbed Hunter's sleeve. The light from the torch in his hand suddenly dimmed and out of the corner of his eye, Hunter saw movement. When he turned to get a better look, it was gone.

Words issued forth from Father Thomas as he stepped in front of Hunter almost as if to protect him. And the torch's light dimmed still further. His breathe caught for a moment as a shape appeared above the fronds, but was quick to realize Larus was making his return over the fronds to land on the tomb in their midst.

He watched as Larus landed safely on the tomb. The erratic movement of the fronds abruptly ceased as every individual frond turned and pointed toward where Larus stood upon the tomb. "Come on!" Hunter shouted as Larus readied to leap again.

Then from beside him, Father Thomas began shouting as he gesticulated with his arms. Shapes moved along the fringe of his vision only to disappear when he turned to look. He couldn't tell for sure, but Hunter felt the priest was fighting to ward off things unseen. Fear gripped him.

Larus readied to leap again. Just as he took his first step to gain momentum for the leap, Father Thomas shouted and threw the torch held in his hand toward the fronds. Hunter watched as both Larus and the torch arched toward the edge of the fronds. The torch landed a foot this side of the leading edge, bounced once, then the flaming end was among them. Instantly, they ignited in a gigantic fireball.

Landing safely on the stone floor several feet from the edge, Larus was thrown to the ground by the force of the frond's combustion. "Get the torch!" he heard Father Thomas yell. Turning toward the conflagration spreading throughout the fronds, he saw where the torch lay.

"We need it!" shouted Father Thomas.

Larus glanced toward him and nodded, then turned back toward the torch. From where he lay a good five feet from the edge of the fronds, the heat coming from them was already quite intense, even for him.

"Hurry!" urged Father Thomas. "We don't have much time!"

Trusting in the good Father, Larus braced himself then quickly scooted forward toward the flames. Scorching heat seared his skin as he reached the torch. Grasping its end, he quickly back pedaled away from the heat.

"This won't last long," Father Thomas said as Larus joined them.

"Did you get it?" Hunter asked. Larus nodded.

Already, the smoke from the burning fronds was thickening and making breathing treacherous. Father Thomas led them from the room and into the next. As they passed through, he had Larus light those fronds afire as well.

Hunter sought movement out of the corner of his eye as they fled, and felt relief when he detected none. At the final room with the lone band of fronds now being directed right at them, they quickly skirted around the edge until they stood at the doorway leading to the altar room with the gigantic spider statue.

Before they passed through the doorway, Larus lit the fronds.

Smoke belched from the doorway as they emerged. Hunter felt a bit light headed which he attributed to the affects of having breathed in the smoke of the burning fronds. The smell was almost the same as what they had encountered back in Shank's place, only subtly different.

Father Thomas led them through the walkway beneath the arching spider legs. At the end, he brought them to a stop. "We have to get out of here fast," he explained. "It knows we are here."

"It?" asked Larus. "Is this the same presence you felt earlier?"

"No," replied the priest. "This is something different. An echo of long ago."

"You mean a ghost?" asked Hunter when Larus quickly gave him the translation.

"You could call it such," affirmed Father Thomas. "The smoke helps mask us from it, but the smoke will grow thinner as we move away from this room and its affects diminish."

"Will it follow us from the temple?" asked Larus.

Father Thomas shrugged. "I do not know," he said.

"Great," moaned Hunter.

"Now," Father Thomas said, "stay close and move fast." Reaching into his robe, Father Thomas pulled forth a piece of wood three inches long and one wide that looked just like part of a wooden plank that had been chipped away.

"Right behind you," agreed Larus.

Murmuring a prayer to Casdralla, Father Thomas headed across the altar room toward the steps leading up. There they found the smoke very thick as the stairwell acted as a chimney, funneling the smoke upward. Coughing, he raised the neckline of his robe to cover his face and pressed it firmly over his nose and mouth.

Following the spiraling steps more by feel than by sight, they at last reached the top of the steps. Emerging from the stairwell, the first thing they noticed was the drop in temperature. It had to have been at least freezing if not below.

Their breath misting amidst the smoke, Father Thomas indicated the table that was visible through the smoke. "The cold emanates from there," he explained. Pointing over to the opening of the passage to their left, "That is the way out. Stay as close to the wall as you can." Then once he made sure they understood, began moving along the wall toward the passage opening. Behind him came Hunter followed by Larus, both with backs pressed tightly against the wall as they scooted along.

Once to the passageway opening, Father Thomas paused and glanced through to the passage beyond. It was dark with a thin obscuring haze of smoke which was ruffled by the passage of air being drawn from the outside to the fire burning below.

The wooden piece of the original High Temple to Casdralla on this world was clutched firmly in hand. Its presence gave him comfort and bolstered his courage. It was almost as if he could feel the presence of his goddess residing within the splinter of wood, though he dismissed such as being the product of having inhaled too much of the noxious fumes.

Death haunted this place. Angry death. It knew they were there and he could feel its desire to not let them leave.

In his mind's eye he saw the rest of the path that lay between them, and the drawbridge and safety. Straight down this passage, through another room, then a final short passage to the drawbridge. Though not a great distance, he feared what they may encounter in the room up ahead. During their last sojourn through that room, he had encountered a stairwell that felt wrong. Now he knew why. Death. Old death. Traces left behind by rites of unimaginable evil resonated where those steps led.

Below where they now stood, in the room with the tombs, they had encountered embodiments of that evil. Traces of evil so powerful that over the centuries had evolved into shades of corporeal entities, spirits if you will. And they hated the living.

Thus far, the smoke from the burning fronds had kept them at bay. But that smoke was diminishing fast and would continue to do so even faster as they made their way down the passage. He could feel their presence, malignant hate radiating outward from them as they sought the living that had so foolishly come visiting. Oh yes, they wanted to greet their visitors in the worst possible way.

"Father?"

Snapped out of his reverie by Larus, Father Thomas turned back to him and said, "Sorry."

"Are you okay?" Larus asked.

"Once we leave this accursed place I will be," he replied. "Now, let us make our way quickly to the drawbridge." Glancing back down the passage, he said a prayer beseeching Casdralla's aid before heading out. "Let us go," he said. Stepping into the passageway, Father Thomas moved quickly, fear of what may lie ahead ever present on his mind.

Bringing up the rear, Hunter followed close through smoke which was rapidly dispersing. As they came to the first branching passageway to the left, the smoke was all but gone. Movement briefly caught out of the corner of his eye caused him to slow as he passed by the mouth of the branching passage. Turning his head, he stared into its dark depths but the darkness failed to reveal its secrets. Suddenly, a shiver coursed its way quickly through him as the hackles on the back of his neck stood on end. Dread came over him and it seemed as if the temperature had dropped several degrees. Realizing the other two were quickly leaving him behind, he cast one last look into the dark passageway before running to catch up.

Twice more they passed passageways branching off from theirs. And twice more, Hunter saw movement in his peripheral vision, only to have it disappear when he turned to look. The feeling of dread which had overcome him back at the first branching passage had increased with each subsequent passage they passed. Until finally they saw where the passage they were following opened up onto a room. Father Thomas brought them to a halt some distance from that room.

He turned and motioned for them to come in close. "You feel it, do you not?" he asked. They didn't have to answer for he could see it in their eyes; the fear, the dread of what was all around them.

In his hand he held the piece of sacred wood from the first High Temple, his thumb caressing it unconsciously. It gave him comfort and strength, and to a lesser degree the other two as well. He could feel how an unseen aura radiated outward from it, enveloping them in a protective shield. He prayed it would be enough.

"Stay close to me, and I mean *close,* as we go through the room ahead," he instructed them. "Once we have made it through to the passage leading to the drawbridge, I want you two to make a break for the drawbridge."

Larus' eyes widened. "What about you?" he asked, worried.

Pointing to Hunter, he replied, "I will give you the time you need to get him out of here. He *must* survive to save my people." He paused only a short moment for Larus to assimilate what he had just told him. Then about to continue, he felt external pressure being exerted on the sacred wood's protective shield enveloping them. Unbidden came the vision of a hungry person poking at a meat pie to see what delicious delectables it may hold. A vision which he quickly banished to the far recesses of his mind.

"But what about you?" asked Larus.

"I am nothing," he replied. "Casdralla will see me through this if that be her will." He took a calming breath as the external pressure began to increase and his fear rise. "Once past the drawbridge...," he began when suddenly he felt a blast of force strike the shield. In his hand the piece of sacred wood felt as if it vibrated ever so slightly. "Casdralla protect us," he prayed.

In his mind's eye he envisioned the shield bowing under pressure as what was outside sought to enter. Then, power surged from the sacred wood and threw back the onslaught.

"Now!" he exclaimed. Turning, he broke into a run for the room followed closely by Larus and Hunter. He could hear Larus speaking to Hunter in his foreign language but had little time to worry about what was being said. His attention was fixed upon the entry to the room ahead, and the darkness beyond.

Around them he could feel ever increasing pressure being exerted upon the shield of protection surrounding them. From out of the darkness ahead indistinct shapes could now be seen, no longer were they only visible in the peripheral. Vaguely man-shaped, their forms were ever changing as if they were but clouds being blown by the wind. But Father Thomas knew these were no simple, gaseous forms. Rather, they were entities, formed of the residual energy left behind by the evil rituals practiced within these halls. And in the most basic understanding of the word, they were *aware*!

Several were just within the room, blocking their way. He could feel their hate and anger radiating outward toward him. Energies inundated the protective shield as others beat upon it, seeking their way to those sheltering inside. With a cry to Casdralla for aid, Father Thomas held forth the sacred wood and charged forward.

"Back!" he shouted with the full authority sanctioned upon him by Casdralla as the leading edge of the shield encountered those waiting within the room. The darkness shattered as light flared at the contact. Unheard shrieks sent splinters of pain through their minds, fighting with their wills to continue on.

A cry behind him caused Father Thomas to slow and glance backward. Hunter had fallen. Larus stood next to him and was helping him up. Forms gathered near to them and in a concentrated assault, threw themselves at the protective barrier.

"No!" cried Father Thomas as he felt the shield buckle. For the briefest moment, the shield caved beneath the onslaught and his two comrades were vulnerable. Entities swarmed forward and he heard their screams of pain.

"By the light of Casdralla I command you...BACK!" Renewed energy sprung from the sacred wood as he rushed to their side. Again, unheard shrieks tore through their minds as the entities were pushed away from their prey.

He found Hunter ghastly pale and unmoving. Only the rise and fall of his chest said he was alive. Larus at least was conscious but seriously weakened, he too bore the pallor of death. Kneeling next to Hunter, Larus struggled to raise him from the floor.

"Can you get him?" asked Father Thomas. Again a concerted attack struck the protective shield, only this time he was ready for it. Though the shield bowed beneath the brunt of the attack, it did not fail.

Larus glanced back to Father Thomas and saw the sacred wood. Energy flowed from it giving him strength and he nodded. Lifting Hunter from the floor, he placed him over his shoulder, then stood.

As Father Thomas turned back to the room, his gaze caught sight of the stairwell leading up. The same stairwell in which he had earlier detected something unpleasant resided in its upper recesses. His gaze lingered only a second upon the opening, yet he could see forms passing through, adding to those already within the room.

"Casdralla," he prayed, "protect your faithful servant and those under his protection…" Moving across the room, a steady stream of prayers issued forth. The room cooled even further by the time they reached the middle of the room. Directly to their left gaped the stairwell; before them lay the opening to the passageway leading to the drawbridge. If they could but cross that drawbridge, he knew they would be safe.

Each prayer coming on the heels of another, he walked quickly to the passageway. Over and over, the protective shield suffered repeated attacks. Yet each time, Father Thomas' faith and the sacred wood kept them at bay. Encouraged, he quickened his pace still further.

They were still several feet within the room when he felt something change. An approaching coldness, a wind as unfelt as the painful shrieks of the entities were silent, flowed from out of the stairwell. With it came despair, mind numbing despair which the protective shield was unable to keep out. It flowed over them like a viscous miasmic wave, sapping their will, fighting to keep them from leaving the room. And it was powerful.

Father Thomas felt his pace slow, the will to keep going steadily draining away though he fought against it. The power coming from the wood was overcome by this new presence. Less than a foot from the passageway, he stopped. So too did the prayers.

"Keep going!" shouted Larus. He felt the energy coming from the sacred wood begin to diminish. As it diminished, the effects of the despair which until then hadn't affected him, began to. When he saw Father Thomas' hand which held the piece of sacred wood drop to his side, he felt a tremor of satisfaction radiate throughout the room.

"Father!" he yelled. Placing a hand on the priest's shoulder, he turned him around. Eyes of despair locked onto his. Father Thomas' mouth worked to say something but grew still before he could speak. Then came a soft thud and as the sacred piece of wood fell from the priest's hand. The shield was gone!

Chapter 27

Pain flared as entities that were no longer held at bay by the shield, attacked. Before him, Larus saw Father Thomas crash to the floor as they surged forward. Lances of pain tore through him as their touch drew forth his very essence. The attacks quickly robbed him of strength causing his knees to buckle beneath the added weight of Hunter draped over his shoulder. Crashing to the floor, he saw them congregating around him greedily.

Over and over pain ripped into him as each entity strove to get as much of his essence for themselves before it was gone. Struggle though he may, he couldn't fend them off. Arms flailed in a futile attempt to ward off beings lacking all properties of corporealness.

Dark blots against the darkness, they fought as much with each other as they did against the three lying upon the cold stone of the floor. Time and again spectral appendages which bore faint resemblance to those of humans reached out and brought pain. Larus screamed as three simultaneously reached within him. The ensuing pain was like nothing he had ever felt before. Shrieking, he felt even more of himself being ripped away.

As the pain wracking his body caused his limbs to convulse, his head flopped side to side. It was then he spied the sacred piece of wood lying upon the floor not far away. Mere inches separated it from where the fingers of his right hand clinched and unclenched uncontrollably as more spectral appendages hungrily entered his innermost being.

His eyes fixated on the wood. The visual contact brought with it a soothing to his pain, enough to quiet the worst of the convulsions. Using the last traces of strength his body contained, he thrust himself across the floor toward it.

One of the entities barred his way. First his fingers, then his hand and arm went cold as it passed through the embodiment of evil until finally coming to rest upon the sacred piece of wood. At the moment of contact, power surged into him. The darkness was shattered as the Qyaendri glow suddenly blazed forth with blinding intensity.

Inaudible shrieks of anger and pain erupted around him as the glow pierced the malignant entities. Those closest to Larus were obliterated outright while the others quickly fled the pain the glow brought them. In a matter of seconds, the room was empty but for the three men lying upon the floor.

As the power coursed through him to quickly heal his wounds it brought strength back to his limbs. Larus gazed at the sliver of wood in his hand and knew it for what it was. In disbelief he realized that what he held had once been part of Casdralla's Temple Prime upon this world! Imbued with the power of many Qyaendris, the Temple Prime was a refuge for Her faithful against the powers of other gods. And now that energy was pouring into Larus like water into an empty urn.

Abilities that had been beyond his reach since Daeson mortalized him returned. He felt the shackles of earthly existence begin melting away as more and more of the residual Qyaendri power imbued within the sacred piece of wood revitalized him. He now understood why his strength had returned to him back in the Ullentite camp, as well as the glow and other minor abilities such as seeing well in the dark. It had been due to the fact he had been in close proximity with this sliver of wood.

Remembering the other two lying motionless nearby, he sent his senses out toward them and could see that though they were weakened almost to the point of no-return, they still lived. Hunter's breathing was shallow and sporadic, his heart beating very slowly. Father Thomas's heart still held a strong beat, he could easily feel every lub-dub, though his body was in a state of shock from the lethal ministrations of the entities.

That brought their situation back to him quickly. Beyond the room, sheltered from the effects of his glow, they waited. Anger and hate washed over him. He could feel their desire to return and end the lives of these mortals who had intruded upon their domain. Then, he felt something else begin to stir.

It was akin to those entities which had attacked them, yet much stronger. In his mind's eye now augmented by his returned abilities, he saw it as a mass of darkness shot through with flashes of red and purple. Larus' eyes turned toward the stairwell leading up and knew it resided somewhere in its upper reaches. A moment later a chill went through him and he knew the being's attention was focused directly upon him. Mist formed in the air as his every exhalation flowed out into a room whose temperature was steadily dropping. The thing that had sent despair to overwhelm them was coming!

Lurching to his feet, he moved to place himself between his two unconscious comrades and that which was approaching. He attempted to reach other Qyaendris nearby for aid, but was soon to realize his returned abilities didn't extend that far. The power gained from the sliver of wood had restored him more fully, but he still had quite a ways to go before he could call himself a Qyaendri. He was only given a brief moment to wonder why the sliver of wood had restored his abilities at all before the stairwell was blotted out by an inky blackness.

The temperature dipped below freezing as a black mass oozed its way into the room, not only from out of the stairwell but also through the very walls and ceiling. Flares of red and purple shot through the growing mass of blackness. He could feel the power of the dark thing, waves of malignant evil rolled over him leaving an unclean feeling in their wake. Not corporeal by any definition of the word, the thing still held a presence which could not be denied.

His mind boggled at such a thing. Never before had he encountered anything even vaguely resembling the frightening mass before him. Not even during his time as one of Casdralla's Celestial Warriors. This was beyond him. His uncertainty blossomed into fear as he realized the glow coming from him was slowly diminishing as the blackness filled the room more and more.

Then suddenly, ice cold pain erupted in his foot causing him to stumble backward. Looking down in shock he saw a tendril of absolute darkness disappearing back through the stones where his foot had been a moment before. Others began emerging from out of the floor in ever growing numbers. And in that blackness, the entities which had earlier attacked them, approached.

"Casdralla!" he exclaimed.

The glow coming from him no longer held them at bay, its radial of affect steadily shrunk in on itself as more of the dark thing filled the room. They had to get out of there and now!

Tendrils writhed throughout the floor of the room. Several now rose between him and his comrades. Leaping over them, he quickly returned to where Hunter lay. Reaching down, he picked up the unconscious man and was greeted by a vision of horror. For where Hunter had lain, two of the writhing tendrils extended from out of the stone floor. Slightly lighter in color than the others, they soon returned to the same blackness as the rest now that they were no longer able to feed upon Hunter.

As the density of tendrils in the room increased, they began fusing together forming greater, thicker bands of blackness. Between him and where Father Thomas lay, one of the larger bands rose amidst more of the lesser. It rose higher than he could safely jump with Hunter across his shoulder.

"Lady!" he cried out to Casdralla. "I need your aid!" Fearing such a cry would be useless coming from a fallen Qyaendri such as he, he was startled by the blinding light which blazed forth from the hand holding the sacred piece of wood. When the initial flash of light vanished, a grin came over him when he saw that his hand now gripped one of the swords of the Celestial Warriors. "Thank you my Lady!" he shouted.

Striking out at the large band of blackness before him, light flared as the ethereal blade connected. Passing effortlessly through the band of darkness, it severed the upper section from the lower. No longer attached to the whole, the upper section dissolved and vanished. Encouraged, he laid about him with the sword, clearing a path toward Father Thomas.

He could feel the rage and hate rolling from out of the blackness as more of the tendrils fell to his blade. A slice to the right severed three, a back hand hack to the left took out four more and then he was at Father Thomas' side. Two pale tendrils had emerged through the priest's body one near his neck and the other through his left leg. Each were feeding on the man's life force.

Larus raised the sword high and called out, "By the sacred name of our Lady Casdralla, save this holy man!" Striking down, he plunged the sword into Father Thomas' body at the neck. He felt the blade connect with the tendril within the priest. Even as the tendril dissolved into nothingness, he passed the ethereal blade through Father Thomas' chest and down to where the second tendril was feeding. In a moment, that tendril was gone as well.

He reached out to take the priest as more tendrils came through the floor, searching for living flesh. Moving the sword in fast arcs, tendrils were hewed asunder. But for each he destroyed, another took its place. He couldn't get ahead of them!

Remember the ways of the Qyaendri. The words of Ftheril came back to him. "Yes!" he cried out as understanding came.

With his free hand, he removed the knife at his belt and cut through his trousers and into his leg. Still using the ethereal sword in his right hand to ward off the outreaching tendrils, he replaced the knife back in his belt. Praying to Casdralla that this would work, he reached through the newly formed hole in his trousers and inserted his fingers into the blood welling from the wound beneath.

It was one of the abilities given Qyaendris serving gods that he planned to take advantage of now. With their blood, Qyaendris could sanctify places, making them sacred to their god. And in so doing, create an area impassable for anything other than mortals and those beings following the god of the Qyaendri whose blood was used. In this case, Casdralla.

"In the name of Casdralla," he intoned as he flicked droplets of his blood outward. Three droplets flew from his finger. He watched one as it flew toward a large band of blackness. Anger and hatred roared unheard as the droplet struck the band, causing it to dissolve into nothingness.

Encouraged, his hand returned for more of his blood. Intoning, 'In the name of Casdralla', he flicked more droplets into the encroaching blackness. Then, he placed a droplet upon the forehead of Hunter and another on Father Thomas saying, "Protect them Lady." No sooner has his blood touched their skin than the black tendrils reaching for them recoiled.

The entities within the darkness went wild as the men were placed beyond their reach. But Larus knew the protection would not last long. The sanctification by Qyaendri blood was not a permanent state. Rather it could be likened to a 'quick fix'. And in his reduced Qyaendri state, would the affect of his blood be strong enough to hold even for a minute? Or would it begin to fade immediately? He didn't plan to remain and find out. It worked for the moment. That would have to be enough.

Bending over, he first picked up Hunter and slung him over his shoulder. Then, he lifted Father Thomas and placed him across the other. Around him, the dark tendrils were coming together to form thicker bands of twisting blackness. Turning toward the passage leading to the drawbridge, he used the ethereal sword to clear a path through the blackness.

Neither of the two men draped over his shoulders moved. His senses told him that they lived, but that their life hung by a tenuous thread. If he didn't get them out of there soon, the thread of life would snap.

Waves of anger rolled over him as he carried them from the room. Intense hate burned into him as he raced along the passageway toward the drawbridge and safety. Up ahead, he could see a faint light that was the way out. Behind him, tendrils now thick enough to fill the entire passageway raced after. Without pausing, he fled with his two comrades slung over his shoulders.

As the distance to the drawbridge narrowed, so too did the hate and anger grow stronger. It did not wish to allow him to leave. In a massive burst of energy, dark tendrils exploded outward from the walls in the space ahead.

"Casdralla!" he shouted as he wielded the ethereal sword of the Celestial Warriors with all the sacred might which was their province. Light flared as every stroke of the blade severed more of the tendrils. A sudden surge of energy behind him caused him to pause and turn back just as a massive tendril of blackness shot forward with incredible speed. Before he could react, it pierced his body.

Pain erupted as the tendril passed through. He could feel it quaver as it encountered the holiness of his god coursing through his body, but such was the density, power, and pure evil of the black tendril that it was able to withstand the contact and remain.

Staggering from the blow, Larus quickly laid into the dark tendril with the sword. Other tendrils came and wrapped themselves around his legs. Though having no substance, still they inhibited his movement. Now less than thirty feet from the drawbridge and escape, he was being assaulted by a mass array of tendrils in a last desperate attempt to keep him within the Temple of the Or'tux.

When he struck out at the massive tendril filling the passageway and threw it back, the ones on his legs grew tighter. Turning the sword upon the ones binding his legs, pain flared anew as the massive tendril pierced him again and drew forth his life force.

Gnashing his teeth, he bore the pain elicited by the massive tendril feeding upon him as he fought to free his legs. Freeing the left, he took a step. Then just as his left foot came to rest and he began working on the right, more tendrils sprouted out of the floor to once again bind his left leg anew.

Alternating from one to the other, he repeatedly freed his legs, each time coming closer toward the drawbridge. All the while his strength continued to wane as the massive tendril's continual sucking of his life force further weakened him. The power coursing from the sacred wood was being sapped by the assault almost as fast as it was pouring into him.

Twenty feet to the drawbridge. Ten feet. He was sweating now. Legs growing rubbery from the strain placed upon them by the added weight of Father Thomas and Hunter. Five feet. Chills wracked his body as his life force grew dangerously weak. Three feet. Stumbling, he went to one knee and was barely able to come erect again. Two feet.

The sword was dimmer now than it had been. As his life force diminished, so too did the power of the sword. Each blow striking the tendrils wrapped about his legs was having less and less of an affect. So close! If he reached out he could touch it.

Then, unable to support the weight of bearing the two men any longer, his knees buckled. Larus cried out as he toppled to the side and slammed into the passage wall. Using what strength was left to him, he thrust Father Thomas and Hunter toward the drawbridge. His heart sank when they came to land with only the upper parts of their bodies having passed through to the outside. Greedy tendrils quickly sprouted and began to feed.

"My Lady!" he cried out. "Help us!"

"Sounded like a prayer didn't it?" Ftheril asked.

Daeson nodded. In the blink of an eye he was garbed in the full battle dress of a Celestial Warrior, sword blazing in the dark. "Grab the priest," he said as he rushed forward to take charge of Hunter. Unable to pass the threshold of another's temple, Daeson was still able to take hold of Hunter's arm which had passed beyond the opening and pull him the rest of the way out.

Tendrils writhed their way from out of the opening, only to be struck by the full might of a Celestial Warrior. Daeson let Ftheril convey the two mortals across the drawbridge to safety on the other side while he stood before the entrance. No more than three inches on the other side rested Larus' hand, out of reach despite being so close.

"Larus!" he shouted. With the Qyaendri glow blazing forth in a blinding light, he sought to get Larus' attention. "Larus! I can't reach you."

Tendrils writhed their way in and around the body of the former Qyaendri. Daeson could sense Larus was fast descending to the point of no return. "Larus!" he shouted again. Then with relief, he saw Larus' eyes open. "Larus, I need you to move closer," he stated. "I can't reach you where you are."

Larus saw the shining light before him and heard the voice. "Move closer?" he moaned. Every inch of his body was on fire and he didn't think he had any strength left to comply.

"Yes," Daeson replied. "Casdralla needs you to move forward."

"My Lady?" breathed Larus.

"That's right Larus," Daeson said. "Our Lady needs you to stretch your hand forward."

The shining light told him his Lady needed him. He couldn't let Her down! The tendrils which had bound him before had relaxed when he was no longer moving toward the entrance. Gazing toward the shining light, he mustered strength he didn't know he had and reached.

Immediately, tendrils locked on him. Having moved the tips of his fingers to within an inch of the temple's border, he fought against the grasping blackness.

"Reach Larus!" urged Daeson. "Casdralla needs you still!"

Then uttering the cry '*Casdralla!*' his fingers crossed the threshold. Before blacking out, he felt pressure being exerted on the ends of his fingers.

It was dusk when he awoke. The first thing he knew was pain. His body ached as if it had been struck repeatedly with clubs from the top of his head all the way to the soles of his feet. A moan escaped him as he turned his head.

Lying nearby were the still forms of Father Thomas and Hunter. With relief he saw their chests rise and fall though they showed no other signs of being alive. Closing his eyes again, he thought back to their flight from the Or'tux temple. Then it occurred to him that he had no recollection of how they had made it across the drawbridge. As he thought hard on what happened, the crackling pop and sizzle of burning wood became apparent.

Opening his eyes again, he sat up quickly which produced a feeling of lightheadedness. Sure enough, there was a fire burning in a ring of stones not very far from where the three of them lay. Another astonishing thing, their horses were tethered to a nearby tree. One turned to look in his direction and snorted. "How…?" he began.

"Just taking care of business," a voice said behind him.

Glancing back, he saw a figure shrouded in a glow. His face grew pale and he drew precariously close to passing out when he realized who it was. "Daeson?" he said with trepidation.

The figure nodded as it came closer. "Thought we might have lost the three of you in there for awhile," Daeson explained. "But there's some strength in you Larus." The Qyaendri came and sat on the ground next to him. His visage was anything but friendly as he gazed upon his one time subordinate. "To be honest I'm surprised you've made it this far."

"However, your task is not over yet," he continued. "You and the others need to rest this day and the next to recover your strength, but no longer. After that make haste to Xith."

Larus gazed at the Qyaendri. "I understand," he said. "Hunter must stand on the walls or Casdra will fall."

"You are correct," affirmed the Qyaendri. "Hunter must be on the walls bearing the ring or all is lost."

"Then…," Larus began before stopping.

"What?" asked Daeson.

In a voice hardly more than a whisper he asked, "Should Hunter succeed in saving Her people, will our Lady take me back?"

"You mean restore you to the ranks of Qyaendri?" he asked.

Larus nodded.

"That is not for me to say," Daeson replied. His face clearly showed how he felt about the former Qyaendri returning to his peerage. Coming to his feet, he glanced back to Larus and said, "Five days." Then he vanished.

Five days? Five days to the walls of Xith? Two days of rest for that is what Daeson said they must have, then three back through the mountains and all the way to Xith. Could they even make it in time?

Groaning, Larus laid back down and closed his eyes. First things first. Recover strength, then we'll see. Closing his eyes, the last thing he thought of before drifting off was the contempt upon Daeson's face when he had asked about being restored to Casdralla's Qyaendri.

Chapter 28

Two days later when the sun was still an hour from breaking over the peaks to the east, three men made ready to ride. Larus had said little about how they came to be where they spent the last couple days, and nothing whatsoever about Daeson's role. Merely stating that he had brought them there after fleeing the Or'tux temple. He said nothing about Daeson and the warning, that they now had but three days to reach the walls of Xith.

It hadn't been easy for him to wait the two days while they recuperated. But seeing how his companions were now able to get around better and with more energy, Larus well understood the need.

Neither Father Thomas nor Hunter had much recollection of the last mad dash to freedom, which Larus figured was for the best. He didn't much care for the memories he had of tendrils feeding upon him. Every now and then phantom pains resurged and he momentarily panicked as the thought they were again sucking away his life. He will be glad to put the whole experience behind and get out of there.

During an earlier discussion he asked Father Thomas, "Can we make Xith in three days?"

"Perhaps," came the reply. "If we set a fast pace and stop for nothing." Father Thomas studied Larus a moment before adding, "You realize of course that the pass will by now be closed?"

Larus nodded. "I thought we could catch a ride on one of the boats resupplying Xith," he stated.

"The town of Pickwood would be the staging area," explained Father Thomas. "We can easily arrive there in two days."

"Excellent."

Leaving that morning, the three riders returned along the route they had followed in their pursuit of Shank. They reached the northern shore of the lake by late afternoon and Sharstan sometime after the sun went down. Larus allowed them scant time to rest in Sharstan. After a few quick words to Mayor Tom about the demise of Shank, and the refilling their packs, they were off.

He pushed them onward for several more hours until Father Thomas began leaning in the saddle. Hunter wasn't much better off either, as he still felt the affects of the ordeal experienced within the Or'tux temple. After finding a suitable place to camp, Larus built a fire to ward off the chill while the other two promptly collapsed beneath their blankets.

The need to reach Xith gnawed at him while the other two slept. Pacing about, Larus continued pondering the words of Daeson. *Five days!* Three of which were now gone. When his sense of urgency to continue could no longer be contained, he wakened his companions and they were off.

"Another two score men just arrived from Hallintock," Sergeant Yerrin announced as he entered the inn that had been commandeered by those in charge of the effort to send supplies and men to Xith.

Captain Hopewell looked up and nodded. "Green?" he asked.

"Very," replied the sergeant. Over the last week, every seasoned soldier and guard that could be spared had long since been dispatched to bolster the defenders at Xith. "I think one hasn't even needed to shave yet."

"Damn," he cursed. "What we need are another thousand fighting men at arms, not wanna be kids filled with dreams of valor." Of course how that many would reach Xith was another matter. The few boats left to ship supplies could hardly ferry a quarter of that number.

The common room of the Inn of the Water Sylph had been cleared of all furnishings except a few tables and chairs needed by the Captain and his subordinates. Maps covered several tables, one being a very detailed representation of Xith and its immediate surrounding countryside.

Captain Hopewell had the unenviable charge of acquiring and organizing the men and supplies being sent down the river to Xith. In the first days when they realized the Ullentites meant to lay siege to Xith, everyone thought they were mad. After all, hadn't Xith withstood every attack since its original construction?

But no one thought that any longer. Ullentite siege equipment soon gave them cause for concern. Wielding stronger arms which hurled larger and more destructive missiles along with a new kind of hellfire that exploded on impact, not to mention their relentless attacks, soon forced everyone to change their attitudes.

Even with the new siege equipment and arsenal of weapons, Casdra's military leaders had been certain of their ability to repel them and drive them back to Ullen. At least so they had thought until the first enemy boat set sail from Cuellyn. Taken when the city fell, the boat was one of the larger crafts built to sail upon the lake and could hold upward to sixty men, a hundred if they packed them in like sardines.

Twenty small craft had been on their way with supplies and reinforcements. When they were just over a mile from Xith, the boat appeared approaching from the southwest. By the time the battle was over, six boats were afire and another two captured. The rest had beaten a retreat back to Pickwood.

Two bands of men had been dispatched with the objective of destroying the enemy's ship. The first band never returned while the second was discovered shortly after their arrival in Cuellyn and set upon. Two men made it back to Pickwood with news the ship remained intact. They also reported several others of lesser size were being constructed in Cuellyn's shipyards. Their best guess was that the first of the new boats would be ready within the week. All this boded ill for their relief effort. Now instead of using what limited space they had on their remaining ships for supplies, they were forced to bring along soldiers, primarily archers for defense. And should the Ullentites gain additional ships, they may not be able to reach Xith at all.

Coming around the table, Captain Hopewell headed for the door. "May as well see if they are worth anything," he said. A glance to Sergeant Yerrin revealed his thoughts on the matter. They weren't good.

Outside, the new men, men of course being a term that could only be ascribed to less than half, stood in four semi-straight rows awaiting the Captain's pleasure. Some wore armor that hadn't seen use in a generation, most likely a legacy handed down from a father or grandfather who could no longer serve.

A few looked to be worth the space it would require to send them to Xith. The rest were a total washout, most of those had fear visibly etched upon their faces. "Alright," announced Captain Hopewell as he stood before them, "who has any fighting experience?"

Four hands rose in the air. Surprisingly, one of them belonged to the group of peach-faced youngsters whom he originally dismissed as being useless. The lad did not bear the look of fear, rather fierce determination stared out from under his unruly brown locks.

"You four," he said, indicating the men with raised hands, "go with Sergeant Yerrin." In a quiet aside to the sergeant, he added, "Check the kid to make sure he can fight. If he can't, send him back to rejoin the others."

"Yes sir," replied the sergeant. Then to the four men, "Fall out and follow me." The remaining men practically breathed a sigh of relief as the four were marched away.

"The rest of you will be sent to the Pass," he announced. "They need brave defenders such as yourselves just as much as does Xith." Turning to his right, he signaled for one of the nearby soldiers to approach.

"These men are to be sent to the Pass," he informed the soldier. "See that they are fed and arrangements made for travel."

"Yes sir," the soldier replied with a salute. Turning to the men he hollered, "Fall out and follow me."

As the men were being led away, Captain Hopewell turned back to the inn, sighed, and shook his head. He doubted if any of them would be more than sword fodder. Still, a man perched high upon a wall in the midst of battle could prove useful. And they were willing to fight, even if the thought scared most of them to death.

Just before entering the inn, he paused and glanced in the direction of the docks. The latest relief convoy had yet to return. They were already an hour overdue and he was growing worried. One, maybe two more such convoys could be sent downriver before the enemy's presence upon the lake became too great. This last shipment had set off two hours before dusk in order to reach the lake once night had fallen in the hopes of slipping past the waiting enemy ship in the dark.

Overhead the sun was already past its zenith and steadily making its way to the horizon. If the boats failed to return soon, there would be scant time in which to load the waiting supplies and men. For too long of a delay would necessitate either risking the boats crossing the lake in the morning hours after the sun had risen, which would increase their risk tenfold, or wait until the following afternoon. Such a delay would be disastrous for the defenders at Xith.

Word from the walled city was not good. Already most of the defender's emplaced siege equipment had been destroyed by the Ullentites. The only good news was that the defensive wall surrounding the city was holding against repeated bombardments by the enemy's catapults. When the boats arrived the day before from bringing supplies to the beleaguered city, he had been informed that the ramparts showed definite wear, but were holding.

Back inside he resumed going over the list of supplies to be sent on the next trip. Sheathes of desperately needed arrow shafts, accompanying sacks of feathers for fletching, and a dozen other items which had to go. Only they didn't have enough room to send it all, not if they were to also ferry reinforcements as well.

An hour went by as he agonized over what to bring and what to leave for the next shipment. In his mind he knew that this upcoming shipment may be the last they will be able to get through to Xith. The waters of the lake were becoming increasingly perilous. Ullentite soldiers were also seen along the river north of the lake.

Putting the list aside, he leaned back in his chair and stretched. The hours spent pouring over dispatches and winnowing down the resupply list were beginning to tell. He was about to have one of his subordinates fetch him a plate of food from the inn's kitchen when three men entered through the front door.

One was definitely a priest, another had a sword hanging at his hip and bore the look of one who knew how to use it. The third looked to be an ordinary citizen completely out of his element.

"Excuse me," said Sergeant Lanfre who was one of Captain Hopewell's aides as he crossed to the door and met the newcomers, "but this inn is for official business only. You will have to find room at another."

"We know that," replied the man with the sword. "Our business is with Captain Hopewell. We understand he is the one with whom we need to speak."

The captain silently watched the interplay between his aide and the three men.

"In what way do you need to speak with the Captain?" Sergeant Lanfre asked.

"We wish to accompany the next resupply shipment to Xith," answered the priest. Then he caught sight of the captain sitting at the table. "Captain," the priest said. "It is urgent that we speak with you."

Sergeant Lanfre glanced questioningly over to Captain Hopewell. When the captain nodded and said, "I'll speak with them," the sergeant stepped aside and gestured for the three men to proceed.

The man with the sword took the lead as the three came before his table. "When is the next shipment due to be dispatched to Xith?" the swordsman demanded without so much as a how do you do.

Captain Hopewell didn't immediately answer.

"Well?" the swordsman asked impatiently.

"Well what?" replied the Captain.

"Are you going to tell us when the next shipment is scheduled to be sent to Xith?" demanded the swordsman.

Once more there was a period of silence between them before the captain said, "I can't think of a single reason why I should." Casting a glance to his aide, the captain silently signaled that additional soldiers may be needed. As the aide left the inn, he turned his attention to the priest.

The priest looked tired. That was the best description he could ascribe to the follower of Casdralla standing before him. His robe looked less than pristine. Several holes and tears dotted fabric stained almost beyond recognition. Only the cut of the robe would have given any indication of who and what he was.

"Father," the captain greeted with a smile.

"Captain," the priest said and silently gave him a quick blessing. "I am Father Thomas, late of the Billin Temple." As he introduced his two companions, the captain's eyebrows raised ever so slightly. "You must excuse my companion," he continued. "We have been on a long journey."

A quick glance to Larus and then his attention returned to the priest. "Were you in Billin when the enemy attacked?" he asked.

Father Thomas shook his head. "No I am afraid," he said sadly. "I was on my way back from the High Temple when they struck. They were gone by the time I arrived."

"I am truly sorry," Captain Hopewell said with heartfelt sincerity.

"Yes," he agreed.

The captain's attention was firmly fixed on Father Thomas. He pointedly ignored Larus. "Why do you and your companions need to reach Xith?" he asked. "I doubt if you would make it out again should the city fall."

His words said more to Father Thomas than perhaps the captain had intended. The way he said, 'should the city fall', indicated he thought it to be a likely possibility. "The situation is that bad?" asked Father Thomas. Fear for the citizens of Xith, not to mention the High Priestess Trystia and the Fathers who had journeyed there with her, filled him.

Captain Hopewell ignored the question. Instead he said, "I can ill spare the space it would require to ferry you and your two companions down the river and to the city. We have little enough room for the supplies desperately needed by the defenders."

"I can appreciate that," assured Father Thomas. "However, we are on a mission for the Lady and our need is dire."

Again, the captain's eyebrows raised in surprise. "You are on a mission for our Lady Casdralla?" he asked.

Father Thomas nodded. "Yes," he replied. "It has brought us out of the grasp of the Ullentites and through a darkness of which I shall not speak. Now, our Lady has directed us to Xith."

He could see the inner contemplation of the captain as he spoke and during the silence afterward. Father Thomas would hate to be in the captain's position right now. Would the captain believe him? Or decide that supplies were more important than three individuals whose path may or may not have been directed by Casdralla. The fact that he was a priest had to bear some influence.

"I can fight," Larus announced when the silence dragged on far longer than he thought it should. "Better than any in your command."

The captain's eyes flicked toward him and studied him for a moment. "Easy enough to say," he replied. "A sheathe of arrows can kill more of the enemy than any one man. And for me to allow the three of you a place in the boats would necessitate leaving more than one behind."

"I assure you," urged Father Thomas, "that if you allow us to travel to Xith, Casdra's fortunes in this conflict will be improved a thousandfold."

Just then, Sergeant Yerrin entered with half a dozen men and started toward the three standing before the captain. With a look and gesture, Captain Hopewell indicated the situation was under control.

Sergeant Yerrin understood and brought the men to a halt, staying just within the inn's foyer. They kept a quiet vigil on the proceedings unfolding in the common room.

Turning his attention back to the priest, Captain Hopewell said, "I am sorry Father, but I cannot afford to sacrifice the cargo which would have to be left behind should you accompany the boats."

The face of the swordsman before him whom the priest named Larus grew red with anger. "But you have to take us!" he heard him exclaim.

"No I do not!" stated the captain. "What more possible aid could you bring that the High Priestess and all the Fathers haven't?"

Larus pointed toward Hunter and said, "Him! We have him."

For the first time, Captain Hopewell took a really good look at Hunter. He found him to be a rather nondescript individual. Lacking a sword or any other type of weapon, he failed to see any significance the man may hold. Despite himself, he couldn't help but laugh.

"This is no joke Captain Hopewell," Father Thomas asserted with all sincerity, drawing the captain's attention. "Amidst the smoldering ashes of the once peaceful town of Billin, I prayed to the Lady for aid." His voice took on a reverent tone, "A Qyaendri appeared before me and delivered Hunter into my care. *'There is a task which this man must complete,'* the Qyaendri said to me. *'You, Father Thomas, must aid him in whatever way you are able.'"*

"We have learned that his task is to stand upon the walls of Xith," he stated. "If he should not stand upon the walls at the appointed hour, then everything we hold dear will come to ruin."

The words were doubtful to his ears, but the intensity with which Father Thomas uttered them gave them credence. "What difference can he possibly make?" asked Captain Hopewell.

"We do not know," admitted Larus. "But we are certain that should Hunter not reach the walls of Xith, Xith…will…fall!" Next to him Father Thomas nodded agreement. Throughout the entire conversation, the one they called Hunter had remained silent, as if he was oblivious to what they were saying.

Father Thomas noted his curious stare toward Hunter. "He does not speak our language," he explained.

The captain's eyes narrowed. "A foreigner?" he asked suspiciously.

Larus nodded and gave him a humorless grin. "From farther away than you might think," he replied.

"Nevertheless," interrupted Father Thomas, "he is on our side and committed to the defense of our people."

What was a couple more sheathes of arrows? pondered the captain. He was doubtful as to the usefulness of a man who could not even speak the language, but there was something very convincing about the priest. His words were hard to dismiss, far harder than one would expect. "Very well," he said, giving in. "But the point may be moot in any event."

"Why is that?" Father Thomas asked.

"The boats are late in returning," he explained. "If they fail to return in the next hour, we will be forced to wait until tomorrow."

"Why so long?" asked Larus.

"The lake between where the river empties into it and Xith is being patrolled by a rather large ship," replied the captain. "We have few enough boats remaining to us and dare not risk crossing the lake during daylight. The last time our boats were caught out in the open, many were lost."

"Then there is only one thing which we can do," declared Father Thomas. "We must pray for their speedy return."

Chapter 29

In the common room of another inn, not far from the one taken over by Captain Hopewell, Larus gazed out the window as the last rays of the evening sun disappeared below the horizon.

"So that's it," commented Hunter. Seated at a table still cluttered with the remnants of their evening meal, he waited for Larus' reply. "We'll never make it in time."

Larus ignored his remarks. The weight of time lay heavily upon him. Ftheril had said five days, four days ago. And with the setting of the sun, Captain Hopewell would not take the risk of exposing his few remaining boats to daytime travel across the lake.

"No," stated Larus as he turned to meet Hunter's stare. "We will not wait and sit idly by while these good people come to ruin."

"But what is there to do?" asked Hunter. "The boats are too late in returning and none others will be sent before tomorrow afternoon at the earliest. If they return at all that is. And according to the serving girl, the boats have never been this late before. She and everyone else doubts whether they will be back at all."

Larus' face grew grave as he turned and resumed staring out the window toward the docks. From where he stood, he had a good view of the pier where they would be loading the boats for their next run. A dozen guards stood watch, all casting worried gazes downriver. If only there was another boat!

As if he was thinking the same thing, Father Thomas asked, "Perhaps there is another boat that has not been appropriated for the relief effort?"

"I doubt it," replied Larus, then paused. Turning about, he directed his gaze toward Father Thomas. "Is there?"

Father Thomas didn't answer right away. When he did, he kept his voice low so as not to be overheard. "Thus far, we have been given everything we need to continue upon the road the Lady has set for us. First, our escape from the Ullentites. Then Father Biern just happened to break his leg so he could aid us in learning the whereabouts of the Or'tux temple. Hunter's finding of the crystal spider, not to mention the way he discovered the entrance to the temple. Every step of the way, we have had guidance and aid from above."

Nodding, Larus began to understand. "So you think a boat may have been 'overlooked' when the relief convoy was created?"

"The Lady provides," replied Father Thomas matter-of-factly.

And so She does as he more than anyone on this world would know. But the sheer amount of help they have thus far received in so short a time was far above anything anyone else has ever been given that he can recall. Could they hope for a little bit more? Leaving the window, Larus crossed to the table and sat. "Where would it be?" he asked.

Father Thomas shrugged. "That I do not know," he replied. "But I am certain that one is out there. We simply have to find it."

"How?" Larus asked. "Pray?"

"How do you think I know for certain that there is a boat available for our use?" he replied. "I know there is one, just not where."

Larus sighed. "It could be anywhere." He believed him. Priests were much more in tune to directions from above, especially this one.

"Perhaps we should take a walk around town," Father Thomas suggested. "I doubt if the boat will be found within the confines of this inn."

"Good idea," agreed Larus. Then to Hunter, "Come on, we're going to see what is going on out there."

"We are?" he asked.

Larus nodded then said, "We aren't going to wait for the boats to return."

Hunter's expression grew grim. "What are you planning to do?"

"Find a way down the river," he explained. "One way or another, we are going to reach the walls of Xith before time runs out."

Hunter grabbed his pack that rested against the legs of his chair before coming to his feet. As he followed Larus and Father Thomas from the inn, his left hand caressed the ring found in the tomb beneath the Or'tux temple. What properties it held that will enable him to throw back the Ullentite onslaught continued to remain a mystery. During their ride to Pickwood, he had slipped the ring on his finger and made several attempts to activate the latent magic they were sure it held. All to no avail.

Father Thomas had been loath to touch it as it belonged to a people that history stated practiced the most evil and vile rituals imaginable. However, when Hunter failed to get a reaction from the ring, Larus convinced him to see what he could do with it. But after several minutes of concentration and prayer, he too failed.

All this gave him cause to worry about what was going to happen when it came time for him to stand upon the walls of Xith. Would the ring react and thwart the Ullentite attack? Or would it remain inert as it had thus far? He and the others were certain the ring was special, held some property which would save the people of this land. If only he knew what it was and how to bring it forth.

Following along behind, Hunter continued rubbing the ring in his pocket until they reached the dock and the relief staging area. Crates, sheathes, and a dozen other items were stacked and ready to load for when the boats returned. He idly gazed at the various waiting cargo while Larus and Father Thomas spoke to the soldier in charge.

Aside from the pier and a couple small warehouses adjacent to the docking area, there wasn't much to grab Hunter's attention. It took but a few moments for him to grow bored. A glance to where Larus appeared to be arguing with two soldiers seemed to indicate that whatever they were discussing, wasn't going in their favor.

Should have stayed at the inn, he thought to himself. He was tired and all he wanted to do was sit down and rest. He couldn't remember a time since coming to this world that he had been able to simply sit and do nothing for any length of time, the two days recuperating after leaving the Or'tux temple didn't count as he was unable to enjoy it. Weary was an understatement of how he felt.

Not far from where the argument was growing more heated, he spied three crates nestled against the side of a warehouse. They looked to have been there for some time and he figured no one would mind if he took his ease upon them. Crossing over, he sat down on one and rested back against the wooden planks comprising the warehouse's side.

The evening was still warm with the hint of a breeze wafting coolly from up the river. Occasional gusts of air felt good and Hunter soon grew quite relaxed. He noticed Father Thomas glancing around, his eyes finally coming to rest on where he sat and Hunter gave him a brief wave letting him know he was okay. Father Thomas returned the wave then turned back to the argument Larus was having with the soldiers.

A minute went by, then two. Hunter grew more and more relaxed as he waited for Larus to finish and perhaps they could return to the inn. Inns had beds and he desperately wanted to avail himself of that particular accommodation as soon as possible.

Whack...whack...whack

As he drifted closer to the realm of sleep, muffled sounds of repeated bangs intruded upon his repose. At first he wasn't sure what he was hearing, but when after a brief pause they began once more, he recognized the sound. It was hammering and seemed to be coming from the other side of the warehouse wall. Intrigued, he turned his head and placed his ear against the wall.

Whack...whack...whack...whack

Bored and with nothing better to do, his curiosity got the better of him. Putting his eye to a gap between two planks, he peered through to the other side. All he could see from this vantage point was a solitary candle burning on a table. Next to it he could barely see someone's backside and the rise and fall of a hammer. What the person was hammering was too far to the side for him to be able to make out. So moving further to his right, Hunter found another gap and put his eye to it just as the hammering stopped.

It was a young man, couldn't have been more than eighteen, maybe twenty at the most. He was moving to where several narrow planks leaned against the table with the candle. There, he picked up one and sighted along its length. Scowling, he put it back then selected another. This time the young man gave a brief nod and mumbled something to himself before returning to a large, somewhat rounded wooden construction.

Hunter watched as the young man set the wooden plank against a gap in the construction, measured it, then took a saw and proceeded to cut off the unwanted section. Once the plank was shortened, he spread a black looking goo along one edge then set the plank flush into the gap with the goo covered edge pressing into a plank already in place.

Whack...whack...whack

The hammer fell several times before the young man returned to the spare planks leaning against the table and proceeded to select another. Hunter could see he was about to start the process over again.

From the pier area came Larus' voice as he continued arguing. About what, Hunter didn't know, most likely boats and such. All he wanted was to reach Xith, get this over with, and be sent home. In his pocket his hand worried over the ring, his thumb continuously turning the ring as it lay in his palm.

Not far down the wall from his position stood the warehouse's door. With nothing better to do, he hopped down from the crate and walked over to it. The door wasn't locked so he opened it and strode in.

Immediately, the hammering stopped and the young man turned toward him. Directing a nervous look toward Hunter, the young man stood still, hammer poised to strike the head of a nail.

Now that he could see the construction in its entirety, he grinned. It was a boat. Damaged to be sure, with most of its surface showing scorched marks and another good sized hole in the bottom aside from the one the young man was working to patch, but this may just be what they were looking for.

"Hi," Hunter greeted. Stepping inside, he closed the door behind him and took three steps before coming to a stop.

Words came from the young man. Though unable to understand the meaning, the inflection of his voice indicated a question was being asked. Most likely 'Who are you?' or 'What are you doing here?'

"Can I help?" Hunter asked in a calm and reassuring tone. Using gestures pantomiming hammering, he slowly drew closer. But when the young man's face grew grim and his hand edged closer to a sword resting against the side of the boat, Hunter stopped.

Another odd thing that caught his eye was the hammer. The head was covered in cloth which seemed odd. But that would account for why the sound of hammering had been muffled. It couldn't have made the job any easier.

A word issued forth from the young man in a commanding tone. Accompanied by the gesture of him pointing toward the door gave little doubt as to its meaning.

Hunter gestured to himself and then the door through which he just entered.

The young man nodded. When Hunter failed to immediately turn and leave, the young man's hand closed on the pommel of the sword.

That was enough for Hunter. Backing up, he quickly left the warehouse. Just as he was closing the door, he heard Larus call his name. He turned to find Larus and Father Thomas coming toward him, Larus looking mad while Father Thomas was more relieved.

"We thought something happened to you," admonished Larus.

"Sorry," he apologized. "But…"

"You shouldn't go off on your own like that," continued Larus, cutting him off in mid sentence. "We can't afford anything happening to you. Not that we're this close."

"I know, but…" he began before Larus cut him off yet again.

"There are two boats available but are being reserved for the next relief convoy. If they send one that is. From what that soldier said, should the boats due back fail to return, they won't send them at all." Scowling back toward the soldier with whom he had so recently been arguing he added, "Father Thomas and I plan to talk with Captain Hopewell and convince him to release one to us. If we get him to agree soon, we'll still be able to make Xith with time to spare."

"Do you think he will?" asked Hunter.

"Between the good Father and myself," stated Larus, "we'll wear him down. Why don't you wait for us at the inn?" And with that, he grabbed Father Thomas by the elbow and together they speedily headed toward the inn wherein Captain Hopewell directed the relief effort.

They were gone before he could get another word out. As he watched them walk away, the whack…whack…whack…of the young man's hammering beat a quiet staccato in the background.

When his two companions finally arrived at the inn from their meeting with the captain, Hunter was nursing a mug of ale in the common room. He had positioned himself so he could observe the front door and saw the way Larus stormed into the inn. The grim set of his face and clenched hands indicated the meeting with the captain hadn't gone off as he had hoped.

"No luck?" he asked as Larus and Father Thomas approached the table.

"He says it would be suicide for us to go by ourselves," spat Larus. "That in all good conscious he cannot accede to our request." Plopping in a chair, he exclaimed in English, "Idiot!"

"So what do you plan to do?" Hunter asked.

"He's left us with little choice," replied Larus. "We'll have to take one by force."

Father Thomas was looking grim. Hunter was sure Larus had already discussed his plans with him and the priest didn't appear to approve. "Maybe there is another way?"

"What are you talking about?" asked Larus.

"Perhaps we could find another boat," he explained.

"We've talked with a dozen different people," argued Larus. "They all say the two boats held by the soldiers are the only ones left in Pickwood."

"Could be they're wrong," Hunter stated, and then grinned.

"I tell you there is...," he began, then something about the way Hunter was grinning caused him to trail off. "What?" he asked.

"There *is* another boat," he said, with a slight emphasis on 'is'. Then he explained about discovering the young man working to restore the broken boat in the warehouse.

"Why didn't you tell us before?" demanded Larus.

"I tried," Hunter replied. "But you kept cutting me off. And then you grabbed Father Thomas and were gone before I could get two words out."

Larus gave Father Thomas a quick rundown of what Hunter just told him. The priest's expression turned to one of relief when he realized there may be a way other than storming the soldiers guarding the two boats. In the ensuing battle, lives assuredly would have been lost.

Once finished filling in Father Thomas, Larus scooted his chair back and came to his feet. "Let's go see this young man and his boat," he said.

"He was a bit nervous," explained Hunter. "Almost attacked me when I didn't leave the warehouse quickly enough."

"Don't worry about him," Larus said patting his sword. "I'm sure we'll be able to handle it. Besides, Father Thomas and I will be able to communicate with him."

"I hope you are right," wished Hunter. Downing the rest of his ale, he came to his feet and followed the other two from the inn. Once they returned to the dock area, he directed Larus toward the warehouse containing the young man and the boat.

As they drew closer, he listened for the whack...whack...whack of the hammer but no sound came from within the warehouse. Upon reaching the door, Hunter urged caution as the former Qyaendri took the handle, turned, and entered.

The candle was burnt down to a nub but still alive. The boat was in the same position as it had been before, upside down on a stand. The holes were repaired, black tar lining the cracks between the new boards giving the underside of the boat a rather ugly appearance. Of the young man there was no sign.

"Where did he go do you suppose?" asked Hunter.

"I doubt if you scared him off," stated Larus. "If that had been the case, he wouldn't have finished patching the holes." Coming to the boat, he inspected the seams and the tar which had formed globules of sticky goo along the cracks. Pointing to the tar, Larus said, "This is going to reduce the speed of the boat." Glancing back to Hunter he added, "Could even make steerage difficult."

Glancing around, he found the warehouse's workbench and removed a trowel-like tool. It had a short handle and a wide, narrow head. Bringing the tool to the boat, he began scraping off the excess tar. "It still won't be a perfect job," he explained as he flicked a mess of recently removed tar off the tool and onto the floor, "but this should improve its maneuverability."

Scraping off more of the tar, he failed to notice the door on the far side of the warehouse open and someone enter. "What do you think you are doing?" a voice demanded.

Three heads swiveled toward the young man who had just entered. At his hip rested a sword and his expression was less than congenial.

"Just removing some of the excess tar," Larus explained.

The young man came forward with hand on the hilt of his sword. "Get away from my boat."

"Your boat?" questioned Larus.

Nodding, the young man replied, "That's right. It's my boat. Now please, step away."

Larus took one step back and dropped the trowel to the floor. Indicating Hunter, he said, "Our friend said you were patching this boat and we thought we would come and see if we could help."

"I don't need any help," asserted the young man. Coming to a stop several feet shy of Larus, he struck as menacing a pose as he could muster. All in all, it did little to intimidate Larus.

"How do you plan to get it in the river?" he asked.

Surprised, the young man's menacing façade slipped. "River?"

Larus nodded. "You have the look of someone on the road to vengeance," he said. "Or am I off the mark?"

Silence hung between the two men as the young man stared at Larus.

"We too seek to reach Xith without the complications of dealing with Captain Hopewell," added Larus. "I'm sure he believes this boat to be beyond repair. Else it would have been fixed already and put to use ferrying supplies to Xith." Gazing into the young man's eyes he asked, "Am I right?"

Still the young man stood silently. His eyes darted from Larus to Father Thomas. He took in the robes which marked him unmistakably as a priest of Casdralla, and finally to Hunter.

"I'm sure it's easily large enough to accommodate four people," Larus said, drawing the young man's attention back to him. When it looked as if the young man was going to balk, he added, "Of course, we could always put the matter before Captain Hopewell and see what he says."

That took the bluster out of the young man and he shook his head. "No," he said. "I don't think that will be necessary."

Coming to stand beside Larus, Father Thomas said, "My son, we are on our Lady's business and must reach Xith as soon as possible. It would seem that this boat is the only way in which we can arrive in time without undue complications."

The words of Father Thomas appeared to soften the young man's attitude still further. "You mean you are on a quest for our Lady Casdralla?" he asked.

Father Thomas nodded. "You could say that," he replied.

The barest hint of a grin appeared on his face. "Then that would mean your chances of reaching Xith are good," he reasoned.

"That's right," agreed Larus. "And any who come with us."

"I'm in," the young man said after only a moment's consideration. "When do we leave?"

Chapter 30

The young man's name was Garin, the second son of a farmer from a small village in northwestern Casdra near Ascet. "My older brother joined the guards a year ago," he explained to Father Thomas. "Two weeks before word came of the Ullentite invasion, we received a letter from him stating how he was being assigned to the garrison at Xith. We have had no word since."

Tears formed in his eyes though he did the best he could to hide them. "He was so excited about the post," said Garin. "He told me that when harvest was over he wanted me to visit and he would show me the sights." Sadness worked to take control but he swallowed and pushed it down. "I hope he still lives."

"So how did you come to be here?" asked Father Thomas.

He gave a rueful chuckle. "My grandfather," he replied. "He used to be in the guard way back when, even made captain before he retired. All our lives my brother and I had been filled with his tales of glory. Whenever we went for a visit, he would teach us sword craft. Of course our mother disapproved but she never directly forbade it."

"When word came that the Ullentites had attacked and Xith was besieged, grandfather gave me his sword and said, *'Garin, the years have taken their toll on me. It's up to you now. Do me proud.'* And with his sword and a pouch full of coins, I made my way here."

As the two talked quietly, Larus stood at a window overlooking the area between the warehouse and the river. A solitary guard stood near the water and they would have to wait until he moved off before making their run to the river. The wait was more due to Father Thomas than anything else. He feared that should the guard attempt to block their passage, that someone would get hurt. And knowing of Larus' prowess with the sword, well knew who that person would be. So they waited.

In the quiet of the warehouse, he continued listening to the tale spun by young Garin. "When I arrived in Pickwood, I learned that my chances of reaching Xith were small. With the boats having yet to return, I realized I had to find another way."

"And that is how you came to find this boat?" prompted Father Thomas.

Garin nodded. "It was in pretty bad shape," he explained. "I don't know how it even made it back up the river with the holes in its bottom. They must have run into trouble for as you can see, most of the outward side has been scored by flames. I even dug two arrowheads out of the rail."

"That guard is still there," interrupted Larus. Turning back to Father Thomas he said, "We'll give him another ten minutes. But after that, we have to get going."

"Then let us pray he moves before then," replied the priest. After quietly saying a brief prayer asking for just that, he returned his attention to Garin. "How did you think to get the boat to the river by yourself?"

"I hadn't figured that out yet," he replied. "But I wasn't going to let that stop me."

Hunter sat over on a crate trying not to feel left out since he couldn't follow the conversation. He knew that if anything important was said that Larus would be sure to let him know. But there had been much discussion going on and not one word of translation had he received. All in all he was getting a bit annoyed.

"You did a good job in patching the holes," Larus said.

Garin shrugged. "That was the easy part," he explained.

"I thought you said you were a farmer's son," stated Larus. "I didn't know there were any shipwrights in your family."

"There aren't," replied Garin. "All farmers have to know how to work with tools and wood. As my father always said, 'A farmer is the most skilled, unskilled labor there is.' Which is true. A farmer has to know how to do everything."

"I agree with you there," Larus said. "Farmers are much more capable than most of those living in cities."

A shout from outside drew his attention back to the window. A guard from over by the main dock area was shouting to the one standing in their way. Larus watched in satisfaction as the guard began walking over to the dock area. In a moment the way was clear to the river.

"Alright people," Larus said. "He's moved off."

"Time to go?" asked Hunter.

"Yes it is," replied Larus. Crossing over to the side of the boat, he had the other three join him in lifting it off the stand. Then they carried it over to the large loading doors facing the river.

After pausing by the window to ensure the route to the river was momentarily free of others, Larus swung the loading door open. As soon as there was enough room for the boat to pass, they made for the river.

"No matter what," Larus said, "don't stop."

"What do you think I am," replied Garin, "stupid?" Across his back was secured two oars which would be needed once they were on the water.

They barely made it a quarter of the way to the water's edge before the cry went up. Soldiers seeing their flight to the water carrying the boat were moving to intercept.

"Move!" exclaimed Larus as he pushed them faster.

"Stop!" one soldier yelled. Larus glanced in his direction and saw that it was the same one he had argued with not very long ago.

"I don't think so!" shouted Garin with a laugh.

Halfway to the water now and the soldiers were gaining fast. It was going to be close. Suddenly, Father Thomas cried out as he slipped and fell. Larus paused only a moment as he and the other two redistributed the weight of the boat. In the bat of an eye, Father Thomas regained his feet. With an apology and a comment about how his robe tripped him up, they were off.

Glancing over his shoulder, Larus saw Captain Hopewell appear. Shouting orders he rallied his men. He wasn't about to allow a serviceable boat to get away.

Now with less than a quarter of the way to go, Garin suddenly let go of the boat. "Get it into the water!" he cried as he drew his sword and turned to face the oncoming soldiers.

Those racing after slowed as they approached this determined young man. With steel held at the ready, Garin faced a score of soldiers, some with many years of experience. Before the first soldier had a chance to close, Garin shouted a war cry and attacked.

"Brave fool," murmured Larus. Those soldiers were going to cut him to pieces. But at least he was giving them the time they needed to reach the water and ready the boat. As the clash of steel on steel rang out in the dark, they reached the water's edge.

Larus waded out into the water several feet where he and Hunter managed to right the boat and set it afloat. "You first Father," he said and helped the priest into the boat. After he was safely in, Hunter climbed aboard. Then, giving the boat a mighty push away from the shore, Larus hopped in. As the current took them and they began floating downriver, Larus suddenly looked back to where Garin still fought. "The oars!" he exclaimed. They were still strapped to Garin's back. "I've got to go back!"

About to jump into the river, the sound of swordplay ceased and a shadow began racing along the beach. It was Garin, the oar handles rising above either shoulder was a dead giveaway.

"Come on!" Larus shouted as the young man kept running.

"Go!" Garin shouted and remained on the beach making no attempt to enter the water and reach the boat.

"What is he doing?" asked Father Thomas.

The shoreline was filled with soldiers in pursuit of Garin.

Racing along the shoreline, he quickly reached the dock area. Jumping up onto the dock without so much as slowing, he evaded three soldiers as they tried to grab him then raced for the second warehouse.

The two story tall structure loomed at the edge of the water. As the three companions floated with the current, they saw the shadow that was Garin merge with that of the warehouse. They kept watch on the warehouse expecting Garin to emerge on the other side. But when he failed to appear,

Larus grew worried. Then, just as hope began to fail, Hunter pointed to the roof and shouted, "Look!"

"What does that fool think he's doing?" queried Larus.

Atop the warehouse, they saw Garin run across the roof toward the river. Just before he reached the end, Father Thomas said, "Oh my," as it became clear what Garin's plan was to be. Racing to the edge, Garin took a flying leap out over the water. Diving in a less than graceful manner, he soared over fifteen feet before impacting with the water.

"Back!" hollered Larus. They were a good forty feet further downstream from where Garin disappeared below the surface. Three pairs of hands dipped into the water and fought against the current to bring them back upstream.

Seconds ticked by and Garin failed to resurface. Larus feared he may have suffered an injury when he hit the water. "Garin!" he shouted. In the dark of night it was hard to see more than intermittent glimmers upon the water from the stars and moon above.

"Father," said Larus, "watch the right side." Switching to English he told Hunter to keep an eye on the left. The expanse of water behind the boat was his province. Straining for any evidence of Garin either swimming or floating, he strained his eyes to the utmost.

"See anything?" he asked. Two voices replied negatively. "Garin!" he again shouted. Then suddenly, the left side of the boat tipped dangerously close to the water. All three lost their balance in the sudden shift and Hunter almost fell from the boat.

"Here," Garin's voice called out. Then he laughed. "Man that was fun!"

Larus turned to find him gripping the side of the boat and pulling himself inside. As he did so, the left side again approached precariously close to the surface of the water. Now that he knew what was causing it, Larus immediately shifted his weight as a counterbalance. In a moment, Garin was out of the water.

Despite the lack of light, Larus could see the young man grinning. "Are you crazy?" he asked. "A jump like that could kill a man."

"Relax," replied Garin. "Did stuff like that all the time back home. Besides it was the quickest way to evade the soldiers and still get to you before you sailed out of reach."

Father Thomas came and sat next to him. "Are you injured?" he asked.

Garin shook his head. "Naw," he assured the priest. "All I did was slow them down so you could get the boat in the water. Once I was sure you were safely on the water, I broke off and ran like He..., uh sorry Father."

Patting him on the back, Father Thomas grinned and said, "Do not worry about it. I am simply glad you are unharmed."

Back on the shore, soldiers stood watching as they sailed away, none were making to pursue. Larus wasn't certain, but he thought he saw Captain Hopewell waving goodbye. Retrieving the oars from Garin, he began rowing vigorously downriver. "Do you know the waters between Pickwood and Xith?" he asked their new companion.

"Sorry but no," replied Garin. "I've only been to Xith once and that was when I was little and we went by way of the pass."

"We have several hours before the river empties out into the lake," explained Father Thomas. "After that it is another hour or two across open water to Xith's harbor."

"I heard one of the guards saying there is a rather large, bowman filled boat that guards the mouth of the river," offered Garin. "He said the last time they passed through they lost several ships to it."

"We heard that as well," replied Father Thomas. Glancing to Larus, he asked, "Any idea how we are going to avoid that obstacle?"

"Not as yet," admitted Larus. "But I am sure we'll come up with something when the time comes." For the following hours until daylight he wracked his brain coming up with a solution.

Three men lay asleep in the bottom of the boat while the fourth kept it centered on the river. The current was moving the boat along rapidly enough so all Larus had to do was use one of the oars as a rudder to maintain their position.

Off to the east, the sky above the treetops was beginning to lighten with the coming of dawn. Over the past several hours, he had struggled to come up with a brilliant maneuver to get them past whatever may lay in wait for them ahead. Unfortunately, brilliance only comes when you know what you are up against.

A few contingency plans had come to mind, depending on the situation. He even thought that should the woods along the last mile of river before the lake prove thick enough in which to hide, that they could take the boat from the water and carry it through the forest to the lake, thereby bypassing the enemy ship that must assuredly be waiting for them at the mouth of the river. None of his ideas were really certain of seeing them through. And as night faded away to dawn, his mind worked overtime.

Black sky turned to a dark blue, then continued to lighten even further. The first to awaken was Father Thomas. He had lain in an awkward position the last half hour and Larus was sure he would have a sore back.

"Where are we?" asked Father Thomas. Sitting up, he glanced to either side of the boat then took a good look downriver.

"Still on the river," replied Larus. "I stowed the oars and let the current carry us so you could have more time to rest before things became…rushed."

"Rushed," replied Father Thomas with a grim chuckle. "That is one way of putting it." Taking another look at their surroundings, he said, "The lake cannot be much further ahead."

"I know," agreed Larus. "Thought perhaps to pull to the shore and scout ahead before we stumble into a trap."

"You think there is one?" asked Father Thomas.

Larus nodded. "There has to be," he replied. "This river is the only avenue your people have of sending men and supplies to Xith. Any commander worth his salt would have men in position watching for any traffic coming down the river. Most likely would even have a bevy of archers available to rain a hail of missiles down upon whatever approaches."

Face turning grim, Father Thomas looked downriver again. This time, his eyes scanned the tree-lined shore on either side. "Maybe we should go ashore now," he suggested.

"Very well," Larus agreed. "East bank or west?"

"Why are you asking me?" he asked.

"You have insights the rest of us lack," explained Larus.

Turning back to Larus, Father Thomas asked, "Because I am a priest?"

Nodding, Larus move the oar slightly to keep the current from altering their position. "Absolutely," he replied. "Ask for guidance and you shall have it."

Never one to need much encouragement to pray, Father Thomas said a brief, quiet prayer for guidance. As soon as he finished, the current suddenly jerked the boat to the right.

Smiling, Larus said, "That's the way to do it." Moving the oar acting as their rudder, he began heading the boat to the right.

"That was...startling," stated Father Thomas in awe. "Did a Qyaendri actually take our boat and nudge it aside?"

"Who knows the workings of the mighty?" he said with a grin. "Any other time I would think that unlikely. But now? With so much at stake?"

As they came closer to the shore Father Thomas asked, "Why would now make any difference?"

"We are working on behalf of Casdralla," he explained. "And according to Hunter's dreams, She has everything staked on whether or not Hunter stands upon the walls of Xith at the appointed time. Rest assured, the entire Celestial might She has to bear will be with us."

Father Thomas grew quiet in awe as he thought about the ramification of what he had heard. For Larus' part, he kept glancing to the empty air around them and wondered how many Qyaendri they had in attendance. A hundred? More?

"Oh how wrong you are Larus," Ftheril said. Unseen and unheard, one solitary Qyaendri traveled with them. That was all they dared have accompanying them. When Daeson had informed him that he would be the sole Qyaendri in attendance on their run to Xith, Ftheril had been shocked.

"Surely I cannot be the only one?" he had asked. "For something this important there must be more!"

Daeson shook his head. "They will soon be entering an area with a large presence of Qyaendri serving Theroch," he explained. "One lone Qyaendri traveling with mortals will not draw attention. We cannot afford for our adversaries to realize your four charges are of special importance to us. You must do this alone."

"I will see them through," vowed Ftheril.

"Also, under no circumstances are you to leave them," Daeson said. He could see the question forming. Forestalling his underling by raising his hand, he said, "You must use your own judgment where their prayers are concerned. Do *not* leave them!"

About to argue, it suddenly dawned on Ftheril the magnitude of the trust which was being placed in him. Not only was he to see them through hostile territory, but the judging of prayers which was reserved for only the most experienced of Qyaendri, was to be his as well. Pride swelled within him. "I will not let you down."

"Just don't let them down," Daeson replied, indicating Ftheril's charges. "Get them safely to Xith no matter what."

"Will you be there?" he asked.

Daeson nodded. "I shall await you in Xith." And with that he vanished.

The abrupt halt caused by landing on the bank of the river woke the other two. "Are we there?" asked a bleary eyed Hunter.

"No," replied Larus. "We are still some distance from the lake." Hopping from the boat, he waited for the others to disembark before dragging it completely out of the water. "I plan to scout ahead and see if the enemy has any surprises for us."

"Good," announced Garin. "I was tired of being in that boat." Stretching, he came forward to stand before Larus. "So, when do we go?"

"*We* don't go anywhere," he replied, with a slight emphasis on 'we'. "You are staying here with Father Thomas and Hunter."

"What?" the young man exclaimed. "Why?"

"Both of us can't go," he argued. Then he pointed to Father Thomas and Hunter. "What if the enemy should stumble across them while we are gone? They would stand little chance."

Garin would rather go with Larus. But when faced with such logic how could he honorably leave two unprotected men alone in dangerous territory? "Very well," he grudgingly agreed. "But don't take too long."

"I shall be back before you know it," Larus assured him. Then after a brief conversation with Hunter about what he planned to do, he entered the trees and disappeared.

Father Thomas watched as Garin stared after Larus' departing back. Coming to stand beside the young man, he laid a hand on his shoulder and said, "I am glad you are with us my son."

Turning his gaze toward the priest, Garin gave him a half-hearted grin. "Couldn't very well leave you two undefended now, could I?"

"How about we have a bite to eat while we wait for his return?" suggested Father Thomas.

"Sure," replied Garin then returned to the boat with Father Thomas.

Moving silently through the trees, Larus kept the water in sight as he worked his way further downriver. Time was a fleeting thing with more and more slipping away with every step. He understood the necessity of what he was doing, it was just that it wasted more time they could ill afford to lose.

Half a mile downriver from where he left the other three, he spied what looked to be a small watercraft lying half out of the water. After a brief pause to make sure he was alone in the immediate area, he went to the edge of the treeline bordering the river. From there he hid behind the bole of a tree while he peered around to take a closer look at the boat.

At one time it had been larger than the one he and the others had sailed in from Pickwood. But now a good portion of its front end was missing and the outside had been scorched similar to the scoring on the outside of their boat.

On the inner port side was a vivid red stain suggesting one of the occupants may have lost a lot of blood. A quick scan revealed no bodies among the debris, only the broken remains of the boat.

Unable to learn anything further, he was about to continue downriver when the sound of someone coughing stopped him in his tracks. It came from further downriver on his side of the river. Searching for the source, he discovered where half a dozen men armed with bows were all but concealed by the trees. If not for the cough, he would have stumbled right into them. They hadn't yet noticed his presence. Hunching down, he worked his way closer to get a better view.

To his surprise, he found the men were also in possession of a catapult. Nodding, he now understood what had happened to the front end of the boat he had just discovered. When alerted that someone was coming down the river, these men would ready the catapult and smash whoever it was right out of the water. The bows would then be used to take out any survivors. Turning his gaze to the other side of the river, he found a similar group of men with a second catapult.

He tried gazing downriver to ascertain if any other catapult crews were in position, but due to the denseness of the trees and curvature of the river, wasn't able to see far. If he was the Ullentite commander, he would have several more similar positions in place just in case boats made it past the first pair of catapults.

He had seen enough. Backing up slowly, he kept low until the men were out of sight then hurried back to the others. Once he returned, he filled them in on what he had seen.

"No wonder the boats failed to return," stated Garin. "They must have been taken out by those catapults."

Larus nodded. "Either that, or by the ship waiting for them on the lake," he added.

"Even if they were lucky enough to reach the city," Garin said, "knowing those catapults were waiting for their return would have prevented them from making any attempt to head back up the river."

"I know I wouldn't try it," affirmed Larus. "Going upriver against the current would be slower and thus would have made them sitting ducks for the catapult crews."

"So what now?" Garin asked. "It's obvious we can't go by boat."

Larus silently thought as he gazed downriver in the direction of the catapults. "We walk," he replied. "Skirt through the forest around those watching the river." Turning to Father Thomas, he said, "You will have to guide us through."

Somewhat surprised, the priest replied, "Me?"

Nodding, Larus said, "You." Then glancing around to the empty air around them added, "And our friends."

"What friends?" asked Garin.

Father Thomas knew what 'friends' Larus was talking about. They were the same friends that had 'nudged' their boat directing them to land on the western side of the river.

"If anyone can bring us through this, it is you," Larus stated matter-of-factly.

In his pocket, Father Thomas absentmindedly rubbed the sacred piece of wood as he met Larus' gaze. For the briefest of moments, he entertained doubt as to the rightness of this course of action. But then holy righteousness filled him as complete certainty banished all thoughts of doubt. After giving Larus a nod, he closed his eyes and prayed that they would find safe passage to the lake.

Garin looked first to Larus, then to Father Thomas, and then back to Larus. "What friends are you...?"

Their unseen guardian smiled when the prayer ended and began wafting away from its creator. Ftheril's first inclination was to take the prayer and deliver it to the High Temple for judgment. But such was not to be. He had explicit instructions from Daeson that he was not to leave them for anything. That should prayers be given, he must use his own judgment in determining whether or not to grant them.

The one so recently uttered by Father Thomas was of little surprise. But now that it had been uttered, he could act. One of the laws of the Compact concerning the interaction between Qyaendri and mortals stated that unless specifically directed from above, no Qyaendri could meddle in their affairs. Even if they thought it was for their own good. Much damaged had been wrought by Qyaendri in times past who acted in what they thought were their charge's best interest. But now that he had been asked for help, and in his judgment decided Father Thomas' prayer was worth granting, he was free to help them.

He already had a sense of the area and where those mortals who worshiped Theroch were lying in wait. Ftheril didn't need to rely on finding the mortals specifically, instead he sought the attending Qyaendri. Any group of mortals would have at least one, and the larger the group, the more there would be.

One of Theroch's Qyaendri was in attendance on the group by the catapults. It was of the lesser Qyaendri, those who oversaw the gathering and execution of prayers such as he. Ftheril knew the Qyaendri was aware of him and his charges, but knew also that it would not act upon that knowledge unless specifically directed to do so by a superior, or if prayer was given by one of its charges that was to be granted. Fortunately, the average mortal seldom prayed. Most were content to make their own way in the world, men being even less inclined than women in giving their fate into the hands of another. Also working in their favor was the fact that all Qyaendri were used to seeing Qyaendri in service to rival gods moving about. For it was very common to find several faiths within any given population.

Off to the west another Qyaendri was visible and it was on the move. Fortunately it was heading in a southwesterly direction away from Ftheril and his charges. He found several others attending various groups and soon had a fairly safe route mapped out from where his charges were and the lake. Returning his attention to Father Thomas, he began guiding the way.

When the warm feeling associated with an answered prayer settled over him, Father Thomas knew they were not alone. Opening his eyes, he turned westward and felt a sense of safety and protection every other direction lacked. "This way," he said, pointing westward as he glanced toward Larus.

Larus gave him a grin. "Lead on," he said. Then noticed Garin and the skeptical look he gave the two of them. "What?" Larus asked the young man.

"How does he know where to go?" asked Garin.

"He just does," replied Larus. "Now stay close." After repeating the same piece of advice for Hunter, he hurried after the departing priest.

Father Thomas worked his way almost due west for a hundred feet before the sense of safety disappeared. It took him but a moment to sense the change to a slightly more southerly heading. Turning toward that direction, he continued leading them through.

Larus for his part was confident that Father Thomas was being given direction that would ultimately lead them either to Xith or provide a way for them to reach the city. Of course, that didn't mean they could relax their guard. On the contrary, he well understood that the best path to Xith may not be the safest. Especially considering the woods was fair teeming with Ullentite soldiers. So with that in mind, he kept eyes and ears alert for any sign of the enemy.

Constantly scanning the woods for danger, he kept only a cursory watch on Father Thomas. So when the priest came to an abrupt halt, he almost walked into him.

Moving his mouth to the priest's ear, he whispered, "What?"

"I do not know," replied Father Thomas. Glancing back to Larus, he said, "I think I may have lost the way." Looking distressed, he was about to continue when the sound of many men making their way through the woods came from almost due south.

"Get down!" urged Larus quietly. Grabbing hold of Father Thomas' robe in one hand, and signaling to the two men behind him with the other, he dropped to the ground pulling Father Thomas down with him. A moment later, a score of Ullentite soldiers emerged from out of the trees.

Lying quietly with hearts pounding in fear of being found, four men watched from hiding as enemy soldiers filed past only mere yards away. Hunter gazed in fear and loathing at the men making their way past. Well did he remember the treatment he underwent while held captive. It wasn't until the soldiers had once again disappeared into the trees to the north did he realize he had been holding his breath the entire time.

"I think they are gone," Larus announced quietly. Coming to his feet, he cast a quick glance northward to be sure they were indeed out of sight, then helped Father Thomas to his feet. "I guess we know what it means now if you 'lose the way'."

Father Thomas nodded. "Get down and hide," he replied.

"How did he know those men were coming?" asked Garin.

Turning to the young man, Larus said, "What? Are you just dense boy?" Indicating Father Thomas, he added, "He's a priest."

"Well I know he's a priest," admitted Garin. "But what does that..." Eyes widening in sudden understanding, he left his sentence unfinished.

"That's right," nodded Larus. "Now," he continued as he turned toward Father Thomas, "where to?"

Eyes once again closed, Father Thomas offered a prayer of thankfulness and reiterated his desire to be led safely through the enemy lines. Almost immediately, the warm sensation of a prayer being answered came over him. Rotating first one way then the other, he soon located the feeling of safety. This time it was coming from almost due south. Opening his eyes again, he gave Larus a grin before heading out.

Twice more the sense of safety disappeared moments before enemy soldiers emerged from deeper in the forest. Both times they hid in the forest undergrowth until the danger was past.

The route made no sense to Father Thomas and if it wasn't for the glimpses of the sun through the forest canopy, he would have been completely lost. Often the direction from which the sense of safety came would change within but a couple steps, which had them taking a very serpentine path through the trees.

At one point, the sense of safety suddenly increased. Accompanying the increase was an urge to hurry and he quickened his pace. "Hurry!" he whispered back to the others.

Larus nodded, relaying Father Thomas' command.

Moving quickly through the trees, Father Thomas soon saw two men moving through the trees ahead of them, directly along the path the sense of safety indicated. He slowed but the sense of urgency only intensified. About to move forward, he felt Larus' hand on his shoulder.

"We cannot stop," he said.

"But there are men ahead," Larus warned.

"I know," replied the priest. "But we need to continue and now." A glance to the trees from which they had just emerged brought a feeling of imminent peril.

Larus saw the look of acute apprehension on Father Thomas' face. Drawing his sword, he said, "Follow me." Moving quickly, he headed for the two men before them.

His eyes were locked on the two soldiers, alert for any sign that they recognized danger was approaching. Larus managed to cover over half the distance before they grew aware of his presence. One even raised his hand in greeting in the mistaken belief Larus was one of the many Ullen soldiers infesting the forest. But the greeting died on his lips when Larus' naked blade came into view.

The shock of seeing him caused the soldiers to hesitate. Using the precious few seconds to his advantage, he threw his sword at one, and charged the other. He and his sword struck at the same time. While the blade embedded itself in the chest of one, he leapt upon the other.

Just as the soldier's sword cleared its scabbard, Larus crashed into him, bowling him over. As they hit the ground, Larus' knee slammed into the man's groin taking the fight out of him. An elbow to the larynx and the man was silenced. After that it was a simple matter of wresting the sword away from the soldier and impaling him with it.

"Damn!" exclaimed Garin in admiration.

"Be quiet!" ordered Larus. Coming to his feet, he retrieved his sword from the other man, cleaned it off and returned it to its scabbard all in a matter of seconds. A quick glance showed Father Thomas practically beside himself with the need to continue.

"Lead on," said Larus and the priest turned and moved into the forest.

They hadn't gone far, when from between the boles of the trees ahead of them, appeared the sparkle of sunlight being reflected off water. They had reached the lake.

Chapter 31

Still ten feet within the fringe of the forest, a cry splits the silence behind them. "They must have discovered the bodies," surmised Garin.

Larus nodded, barely giving Garin more than a passing glance. His attention was on Father Thomas who had come to a stop. "Where to now?" he asked.

Looking first one way then the other, Father Thomas sought the sense of safety which had been directing their path for the past hour or so. But all he felt was an almost overpowering sense of dread and impending doom. "I do not know," he replied. Turning his attention full onto Larus, he said, "I think this is as far as it is going to take us."

More voices were arising in the forest indicating others were joining in the pursuit. From the sound of them, soldiers were all over the place.

Hunter came and grabbed Larus by the shoulder, turning his attention toward the lake. "Look!" he exclaimed quietly as he pointed down the beach to their right. One small watercraft sat on the sand, next to which stood six men with swords drawn. Their attention was currently fixed toward the forest, searching. He then indicated a second vessel, much larger than the smaller one, moored a hundred feet from shore. "I think that's the boat that has been giving Captain Hopewell's men such problems."

It was a merchantman suitable for plying the waters between towns bordering on the lake. Its deep draft kept it from coming too close to shore, but such would prove beneficial for sailing through the deeper water. Larus caught sight of a catapult's arm just behind the prow. A dozen archers stood at the railing gazing toward the hullabaloo transpiring within the forest.

"We have to take that ship," Larus stated.

"No way can we do that," argued Garin. He too had seen the catapult. "If the catapult doesn't get us, their arrows will."

Father Thomas' anxiety and sense of dread was increasing exponentially as they stood idle within the trees. They had to get moving. "Larus," he began but was interrupted by the sudden appearance of armed men appearing amidst the trees some two hundred feet deeper within the forest.

"There they are!" one man cried as he spied them.

"Move!" Larus ordered and practically shoved Father Thomas all the way from the trees and onto the beach. As he and Father Thomas left the shelter of the trees, the six men guarding the smaller craft immediately took notice and charged.

"Hunter!" Larus shouted. "Get the boat!" Then switching from English he said, "Garin, let's go." With the young man quick to follow, he drew his sword and raced to engage the enemy. As Garin sped to come abreast of him he heard the young man give out with a war cry. "Do this fast," he advised. He just had enough time to see Garin nod before the battle was joined.

Moving with speed greater than that of any human, Larus knocked the sword of the first man to engage him aside before running him through. Kicking the soon to be dead man off his sword, he ducked under an overhand hack delivered by another. With his free hand, he struck out and connected with the soldier's chest. He heard an 'oomph' as the soldier was knocked backward into two of his comrades.

Metal rang on metal as Garin's sword deflected a thrust by one of the two men engaging him. A quick dodge to the side to avoid a follow through slice by the man's partner, then he brought his sword back around and opened a six inch cut along the first man's upper arm.

"Yeah!" he cried as he kicked out at the second soldier, causing him to dance backward.

As the two men fought, Father Thomas and Hunter raced around the combatants to the small boat several yards up the beach from the water. One of the soldiers started moving to intercept them but was stopped by a sudden attack by Larus. His death cry sounded above the clash of metal as they reached the boat.

It had three benches and could comfortably seat half a dozen men, a full dozen if they squeezed in. Lying along the bottom beneath the benches was a pair of oars.

"Get in Father," Hunter said, gesturing for the priest to enter the boat first.

Dozens of men began boiling out of the forest all along the beach. Father Thomas scrambled over the side and took position on the middle seat. Hunter made ready to push the boat into the water when suddenly, Larus and Garin were there beside him, having taken out the remaining soldiers.

As one the three men pushed the boat into the water. First Garin then Hunter jumped in. Father Thomas had the oars in position by the time Larus was out of the water. Rowing for all he was worth, the small boat began pulling away from the shore.

Soldiers rushed into the water in pursuit. Their shouts and cries warred with the sound of their splashing as they made for the boat. At the stern, Larus and Garin made ready to meet them.

"Pull harder!" Larus shouted. Striking out as the men drew near, he took one in the neck while the lethality of Garin's blade felled another. The water turned red as a third man fell to Larus. Garin thrust at one but the man dodged backward just in time to avoid being struck.

The water was growing deeper and the soldiers were now up to their chest and grew increasingly unable to close the distance to the boat. Finally, the men in the water realized they were not going to reach the fleeing boat and stopped their watery pursuit. Shouts of anger, of warning, and even demands for them to stop spewed forth as the small craft steadily pulled away from shore.

Cleaning his blade in the water of the lake, Larus gazed out toward the large merchantman. Up in the riggings men were quickly unfurling sails and he saw where the anchor was being drawn from the water. Still too far away for their arrows to be effective, the archers stood watching, waiting for the time when the ship was underway and the distance was no longer so great. Once his blade was clean, dry, and back in its scabbard, Larus relieved Father Thomas at the oars.

Upon his first pull, the boat practically leapt from the water. As his fourth stroke propelled them along, the merchantman's sails filled with wind and the ship turned in pursuit.

"We'll never outrun them," Garin asserted. From his position in the rear of the boat, he watched as the merchantman finished coming about, and with full sails, rapidly began closing the gap.

Larus knew the truth as well. It was only a matter of minutes before the merchantman came within catapult range. And when that happened...

Ullentite soldiers up and down the shoreline stood watching the events unfolding upon the water. Any attempt to land their small craft would be met with heavy resistance. Somewhere to the south, too far to as yet be visible, was the relative sanctuary of Xith. Pulling hard, Larus struggled to maintain what distance he could between themselves and the ever approaching, archer filled, catapult bearing, merchantman.

Struggle though he may, the distance between them steadily decreased. Scant minutes passed before an archer launched an arrow toward their small craft. Not nearly close enough, the wind altered the trajectory of the missile causing it to miss its target by a wide margin.

Whum!

Father Thomas turned his gaze toward the merchantman and watched in horror as from its prow, the enemy catapult sent forth a rain of small stones. "Casdralla preserve us!" he prayed. The aim was true and the deadly missiles arced straight for them.

"Thank you Father," Ftheril said as he moved to interpose himself between his charges and the rain of stones. Time slowed as he altered the course of the deadly missiles so they splashed harmlessly into the water scant feet from the wooden stern of the small watercraft.

He grinned at the Qyaendri who accompanied the enemy's ship. Theroch's servant glared impotently back at Ftheril, unable to act due to the lack of prayers of his charges. A single uttered prayer by even one of the men on the merchantman, and the outcome could have been quite different.

As a volley of arrows followed a short time later Ftheril caused them also to miss their target since he was free to act because of the beseeching prayers of Father Thomas. But there was only so much even a Qyaendri could do. He simply could not bat them out of the air. It had to be done in such a way that the mortals who were watching would not suspect Qyaendri involvement. So as the merchantman drew closer, it became more difficult to protect his charges.

Whum!

Another volley of stones arced toward the small craft. Once again slowing time, Ftheril continued working to protect the men fleeing in the small watercraft.

"We have to do something!" Hunter shouted to Larus.

Cutting through the water at a speed greater than any thought possible, the small craft practically flew across the surface. But still, the merchantman continued to gain. Larus realized that desperate times called for desperate action.

"Garin!" he shouted to get the young man's attention.

His gaze drawn from watching the approaching merchantman, Garin turned toward Larus.

"When I fall, signal the ship that you surrender!" Larus ordered.

"But..." Garin began before the meaning of Larus' words registered. "What do you mean?"

"Arrows!" shouted Hunter as another flight was launched from the merchantman.

"Just do it!" insisted Larus. Then, the arrows fell among them.

Ahhhh!

Father Thomas turned toward the cry just in time to see Larus flop over the side of the boat and into the water. Before Larus completely disappeared from sight, he saw the feathered end of one of the enemy's arrows. "No!" he cried as he moved to where Larus disappeared. Looking over the side, all he could see was an ever widening ripple from where Larus had gone under. "Lady no," he prayed. Eyes scanning the water, he failed to find any sign of their friend resurfacing.

Saying a prayer for the Lady to watch over Larus and not let him die, a warm comforting feeling settled over him. But such was his anxiety and fear caused by the sudden loss of Larus and the imminent peril posed by the merchantman, that he failed to consciously register the sensation.

With Father Thomas' prayer still floating buoyantly in the air, Ftheril sought Larus in the water. To his surprise, he discovered him to be unhurt. Quickly deducing the plan of the former Qyaendri, Ftheril reoxygenated the air in Larus' lungs, enabling him to remain submerged longer, then moved toward the ship.

The antipathy Theroch's attending Qyaendri exuded at his approach was a palpable presence. But with no prayers giving him freedom of action, all he could do was glare. Hopefully the men on the merchantmen would believe Larus hit by an arrow and that his dead carcass was even now enroute to the lake's bottom. Ftheril had to find a way to aid Larus in reaching the deck of the merchantman. Already men were up in the rigging furling the sails, slowing the ship. Sending his senses forward to the three men remaining in the small watercraft, he found the oars to have been brought in and the boat had come to a stop.

A quick scan of the deck of the merchantman revealed a long length of rope coiled at the base of the port side near the stern. Moving toward it he made sure no mortal would bear witness, then secured one end to the ship and tossed the other over the side.

"Don't try anything funny," a soldier at the ship's side ordered the three men in the small boat.

Ftheril heard Father Thomas reply, "We will not."

As the starboard side of the merchantman came alongside the smaller boat, the rope dangling over the port side suddenly went taught.

Father Thomas looked up at the archers with arrows directed toward him as the merchantman came alongside. A rope ladder was cast down and a soldier quickly descended into their boat. Drawing his sword, the soldier held it toward Garin and said, "Drop your weapons."

Without hesitation, Garin unbuckled his sword belt and let it fall. A knife sheathe appeared from his waistband and that too joined the sword in the bottom of the boat.

Turning to Hunter the soldier asked, "Are you armed?" His question was met with a blank, though nervous, stare.

"Neither he or I are armed," Father Thomas assured the Ullentite soldier.

The man gave them a quick visual check then directed Garin to climb the rope ladder. "You first," the man said.

Garin moved to the ladder and began climbing up to the deck above. He could feel the eyes of the archers upon him as he ascended the rungs one at a time. Then as he reached the second rung from the top, all hell broke loose.

Men started crying out in surprise, pain, then ultimately fear. As the archers fell, Garin caught a glimpse of Larus. Wet hair pressed to the sides of his face and droplets of blood splattered across one cheek, his sword was quickly felling the men on deck like cordwood.

"Cear!" the soldier in the small boat shouted. "What's happening?" Looking up toward the deck, the soldier knew something was going on but not what. Grabbing Father Thomas, he held him close all the while menacing him with his sword.

Garin quickly assessed the situation and knew the greatest threat at the moment was from the soldier who held Father Thomas. Up on deck Larus was wading through the enemy like an angel of death and didn't look as if he needed any help. Then just as an Ullentite body flew over the side of the merchantman, he pushed outward from the hull, then fell toward the boat below.

Distracted by the falling body of his comrade, the soldier below failed to realize what Garin was doing in time to react. When he did, he barely had time to raise his sword before Garin slammed into him. The resulting impact knocked Father Thomas from the boat.

Immediately, Garin fought for control of the soldier's sword. The soldier struggled against Garin's attempts as they wrestled in the bottom of the boat. Hunter scrambled back out of the way when the fight for the sword brought it perilously close to impaling him.

Left hand grasping the wrist of the hand holding the sword, Garin's right fist pummeled into the man's face. Cartilage snapped as he broke the man's nose. Then the soldier's free hand slammed into the side of Garin's head, slightly dazing him. But shaking it off, Garin spied his knife and sword where they lay not two feet away beneath the center bench. Still retaining a strong grip on the soldier's swordarm, he reached for the knife. But in so doing, he opened himself up to another strike to the side of the head.

Vision blurring, he continued reaching for the knife. Again the soldier's fist slammed into him just as his hand grasped the hilt of the knife. Spots appeared before his eyes and the world dimmed momentarily, but he now had the knife. Bringing back his arm to block another blow to the head, he then lashed out. Eyes widening in surprise, the soldier tried to ward off the attack but reacted too late. The knife sank into the soldier's chest and the fight was over.

"Are you okay?"

Looking up, he saw Larus peering down from the deck of the merchantman. With streaks of blood intermixed with water dripping from his hair, he was a ghastly sight. A quick glance to where Hunter was helping Father Thomas from the water revealed they were both unhurt. "I think so," he replied.

"Good. Once Father Thomas gets out of the water, help him and Hunter up to the deck," Larus said. "We still have a ways to go."

Glancing up to the rigging Garin asked. "Can we sail this?"

"Should be able to," Larus replied. "Either way it's still better than rowing along in that small boat."

"You have a point there," Garin agreed.

"Hunter," Larus said, "take the helm."

Casting a look to the wheel, Hunter nodded and replied, "Aye, aye Captain."

To Father Thomas Larus said, "Keep a look out for any more boats."

"I shall do so," assured the priest. Moving to the center of the boat, Father Thomas began casting his gaze back and forth over the water.

Larus and Garin began raising sail and when the wind filled the canvas, the merchantman began to move. "Hunter," Larus shouted, "head southeast."

"Southeast?" Hunter asked. "I thought Xith was more directly to the south."

"It is," replied Larus. "But we need to move out of sight of those on the shore." Indeed, there were quite a few Ullentite soldiers on the beach watching.

"Got you," Hunter said. Turning the wheel, he soon had the boat moving at an angle away from the shoreline.

After tying off the rope used in controlling the amount of sail deployed, Larus joined Father Thomas. "Anything?" he asked.

Shaking his head, Father Thomas replied, "No."

Judging by the sun, it was a little past noon. "We could be there in a couple hours if the wind holds," Larus surmised.

Next to him, Father Thomas nodded. "It will be good to at last reach the city and have Hunter do that which he is destined to do."

Staring out across the water in search of other enemy crafts, Larus wondered just what part the ring had to play in all this. Every attempt to activate any latent powers it may hold met with failure time and again. He was certain Hunter and the ring had to reach Xith, all signs pointed toward that goal. Larus simply wished he knew what was going to happen.

Disturbing his reverie, Garin appeared at his side. "You sure took those archers out fast," he said in admiration.

Larus just shrugged. "They were so intent on capturing you three that I was upon them before they realized their danger," he explained. "By the time they did, it was too late."

"Still, it was quite a feat of swordsmanship," the young man insisted.

"I suppose so," Larus replied.

Time passed and the shore eventually disappeared into the horizon behind them. Hunter was less than perfect in his steerage of the boat, for Larus twice had to correct his heading as Hunter tended to drift more to the west than south.

"I'm doing the best I can," Hunter exclaimed defensively after the second course correction.

Larus grinned. "When land comes into view again your job will be easier," he assured.

"Either way, I'm having a heck of a good time." Standing at the helm with the large circular steerage wheel grasped in both hands, he felt just like a pirate right out of the Age of Sail. For a time he was able to put what lay ahead of them once they reached Xith to the back of his mind and just enjoy sailing across the water.

In the single cabin the merchantman boasted, Garin found the soldier's food stores. Dried beef, cheese, bread, and ale made up their midday meal. They made sure to fill their packs as well, just in case.

A little over two hours from when they commandeered the merchantman, a dark shape appeared out of the horizon to the west. Larus' keen eyes were the first to see it. "Ship!" he hollered. A glance to the south revealed the lake's southern shore was still hidden in the horizon.

"Head due south!" he shouted up to Hunter.

"Isn't that the way we are going now?" he asked.

"You've drifted eastward again," said Larus. Pointing to a point several degrees left of their current course he added, "That way."

"Okay," Hunter said and turned the wheel to point them in the proper heading.

"It's a bit far," Garin said.

"I do not believe it will be able to catch us," surmised Father Thomas.

"Why should they think they need to?" questioned Hunter. "For all they know, this boat is crewed with Ullentite soldiers."

"Good point," agreed Larus. "Let's hope they continue under that misunderstanding." Glancing to the sails above, he found them billowed out to their fullest extent. Prayers issued from Father Thomas and it felt as if the wind blew all the harder.

It wasn't long before the new boat altered course and was heading straight for them. "Might be a coincidence," offered Garin hopefully. But as time passed and the other boat continued maintaining a course in their direction, they knew it meant to close with them.

Time passed slowly as the two ships raced southward. Despite their best efforts, the gap between them gradually closed. When land finally came into view to the south, their pursuer had closed a third of the distance.

All but Hunter stood at the prow, scanning the horizon for any sign of Xith. Hunter remained at the wheel, unwilling to relinquish his position. Father Thomas prayed for sight of the walled city, but it took another fifteen minutes before it came into view.

Smoke rose from the area and at first they feared the city had already fallen. But as they drew closer, they realized that though fires were burning within the city, the defenders still held. Arcs of flame flew from the besieger's ranks, balls of burning pitch launched from the many catapults encircling the city soared over the walls igniting even more fires.

"Lady," breathed Garin in troubled awe at the sight.

Larus expected to see answering catapult fire from the defenders, but was soon to realize the attackers had destroyed every defensive siege equipment the city might have held. "It's not going to last much longer," he replied.

"The city will not fall before the descending moon reaches the horizon," Father Thomas stated with conviction. "Or so Hunter's visions would have us believe."

Nodding, Larus glanced to the sun which was still several hours from reaching the horizon. Barely seen to the east, the moon had already peaked over the horizon and was beginning its arc across the sky. It wouldn't be much longer after sundown before the moon set.

"Have you given any thought on how we are going to enter the city?" Garin asked. "We are after all in a boat which Xith's defenders may recognize as one of the enemy's."

Larus turned his gaze upon their newly acquired comrade. "That will be up to Father Thomas." Turning to the Father he said, "If I recall, you once mentioned having a friend within the city. A fellow priest?"

"Father Terrance," affirmed Father Thomas. "He would vouch for us."

"Fortunately the enemy has destroyed the lakeside catapults," observed Garin. "That should enable us to come in close so you can shout up to the guards and ask for your friend."

"With any luck he may already be there on the wall when we arrive," offered Larus. "Pray that he will be Father."

"Yes," said the priest. "I shall do that." Closing his eyes, he began to pray.

They remained quiet while Father Thomas beseeched higher powers to arrange for Father Terrance to be upon the lakeward wall.

The silence was suddenly shattered when from the rear of the boat, Hunter shouted, "Larus!" Glancing back, Larus saw Hunter pointing toward the city. Moving his gaze to follow Hunter's direction, he saw two smaller boats upon the water not far from the walls of Xith.

It looked as if the two boats had been stationed outside the opened area of the defensive wall where ships could pass through to the safety of the harbor within. Easily a hundred feet wide, the harbor opening was currently blocked by an immensely thick chain whose links were the size of a fully grown man. The chain stretched from one side of the port entrance to the other, and at no point did it rise more than two feet above the water. Massive winches built within the wall on either side were used to raise and lower the chain.

Behind them, the pursuing boat continued to close the distance.

"What do we do?" asked Garin. The appearance of the two boats lying in wait between them and the city created a much more problematical situation. It was apparent that they were crewed by Ullentites.

"Nothing," Larus replied. "I doubt if they suspect us of not being part of their attack force. They must know we carry a catapult, yet they are making no attempt at evasion."

Garin flashed him a grin. "Easy pickings you might say," he said with relish.

"Very," he replied before turning toward Hunter. "Keep heading straight for Xith."

Hunter nodded then turned the wheel slightly to keep the appropriate heading. Now that he had their goal in sight, it was much easier to maintain the proper course.

Garin gazed longingly toward the catapult, the eagerness he felt to turn it upon the two smaller craft was obvious.

Larus, Garin, and Father Thomas moved forward to stand at the prow. The one-time Qyaendri gazed out over the water and gauged the distance between them and the two smaller boats. Still out of the catapult's reach, it wouldn't be long before they were within range. Beyond the two craft stood over a hundred yards of open water to the wall of Xith. Behind them, the pursuing boat continued closing the distance.

"Let's do it," he said. "Find the shot for the catapult and have it ready."

"Yes sir!" Garin cried out in glee.

"Hunter!" shouted Larus. "We're going to fire the catapult. Watch me for directional changes."

"You got it," replied Hunter. Unable to control himself, he gave a deep throated "Yar".

Garin found two bins of shot situated near the catapult. Each held a full supply of rocks ranging in size from the size of a man's fist to three that would take two men to lift into the catapult's cradle.

Larus went to the catapult's crank and began lowering the arm into position. Once it was fully retracted, he and Garin began transferring the shot. "Fill it with the largest rocks you can," he advised.

Using both hands, Garin lifted a rock twice the size of his head out of the bin and placed it in the cradle. "Think we'll have time for two shots?" he asked.

"I doubt it," Larus replied. "Our speed is too great." In fact, they were quickly reaching the point where the catapult would have to be fired. While Garin continued filling the cradle the rest of the way, Larus moved directly behind the arm and sighted down its length to the small boats.

Raising his left hand he indicated for Hunter to turn a degree in that direction. As the boat swung into line, he quickly dropped his hand at which point, Hunter brought the tiller back to even.

"Stand back," Larus warned as he reached for the release lever. Another sight down the catapult's arm and he saw that it was lined up perfectly on one of the small boats. Pulling the lever, the arm was released. The merchantman seemed to shudder as with a 'whoosh!' the catapult shot its load of rocks up and forward.

The hail of deadly missiles reached its apex before the crew of the small boat realized their danger. A few of the men were able to jump over the side and into the water before the rocks hit, but the majority reacted too late.

Stones slammed into the boat and crew, pulping flesh and smashing wood. "Yes!" exclaimed Garin as the sea turned red and the boat began to sink. The second boat quickly swung wide and raced from the path of the merchantman that had just delivered so much destruction, its rowers pulling with every ounce of strength they possessed.

"Too bad we can't get the other one," lamented Garin as he watched it flee.

Racing through the wreckage, the merchantman cut through water littered with the remains of a dozen men. Larus was more concerned with gaining the city than in taking out any more of the enemy. "Are you praying for your friend to be on the wall?" he asked Father Thomas, turning his eyes to the wall's ramparts.

"I have," he replied. "Many times."

Larus just nodded as his gaze searched the wall for a sign of Father Thomas' friend. The silhouettes of over a score of men were crowded upon the wall. Drawing closer, Larus could see the men staring their way. He hoped they had observed the destruction of the smaller boat. It would make gaining the city that much easier.

Still over a hundred yards away, the crowd upon the wall began to grow as it became clear the merchantman was headed straight for them.

At a hundred yards, Hunter altered the course of the merchantman ever so slightly and aimed for the harbor entrance.

"No!" shouted Larus. Then with hand signals, he had Hunter return them to their original heading.

"Would it not be better to sail into the harbor?" questioned Father Thomas.

"Can't take the chance that they are going to let us in right away," he replied. "With that other ship gaining on us, we can ill afford the time it would take to convince them to allow us in." Turning toward the priest, Larus grinned and said, "Hold on."

"You mean…?"

Larus nodded and returned his gaze to the rapidly approaching stone wall. "Being followers of Casdralla, those upon the wall will put aside all thoughts of suspicion when people are in need. We are going to ram the wall!"

Ever since they had come within visual range of Xith, Ftheril has kept a constant watch on the ring of Celestial Warriors serving Theroch encompassing the walled city. They had paid scant attention to the lone Qyaendri and the boat quickly advancing toward them. But when their followers were slain in a withering shower of missiles, their attention was drawn.

Half a dozen broke from formation and moved toward the advancing boat. Ftheril looked on with growing anxiety as they quickly drew closer. Should he dare their wrath and stay with his charges? Or give ground to them because with the increase in the number of Theroch's faithful in the area, his Qyaendri held sovereignty? Would he risk war between Casdralla and Theroch by staying? Would he doom his charges by leaving?

Adding his power to that of the wind, he gave the merchantman additional speed on its way to Xith while debating what he should do. There would be no help forthcoming from above. Daeson had said he would be on his own until they reached Xith. Within the walled city he could sense many Qyaendri loyal to Casdralla, both Celestial Warriors and those attending to the mortals. Ftheril knew they were aware of his presence, yet none made even the slightest move to come to his aid.

His indecision finally came to an end when the approaching Celestial Warriors drew their swords. Faced with imminent destruction, he vanished.

"You're going to kill us!" Garin shouted at Larus. "At this speed the boat will break apart like kindling."

"Probably nothing as dramatic as that," the one time Qyaendri assured him. Turning his gaze back to the fore, he gauged they had less than a minute before collision. "Pray that we will survive without injury Father."

"Yes," said the priest. "I shall do that."

Ordinarily for one to push providence so far would prove foolish, but Larus had a feeling their particular group could go further than others would be allowed. After all, weren't they on the business of the Lady? Assuredly Her Qyaendri would not allow them to fail so close to the goal. Not with the prayers of Father Thomas enabling them into action. Unbeknownst to him however, Father Thomas' prayers were now left to drift uncollected until they were no more.

He rushed up the steps to where Hunter stood at the wheel. "Maintain this course," he advised. Hunter nodded.

Fifty yards and everyone but Hunter found something to hold on to.

At twenty yards, Hunter let go of the wheel and rushed toward the guy ropes secured to the side. Taking a firm grip, he watched the now towering wall fly toward them.

Five yards. The world fell into a hushed silence, the only sound being that of the wooden hull cutting through the water. Then...

Wham! Crack!

...the prow slammed into the unyielding stone wall. The front of the merchantman cracked open. Rocks from the catapult shot storage went flying into the wall with a rat-a-a-tat-tat. Almost immediately the deck began tilting forward as the prow filled with water.

All but Larus lost their holds when the ship rammed the wall and flew forward. Garin was thrown to the deck and rolled into the catapult. Hunter flew off the steerage deck and slammed onto the main deck. Father Thomas hit the deck rolling and gently came to rest midway to the prow.

As soon as he regained his balance, Father Thomas was on his feet and fought against the rapidly tilting deck. Larus was quick to his side and offered a steadying hand. Turning his face toward those on the wall above, he shouted, "I am Father Thomas, priest of Casdralla! I and my companions seek entrance into Xith."

"Thomas?" a voice cried out. It belonged to a man in priest robes who stood with the others gazing down at the wreckage.

"Father Terrance," breathed Father Thomas in relief at seeing his old friend.

Suddenly, the deck of the merchantman shifted precariously as the prow dipped below the surface, gushing water onto the deck. As Father Thomas lost his balance and fell forward, Larus reached out and grabbed him. Dragging the priest after him, Larus backpedaled toward the stern.

Garin was on his hands and knees working to keep upright as he too moved away from the water. Hunter still remained far enough back that he was in no immediate danger.

"Here!" the voice of Father Terrance shouted. The end of a rope dropped from the top of the wall and hit the water. "We will pull you up!"

The second small boat was beginning to return, its six archers readying their bows. Larus saw them and saw too that the boat which had pursued them for so long was taking in sail as they slowed their approach. Beneath him, the deck was still tipping as the prow of the merchantman continued its descent beneath the water.

"Can you swim?" asked Larus of Father Thomas. He has his arm around the priest to prevent him from slipping forward into the turbulent water caused by the sinking of the ship.

"Yes," came the reply.

"Then get to the rope." With that, Larus took a firm hold on Father Thomas' robes and launched him over the side. Then before the splash of Father Thomas hitting the water could be heard, Larus was on his way back to where Hunter held onto the main mast.

It was difficult for him to work his way across the precariously slanted deck but he made it to Hunter's side. By this time, Father Thomas had reached the rope and was already being pulled out of the water and up to the top.

"Time to get wet?" Hunter asked with a nervous grin.

"You might say that," replied Larus just as the deck shuddered and pitched even further. "As soon as the rope comes down again, I want you to make for it and get to the top of the wall."

A glance back to the other boats upon the water revealed that they were closing fast. "What about you and Garin?" he asked.

"We can handle ourselves," Larus assured him. "Once you are on the way to the top, we'll make for the harbor entrance." Even though the distance was but forty feet, the harbor seemed quite a distance away with the enemy boats closing fast. "Oh, and try to sway back and forth on your way up," he added. "A moving target is harder to hit."

"Thanks," replied Hunter.

From the stern, a hissing noise began to be heard as air was forced out between the planks of the deck. "Here we go," Larus said as the boat started its final plunge beneath the surface.

Garin's position was the first to be submerged. Before the water engulfed him, the young man jumped out and away from the sinking boat. No sooner had he hit the water than Larus and Hunter also leapt to safety.

Geysers of water exploded upward as pockets of air escaped from submerged portions of the sinking vessel. A moment later, the last of the merchantman sank beneath the surface.

Larus was quick to break the surface again. Hunter's head appeared nearby a second later. "Larus!" a voice shouted from the top of the wall. Glancing up, he saw a waterlogged Father Thomas standing among the defenders and waved in acknowledgment. "Hunter," Larus said. "Get to the rope."

Without replying, Hunter began swimming toward the wall and the rope that was even now on its way back down. Larus accompanied him. Nearby Garin moved to join them, but Larus shouted, "Garin!" Drawing the young man's attention, he gestured for him to make for the harbor entrance instead. Seeing Garin understand and alter his course accordingly, Larus resumed swimming for where Hunter now treaded water as he worked to get a firm grip upon the rope.

"Here," Larus said as he reached Hunter's side. Taking the rope, he looped it beneath Hunter's arms and tied it off. Then turning his head toward the ramparts above, he shouted, "Okay! Haul away."

Immediately, the rope grew taut and Hunter began to be drawn from the water. "Remember, use your legs to swing back and forth." As if to accentuate the necessity for that action, an arrow ricocheted off the wall not six inches from Hunter's head.

Larus turned to find the smaller boat had closed within arrow range and its archers were drawing aim upon Hunter as he was drawn up the wall. Hunter for his part was not only using his legs but hands too in an attempt to provide a moving target. If the situation hadn't been so dire, Larus would have found his flailing of limbs to be quite comical.

Trusting in Casdralla, or rather in the Qyaendri serving her, to see to Hunter's safety, Larus dove under the water and swam for the harbor entrance. An arrow shot through the water before him and stuck the stone of the wall. Then another.

Swimming with all his might, he followed the portion of the wall beneath the water until he came to the harbor entrance. Coming up for air, three arrows flew past within inches of his head before he could submerge once more. Then, again following the stone surface of the wall, he swam through the harbor entrance and beneath the massive chain barring ship traffic.

As soon as he reached the inner side of the wall, he came up again and was greeted by the sight of four armed men bearing the insignia of Casdra. They stood upon a platform running along the base of the inner wall just above the waterline. Each held a bow with arrow knocked and aimed straight for him. He found Garin lying on the platform behind the archers with another two men wielding naked blades standing on either side of him.

A moment passed as Larus treaded water, staring at the archers before him. None bore even the remotest attitude of welcome. Then one of them said, "Get out of the water. NOW!"

Chapter 32

The archers stepped back with arrows knocked and ready as Larus climbed from the water. "Quickly now!" one of them commanded. He was just drawing his legs from the water when a shout came from above.

"Stand down Keller," ordered a Cardri officer.

One of the two men wielding drawn swords looked up at the words. "Sir?" one of them replied.

An officer along with two priests, one of whom being Father Thomas, Hunter, and the officer's three aides, were making their way down a flight of steps. "Stand down I say," repeated the officer. "These men are ours."

Sheathing his sword, the soldier whom the officer addressed as Keller nodded to the others standing on the platform. "Put them away," he said.

No longer being menaced with swords, Garin sat up and pushed an errant strand of wet hair back to where it belonged. "We made it," he said with a grin.

Larus nodded and proceeded to get to his feet.

"Sorry about this," apologized Keller as he offered Larus a hand.

"Don't worry about it," Larus assured him. Taking the proffered hand, he came to his feet.

"Thank the Lady you two are safe," Father Thomas said as he rushed down the remaining section of steps. The priest behind him had to be none other than his friend Father Terrance, followed in turn by Hunter.

Larus nodded to the priest then turned toward the officer. "What's the situation?" he asked.

Coming to a stop, the officer looked Larus up and down as if contemplating who this man might be that would ask such a question.

"The situation is not good," replied Father Terrance. Then to his fellow priest he said, "This may not have been the best time to come calling."

Father Thomas gave him a grim grin as he turned his gaze toward the city.

Hazy smoke filled the air and at least four separate fires burned in various parts of the city. Screams sounded as another flaming ball of pitch sailed over the wall. As it struck the rooftop of a building on the far side of the city, it splattered, spreading its burning material to neighboring structures.

"First they fling a dozen or more such missiles," began Father Terrance, "then they storm the walls." Sighing, he watched as another flaming ball sailed over the wall, this time landing in a plaza. People congregated within the plaza scrambled to escape, unfortunately one man didn't move fast enough. For when the burning pitch hit the ground and flew apart, he was hit by the burning mass and went up like a Roman candle.

Fathers Terrance and Thomas simultaneously voiced prayers for the man and the fate of Xith.

"We should see two more before the next attack commences," said Keller.

"Then there is no time to lose," Larus said.

"Yes," agreed Father Thomas. "Our Lady has sent one to deliver us from the Ullentites." Indicating Hunter, he said, "In the ruins of my village, a Qyaendri delivered him unto me."

Several gasps came from those gathered about. Even Father Terrance looked shocked by his statement. "A Qyaendri?" he asked, as if he couldn't believe his ears.

"Yes my friend," answered Father Thomas. "He bears an item of great power wrested from the clutches of the dead. This day, he must stand upon the walls of Xith or all is lost."

"What can one man do?" asked the officer.

"It is not he that will do this thing," replied Father Thomas. "He is but an agent for our Lady."

"Then should he not speak with High Priestess Trystia?" Father Terrance suggested.

"Does she still live?" asked Father Thomas.

"Yes," Father Terrance assured him. "She and the Fathers have been in the Temple fasting and praying since they first arrived. It has been a great boon for our people that she is here."

"I doubt if we could have withstood the onslaught this long had she not come," agreed the officer.

"Things are that bad?" asked Garin.

Nodding, the officer gestured toward the burning city. "Look for yourself," he said. "Fires have burned almost non stop since the initial attack. Our forces dwindle with every attack while theirs seem to swell." Turning to Hunter he added, "I hope you can turn this tide."

After Larus gave him the translation, Hunter said, "I'll do my best."

Up to this point he hadn't really understood the reality of the situation. True, he knew Xith was besieged, but now that he was there, the gravity of it sank in all the deeper. The odor of smoke in the air, screams and cries of the people, and the terrible sound of pitch balls exploding made the danger seem all the more palpable. He wiped away nervous perspiration that he hadn't even known was forming on his forehead. Now that Hunter was there, within the walls, the sense of urgency which had dogged him for days had vanished.

"Are you ready?" Larus asked.

Turning to meet his gaze, Hunter swallowed and nodded. "Yeah," he replied. "Let's get this over with."

Larus gave him a reassuring grin and patted him on the shoulder. "Casdralla would not have brought you all this way for nothing," he assured him. "Trust in Her." Then to Garin and Father Thomas he said, "Perhaps you two should stay at the Temple where it will be safe."

"No," Father Thomas replied while at the same time Garin exclaimed, "Are you kidding?"

"We have come this far together," continued the priest, "we shall finish it together."

"That's right," agreed Garin. "I may have joined this late, but I'll not be shut out now."

"Okay then," Larus said, giving in. Turning toward Garin he added, "Your charge is to watch over Father Thomas. No matter what, you keep him safe. No running off to be a hero. Is that understood?"

"Perfectly," Garin responded.

"I shall hurry to the Temple and inform High Priestess Trystia of your presence," said Father Terrence.

"Keller," the officer said to the younger soldier, "Take your men and accompany them. See that they reach the wall."

"Yes, sir," replied Keller.

"I'm not sure if any of this will do any good," the officer said to Father Thomas.

"We must trust in the Lady," stated Father Thomas.

Three more burning balls of pitch arced over the wall and slammed into the city. Men rushed to put the fires out. Then, horns sounded and a great cry went up from the south.

"The attack has begun," said Keller.

Wending their way through the city, Keller led them unerringly toward the southern wall. Father Thomas looked sadly upon the faces of the people they passed. Men, women, and children were out and about, each bearing a look of hopelessness. Prayers issued forth in an almost non stop procession.

As they drew closer to the wall, they began hearing a deep, intermittent, thumping sound. "Catapults," explained Keller. "They've launched almost a constant barrage against one section of the wall ever since first arriving."

"Trying to smash their way through?" asked Larus.

"You could say that," he replied. "They have launched so many that a pile has begun to form at the base of the wall. Last I heard it was a third of the way up."

"And the wall?"

"Still holding," Keller said. "A crack here and there the stonemasons repair as best they can."

All in all a dire situation indeed. Father Thomas prayed for Hunter to be successful and that his people would win the day.

The plight of the city and the status of the wall held only minor concern for Garin at this particular moment in time. First and foremost on his mind was his brother Stephen and whether he still lived. The guards he questioned after being dragged from the water as to Stephen's whereabouts knew his brother, but did not know if he yet survived.

Eyes scanning the city, pausing for only the briefest instant on any wearing the colors of Cardri, he sought his brother. He was torn between the desire to find his brother and the need to remain with these newfound comrades. If they were truly in the service of the Lady, and several inexplicable happenstances which had occurred since first they joined together seemed to give the supposition validation, then this was where he needed to be. Not to mention the fact that he had pledged to ward the priest. And so he remained true to his word and kept close to the priest all the while searching for any sign of his brother.

As they drew closer to the place where the wall was being repeatedly hammered, over the sound of fires burning and a plethora of other noises, the clash of swords began to be heard. From between buildings as they rushed forward, the upper ramparts of the wall became visible. Soldiers of Cardri fought with men who tried to set foot upon the wall. The tops of scaling ladders peaked over the wall where the fighting was fiercest.

Then they were out from between the buildings and entered the street running along the base of the wall. An entrance to a guard tower stood nearby. Reinforcements rushed into its doorway on their way to the top.

A Cardri officer stood below, gazing at the fighting, gauging its ebb and flow. Nearby were another hundred men held in reserve, ready to go at a moment's notice.

"Captain Hollin!" Keller hollered as they drew closer.

The officer turned and saw them approaching. "Sergeant Keller," the officer replied. "Didn't you and your men have the duty at the harbor?"

"Yes sir," Sergeant Keller replied, then gestured to Father Thomas. "But Captain Osterman ordered us to escort Father Thomas here and his friends to the wall."

"Why?" asked the captain.

"Captain," interrupted Father Thomas, "there is no time to explain. We are sent by the Lady to stem this tide."

Arching his eyebrows, the captain looked at him skeptically. "I don't see what you would be able to accomplish Father. Other than to get yourselves killed." Drawing Father Thomas' attention to the wall, he said, "It's nothing but butchery up there. No place for one of the Lady's priests."

"Nevertheless…," replied Father Thomas, leaving the statement unfinished.

Captain Hollin met Father Thomas' gaze. After a moment he shrugged. "Suit yourself Father. Only be careful."

"We shall," assured the priest. Father Thomas began to turn toward the nearest guard tower which would allow access to the ramparts but was stopped by Captain Hollin.

"Not that way Father," the captain said. "Fighting is at its worst up there." He then indicated another guard tower a hundred feet further down. "Use that one. It will lead you to the fringe of the assault and you won't be in as much danger."

Father Thomas glanced to Larus and received a nod. "Thank you my son," Father Thomas said. Then with Larus leading the way, they quickly headed for the tower.

The screams of men cut through Hunter like a searing hot knife. Blood dripped down the surface of the wall from the carnage going on up top. But that was not the worst of it. His gorge rose when he saw a hand with several inches of forearm still attached lying on the cobblestones and he thought he was going to lose it right there.

Ahhhh!

A cry from above caused Hunter to look up. A soldier bearing the colors of Cardri was plummeting from the wall. Dancing to the side, Hunter barely missed being struck by the man. The sound the body made when it impacted with the ground was more than he could bear. Doubling over, he started to heave uncontrollably.

Before he was finished, Father Thomas came to his side. "Are you alright my son?" he asked.

Nodding, Hunter worked to get his stomach under control once again. When he did, he looked up to find everyone staring at him.

"This is the man who is supposed to save us?" Keller asked questioningly.

None replied as Larus came to Hunter's side. "You can do this," he said.

"I think so," agreed Hunter. A glance to where the man lay that had almost fallen upon him caused his gorge to rise once more. Immediately, he closed his eyes and took several deep breaths. A gentle tug on his arm by Larus and he was once more on his way toward the tower.

Memories of dreams drifted back as he passed through the tower's door; the guard, the shattering of the wall, the invasion by the darkness that swept everything aside. Fear that had been with him since first seeing the battle upon the wall grew. And with every step he took upward, his fear grew even more.

Without the physical presence of Father Thomas on the right and Larus on the left, he doubted if he would have been able to make it so weak from fear were his legs. But they gave him strength and allayed much of the fear that sought to take him. Concentrating on simply putting one foot in front of the other, they reached the top before he even knew it.

The wind sweeping over the ramparts was anything but soothing. Bearing the smell of smoke, blood, and death, it only worked to intensify the feelings of fear which had hold of him.

To either side lay the dead and dying. Garin searched their faces for his brother, praying that he would not find him in such circumstances. With relief, the dead failed to reveal his brother. Turning to the living fighting the invaders, he again sought Stephen.

Blood-spattered soldiers at the wall fought those who sought to breach the city's defenses. Thus far at this section of the wall, the enemy had been unable to make it any further than the top of the ladders before being cut down.

Men with pikes worked to push the ladders away from the wall while men with spears struck the enemy as they came within reach. Arrows soared over the wall, at times finding their mark in the defenders. Each time a defender was struck, an enemy was able to get further up the ladder before another defender appeared and the battle continued.

Then suddenly, a soldier went down and a gap formed in the defender's ranks. Without thinking, Garin immediately drew his sword and was about to fill the gap when he was unexpectedly stopped. Turning, he saw it to be Larus who had hold of him.

"No!" Larus shouted. "You are to protect Father Thomas!"

Garin's gaze bored into him.

"Do not foreswear *this* vow!" Larus said with great intensity.

Bloodlust melted away as reasoning reasserted itself. Nodding, he said, "Fear not. I am a man of my word." Returning to his place next to Father Thomas, he prayed for the flux of battle to bring an Ullentite soldier to him. In a matter of seconds, another defender appeared to mend the line and the battle for control of the wall continued.

Battle raged along the ramparts as Ullentite soldiers continued swarming up scores of ladders in an attempt to breach the line of defenders. Arrows buzzed like insects, occasionally finding its mark. Blood soaked the stone walkway, men of both sides lay moaning and screaming for help as their life slowly drained from them. Those of Cardri were taken away to the surgeons by women and young boys. Men of Ullen were left to die, or if a lull in the battle permitted, tossed over the side.

Wham!

Boulders continued slamming into the outer wall sending shockwaves coursing through the stone. Not far from where they emerged from the guard tower, one of the hurled projectiles struck a merlon, shattering it. Shards of stone flew from the point of impact and laid waste to half a score of Cardri soldiers. Immediately, the tops of ladders appeared and the fight was on.

"Not that way," Larus said as defenders moved to push back the ladders and repel those who sought to reach the top. Moving in the other direction, he brought them to a place still close to the fighting, yet was experiencing a momentary lull.

Turning to Hunter, he said, "Now it's up to you."

Nodding, Hunter tried to quiet the trembling he felt as fear sought to take him. Death surrounded him. Out on the plains surrounding Xith was arrayed the enemy army. His fear rose as his eyes took in the thousands upon thousands of men waiting their turn to assault the wall. Pockets of siegecraft spaced about the walls hurled their missiles.

With trembling fingers, he removed the Ring of the Or'tux from his pocket and held it before him. The oval shaped stone with a single thread of red marring the blackness brought little comfort. *What was he supposed to do now?*

Father Thomas looked to him with a surety of purpose, Larus had his attention turned toward the enemy, and Garin stood between the edge of the wall and Father Thomas praying for an Ullentite to appear. None were able to offer him any help on the matter of the ring.

Closing his eyes, he concentrated on the ring while sliding it onto his right ring finger. It fit perfectly, almost as if it was made for him. He sought to make a mental connection with whatever powers it may hold. When after several minutes his attempt proved futile, he opened his eyes once again. The ring remained unchanged and static on his finger.

"What am I doing wrong?" he asked. In all the stories he had ever read, and movies watched, rings of prophecy always held amazing powers waiting to be tapped. Yet, this one seemed to ignore all his efforts.

He tried holding his hand at arm's length and shouting for the power to come forth. Nothing. Tried waving it back and forth, then pressing it to his forehead. Still nothing.

Nearby he heard one of Keller's men whisper, "Is something supposed to be happening?"

"Quiet!" Keller commanded. "Leave him be."

Doubt began creeping in as repeated attempts met with failure. After ten minutes of being upon the wall and still having failed to summon the power of the ring to turn the Ullentite tide, he saw the confidence Father Thomas had initially exhibited begin to fade.

Hunter knew everything was riding on him. ***But what was he supposed to do?!*** It was inconceivable that he would have been brought to this world and taken on such a perilous journey, only to meet failure. How was he to get home if he can't make this damn thing work?

Holding out his hand outward once again, he concentrated on the ring...

Unseen armies faced each other on either side high above the wall. Celestial Warriors of Casdralla stood toe to toe with Celestial Warriors of Theroch. Neither side advancing, each held their ground as the mortals below them fought. Whosever mortals won the day would hold sway while the losing side, by long held tenets of the Compact by which all Qyaendri must abide, would withdraw.

Already it was a foregone conclusion. The Ullentite presence was simply much too strong for the Casdra army to repulse. Also, fissures deep within the wall grew with each stone hurled by catapult. It was only a matter of time. But until such time as the wall gave way and the Ullentite army overran the defenders, no Qyaendri of Theroch would be allowed past.

A small army of lesser Qyaendri busied itself throughout the city as it took charge of the almost continuous stream of prayers being offered by the defenders; prayers beseeching aid, prayers asking for deliverance and victory, and a host of others. But each prayer delivered to the High Temple on Casdralla's plane of existence went unanswered, much to the chagrin of the attending Qyaendris.

Atop the wall bearing the brunt of the catapult assault, a small knot of Qyaendris were gathered. Neither facing off against those of Theroch, nor busying themselves with the prayers of the faithful, instead they oversaw a small group of humans who themselves were doing little as far as the battle was concerned.

Daeson and a score of Qyaendri whom were subordinate to him, watched as Hunter sought to use the ring. Occasionally, an arrow's trajectory was altered by them to ensure the safety of those they watched. Such was the need to preserve these particular mortals that efforts to protect them would at times not be so easily dismissed by the mortals as mere chance. Fortunately however, so engrossed were the mortals by what was transpiring around them, that none paid much attention to an arrow that suddenly defied the laws of physics.

Minutes rolled by as the battle raged. Men died, feats of heroism abounding up and down the wall as the defenders repulsed the attack, and still, the ring remained impotent. Daeson held little attention to the mortal known as Hunter and the man's attempts to utilize the ring. Instead, he was focused on the enemy arrayed across the field outside the wall.

He watched the ebb and flow of its soldiers, felt the emotions and tensions coursing through each as the fortunes of battle change for good and bad. Then, when he finally detected that which he was waiting for, he turned to Ftheril who stood beside him.

"It is time," he said.

Without a word, Ftheril disappeared.

Chapter 33

"They're breaking off the attack!" exclaimed Garin. Up and down the wall, soldiers began drawing back to the sound of enemy horns. A cry went up as the defenders once again successfully thwarted the enemy's assault.

Wham!

Though the attackers were falling back, the barrage of missiles continued.

Wham!

The wall shuddered again and again as massive boulders slammed repeatedly into it. Cracks formed, flecks of masonry broke away, and still the wall held. As women, boys, and anyone who could lend a hand came for the dead and dying, the few stonemasons remaining within the city worked to shore up the wall as best they could; a beam of support here, a patchwork of stone there.

Men who but minutes before were fighting for their very lives, now had a chance to relax their guard and get what rest they could. Girls bearing water buckets and sacks of rations appeared to give weary soldiers food and drink.

Wham!

Feeling the wall shudder beneath him, Hunter lowered his arm. Face bearing the look of failure and a trace of fear, he turned toward Larus. "What did I do wrong?" he asked. All attempts to utilize the ring had failed. He would have liked to think the withdrawal of the enemy was his doing, but Hunter knew better. The ring had remained impotent despite his every attempt to draw forth its power. He had failed.

"I don't know," replied Larus. He too was at a loss.

Father Thomas was mystified as well. Did not Hunter stand atop the wall as he was ordained to do? Having come from the Or'tux, a people said to have deep roots in the practices of death, he had thought being around such death as the last battle had wrought would have brought something about. The souls of enemy and friend alike breaking their mortal bonds could perchance have influenced the ring, but such did not happen. Nothing happened.

"Could we have missed something?" asked Father Thomas. "Some clue buried deep within Hunter's mind that we failed to retrieve?"

Larus kept his attention focused on Hunter as he nodded. "Perhaps," he admitted. It was certainly possible. Maybe Hunter knew something that even he did not know he knew? Though he admitted the possibility, Larus doubted such to be the case. He and Hunter had gone over his dreams time and again until he knew them better than Hunter did. In every one he could see the hand of Qyaendri, directing Hunter's thoughts as they implanted the visions.

Garin for his part wasn't sure why nothing had happened though everyone had thought something should. Now that Father Thomas was no longer in harm's way, his attention was focused inside the walls scanning the many faces passing on the street below. Injured soldiers, civilians doing what they could to help, even children had little time to play as they too worked for the city's defense. Nowhere amongst the hustle and bustle did he see the face of his brother, Stephen. In the back of his mind, fear worked to convince him his brother had already fallen though he refused to believe such a thing. The only thing which would convince him his brother was dead was to see his lifeless body. Until then...

As he continued scanning the faces below, his attention was drawn by hurried movement moving at odds with the flow of people. A man in priestly robes stepped quickly through the throng on his way toward the nearest guard tower.

"Isn't that your friend?" he asked, turning toward Father Thomas while at the same time pointing to the approaching priest. "Father Terrence wasn't it?"

Father Thomas moved to the side and looked down in time to observe Father Terrence disappearing through the tower's door. "Yes," he replied. "That is him."

"He seemed in an awful hurry," Garin commented.

They had a short wait before Father Terrance emerged from the tower's door there atop the wall. When he spied Father Thomas, he immediately moved toward him.

"Thomas!" he said, voice filled with urgency. "High Priestess Trystia requests for you and your comrades to attend her at your earliest convenience."

Larus glanced to Father Thomas and asked, "I suppose that means right now?"

"I would think so," agreed Father Thomas. To Sergeant Keller he asked, "How long before they launch the next assault?"

"An hour, maybe longer," the sergeant replied. "After the drubbing we just gave them, it will take them that long to regroup."

Wham!

The wall shuddered under the impact of another boulder. "Very well." Turning to his friend, Father Thomas said, "Let the High Priestess know we are on the way."

With a final look cast over the wall to the mass of enemy troops spread across the field, Father Terrence immediately hurried to return to the temple.

As his long-time friend disappeared back into the guard tower, Father Thomas turned his attention back to the lost looking Hunter. He could see the sense of failure the man felt written across his face. To Larus he said, "Tell him it was not the appointed time and to have faith in our Lady."

"Are you sure it wasn't the appointed time?" asked Larus.

About to answer, Father Thomas suddenly stopped as he considered the possibility. After a moment, he nodded. "Yes, I do," he replied. He *had* to believe that the time had not been right. Looking out over the massed enemy who were reforming themselves into battle formation in anticipation of launching another assault, doubt gnawed at him. What if it had been? *No!* He refused to believe such a thing. It was not yet time!

When Larus finished assuring Hunter that he had not bungled things, that their arrival on the wall had been merely premature, Father Thomas led them from the wall.

"You and your men may return to your duties at the harbor Sergeant Keller," he said.

"Perhaps we should stay with you until you reach the temple," Sergeant Keller offered.

"That is not necessary my son," replied Father Thomas. "I know the way and do not believe we will be in any danger in the interim."

"As you wish Father," replied the soldier. He and his men escorted them down through the tower and once on the street, began making their way back toward the harbor.

"Sergeant!" shouted Garin before the soldiers had a chance to disappear into the crowd.

Sergeant Keller paused and glanced back to the young man. "Rest assured Garin," he said, "If I should see your brother, I will tell him where you can be found."

"Thank you."

Nodding in reply, Sergeant Keller resumed leading his men back to the harbor.

"Your brother is still alive within the walls of Xith," Father Thomas assured him.

With hope gleaming in his eyes, Garin turned toward the priest. "Are you sure?"

"Yes my son," replied the priest most matter-of-factly. "He still lives."

Larus glanced first to Father Thomas then to Garin. "If he says it, believe him," he assured the young man. "Xith's a large city and he most likely has duty on another portion of the wall."

"Yes," stated Garin. "He must be." Bringing up the rear of the foursome, his eyes remained ever vigilant for any sign of his brother. For the first time in many a day, there was a slight bounce in his step.

Father Thomas led them unerringly through the streets of Xith toward the city's temple. It was like a second home to him as he had visited Father Terrence many times over the years. He knew the inner passages of Xith's temple almost as well as those of his once beautiful temple lying in the now charred remains of Billin.

Memories came unbidden as he walked the streets. So much had been lost in so short a time. Would he ever again return to see the sun rise over the tops of his beloved mountains in whose loving arms his home had been nestled? If so, it would never be the same without the people who have been lost.

Faces of the dead lying among the ruins of his home, the looks of hopelessness and sorrow on those few who had survived, and worst of all the looks of abandonment on the faces of those left in the less than gentle care of the Ullentites when he and Larus fled with Hunter. All that and more plagued him as he made his way to the temple.

But, he had faith that Casdralla would see Her people through despite the suffering. As in the treatment of an illness, sometimes it was necessary to momentarily increase the suffering as you ministered to the wound. She would not, *could not*, abandon them in their hour of need. Hunter was there with them, brought by the hand of Her Qyaendri. After all was said and done, he was certain his people would be triumphant.

When they came to Temple Square situated before Xith's temple, Father Thomas saw Father Terrence waiting for them atop the short flight of steps leading up to the large, double door which was the main entrance into the temple. Beside him stood a second priest whom he recognized as the seniormost of the Fathers, those priests counted among the council who aided the High Priest or Priestess. It was Father Bennon. Though stooped with age, leaning heavily on a stout staff for support, and being by all accounts the oldest living priest in memory, his mind was sharp and his grasp of religious doctrine unparalleled.

"Father Thomas!" waved Father Terrence when he saw their group approaching. With one hand aiding the aged Father to remain upright, he motioned for them to hurry with his other.

Keeping a pace ahead of the other three, Father Thomas was the first to the steps. Taking them quickly, he was soon standing before the two priests. Giving the aged Father a deep bow of respect, he said, "Reverend Father."

"Bah!" exclaimed the Father. "No time for such folderol. We have business that needs doing young Thomas."

Despite the gravity of the situation, Father Thomas couldn't help but grin. Father Bennon had always been his favorite of the Fathers. In fact there wasn't a priest who didn't hold a place dear to their heart for him, even though he could be a bit abrasive at times. "Business Reverend Father?" he asked.

Shrugging off Father Terrance's support, he immediately motioned for Father Thomas to come to his side and take over. "That is correct," he said. "Everything is in place, we must not dally. I know how much you younglings get distracted by every little thing, and let me tell you, this is not the time for such nonsense!"

"No Reverend Father," replied Father Thomas. Glancing to Father Terrance, he saw him grin which he couldn't help but return. Being in Father Bennon's presence made them feel as if they were Novices again being reprimanded about one thing or another. For a brief moment, they enjoyed if not a small interlude of happiness, at least a warm feeling from long ago.

"Come," Father Bennon said as he turned for the large doorway leading into the temple. As the Father turned, his large staff beat a staccato upon the stone flooring as his feet made minor turn corrections which another person could manage in a tenth of the time.

Moving with him, Father Thomas soon had him positioned correctly and headed through the door. "What is happening?" he asked the aged Father.

"Young Trystia has everything in hand, she does," he replied with no further explanation.

In all the years he has known Father Bennon, he couldn't ever recall hearing him address another priest by anything other than their given name. Never once has the appellation of Father or High Priestess ever passed his lips. Perhaps being the oldest living man in Casdra gave him the right for none ever sought to correct him.

Their progress through the temple was slow due to the small steps of Father Bennon. Priests, novices, and a mass of fearful worshipers filled the halls. Those not of the priesthood sought refuge while those serving the temple worked as best they could to meet their needs.

Though densely packed, the sea of people easily parted for Father Bennon. When they realized the old priest was approaching, people grew hushed and an unobstructed cordon opened up almost as if it was the hand of the goddess. Which given the situation, it may just have been.

Heads bowed and words of respect were given as they passed. The slow shuffling gait of Father Bennon eventually brought them past those areas in which the uninitiated were allowed to gather and into the more private area in the heart of the temple. There, the corridors were much less tempestuous.

From a branching corridor appeared Father Correll. A priest of middling years, he was one of the many other priests along with Father Terrance who saw to the spiritual needs of Xith.

"Father Thomas," he said as he moved to walk alongside. "I am so sorry for what happened to your home. I have prayed for you and your people every night since word reached us."

"Thank you Father Correll," responded Father Thomas sadly.

The aged priest suddenly came to a halt and turned a head all but devoid of hair to gaze at the newcomer. Looking out from beneath bushy eyebrows showing a mixture of gray and white, he asked, "Correll?"

"Yes Reverend Father?"

"Do you not have some place to be right now?" he asked impatiently. "We are almost ready to begin."

Giving Father Thomas a knowing look that said volumes, he replied to the elderly priest. "Yes, Reverend Father." Then to Father Thomas he said, "Good to see you alive and in good health."

"You too Father Correll," replied Father Thomas.

Once the aged Father saw Father Correll moving off, he resumed his shuffling gait. Eventually, they arrived at a large door in the shape of an arch. Many arcane symbols and pictographs were engrained in gold leaf across its surface. Two Novices in light brown robes stood before the door.

"Is everything ready?" Father Bennon asked them.

"Yes, Reverend Father," one of them replied.

Coming to a halt, he motioned for the door to be opened. Then to Father Thomas he said, "You and he are to enter with me." When he said 'he', the aged Father pointed toward Hunter.

"But what about us?" asked Larus. "Are we not to go in as well?" For the first time Father Bennon's gaze turned directly upon Larus. His eyes bored into Larus' with more intelligence than anyone the former Qyaendri had ever encountered. He was a bit taken aback by it.

"Have we met before my son?" the aged Father asked.

"I do not think so," he replied, then quickly added, "Reverend Father."

"Hmmm. Your face looks familiar..." Remaining silent for a short time, the aged Father continued scrutinizing Larus' face. Then with a shake of his head, he said, "No. You and the young swordsman are to wait elsewhere until we are through."

Stepping forward, Father Terrence said to Larus, "I am to take you both to a room where you can relax with food and drink until the rite is completed."

"What rite?" asked Father Thomas.

"The Rite of Blessed Holiness," Father Terrence answered.

"The Rite of Blessed Holiness?" questioned Father Thomas as if he couldn't believe what he was hearing. "Are you sure?"

Catching a note of something untoward in the way Father Thomas asked the question, Larus asked, "What?"

Turning to the one time Qyaendri, Father Thomas replied. "It is simply the longest and most monotone ritual we have. Novices are at times forced to perform it as a punishment. It can take hours."

"Hours?" asked Larus. Even though he couldn't see outside from where they were now, he knew the sun had to be close to the horizon. "But...

Before he could say another word, from the other side of the door, a chime rang three times. "It has begun," stated Father Bennon. Moving forward and forcing Father Thomas to accompany him, he moved for the door.

"Come along Hunter," Father Thomas said.

Hunter looked to Larus who said, "You better go with him. You are going to take part in some sort of ritual. Garin and I are to wait elsewhere."

With a look of panic, Hunter asked, "But how am I to know what to do? I can't speak the language?"

"I am sure they will be able to convey what they wish you to do," he assured him. "Besides, Father Thomas will be with you."

At the door, Father Bennon's staff tapped, hard, three times upon the floor. Larus and Hunter turned toward the sound and saw him looking impatiently in their direction. With a 'good luck', Larus gave Hunter a gentle shove forward.

Nervous, Hunter joined Father Thomas and the aged priest as they passed through the door and into a corridor on the other side. Forty feet long with pairs of candles spaced every five feet, it bore neither door nor archway until opening onto a room at the other end.

The odor of burning incense grew stronger the further they went. Forms began to be discernible within the room ahead. Many priests and priestess stood in circular formation around a chair sitting in the center of the room. It soon became clear that the chair was to be Hunter's destination.

Hunter grew nervous as when he emerged from the corridor and into the room, every eye turned toward him. A priestess of short stature wearing a robe bearing golden embroidery had to be none other than the High Priestess. Much more petite than Hunter had expected, yet she maintained an air of command and power that was hard to ignore.

"Hunter," Father Thomas said softly. Laying his hand upon Hunter's arm, he gestured with the other toward the chair. "Please, sit."

As the old priest was led to his place in the formation of robes surrounding the chair, Hunter was led at a slow and stately pace by Father Thomas forward to the chair. With each step he took, a chime sounded and the assembled priests intoned a single, unintelligible syllable. Once at the chair, the priests grew silent as Hunter took his seat. Immediately, the voices of those assembled began chanting in a flat, and rather monotonous, tone.

He uncertainly looked to Father Thomas. One of two not participating in the chanting, he gave Hunter a reassuring smile. The second individual who remained silent was the High Priestess. She held a silver filigreed chalice which looked to contain a clear liquid. Hunter wondered if it was this world's equivalent of holy water. She came forward, and while her priests continued chanting, anointed his forehead and each eyelid with the clear liquid.

Once his anointing was completed, she passed the chalice to Father Thomas. Then she raised her hand and the chanting suddenly stopped. Her eyes turned to Father Thomas who said, "Hunter" which was echoed by those gathered as they resumed their monotonous chanting, this time with the added voices of High Priestess Trystia and Father Thomas.

Ten minutes passed and still the chanting continued. Twenty, and Hunter did his best to suppress the yawn that had begun wanting to be released, the constant droning of voices only subtly varied in pitch and speed having its affect. At thirty and his head began to droop as the monotonous chanting continued. At forty his head drooped forward for the last and final time. When it became clear that Hunter would not immediately reawaken, High Priestess Trystia gestured for Father Thomas to follow her.

Through the ranks of chanting priests and priestesses, he silently followed her. Then before exiting from the room by a door other than the one through which they had initially entered, he cast a final glance to the still sleeping Hunter who was all but completely encircled by robed individuals.

Entering a short corridor, they were soon at another small room quite similar to the Silver Leaf Room at the High Temple though without the murals. This one contained only two benches and three alcoves, one which held a pair of burning candles. The alcove opposite the door through which they entered held but one.

Father Thomas crossed to a bench and sat when High Priestess Trystia gestured for him to do so. She took her seat opposite him upon the other. Silence hung between them, broken only by the drone of the chanting priests in the next room. This was the first time he could recall ever having been alone in the presence of the High Priestess. It made him decidedly uneasy.

"Father Thomas," she began in a voice filled with compassion underlined with something else, something that made the hair on the back of his neck stand on end. "Do you trust in our Lady Casdralla?"

"What?" he asked, taken aback by such a question. "Of course I do."

She nodded. "You always did have great strength of faith in you," she said. "Even before you were sent to Billin we knew there was a spark in you, something that many of us strive for but never fully attain. When Father Velryn passed on and Billin required a new spiritual leader, I and the Fathers gathered together to choose his successor. As you know, when a position of such authority opens up, there is usually quite a bit of wrangling as different priests are put forward whom the Fathers deem worthy. Only once has there been but one name put forward. Yours."

"Mine?" he asked.

"That is correct," she replied. "Quite often the debates around such decisions can grow quite heated, but for the post of Billin, there was but one name proffered. It received a unanimous vote."

"Mine?" he asked again.

"Yours." Giving him a small grin, she nodded. "At the time I felt fortunate that the decision was made quickly and easily. But now I think there may have been more to it than your being favored among your peers. Perhaps you were meant to be there at the start of this conflict."

Father Thomas was amazed by what he was hearing. He had never considered himself overly pious or anything more than a common priest. During his tenure at Billin, he tried to serve Casdralla to the best of his ability, and didn't think he had accorded himself better than any other priest would have.

"Why are you telling me this now?" he asked.

Sighing, High Priestess Trystia said, "Much will be laid upon your shoulders and I wanted you to know that you have the strength to see it through."

Father Thomas didn't know what to say. "What about Hunter?" he finally asked. "What part does he play in all this?"

She sat still for several seconds before saying, "We have much to discuss and very little time to do it."

"About Hunter and the ring?"

"In part," she said. Then she began to speak.

As Father Thomas listened, he began to understand.

The sun had long since dipped below the horizon. Larus stood impatiently staring out the window toward the wall in the distance where arcs of flame could be seen flying over as the enemy loosed its catapults. Even from this distance the cries and shouts of men locked in battle could be heard. The enemy had launched another attack a short time ago and from the looks of it, was assaulting a wider stretch of the wall than the time before.

Garin stood beside him as he too stared out over the city. Where could his brother be? Had word reached Stephen that he was within Xith? Did he still live? With the heated battles raging along several hundred feet of wall, he prayed that he did.

"It's been hours!" exclaimed a very frustrated Larus. "What could they be doing?"

"Father Thomas did say that the ritual they were performing was rather long," said Garin. "All we can do is wait until they are finished."

"No," stated Larus. "We cannot remain here much longer." Gazing out from the window again, he could see the moon as it reached the top of the wall. Another hour, maybe less, and it would be at the horizon. In Hunter's dreams, at least those in which he stood upon the wall, the Ullentites always gained the city when the sun was at the horizon. If his dreams were to be believed, then they had little time to do anything.

"Ftheril," he said to the air about him, "if you hear me, we need to get out of here."

"All in due time, Larus," came the reply.

Turning around, he found the Qyaendri Ftheril standing just within the room by the door. A glance to Garin revealed him to be motionless, frozen in place.

"We must be certain that Hunter gains the wall at the precise moment," he stated. "Not a second either earlier or later."

"Why?" Larus asked.

"An important juncture of events is about to take place and timing is critical," he explained. "Everything rests on two things."

"What?"

"That Hunter stands upon the wall you already know," he explained.

"And the other?"

"Father Thomas must survive this conflict."

"Father Thomas?"

Ftheril nodded. "If either of these two events fails to come about, then the light of Casdralla will be extinguished from this world."

"But…" he began.

Cutting him off, Ftheril said, "My time is up." And with that, the Qyaendri disappeared.

He stood still and quiet for several seconds after the Qyaendri departed. Garin, now freed of the paralysis imposed upon him during Ftheril's visit, saw the way Larus remained motionless looking into the room instead of out the window as he had been but a moment before. "What is it?" he asked.

Shaking his head, Larus said, "Nothing." Turning back to the window, he looked for the moon, but found it to have already descended out of sight.

Just then, the door opened and a Novice stuck his head in. "High Priestess Trystia has requested your presence." The lad was nervous, that much was evident from the quaver in his voice and the way he couldn't remain still.

"Are they done?" asked Garin.

"You are to follow me," was all the reply the Novice gave. Then without waiting to see if they were coming, turned abruptly about and disappeared back through the door.

"Come on," Larus said to Garin as he quickly headed for the door.

Chapter 34

The chanting droned on.

High Priestess Trystia sat before him, eyes filled with sorrow softened by the love of a mother. For that was how she saw herself in the role of High Priestess, mother to all her people. And so it was with great sadness that she now looked upon Father Thomas.

Eyes red rimmed from tears, sobs continued to wrack him as he sought to come to grips with what had just been revealed. The weight of that knowledge weighed upon him like that of a mountain, seeking to crush him into oblivion.

Gently, she moved her hand beneath his chin and raised his head so their eyes could meet. His was a face of unendurable sadness. A smile came to her as she sought to assuage the feelings plaguing him. "You must be strong," she said, eyes searching his. "Casdralla has much faith in you and knows you will not fail."

"But…," he began before sobs once again took him.

Coming forward, she knelt before him and embraced her aggrieved child.

Knock! Knock!

Two raps upon the door were shortly followed by "It is beginning so you better not be dilly dallying in there." The voice of the elder priest Father Bennon broke the spell of heartache that had hold of Father Thomas. The Father's staff rapped on the door twice more before they heard him returning down the short corridor to the room in which they left Hunter.

"We need to return," High Priestess Trystia said.

Father Thomas nodded. Then with a mischievous smile he asked, "Or he might come back and drag us by our ears?"

"You heard about that did you?" she asked.

"I think everyone has," he replied.

During her early years as a novice, the future High Priestess had lost track of time and failed to arrive for a time of study with Father Bennon. So piqued at her was he, that he searched the temple until he found her. When he did, he took her by the ear and led her back to his study on the most circuitous route through almost every major hall, berating her the entire time. It goes without saying that she never again, nor did any other novice for that matter, arrive late for a lesson given by Father Bennon.

Coming to their feet simultaneously, they left the room.

Once in the small corridor connecting the small room of quiet reflection in which they had just left and the room in which the priests droned on with the Rite of Blessed Holiness, the momentary alleviation of his sadness at the High Priestess' expense vanished.

His steps grew heavy when they arrived in the room and saw Hunter still asleep in the chair. Father Terrence came forward with Father Bennon on his arm. To Father Thomas he said, "Your other two friends have been summoned."

"Excellent," replied the High Priestess.

Of his friend's words he barely heard for his attention was fully fixed upon Hunter. No longer was the poor man sleeping peacefully. Instead, his arms and legs twitched, eyes moving rapidly beneath the lids, and intermittent small noises could be heard coming from him. Father Thomas recognized the signs, he had seen them before. Many times had he and Larus watched Hunter act in a similar manner just before awaking to periods of madness. At the time they assumed it to be a reaction of his translocation from his world to theirs. But they now knew better. It had been a reaction to the implanting of visions by Qyaendri, a thing rarely documented and almost never seen. Truly, what they were seeing before them was the hand of Casdralla. Only, Father Thomas couldn't help but wonder if like the times before, Hunter would awake to madness.

Just then a novice entered the room quickly followed by Larus and Garin. Father Thomas waved them over, motioning for them to remain silent.

Larus too recognized the signs Hunter exhibited. Coming close to the priest, he moved his mouth next to Father Thomas' ear and in the breath of a whisper asked, "What's going on?"

Father Thomas turned eyes of deep sadness upon Larus. For a moment he debated about whether to impart the knowledge to him or not. When after several agonizing moments of weighing the consequences, he came to the decision that Larus had the right to know. Turning his head, he was about to answer when the chanting suddenly stopped.

Hunter awoke to utter darkness. He could feel the chair beneath him but of Father Thomas and the other priests there was no sign.

"Hello?" he said. His voice seemed to echo back to him, but of an answer there was no reply.

"Father Thomas?" he shouted, this time with a tinge of panic. "Larus?"

Then from out of the darkness before him, a silver light appeared. It grew brighter as it drew closer, its light banishing the darkness and allaying his fear. Soon it became apparent that a single man walked toward him.

A sword hung at the man's hip and he was dressed in armor that was somehow familiar. The coat of arms emblazoned upon his chest was that of five stars forming a semi-circle. The light was coming from the stars.

"Are you ready?" the man asked.

"Ready?" asked Hunter, not sure as to what the man was referring.

"You have it do you not?"

Lifting his hand before him, he saw the ring upon his finger. Its oval shaped stone with a ribbon of red seemed to draw in the light of the stars. "Is this it?" he asked. Looking up from the stone, he gazed to the man.

The man nodded. "We must hurry for the appointed hour is at hand."

Hunter saw the man hold out his hand. Hesitating only a moment, he took it.

The cessation of the chanting coincided with Hunter rising from the chair.

"Hu...," began Larus when Father Thomas took him by the shoulder and shook his head. "Leave him be," he whispered.

Larus turned his gaze toward Father Thomas and could feel the sadness radiating from the man. Before he could say a word, the sound of Hunter's steps heading for the door commanded his attention.

"He must reach the wall," stated High Priestess Trystia. "Let no harm befall him."

Larus nodded. "Rest assured," he said, "none will." And with that he and Garin hurried after Hunter.

Father Thomas didn't immediately follow.

"You must go with them Father," said High Priestess Trystia. "It is upon you to see him through until the end." She then approached and gave him a comforting embrace. After patting him upon the back as a mother would a forlorn child, she held him at arm's reach. "It is the will of Casdralla. For Her, are all things done."

Unable to speak, he simply nodded. Turning to follow his three companions, he was abruptly stopped by Father Bennon. "Take care young Thomas," the elderly Father said with uncharacteristic kindness. Then his face did something that few had rarely seen. He smiled.

"I will Reverend Father," Father Thomas replied.

"Now get going," barked Father Bennon, having returned to his former, grumpy self. "You would think it was time for tea by the way you are lollygagging about." With a shove lacking in any impetus, he encouraged Father Thomas toward the door.

Moving quickly, Father Thomas hurried after his companions. He caught up with Larus and Garin just as they reached the crowded outer area. Hunter was standing motionless, the hallway before him was choked with people, citizens of Xith who had come seeking refuge.

Larus noted Father Thomas' appearance. Gesturing to Hunter he asked, "What is he doing?"

Suddenly, the crowd before him opened and he resumed his way. Walking at a steady pace, the crowd continued to part before him almost as if it was a choreographed ballet. When Hunter approached, the people parted.

Father Thomas heard Larus mutter a word that sounded like 'Ftheril' though he couldn't be certain.

Those following after Hunter were not so fortunate. For once Hunter passed, the hallway returned to its former, congested state. Larus and Garin were at times forced to use less than gentle means in order to keep Hunter in sight. An elbow here, a shove there, though nothing too unpleasant for the people in their way. Father Thomas followed through the wake they created.

Once he emerged from the temple, Hunter's step quickened. It didn't appear as if he was completely conscious as he made his way through the streets. He moved in almost a completely straight line toward the wall, the only obstacles he circumvented were buildings. Everything else moved of its own accord out of his path.

The city was in complete disarray. Fires burned unchecked in multiple areas, people raced along the street in fear and panic. Fighting atop the southern wall was frenzied. Unlike the times before, flaming balls of pitch continued being launched over the walls as Ullentite soldiers scaled ladders. In one place the enemy had secured a foothold atop the wall and fighting was fierce as defenders fought to throw them back.

Wham!

The wall continued to be hammered by boulders.

Wham!

Again and again the wall shuddered under the relentless bombardment.

As they drew closer to the wall, the ramparts of the area under bombardment became clearer through the smoky haze covering the city. Most of the merlons which had stood when last they were upon the wall were shattered, some gone altogether. Men, stonemasons from the looks of it, worked furiously to repair the damaged wall. Arrows from enemy bowmen picked them off one by one until by the time Hunter reached the street running beneath the wall, they were gone.

It was utter pandemonium.

Wham!

High above their heads, a section of the wall blew apart. Screams filled the air as large sections of stonework rained down upon the people below. Men and women alike ran to get away, everywhere were the wounded and dying. Soldiers no longer able to fight had been carried this far before those who brought them down were forced to return for others. One man with a gash across his face was crushed to death when a stone the size of a small cart fell upon him.

But it was not only among the wounded. Even small children with arms in slings and bandaged wrapped heads stained a horrible red were seen here and there. There was no one free to take them from this place. All the free hands were upon the wall either fighting or removing those wounded that could be reached.

And through this all, Hunter walked. Neither seeing nor hearing the pleas of those by which he walked, his eyes were focused straight ahead toward some unfathomable point.

When it became clear his destination was to be the door of the guard house, Larus turned to Garin. "I'm going ahead to make sure he reaches the wall alive," he said. "Stay with Father Thomas and keep him safe."

"But you are going to need me," he insisted. Indeed, the section of the wall whereupon the guard tower led was locked in furious battle. The enemy had established a foothold and more men were appearing atop the ladders every second.

"Stay with the Father!" he shouted as he raced past Hunter. A glance to Hunter's eyes in passing revealed them to be glazed over.

Garin slowed and allowed Father Thomas to catch him. "Father?" he asked.

Nodding toward the tower's door, the priest said, "We too must reach the top." *It is upon you to see him through until the end,* the words of High Priestess Trystia echoed in his mind.

Larus was already within the tower working his way to the top, and Hunter's backside was just passing through the door. "Let us hurry," he told the young swordsman.

Wham! Wham!

The wall above them shuddered and masonry rained down. One ill fated hand-sized stone striking Father Thomas in the left shoulder, knocked him backward to the ground.

"Father!" Garin exclaimed. Moving to the priest's side, he quickly pulled back Father Thomas' robe to inspect the wound despite the priest's protestations. Underneath he found an ugly black bruise that was beginning to swell.

"I am alright my son," Father Thomas asserted. Offering his right hand he said, "Help me up. We must reach the top of the wall!"

"Are you sure you can make it?" Garin asked.

"We have to!" Father Thomas uncharacteristically shouted. "Now help me up!"

Taking the proffered hand, Garin helped the priest return to his feet.

Wham!

They had barely started for the door when another rain of masonry peppered them with a barrage of small, stinging stones.

"Quickly," Father Thomas urged. Together, they raced for the tower door. Only feet away, the door swung shut of its own volition.

Garin immediately grasped the handle and tried to open it. "It won't open!" he shouted.

"Don't let them enter," Daeson said to the Qyaendri holding closed the door.

"As you wish," the Qyaendri replied.

Unseen by the pair before the tower door, scores of Casdralla's Qyaendri worked to hold up the wall, preventing it from collapsing while on the opposite side, an equal number of Theroch's Qyaendri strove to see it collapse. Both sides being bolstered by the prayers of their faithful into action.

Within the tower, one lone Qyaendri led a mortal through a waking dream toward the ramparts. He didn't have long to get his mortal to the precise spot. A second late and everything would be for naught.

Wham!

The tower shook as this time, a catapult's missile impacted against its outer side. Fissures spiderwebbed the outer wall and Ftheril had to keep his mortal from slipping from the steps and tumble to the bottom. Such a fall would bring their carefully laid plans to ruin. Once the shaking of the tower subsided, Ftheril worked to get his mortal moving once more.

Swords clashing and men swearing greeted Larus as he reached the tower's upper door leading onto the wall. Not far from the other side of the door was the back of an embattled Cardri defender. Clash, clang, hack, the Cardri defender went down as the Ullentite's sword, cleaved him from neck to breastbone. With the way to the tower's door now clear, the attacker gave a mad shout of victory and bolted forward. He died before he could pass the threshold, Larus' sword shot through the opening and impaled him.

More of the enemy surged forward as Larus moved through the doorway. Other Cardri defenders stood to either side, oblivious to his appearance as they were in their own lethal duels.

Kicking the soldier from off his sword, Larus glanced back within the tower and saw Hunter was now almost to the top of the steps. Another attacker approached and his attention was drawn back to the battle. Two quick passes of his sword and the man joined his comrade on the cold, blood soaked stone of the wall.

Hunter now stood at the doorway, his eyes remained glassy and unseeing.

"The time is at hand," the guard said. "Do you have it?"

Hunter held out the hand bearing the ring brought forth from the Or'tux temple. "I do," he replied.

The guard began to fade as the real world came into focus; the battered ramparts, arcs of flame soaring over the wall, men locked in battle. To his surprise, one of the sword bearing men battling upon the wall was none other than Larus. Glancing left and right, he searched for Father Thomas but failed to locate him.

As the world grew ever more real and the dream-like state which held him in thrall diminished, his gaze caught sight of a low lying glow far to the west. Stepping through the doorway for a better look, he stepped upon the wall just as the moon reached the horizon.

Wham!

"Hunter!" Larus shouted. Parrying a thrust, he immediately retaliated with a crossover hack. As his blade bit deep into the soldier's unprotected armpit, he kicked out and propelled the man away. "Get back inside." An enemy's sword lashed out toward Hunter but the arm which held it was severed at the elbow by a well aimed blow by Larus. A fraction later and Hunter would have died. Fighting was fierce as more men rushed forward against the dwindling defenders. Those standing with Larus before the tower's door were growing fewer and fewer.

Wham!

The battle raged furiously. The enemy, having obtained a foothold upon the wall, was now throwing everything they had into it. Fifty feet from where Hunter emerged from the guard tower, the wall was devoid of all Cardri defenders. Ladders rose edge to edge against the Ullentite controlled section of wall, each bearing a steady flow of men to join the battle. Dozens topped the wall every minute.

Wham!

Larus and a mere half dozen Cardri defenders now held the onslaught at bay, but barely. Had Larus not joined the fray atop the wall, the enemy would have already overrun this section and taken control of the guard tower. Such a thing would have given them access to the city below. And with every able-bodied swordsman battling atop the wall...

Wham!

A boulder struck the top of the guard tower and shattered. Fragments rained down on those below. Then, a crack was heard and Hunter looked up to see a fissure form in the upper section of tower. The stone was giving way.

"Larus!" shouted Hunter as he leapt forward to avoid the falling masonry. He felt the wall shiver as the tower tipped to the side and slammed into the inner edge of the wall. From the street below he heard screams as the tower fell.

Wham!

One of the six standing with Larus fell, then another. "Back!" shouted Larus. They could not hold. Even one with his skill could not hold out forever against overwhelming odds. Five against fifty? With more coming every second.

Wham!

Hunter stumbled as the wall shuddered with the impact. There was a popping sound and a glance toward the stone between his feet revealed a three inch fissure. Backing away from where Larus and the last few defenders held off the enemy. Hunter lurched to the edge, grasped hold of a merlon for support, then raised the ring. He looked out over the swarming mass of enemy soldiers extending outward from the base of the wall. There had to be tens of thousands yet to join the battle.

Swallowing hard against the fear, Hunter held out his hand. "Work damn you!"

"Now," ordered Daeson and the Qyaendri which had worked to keep the wall from collapsing ceased their efforts. "It is time." To Ftheril he said, "See to the priest."

"As you wish," Ftheril replied.

Barely having escaped the fall of the tower, Father Thomas and Garin stood among the rubble. The tower door was blocked, chunks of fallen stone in sizes too great for them to budge now all but hid it from view. Around them, people screamed and fled. On the wall above, the presence of the enemy multiplied.

"Father!" shouted Garin. Pointing to a tower fifty feet away he said, "We can reach the wall through there."

Father Thomas stood transfixed as his gaze settled upon Hunter. Standing alone behind a fast dwindling line of defenders, Hunter had his arm outstretched toward the enemy as he sought to bring forth the power of the ring.

Wham! Crack!

The wall beneath Hunter suddenly sagged inward. Father Thomas held his breath as Hunter held onto the merlon to keep his balance. The blow knocked the three remaining defenders standing with Larus to the stone walkway, one was unable to catch himself in time and slipped over the edge. His scream ended upon impacting with the ground.

Larus kept his feet, though barely. The enemy ceased their attack and began edging away from the sagging section of wall.

Wham!

Another catapult flung boulder slammed into the outer side of the wall. Cracks spiderwebbed their way across the inner surface of the wall and chips of masonry filled the air.

"Father, we can't stay here," urged Garin. "The wall is coming down."

Almost as if fate was waiting for just such a statement to be uttered, another boulder struck the wall.

Father Thomas gasped when he saw the section beneath Larus began tipping in toward them. Larus made a mighty leap as the stone gave way and came to land next to Hunter.

"Come on!" shouted Garin. Not waiting for Father Thomas to reply, he grabbed the priest's robe and pulled him away from beneath the collapsing wall.

"Larus," Hunter asked, "what is wrong? Why won't it do anything?" With the upper section of the wall gone not five feet away and the portion upon which he stood leaning at a precarious angle, he held onto the merlon with a death grip.

"I don't know," replied Larus. "But we can't stay here."

Wham! Wham! Wham!

Boulders slammed in rapid succession against the broken wall. Each blow brought more of the wall down and the section upon which Hunter and Larus stood continued to lean at an ever greater angle. Now that a portion of the upper wall had been taken out, the enemy catapults sought to reduce it all the way so their army could enter the city.

Larus worked his way to the next merlon further away from the broken section of wall. Once he had a secure grip, he held out his hand toward Hunter. "Take my hand."

Fear practically freezing him into immobility, it was all he could do to pull one hand away from the merlon and reach out for Larus'. Stretching as far as he could, he took hold of the proffered hand.

Wham! Wham!

The wall shuddered. The merlon to which he clung and the stone beneath his feet gave way. Hand slipping from out of Larus', Hunter fell.

"Hunter!" cried Larus as he watched Hunter seem to disappear in a cloud of dust and the roar of falling stone.

Wham!

"Hunter!" he shouted again. Eyes working to pierce the darkness, he began working his way down the jagged edge of what remained of the wall. "Hunter, I'm coming!"

Then from below, he heard a weak voice. "Larus?"

"Thank goodness you are alive." Finding ample hand and footholds in the jagged cracks, he descended the wall until Hunter came into view. He had landed on a portion of the wall that still stood. A large block of stone overlay his lower extremities from his belly down. Blood welled from his mouth and the only thing moving was his eyes.

"I'm not going home am I?" he asked when Larus drew near.

Larus was aghast. How could this be the end? After all they had gone through he would not let it end this way. "You are not going to die!" he shouted. Moving forward, he gripped the edge of block crushing Hunter and with all his strength, strove to lift it.

"Tell Father Thomas that I am sorry I was not able to save his people," Hunter said sadly, voice growing fainter. A coughing fit took him as Larus tried to move the block covering him. When it subsided, he looked at Larus forlornly and said, "I always wanted to be the hero."

Wham!

Shards of stone rained down as more of the wall shattered beneath the onslaught of the catapults.

"Now, I guess I never will."

Wham!

Those below watched in horror as masonry exploded outward. In the moments of stunned silence that followed, a groan came from within the wall just before an entire section gave way and collapsed. Tears flowed freely from Father Thomas' eyes. Garin stood in shock. *The wall of Xith had fallen!*

Chapter 35

"No," said Garin. "This cannot be happening!"

You must be with Hunter until the end. Again the words of High Priestess Trystia returned to Father Thomas. *After that, all will rest upon your capable shoulders.* A cloud of dust raised by the falling stone enveloped the area blotting out all sources of light. Garin's hand rested upon his shoulder and he could hear the disbelief in the young man's voice.

"Father?" Garin asked when the priest failed to speak.

"We...," he began when from out of the darkness before him, a faint light caught his eye. Not that of a flame, this was more of a glow. For the briefest moment he watched as it moved through the dust cloud before finally disappearing.

Shhhhht!

The sound of Garin's sword leaving its scabbard was followed by the sound of footsteps coming toward them. Father Thomas felt more than saw Garin move between him and the one approaching. "Stay behind me Father," he heard Garin say.

As the dust began dispersing, light from nearby fires cast the world in shadows. One shadow moved toward them.

"What are you going to do?" asked Larus as his form grew more distinct in the limited light. "Kill me?"

"By the Lady!" exclaimed Father Thomas. "You are alive."

Drawing closer, it soon became evident that though he was alive, he was the worse for wear. Abrasions marred most of his exposed skin. Blood dripped down the side of his forehead from a mass of blood-matted hair. And from the way he was walking, his left leg had suffered damage for he was favoring it.

"What about the other guy?" asked Garin.

Larus gazed sadly at Father Thomas. Shaking his head, he said, "Crushed when the wall fell."

"Then this has all been for naught?" asked Garin.

Before an answer could be given, war cries of Ullen sounded as soldiers poured through the newly formed gap in the wall. Almost by the will of god, a breeze appeared to further disperse the dust. Enemy soldiers saw them standing exposed within the glow of nearby fires, and charged.

Larus drew his sword and turned to face them. Garin moved to take position next to him but Larus said, "No." Then he gestured to the priest. "You must get Father Thomas out of here."

"But you can't take them all by yourself!" argued Garin.

"No," agreed Larus, "but I can give you two the time to get away. Now go!" Returning his attention back to the enemy, he raised his sword and raced to meet them.

"We must go my son," Father Thomas said.

Garin paused only a moment before nodding. He had given his word. "Let's go." With the sound of swords clashing and men screaming in pain behind them, he and Father Thomas fled the area.

Running with sword drawn, Garin led the way away from the battle and quickly ducked down a side street. "Where are we to go?" he asked. "The city is surrounded and shortly will be overrun with enemy."

"Out of the city," he replied. "We have to get out of the city."

"The harbor?" suggested the young swordsman.

Father Thomas nodded. "It may be our only chance. This way." Having a greater knowledge of Xith's streets than Garin, he took the lead.

People were running this way and that as word of the enemy's presence within the city spread. No one knew where to go, all they did know was that the situation would only get worse, and fast. Some raced for the gates, some headed for the safety of the temple, while others of like mind fled toward the harbor.

People came to Father Thomas for help as he was a priest. Despite their pleas, he only slowed minutely to offer a brief word of encouragement and prayer for their well being before continuing on. Such action weighed heavily upon him, as first and foremost he had became a priest to help people as well as serve the goddess Casdralla. He wished desperately to do something for them, and it cut him to the core that he could not.

"There's the harbor!" shouted Garin as the ships' tall masts came into view over the city's skyline.

"Let us hurry," urged Father Thomas. A sense of doom was settling over him and he knew they had little time to affect their escape. But when the street opened onto the docks, pandemonium was what they encountered.

People jammed the wharf area. Swords and knives flashed as people fought to board what few ships remained. The massive chain barring the harbor's entrance was down and the way to the lake wide open. Casdra soldiers strove to maintain order but hysteria had overcome the people. The enemy was in the city and everyone wanted out.

When a trio of soldiers positioned before the one ship's gangplanks were cut down by a score of armed citizens, Garin knew there would be little chance of them gaining freedom this way.

On the water he spied a ship making for the harbor entrance. Listing heavily due to being packed to the gills with refugees, it was very sluggish in its movement as it crossed the inner harbor. It reached less than a hundred feet from the harbor entrance before a hail of stones soared from the enemy ship guarding the lake and shredded those on board. Another volley quickly followed, this time with much larger stones. Amidst the screams of people which had been torn asunder by the first volley, came the sound of wood being smashed apart as the larger stones took out the hull. It didn't take long before the ship went down.

"Father?" asked Garin. "Should we make for the temple?"

Glancing toward the temple, Father Thomas shook his head and said, "No. There will be no safety there."

With the harbor no longer a viable avenue of escape, and with the walls completely encircled by the enemy, there was no way out. Father Thomas then did what he always did when faced with a situation to which there seemed no solution. He prayed.

On the other side of the city, the Ullen incursion had come to a stall. It was beyond belief that a handful of defenders could hold back a force of their size. Little over a dozen battle hardened Casdra soldiers and a single civilian fought off every attempt of the enemy to push down the main thoroughfare. The side streets were equally defended, but despite that fact, progress was slowly being made along those fronts. It was this group holding the center which would not budge.

The civilian fought as a man possessed. The Casdra soldiers didn't know who he was, but they were thankful that he was on their side. His blade moved faster, and struck more deadly, than any they had ever seen. One pass, two, and an enemy fell.

His eyes were laced with what many believed to be madness but was in fact nothing more than unbridled anger. Expletives issued from him in a steady stream as he vented his wrath on any who came before him.

All his dreams of rejoining Casdralla's Qyaendri were gone. He had failed and failed utterly. Casdralla's people on this world were going to suffer, if not perish altogether, and it was all his fault. *Hack!* Cleaving a man from shoulder to breastbone, Larus barely even noticed.

Anger at Xi for choosing him. *Stab!* Run through, a soldier fell.

Anger at Daeson for making him mortal. *Slice!* Nearly cut in half, an Ullen soldier's upper torso fell away.

But most of all, anger at himself. *Hack! Hack! Hack!*

He had been the one to fail in the mission. *He* had been the one who failed to see the signs in time. It was *he* who doomed an entire people because he wasted the time given him to find the Chosen One.

Hunter had died because of him! Death and suffering of thousands more would all come about because of him!

In a rage of despair so intense as to be likened to a death wish, he began wading forward into the ranks of Ullen soldiers. And as he went, swords shattered and men died.

A tug on his sleeve broke his concentration and the prayer remained unfinished. Even though it hadn't been completed, Father Thomas felt a calmness settle over him "Father," he heard Garin ask, "what are we to do?"

Fires raged throughout the city. Whether because of malicious acts of the enemy or simply due to people's careless hysteria mattered little. Xith burned.

Just then a group of soldiers emerged from a nearby street. Seven men threaded their way through a sea of humanity clogging the wharf area as quickly as the densely packed people would allow.

As he had done many times before, Garin automatically scanned the faces of the soldiers for his brother Stephen. Then when recognition came that his brother was the one who led the others, he gave out with a whoop.

"Stephen!" he shouted with all his might. Moving forward, he kept calling his brother's name over and over.

"Garin?" replied Stephen as he heard his brother's voice over the din. Turning, he spied a figure shoving people left and right in his desire to reach him. *"Garin!"* he cried and raced forward as he too shoved people indiscriminately out of the way.

The two brothers met and clasped each other in a fierce embrace.

"I didn't think I would find you," Garin said. "Praise the Lady I did." Tears of thankfulness rolled down his face.

When they broke apart, Stephen had matching tracks in the soot covering his face. "Heard you were in the city," he said. "Figured you would be down here trying to get out."

"We can't leave this way," Garin replied. Gesturing toward the mouth of the harbor, he said, "The enemy's boat is keeping everything bottled inside." As if to accentuate his words, a rain of stones flew from the lake and peppered another ship trying to get free.

By this time Father Thomas had joined them as well as Stephen's six comrades. A quick exchange of greetings was given. "As it would happen, Father," Stephen said once the formalities were out of the way, "there is another way out of the city."

"What?" asked Garin. "Where?"

One of the soldiers, a young man close to Garin's own age stepped forward. "There is a smuggler's route that will take us out past the wall," he said. "If we can reach the entrance, we should be able to make it out of here."

"Why haven't you already left then?" asked Garin.

Stephen smiled. "I couldn't run out and leave my little brother could I?" he asked with a grin. "What would mother say?"

"Let's not spend time standing here," another soldier said. Casting glances back to the south, the presence of the enemy was ever present on his mind. They had to reach the entrance before the enemy had a chance to enter that part of the city.

"I agree," replied Stephen. Turning to the one who had spoken of the smuggler's route he said, "Lead on."

The soldier nodded and turned toward an avenue heading in the general direction of the eastern wall. As they made their way through the wharf area, Stephen glanced to his brother. "You picked a heck of a time to come calling," he said.

"You did say you would show me the sights," Garin countered.

Stephen gave him a nod and then the two brothers began catching up. Talk of home and more mundane things provided a moment where the immediate cares could be forgotten in lieu of better times.

Twice they turned onto different streets as they sought a way around the tide of people fleeing the enemy. When at last the soldier brought them to a halt, they had reached an area already deserted by the populace. The street running along the base of the outer defensive wall was less than a block away.

The soldier pointed to a nearby building. In the dark it looked to be a residence. "The entrance is in there," he announced quietly.

"Where does it lead?" asked Garin.

"To a broken down farmhouse amidst a grove of trees about half a mile from the city," he explained. "Naught much left but part of one wall and most of the chimney."

"And no one else knows of it?" asked Garin.

"Only my family," he replied. "And they left when Xith was first surrounded."

Father Thomas gave the soldier a most disapproving look. "More people could have been saved if you would have divulged its secret sooner."

Shaking his head the soldier said, "With all due respect Father, the grove in which the smuggler's route exits has been continuously harvested by the enemy since they first arrived. A mass exodus would not have gone unnoticed. Not to mention the risk of giving the enemy a way past the wall and into the city."

Looking little convinced, Father Thomas remained quiet.

When no retort materialized, the soldier turned his gaze toward Stephen, then roved over each of the other five soldiers in turn. "Are you sure you want to do this?" he asked.

One man nodded. "Our dying here will make little difference."

Another added, "The city is lost."

Each felt no small amount of shame in their decision to flee the city. To assuage their guilt, another said, "It isn't deserting. Merely repositioning forces to a place of strength where we can do more damage."

Despite such words, each knew the truth. They were deserters who didn't want to die defending a city they had sworn to protect. The fact that the city had already fallen offered them little comfort.

Silence hung between them for a brief moment before Stephen said, "If we are going to get out of here, let's do it."

"Right," said the soldier who had led them there. "Let's go." Stepping out of the shadows, he hurried across the street followed closely by the others. At the building's entrance, he produced a key and unlocked the door.

The interior was dark and the glow of nearby fires did little to dispel it. Holding open the door, he motioned for them to enter. Scanning the area, he said, "Quickly now, before anyone sees."

Father Thomas hurried behind the two brothers and was soon entering a small room, a residence's foyer if the hat stand and small table set just within the door were any indication. Stopping near the hat rack, he waited for the last soldier to enter and for the door to close.

"Stay where you are for a moment," their guide said. "I'll get a lantern."

In the darkness of the foyer, Father Thomas stood quietly and waited. From outside he could hear the sound of a child crying for its mother. So much sorrow, loss, and death. He didn't know if his heart could take it. Again he was fleeing while people in need were left behind. Then from the other room a lantern blossomed to life and the soldier called them forward.

The light from the lantern revealed that they were indeed within a residence. The foyer opened onto the front room of the home. The modest furnishings within the room indicated that those residing within were not the most well-to-do citizens of Xith. Despite their meager possessions, the home was neat, clean, and tidy.

"This way." Moving toward a hallway off the main room, the soldier led them to a storeroom in the back of the house. Within they found many barrels and crates positioned across the floor. Coming to one barrel set against the back wall, he set the lantern on a neighboring box and motioned for the others to help him. "We have to move this barrel," he explained. "Beneath lies a trapdoor which leads to the tunnel."

Stephen and another soldier moved forward and together, the three of them moved the barrel aside. "What's in this?" Garin's brother asked when the barrel proved exceptionally heavy.

"Sand," answered the guard. Moving it aside, the trapdoor was revealed.

So masterfully crafted was the door to blend in with the surrounding floor, that if one didn't know it was there, it probably wouldn't have been noticed. To raise it, the soldier produced two narrow, three foot rods of metal. He handed one to Stephen then indicated a barely seen crack running along the outer fringe of the trap door.

"Slide it through there until you hit resistance," he said, "then pull the rod toward you."

"Alright," replied Stephen. Doing as he was told, he inserted the thin metal rod until he met resistance, then pulled. The soldier did the same simultaneously and both felt something being pushed aside. When a barely audible, 'click' was heard, the soldier removed his rod. Stephen did the same.

"A pin had to be released in order for the way to be opened," the soldier explained. Tossing the rod aside, he placed his foot along the edge of the trapdoor and applied pressure causing the opposite end to come up.

He gave the others a grin at the ingenuity of the trapdoor's construction as he moved to the edge jutting from the floor. There he took hold of an indented handhold in the side and easily opened the trapdoor the rest of the way.

"Pretty neat," commented one soldier.

"My grandfather was a very ingenious smuggler," he replied. "Smarter than most." Bringing the lantern's light to shine down into the opening he revealed a ten foot drop, at the bottom of which began a tunnel heading almost due east. A wooden ladder badly in need of repair ran down the side opposite the tunnel.

"Be careful as you climb to the bottom," he stated. "The ladder is quite old so take it one at a time." Moving into position, he pointed out a handle on the underside of the trap door. "Whoever is last, make sure you shut the door hard. We might want to keep this way into the city from becoming known."

Stephen nodded. "Makes sense," he agreed.

One by one, they descended into the darkness below. Father Thomas was the second down followed by Garin. He was startled when at the bottom of the ladder, his foot stepped into six inches of cold water covering the floor of the tunnel.

"My grandfather said that when the tunnel was first dug, it used to flood with the rains," he explained while the others made their way down. "Then he came up with the idea to dig a cross channel to Xith's sewer so it could drain."

"That was smart," Garin remarked.

The soldier chuckled. "It was until a massive downpouring of rain came through and flooded the sewers," he said. "My grandfather said that he was forced to bring a load of ...uh...well... never mind... through a tunnel chest high in sewer backflow."

"Did they abandon the tunnel then?" asked Father Thomas.

"After all the work they put into digging it? No. My grandfather devised a series of weights and pulleys that would shut off the cross channel to the sewers should the flow be reversed. Unfortunately, in doing so the tunnel was no longer able to be completely drained."

"Why?" asked Father Thomas.

The young soldier just shrugged. "I don't know, Father," he replied.

A thud from above sounded as Stephen slammed the trapdoor closed. "Push on it to make sure it won't pop back open," the soldier shouted up to him.

"It's secure," came the response.

"Good."

Turning the light to shine down the tunnel, the soldier said, "The other end is slightly higher than this one so the water should be gone by the time we reach the exit." With that, he began leading the way.

Father Thomas fell in behind and followed him through a narrow tunnel barely high enough to accommodate the tallest of them. Silence hung heavy in the air as each contemplated the fate of those being left behind, as well as their own futures. Would any of them survive? Would Casdra?

Heavy on Father Thomas' mind was the death of Hunter and having left Larus to guard their retreat. Even one of Larus' skill would be unable to survive long before the might of the Ullen army. Though he had to admit, if anyone could, it would be he.

The tunnel seemed longer than what the young soldier had claimed. But at least he was correct about the tunnel's slope. By the time he announced they were directly beneath the city's wall, the water was already less than three inches deep. Another hundred feet and the water was behind them. And still the tunnel went on. Garin was amazed at how far it extended. It must have taken years for them to dig it.

After walking for what seemed a very long time, a dim light began to be noticed far in the distance. "It must be dawn," the young soldier explained. "That light you see is filtering down through the cracks of the door hiding the other end."

"I do not think so," responded Father Thomas. "Dawn is still an hour away."

"Are you sure?" asked Garin.

Father Thomas nodded. "I have a sense about such things," he replied.

"If it isn't sunlight," queried Stephen, "then what is it?"

It wasn't until they drew closer to the end of the tunnel before they began to realize the source of the light. The faint odor of charred wood that soon became apparent intimated that it was the light of a fire which was filtering through the other end. Then voices too faint and muffled to be made out clearly were heard.

The young soldier brought them to a stop before reaching the end. "Wait here," he said then went forward alone to check it out.

The others watched as he reached the partially illuminated end of the passage and paused to look up. Then he climbed the ladder set into the wall for a closer look. They didn't have long to wait before he reappeared on his way back to join them.

"Well?" asked Father Thomas.

"The light is coming from a fire burning in the farmhouse's old fireplace," he explained.

"What about the voices?" asked Garin.

"I couldn't clearly make out their words," he replied, "but based on their accent I think they are part of the Ullen force."

"Why would they be there and not taking part in the sacking of Xith?" Garin wondered.

"I don't know little brother," replied Stephen.

"This complicates things," said one of the soldiers.

"You could say that," agreed another.

Glancing down the tunnel toward the exit, Stephen said, "There can't be very many. The bulk of their men would have to be at Xith. We should get out before the attack is over and more return."

"And the sun comes up," added Garin.

Stephen nodded. "Which from what the Father said, isn't far away."

"Less than an hour," affirmed Father Thomas.

"Then what are we waiting for?" Garin looked at the others and could see a hunger in their eyes. To shed the blood of the enemy would in some way assuage the guilt each felt at having abandoned Xith to its fate. He almost felt sorry for the first few they encountered. Almost.

Chapter 36

The red hot anger which suffused him at the outset had cooled off gradually with every Ullen soldier slain. Sword arm rising and falling, Larus continued battling with incredible speed and accuracy. Whirling, twisting, thrusting, hacking, any who came near soon felt the bite of his blade.

Another would have succumbed to fatigue long ago for no mere mortal could hope to sustain the intensity with which he fought for any length of time. Fortunately for Larus, he was no mere mortal but a mortal who had once been counted among the Qyaendri of Casdralla. But such a history alone would not account for his abilities. If not for the fact that a fragment of Casdralla's temple prime was nearby, and the power derived from it, he would be little different than the men lying slain at his feet.

Sword lashed out and another man falls.

Those Casdra soldiers who had stood with him at the time Father Thomas and Garin went in search of a way from the city were dead. For some time now he had battled alone, an island of death in a sea of enemy.

Senses heightened by the power of the sacred piece of wood detected an arrow in flight. Twisting slightly at the last minute, he allowed it to pass a mere inch from his flesh.

Soldiers charged from every direction. Stepping forward he struck out with a cry and forced one back. Turning, he lashed out at another catching the man in the knee joint. Twisting, he avoided a blow coming from the other side. Then ripping his sword from the knee joint to a cry of pain, he struck out in time to deflect the thrust of yet another.

Back and forth, he was always where their swords could not find a target, his sword on the other hand found targets aplenty. Yet, still they came. Kicking out at one, striking another, he soon threw back this attack and for a moment was surrounded in relative calm.

A dozen men ringed him, each standing just out of sword range with weapon at the ready. Larus paused a moment to catch his breath and to assess the situation. Around his island of calm, scores of Ullen soldiers poured past on their way into the heart of Xith. Of those encircling him, he could see apprehension in each of their eyes. His prowess was a fearful thing and none wished to be the next to face it.

Blood dripped from the end of his sword as he stood staring at the men ringing him. Almost without thought, his sword suddenly moved and knocked an arrow aside before it could reach him. A gasp ran through the enemy, for his eyes hadn't even so much as glanced in the direction of the arrow when it was struck.

Then his eye caught sight of movement moving at odds to the main flow of incoming Ullen soldiers. Two men, one wearing dark red robes was obviously a priest of Theroch, the other a large swordsman with dead black eyes, were moving directly toward where he stood.

When those soldiers surrounding him noticed the new arrivals, it seemed almost as if they gave a collective sigh of relief. Those closest to the two moved aside and opened a way to Larus. Relieved grins were observed on the face of many.

The priest was a step in front of the other as they entered the circle of calm surrounding Larus. "One man?" the priest asked as he glanced around at the others. His expression was hard and the grins quickly disappeared.

"Yes Dark One," one soldier replied. "He fights like a Ka'Drach."

Turning his gaze once more to Larus the priest said, "Indeed." Then turning to the soldier with the dead black eyes, the priest intoned an invocation. Bending over, he dipped two fingers into an open wound of a man Larus had recently slain. With blood covering his fingers, he stood and reiterated the invocation while simultaneously drawing two lines across the man's forehead.

Larus watched the priest perform his ritual, all the while contemplating whether Theroch's servant should be his next victim. Then, a barely seen glow appeared to settle over the man with the dead eyes, drawing his gaze.

His eyes widened in shock as for a split second, he saw the ethereal form of a Qyaendri settle into the man. And it wasn't a regular run of the mill Qyaendri either, but a Celestial Warrior! His mind barely had time to register such a thing before the priest completed his invocation. A split second later the man's eyes were no longer dead black. Now, orbs of deep red stared out from under dark, bushy eyebrows.

The priest turned toward Larus and spoke a single syllable. Faster than a bird in flight, the man's sword leapt from its scabbard as he stepped forward. A cry went up from the soldiers when Larus barely managed to avoid the blow. He hadn't expected the man to move with such speed nor to wield a sword half a foot longer than his own.

Leaping back, he danced away from the flash of steel and then lashed out with his own. Before his blade could even come close, it was struck to the side. Once more he was forced to dodge and twist as the long blade flew toward him, barely avoiding its less than gentle caress.

Using every ounce of power and skill at his command, Larus went on the attack. Thrust, slice, hack, each one being beat aside long before they could come close to connecting with his opponent.

"You have great skill, dog," the priest said as his man went on the offensive. "But none have ever defeated one of the Ka'Drach!"

In a blur of steel, he barely kept the Ka'Drach's blade from striking home. Dodging to the side, he felt his tunic part as another lightning quick thrust came perilously close to ending him then and there. Dancing away from his opponent, he neared the ring of soldiers and was almost impaled through the back by an onlooker's sword. Realizing his error in time, he twisted to avoid the blade and moved further toward the middle.

The red eyes of the Ka'Drach tracked his every movement and the longer sword flashed forward. Knocking it to the side, Larus suddenly felt a flare of pain. A quick glance down showed a red stain beginning to form where the longer sword had opened a wound in his side. He had been a fraction of a second too late. It wasn't a deep wound by any means, but it was the first he had sustained of any consequence since just after the wall collapsed.

"Lady, give me strength!" he cried as he launched into a series of lightning quick attacks. To his amazement, his onslaught left a red line along the Ka'Drach's arm. The sight of the small welling of blood gave him hope that he could win this fight despite the aid given to the Ka'Drach by one of Theroch's Celestial Warriors. With renewed determination to see his opponent fall, he stepped forward and pressed the attack.

"It's their baggage train," the soldier whispered down to the others. Being the one who knew the workings of the secret trapdoor best, he stood at the top of the ladder and was looking through the now opened trapdoor to see what lay beyond.

Not far from where he peered through, five men sat before the fireplace in the ruins of the old farmhouse, the closest being not more than a foot away. It was a lucky thing that none of the men had actually been sitting upon the top of the trapdoor when he lifted it. Their bacon would have been cooked for sure had such been the case.

He took a moment longer to scan the rest of what was visible from his vantage point before carefully closing the trapdoor and returning to the bottom of the ladder where the others waited. "Five men are sitting close to the trapdoor," he explained. "We will have to take them out first."

"Soldiers?" asked Stephen.

He shook his head. "No. I think they are the teamsters who drove the wagons. There are soldiers however closer to where the wagons are gathered. I counted half a dozen."

"Most likely keeping watch in the event our people tried something," suggested one of the soldiers.

"How about horses?" asked Father Thomas. "We will need horses if we hope to make it far."

The soldier turned toward the priest. "They are picketed near the wagons," he said.

"I don't suppose they are saddled?" asked Garin hopefully.

"We aren't that lucky," replied the soldier, shaking his head. Glancing to Stephen he added, "And by the way, the sky is beginning to lighten with the coming of dawn."

"Then we better make this quick," said Stephen. "You and the others keep them off us while Garin, Father Thomas, and I ready the horses for travel."

Giving him an evil grin, the soldier said, "No problem." Moving to the base of the ladder, he quickly climbed to the top. Another soldier climbed up after him, then a third.

From below, the rest watched as the soldier reached the top and drew forth his knife. Father Thomas looked on as the man released the pin holding the trapdoor closed. Then with a mighty heave, thrust the trapdoor open.

Immediately, the soldier lashed out with his knife and a grunt was heard as it struck home. Then all hell broke loose on the surface as men began crying out they were under attack. Moving quickly, the lead soldier was on the surface with the next man already topping the ladder.

"Come on!" they heard from above as the clash of metal rang forth.

Stephen was halfway up the ladder when the last soldier passed from the secret smuggler's way to the surface. Behind him came Garin followed closely by Father Thomas.

At the top, he found his six comrades engaged with as many Ullen soldiers. Once out, he drew his sword and waited for his brother to exit. Eyes scanning the battlefield, he saw an enemy fall, then another. When one broke and tried to run, he shouted, "Don't let them get away!" One of Stephen's comrades quickly overtook the man and struck him down from behind.

Garin's head appeared and was followed by the rest of him. Then, Father Thomas emerged into the open. Off to the east, the sky had already grown quite bright. Just above the horizon the sky was beginning to glow with the first emergence of the sun.

Stephen lent Father Thomas a hand the rest of the way out then slammed the trapdoor closed. The immediate vicinity had been cleared of the teamsters, five dead bodies lay before the fireplace. Four of his comrades held off enemy soldiers while the other two were heading toward the pair of soldiers at the wagons.

"Shall we little brother?" he asked.

"Let's," Garin replied. With Father Thomas between them, they headed for the picket line of horses.

Civilians fled and in the distance more soldiers could be seen on their way. One of Stephen's two friends heading toward the soldiers guarding the wagons snagged a burning brand from one of several campfires in the area and tossed it onto a nearby wagon, setting fire to the enemy's supplies. Seeing how well the fire spread among the goods, his comrade did the same to another before forced to engage the enemy.

Saddles for the horses were conveniently stacked on a wagon next to the picket line and Stephen was the first to reach them. Taking one off the top, he moved toward the nearest horse and began readying it for travel. Father Thomas and Garin quickly followed suit.

Stephen had his first almost completely secured when he heard one of his buddies yell his name. Glancing toward the call, his friend pointed toward a soldier coming up behind him. "Garin!" Stephen hollered, alerting his brother to the approaching danger. "I'll take care of this. You and Father Thomas continue getting the horses ready."

Garin cinched the final strap tight securing the saddle in place when the ring of metal announced his brother had engaged the soldier. A glance over his shoulder toward Stephen locked in battle revealed him to be holding his own. Though he longed to join his brother, Garin knew speedily getting the horses ready to ride was paramount. Returning to the wagon containing the saddles, he tossed several more toward the picket line before hurrying over and readying another horse.

"You better hurry!" one of Stephen's buddies shouted to Garin. Garin looked to see a fast moving force of over twenty enemy soldiers heading their way.

Father Thomas had three horses ready and was beginning on a fourth. Garin cinched the strap tight on his second then grabbed a saddle lying nearby to begin his third. Behind him, the sound of battle abruptly stopped. A second later, Stephen appeared beside him, shirt stained a dark red.

"Is it bad?" asked Garin.

His brother shook his head. "The blood's not mine," he said. "The damned idiot fell on me after I ran him through." Taking one of the saddles Garin had tossed over, he set to work readying another horse.

As he worked, he kept an eye on the advancing force. Aside from them, there were no other enemy in the immediate area except the backs of a few fleeing civilians. "Jimmy!" he shouted to the one who had led them through the smuggler's route, "Time to go!" Pulling the strap tight, he leaped up into the saddle.

Garin was still buckling the strap beneath his horse's belly when Stephen mounted. "Best be hurrying little brother," he advised.

"I am!" he shouted back.

Father Thomas, having finished saddling his fifth horse, now climbed into the saddle as well.

Jimmy and three others raced across to the prepared horses and quickly mounted.

"Where are Matt and Yarma?" Stephen asked.

"They won't be coming," Jimmy replied.

"Damn!" he cursed, then spied their dead bodies lying among twice as many of the enemy. At least they took a couple with them. Glancing back to his little brother, he saw that he was still having trouble with the cinch. "Leave it," he said. "We won't need it."

As his brother moved to mount a saddled horse, Stephen turned his gaze toward the approaching Ullen force. If they numbered but a few less, he would be inclined to run them over during their escape. Unfortunately their force was too great for them to take the chance.

Once Garin was in the saddle, Stephen said, "To the Pass!"

"No!" shouted Father Thomas. "We must go east."

"East?" asked Jimmy.

"An Ullen force is already in position at the Pass," he explained. "We will never reach it. I know the mountains to the east and there are little known trails which will take us through to the other side. We must go east."

Stephen only hesitated a moment before saying, "East it is then." The sun was just peeking over the mountains as eight riders made a break for it. Being the only ones on horseback, it was easy to avoid those soldiers who sought to bar their escape. As they raced to the east, clouds of dark smoke rose behind them. Xith, once the staunch guardian of Casdra, burned.

Blade singing through the air, Larus' blade found its mark. Leaving behind a three inch line of red, it quickly parried another strike by the Ka'Drach, narrowly avoiding a blow to the head.

Both men bled from multiple wounds, the worst was coming from that of the Ka'Drach. The power from the piece of sacred wood helped to heal his own wounds while those of the Ka'Drach did little more than bleed. The Celestial Warrior may be giving his opponent great skill in battle, but it did little to heal his wounds. During a lull in battle, the thought came that perhaps those who originated the ritual which summoned the help of a Celestial Warrior didn't believe such would be needed. And once a ritual was set in the minds of mortals, it was difficult for it to be altered, certainly not during the heat of combat.

Thrust, parry, hack, parry, dodge. Around and around the two combatants went as each sought to pierce the defense of the other. While on the defensive, Larus would look for an opening which could be exploited. When one presented itself, he struck hard and fast. As his sword opened another gash on the Ka'Drach's forearm, he danced backward, barely avoiding the slash of the Ka'Drach's longer sword.

For a brief moment he began to entertain the thought that he may just win this. Again he saw and opening and struck. Again blood flowed. Parrying a backswing, he easily maneuvered the Ka'Drach into opening his guard yet again. Thrust! Six inches sank into the man's side a moment before the Ka'Drach's sword struck the blade, causing it to rip its way out the side.

Dodging a backhanded blow, Larus saw the flap of skin dangling from the Ka'Drach's side, blood pouring from the wound. The battle wasn't going to last much longer. If not for the presence of the Celestial Warrior bolstering the Ka'Drach, it would be over already.

Seemingly unfazed by the wound, the Ka'Drach went on the offensive. Larus parried each blow, knocking the blade first one way then the other as he bided his time. Then, an opening appeared. Without hesitation, he thrust only to have his sword knocked aside before it could connect. Again the Ka'Drach went on the offensive.

Parry, dodge, parry, twist, Larus managed to avoid the blade as he awaited another opening. When one appeared, he moved to thrust only to have the Ka'Drach's blade seem to come out of nowhere and take him in the shoulder. It was the left shoulder so didn't impair his fighting ability greatly, but it forced him to grow more cautious. He couldn't afford another such blow.

The wound throbbed with pain and blood flowed freely. As his blade wove a metal barrier, the wound continued to throb. It wasn't healing like previous wounds had. The times before there would be an initial burst of pain followed by a balming affect which dulled the pain until it was no more. This time however, the pain did not diminish. It remained.

Parry, dodge, parry, *stab!* The Ka'Drach's sword breached his defense and scored along his side. Backstepping quickly at the unexpected blow, he came perilously close to the ring of onlookers and the swords they held. Dancing to the side, his sword knocked aside the Ka'Drach's which had been heading for his chest. He was a moment too slow and the point grazed the front of his tunic as it was batted aside.

His senses were growing dull, his speed lessening. It grew harder and harder just to maintain a defense. Small cuts began dotting his exposed skin as the Ka'Drach's sword breached his defenses with greater frequency. Fatigue began setting in. Once having been certain of victory, he now fought merely to survive. The power of the Qyaendri was leaving him.

As the Ka'Drach's sword again penetrated to leave an angry red line across his cheek, he realized what was happening. The sacred piece of wood from Casdralla's temple prime was no longer near. It was moving away in the pocket of Father Thomas. And as the distance between them grew, so too did his abilities weaken.

Parry, *stab!* Dodge, *slice!*

He was no longer able to avoid the blade. As his own sword was knocked from his hands, and the last vestiges of ability left him, he knew that Father Thomas had made it from the city and was riding with all speed to safety.

Seeing the Ka'Drach's sword descending to finish it, he raised his head and shouted to the sky, "Forgive me!" Then the blade struck and the battle was over.

Later that afternoon, a group of riders reached the relative safety of the foothills and paused for a brief period to rest. Far to the west the smoke rising from Xith remained visible as it rose to a great height before being blown westward by the wind. Eight men stood upon a ridge as they gazed back toward what was left of a once great city.

With Xith in ruins, it was only a matter of time before the rest of Casdra fell to the invaders. One man among the eight, clad in worn robes that had seen better days, wept.

Invaders spread throughout the city rounding up the men, women, and children. Groups of captives were led from the city and placed in slave lines. Already two slave trains, comprising several lines each, were on their way south while more were still being put together. Once the entire population of Xith was on its way south, the campaign for the rest of the country would commence.

In the center of the city, the remainder of the defenders held up in the last bastion available to them, the temple. Unwilling to waste good men to root them out, the Ullen leaders decided to let fire do their work for them.

Barrels of oil and pitch were gathered and set around its outer perimeter. Small casks were tossed through every available window. Archers were set in place to pick off anyone attempting to throw them back out. Many defenders died in such attempts.

Once all was in readiness, the barrels were set afire. Arrows of flame were directed through the windows, many of which ignited the smaller casks which had been tossed through earlier.

It didn't take long before flames spread throughout the entire structure. Screams came from those caught within. Any who attempted to flee fell to a hail of arrows. When the fire grew more intense, the screams grew silent and no further attempts were made by the defenders to escape.

In the heart of the temple, in a room seldom seen by any who did not serve Casdralla, High Priestess Trystia stood with the Fathers as well as those priests who served at the temple in Xith.

Words were useless at this point. Everyone knew full well what fate was to befall them. Already, smoke had found its way into the room and was growing thicker by the minute.

Then, one of the Father's began a hymn from his childhood, one which he had learned at his mother's knee. His solitary baritone was soon joined by an alto. One by one, the others joined in until every voice sang as one. As the smoke became thicker, voices cracked, but still they sang.

When the fire finally reached the room, and a wall erupted in flames, the voices sang all the louder. Then the room was filled with a glow not of this world, one which outshone the fire. Qyaendris appeared, one for each of the priests. They enveloped their faithful servants in soothing comfort as fire began licking their robes.

Father Bennon, the oldest living man in Casdra, felt neither pain nor fear when the fire came to claim him. For he was no longer there. Standing barefoot on the muddy banks of a river, he saw a boy coming toward him. It was his older brother, a vision from a time when he was but a boy himself.

"Where have you been?" his brother asked. "Ma's been worried about you."

Father Bennon grinned as he felt the familiar sensation of mud oozing between his toes. No longer was he old and frail with a body bent with age.

Youth surged in his veins and he gave out with a whoop and holler as he raced forward to greet his brother whom he had not seen for thirty years.

"Come on Toad," his brother said, using the name he had called his younger brother in a time long past. Taking his younger brother by the hand he said, "It's time to go home."

Some distance south of where Casdralla's temple burned, an Ullen junior officer with five subordinates moved among the rubble of the collapsed portion of the city's defensive wall. The young officer was doing what many others were doing throughout the city, looking for valuables. Two pouches hanging from his belt were already filled to bursting as were his pockets. Coins, gems, and jewelry were up for grabs. If a man was quick enough, he could bring home a fortune in a place like this.

Of course, each man must give an account of what he took. Ten percent of all they found was to be handed over to the King's representative which always accompanied an army on the move. He was there to ensure everyone's compliance with the 'Loot Tax' as it was called.

The young officer had a keen eye and could spot treasure a mile away. So when he spied a hand protruding from a pile of stone, he was quick to notice the ring adorning one finger. Making sure no one else had yet noticed this piece of treasure, he moved forward and pulled the ring free.

It was a simple, plain ring bearing but a single, black oval stone with a thread of red coursing its way through. Not figuring it to be worth much, he still placed it within his pouch and continued on in search of other, hopefully more valuable, items.

Unseen by the officer, two Qyaendri watched as the ring was taken.

"It is done."

"You never intended for the people to be saved."

Xi looked at Larus and shook his head. "No."

"Hunter was brought to this world, and all that we went through was so the ring could be found by that officer?" he asked.

"Yes," replied the mightiest of all Casdralla's Qyaendri. "By the time we discovered Theroch's plans to have his mortals invade Casdra, it was too late to set into motion events that would lead to their salvation."

The two Qyaendri faded from the ruins of Xith and reappeared within the great Rotunda of Casdralla's High Temple, the one on her plane of existence. "So we did what we could to ensure our Lady's presence would not be extinguished from that world. The chance of success was small, and we took it."

Xi glanced to Larus as he said, "Sending you to Earth was not a mistake Larus. You were the only one whom we could send in order for the plan to come to fruition."

"And was making me mortal part of the plan?" he asked.

"A large part, yes," he admitted. "It was in your nature to become so immersed in Earth's culture that you failed to search for the Chosen One. We counted on that."

Larus didn't like what he was hearing, that his ineptitude made him the perfect candidate.

"I know you suffered," Xi said. "Had there been any other way, we would have taken it. But a regular mortal could not have brought the ring out from the Or'tux temple. A mortal simply would not have survived what had been left behind. Since the Or'tux temple was also a 'prime' temple to another god, no Qyaendri serving Casdralla could enter to fetch the ring without breaking the Compact. We needed someone who was neither mortal nor Qyaendri, but a blend of both."

"Which was me," concluded Larus.

"Exactly," agreed Xi. "With Father Thomas carrying a remnant of our Temple Prime on that world, you had the ability to get everyone out safely, which you did." Glancing at Larus, he said, "You did well."

"Then, I am restored to the ranks of our Lady's Qyaendri?" he asked.

"Could you be here otherwise?" asked Xi. "You are a faithful servant of our Lady, Larus, and as such deserve a place among her Qyaendri."

"But I lied."

"True," agreed Xi. "And you have reaped the fruit of such action. But one does not idly discard a servant as faithful as yourself, provided he has learned from his mistake?"

"It won't happen again," Larus said with all sincerity.

Xi nodded. "Now," he began, "what should I do with you?"

"What do you mean?" Larus asked.

"After the way you acquitted yourself against one of Theroch's Ka'Drach, it would be possible to return you to the ranks of our Celestial Warriors."

"That would indeed be an honor," replied Larus, with a hint of misgiving.

"Would it?" asked Xi, then he gave Larus a disarming grin. "You have but to say the word and you would again be among their exalted ranks."

"Well," thought Larus, "if it's all the same to you..."

The harvest was over. Now that the days were growing shorter and the warm, carefree days of summer past, a boy faced the moment which had lent an air of dread to times of pleasure during the last few days. He had known it was coming, and despite his best efforts to avoid the consequences of having another year added to his tally, could not escape his fate. For today was his first day of school.

Earlier that morning, his mother woke him before the sun had even begun its rise over the horizon. He dragged his feet as he put on his best clothes which had been laid out for him the night before. Not even the prospect of sitting down to his favorite breakfast of fried dumplings with berry preserves could make him move any faster.

"It's not going to be that bad," assured his good friend Stymie.

With breakfast behind him and the sun making its way over the horizon, he and Stymie walked along the dirt road toward town. There, he would find Old Widow Harpin who had been the school teacher when his parents had walked this walk. True, everyone said she was a dear lady who rarely said a cross word to anyone, but he had his misgivings nonetheless.

"I'm no good around others," he stated, and not for the first time.

"You will do fine," Stymie said encouragingly.

Sighing, Allen walked. Butterflies, or rather dragons bent on destructive mayhem, swarmed in his middle. He could feel the comforting arm of Stymie about his shoulders. And as the schoolhouse came into view, his steps grew more leaden.

Other children, both boys and girls, were headed to the same destination. One such boy whom Allen recognized as Trevor, the miller's son, spied his approach. "Allen!" he shouted and raced over to meet him.

Trevor was one of his few peers whom didn't generate the immediate urge to flee. His father sold his grain to Trevor's father so the two boys knew each other if not actually spent any great deal of time together.

"First day of school too, huh?" asked Trevor when he came to walk next to Allen.

"Yup," Allen replied.

"My brother was telling me that Widow Harpin bakes cookies for the new kids," he said excitedly.

Allen perked up at that. A whiff of odor in the air brought to mind his mother's molasses drops, cookies she makes on occasion which Allen absolutely could not resist.

"Come on," said Trevor. "If we get there quick they may still be hot."

The prospect of hot molasses drops seemed to dispel the lethargy which had dogged him since morning. With Trevor a step ahead, Allen broke into a run for the schoolhouse. Then he paused and glanced back at Stymie who had not accompanied him.

"You go on," Stymie said. "You can tell me all about it when you get home."

Panic set in at the thought Stymie would not be there. But then Trevor returned and grabbed him by the arm. "What are you waiting for?" Spurred on by Trevor's fervor, Allen waved to Stymie before racing for the schoolhouse.

Larus grinned as he watched the young boy run. This is what he liked to do, help mortals. Some Qyaendri would think him insane to turn down the honor of joining the ranks of Celestial Warriors. But to Larus, being the one who brought a prayer to fruition was far more important, and satisfying.

He watched Allen run next to the boy who would most likely become his best friend. 'Stymie' may not be needed much longer. But then, there were always more prayers to fulfill, and more mortals to help.

Epilog

Three men crouched huddled in the lee of a hill. Clothes ragged, dirty, and torn, they had not known a moment's peace for quite some time. One clutched tightly a satchel to his breast. Within was the hope of Casdra, a once tranquil kingdom now ground under the heel of a conquering army.

It had taken the Ullen army less than two months to break through the pass and subjugate the entire population. The Casdralla's High Temple was destroyed, as were every other temple to the Lady which they encountered. If not killed outright, priests were made into objects of ridicule and forced into the most degrading and demeaning labor their new masters could devise.

"You must survive."

The words of High Priestess Trystia came back to him as he, Garin, and Stephen hid from an Ullen patrol.

"Reach the High Temple and save the Book."

He knew of which book she spoke. Within its sacred pages were the rituals, and wisdom of Casdralla. Without them, Her light would dim and ultimately fade from this world forever.

"Wait here," Stephen said as he quietly moved to the top of the hill to see if the patrol had moved on.

Clutching the satchel in which the Book rested tightly, he watched Stephen climb to the top of the hill, pause a moment, then return.

"It's clear," he said. "Let's go."

Heading north away from the enemy occupied lands, they fled during the nighttime hours, resting only when the sun was at its highest.

"Find a place hidden from the eyes of our enemy and wait."

"Wait for what?" he had asked.

"When the time comes, you will know."

There was only one place he felt would be safe from enemy incursion. Nestled in the satchel next to the Book was a decorative box containing powder of the theshil plant having also been retrieved from the High Temple. It would be needed when they reached their destination.

Deeper into the northern mountains they went until finally reaching their destination. Father Thomas led them through the hidden passage off the ancient road, past the waterfall, and along the underground river until coming to a drawbridge spanning a deep chasm.

"What is this place?" asked Garin.

"A place not to be taken lightly," replied Father Thomas. From the satchel he removed a brazier and filled it with theshil powder before igniting it. When the familiar noxious fumes began to rise, he stepped toward the drawbridge.

"How long are we to stay here?" Stephen asked.

Father Thomas paused and glanced back. "For as long as we must." Turning back to the drawbridge which would take them into the Or'tux temple, he steeled himself, and entered.

Check out the other epically adventurous worlds of fantasy author

Brian S. Pratt

The Morcyth Saga

James, a high school senior, went looking for a job. But instead, he begins what turns out to be an adventure of a lifetime. Whisked unexpectedly to a world where magic works, he must learn to master its power, all the while searching for the meaning of why he was brought there and what he must do.

The Broken Key Trilogy

Four comrades set out to recover the segments of a key which they believe will unlock the King's Hoard, rumored to hold great wealth. Written in the style of an RPG game, with spells, scrolls, potions, Guilds, and dungeon exploration fraught with traps and other dangers.

Dungeon Crawler Adventures

*For those who enjoy dungeon exploration
without all the buildup or wrapup.*

Fans of his previous works, especially *The Broken Key*, will discover *Underground* to be full of excitement and surprises. First in a series of books written for the pure fun of adventuring, *Underground* takes the reader along as four strangers overcome obstacles such as ingenious traps, perilous encounters, and mysteries to boggle the mind.

The Adventurer's Guild

Jaikus and Reneeke are ordinary lads whose dream in life is to become a member of The Adventurer's Guild. But to become a member, one must be able to lay claim to an Adventure, and not just any adventure. To qualify, an Adventure must entail the following:

1-Have some element of risk to life and limb

2-Successfully concluded. If the point of the Adventure was to recover a stolen silver candelabra, then you better have that candelabra in hand when all is said and done.

3-A reward must be given. For what good is an Adventure if you don't get paid for your troubles?

Jaikus and Reneeke soon realize that becoming members in the renowned Guild is harder than they thought. For Adventures posted as Unresolved at the Guild, are usually the ones with the most risk.

However, when they hear of a party of experienced Guild members that are about to set out and are in need of Springers, they quickly volunteer only to discover to their dismay that a Springer's job is to "Spring the trap".

If they survive, membership in the Guild is assured.